3

Broken Line

A Chronicle of Tala

Matthais Carr

Runebear Publishing Inc

Book Cover artwork by Ryleigh Crockett and Sugarnuts International

Cover Design by Mahmuddidar

Map Design and artwork by Inspirat_nforge

First Edition 2022

Dedications and Acknowledgements

I want to thank all the people who helped me along this long journey to finishing this book. Most importantly my wife Crystal for standing by me and believing in me this whole time.

This book is dedicated to my late father Charles Richard Crockett who instilled in me a love of books.

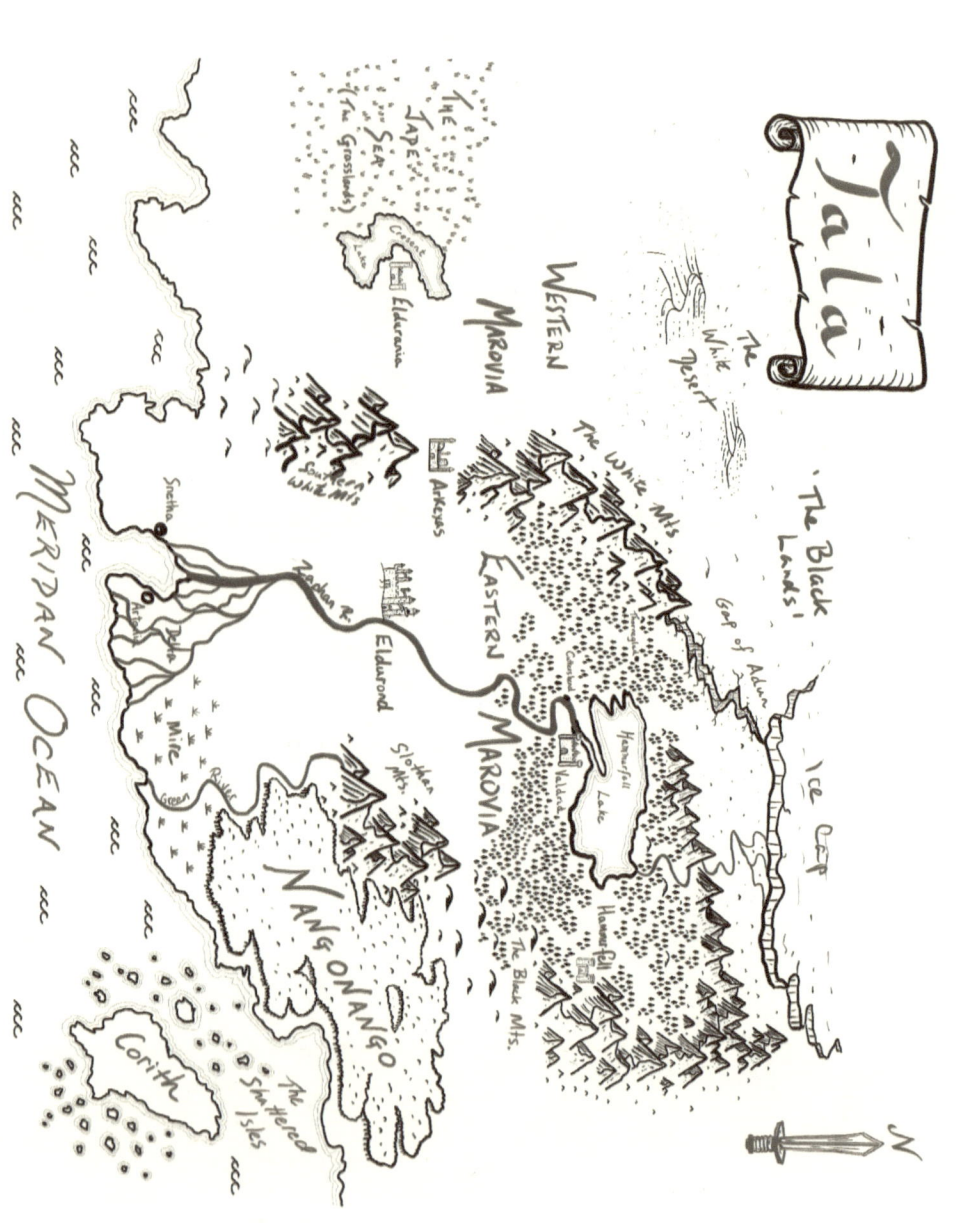

Broken Line

A Chronicle of Tala

CHAPTER ONE

The *lives* *of* *men* *are* *but* *playthings* *to* *the* *gods.* Warrec chewed over the quote, mulling the words over in his mind. He had no idea why that old saying from one of his old instructors was rolling through his thoughts. It had been an offhand remark one of his training sergeants had said to him and the rest of the squad years ago during training one day. *Probably meant to simply motivate us, damn if I can't remember his name,* he thought. Warrec absently toyed with the reins in his hand, twisting the bit of leather around his gauntleted fingers. As he and his traveling companion, Joenair, got closer to Thornglade the quote had been popping into his head more and more.

Warrec wiped the sweat from his brow with his saddle handkerchief and scratched at the two months growth of beard on his face. It was neatly trimmed and groomed, light brown with a tint of red running throughout it. Though there was a hint of wildness creeping in.

It was a slight indication that its bearer came from the wilderness of the northern expanse around the great lake. He had decided to keep the beard full, forgoing the traditional goatee worn by most knights, though it did partially cover the tattoo that he was so proud of that ran along his left cheek to his left ear.

His arm made a slight clinking sound as he moved it. Warrec wore his full set of plate armor. A black gambeson formed the base layer, not counting his undershirt and green uniform coat. Over the thick quilted coat was a hauberk of simple steel chainmail that covered his upper arms and dropped down almost to his knees. Over the relatively simple, yet sturdy hauberk and gambeson were several sections of integrated plate and his green with gold trim cloak.

The armor was a masterwork piece of Dwarven craftsmanship, far beyond what a normal knight would wear or could even afford. It had taken Warrec well over a year to assemble the set, buying it piece by piece. Forged of valentium, Dwarven high steel, the set had cost a small fortune but was worth every copper. Stronger than normal steel, the valentium armor was all but impervious to damage.

The silvery metal gleamed as the sunlight hit it. It was warm wearing the armor in the direct sunlight but not unbearable. Even though it was midsummer the air was pleasant and mild and had grown steadily cooler the farther north they rode. It was simply easier to wear it than to try to pack it up on the back of the horse. Besides, his homeland in the north wasn't the most civilized part of the empire.

He told himself that it was better to be prepared in case the worst happened. Though for most of the journey he had packed it. He had only recently started wearing his full kit as he approached his ancestral home. Bandits were not unheard of in the interior though most had the sense not to attack a knight. There had also been a strong swell of pride within as his countrymen had gawked and stared at a knight riding by. Though his title was a military one, earned through distinguished service; it held no lands or political power. He was still just as far below the nobility as everyone else. *And yet Addie still loves me,* he added mentally.

Still, only two days out from the river he and Joenair had already run into a pack of the stupidest bandits the AllFather had ever made. Two days ride from the Zaphan River they had been ambushed. Warrec still wasn't sure if it had been a lack of sense, ignorance or desperation that had caused the highwaymen to accost the two of them. Four bandits had offered to spare their lives in exchange for their gold and weapons. The idiots were dead before they had even finished the last sentence of their ultimatum. Bandits were more nuisance to the two of them than a real threat. Warrec was more worried about running into a bearcat or a rogue mammoth, but his worries lessened as they grew closer to his home village.

His mind drifted to thoughts of his boyhood home as he rode on. *Thornglade, it has been almost four years since I have been home,* he thought. He had left for the capital of Eldurond to join the legion and train at the military academy ten years ago when he was seventeen.

He had been home only twice since then. There had been other opportunities of course. It was just that those two times had been unpleasant at best. Of course, seeing Aluna again on his first visit had been wonderful. She was such a cute and happy kid. Warrec sat upright in his saddle as he did the math in his head. The last time he had seen her she hadn't quite turned thirteen. Warrec sighed, which was a decade ago.

Kid, ha, he thought. *She won't be a kid anymore; she will be all grown up, a young woman of twenty-three. Feels odd to think of her as a woman grown, hell she'll probably be married now with a litter of children of her own now.*

Last time he had visited he had been unable to see her because she was on a spirit walk in the forest. She had been off training to be the village's next shaman like her father, learning the ways of the wyrd.

He liked her father. The man was a little crazy, magic does that to a lot of wielders. He was a happy funny man, nonetheless. The old shaman always seemed to be bursting with joy, full of life. *Not like my father,* he thought as an unconscious frown crossed over his face.

My father, the great warrior, protector of the village and guardian of the temple. Well, he used to be now he is just a pathetic old drunk. Trying to kill himself with a bottle.

Warrec slightly shook his head at the thought. *Though maybe he has that right now. He took it pretty hard when Everett was killed by the Lord of the Black Lands, Argis how I hate him. You killed my brother you bastard and someday, immortal, or not I'll find a way to end you.* Warrec gritted his teeth as his mind dwelled on Argis.

His knuckles turned white as he gripped the reigns. Argis had killed Everett as Everett had been leaving home to return south for another tour of duty. For centuries Argis the Dread Lord and ruler of the Black Lands in the frozen uninhabitable north had been the predominant boogie man of the empire as far back as anyone could remember.

His father had told him that Argis had caught Everett in an ambush with a few others as they traveled south. *He is rarely seen anymore, but one of the few times he leaves the Black Lands and it's to murder my brother.* A glint of fire and malice flashed across Warrec's eyes.

That was the reason the old man forbid me to go south and join the legions. But I had to go be a knight. I had to do it, for Everett, I had too. Then mother died while I was away. He resents me for not being there, I know he does, but it wasn't my fault dammit. The pain became too much to hold in any longer and the anguish showed itself on Warrec's face as a low growl escaped his lips.

"So, the guy goes, what you think I wished for a giant rooster?" Joenair burst out laughing as he finished his joke. Warrec jolted in his saddle, reflexively grabbing the greathelm that was perched on the saddlehorn in front of him to keep from knocking it off, as his friend's laughter snapped him back to the present. Warrec glanced sideways at Joenair as he realized that the smaller man had been talking for quite a while now and Warrec had no idea about what. Joenair groaned as he saw Warrec wasn't laughing.

"Oh, come on that one is great. How are you not laughing?" Joenair asked.

Warrec shook his head. "Sorry I was off in my head. Go ahead and tell it again."

Joenair rolled his eyes and waved his hand dismissively. "No, never mind it'll just lose all its flavor. What's eating at you anyway? You have been quiet, even for you."

Warrec gestured at the road ahead of them, but to call the dirt path a road was generous. The empire hadn't gotten to building roads in the northern expanse yet, that vast stretch of wilderness surrounding Hammerfall Lake, or simply referred to as The Lake by the locals. The few roads up here weren't like the engineering marvels that criss-crossed the interior.

"Just thinking of home...and Argis," he said.

Joenair looked at his friend but said nothing. He knew that coming home was painful for his old friend. Warrec wasn't the type to talk about such things, even to his best friend. Of course, that hadn't stopped Joenair from gently prodding every now and then. It was his nature after all to read people and find out what makes them tick.

Warrec glanced sideways at his friend. He had known Jay for almost ten years and still he knew very little about him. The man was practically unreadable, at least when he wanted to be and wasn't putting on an act. Warrec mentally shrugged. *Guess it comes with the territory of master assassin and spy.*

Joenair wore simple brown breeches and a long grey tunic belted at the waist with a plain black belt to match his short boots. A large floppy hat tended to conceal his face in shadow. The man was clean shaven and kept his hair short and neat. Neither ugly nor handsome Jay was the type of man that you could look right at him and not see him, though that simple attire hid a large assortment of knives and other nasty weapons.

"Jay I'm glad you came along," Warrec said.

"Well of course you are. I'm awesome," Joenair said with a

laugh. He then sniffed loudly and nodded. "No, but seriously, from what you told me about your father and brother...I can see how this would be difficult. Though honestly, I don't know why you didn't bring Addie along. You would think you would want your future wife to meet your family, after all."

Warrec grunted. "I had no intention of dragging her up here, too dangerous."

Joenair cocked his head. "Really? But you have no problem risking my neck I see. Besides, you do remember she handled herself perfectly well in the Orc jungles down south."

"It's different now."

"You're being overprotective."

"No, she has duties and planning to do. I'm going to see my father, tell him and be done with it."

Joenair turned and looked at Warrec. "And you think he is going to pack up and go on holiday and travel all the way south for your wedding?"

Warrec shook his head. "Nope. Not at all, I expect him to grunt and grouse and then ignore me till I leave." Warrec let out a long sigh. "And then I expect I probably will never see him again." Joenair frowned to himself and gently shook his head.

Warrec had tried to assimilate himself into the culture of the empire as much as possible, but he was a Vatninu man through and through. Not only did he have the look and heavy build, but he also had the passion and stubbornness. One could always spot a Vatninu in a crowd, no matter where in the empire one was. Warrec rolled his shoulders and felt the large muscles bulging underneath his plate.

Fair skinned with wild shocks of red and blonde hair that they usually kept long and braided; the Vatninu stood out from the more normal tannish complexion and dark hair of most of the rest of the humans in the empire. Of course, it also helped that both the men and the women stood a head taller than the majority of their southern cousins. The men wore their beards long and often wove silver beads and rings through the braids, gold if they could afford it.

They had a reputation of being wild barbarians, unruly, unwashed, and unkempt; though Warrec had told Joenair several times that was nothing more than imperial gossip. Most of the Vatninu took considerable pride in their grooming and were meticulous when it came to the care of their beards. While Warrec usually kept his beard and hair longer than most imperials it was well brushed and groomed far beyond what most others kept theirs. Also, Warrec had an affinity for water that most imperials found strange and preferred to bathe every day.

Legends spoke of the Vatninu ancestors being giants and while Joenair had doubted the veracity of such claims it was easy to see how they had started. Warrec was easily one of the biggest men in their legion and had strength to match. Several times he had been recorded moving weights that even Dwarven laborers had been hard pressed to lift. Warrec was rather proud of that.

Warrec cocked his head at the thought as he mulled it over. He found it curious how similar both races were. Both shared similar artistic designs and fashions. Except for the significant height difference, both races had comparable heavy muscular builds. Though they did differ in the face, Dwarves had broad, almost flattened noses and deep-set eyes under a heavy brow, while the Vatninu had much sharper and angular facial features. In a way the Vatninu almost resembled a Dwarve that had been stretched out. Granted they shared a long border with each other and had been trading with each other as far back in history as could be remembered.

Warrec slightly shook his head. Physically they were akin to one another, but in disposition they couldn't be more different. While somewhat surly, Dwarves were naturally more reserved and solemn, when they weren't drinking that is. The Vatninu tended to be passion incarnate, loud and boisterous. They dominated the room when they entered, both by size and personality. The difference showed the most on the battlefield. The Dwarves marched and moved like an advancing glacier, unwavering and unstoppable. The Vatninu attacked with the ferocity of a blizzard, howling and half mad with rage.

The rage was what the Vatninu warriors were famous for, that and stubbornness, he couldn't forget the stubbornness. Though even among the Vatninu clans Warrec's family, the Vornirulfs, were legendary in their battle prowess and rage.

His people called it the grimmig, though Warrec always thought of it as simply shifting; a change in thinking that overwhelmed the logical and civilized parts of his brain. Grimmig unchained the beast inside, the wildness that men kept locked away. In a way everything crystallized, time slowed, and the world snapped more into focus and became simpler. There was himself and everyone else and everyone else was a threat that had to be destroyed. In the heat of battle his rage would consume him. He destroyed and killed everything in his path, the whole time howling and snarling like a wild beast.

However, through years of training and mental focus Warrec had learned to direct if not control it. As he had moved along in his training Warrec had gone berserk less and less until finally it had all but disappeared. Legion discipline had hammered out the slag as it had forged Warrec into a fine warrior. He only slaughtered his enemies, which was a blessing.

It was a somewhat uncommon feat to be able to direct it. By most accounts, the Vatninu when overcome by rage and fury would tend to attack anything that moved smaller than themselves, avoiding their comrades, unless those comrades happened to be tiny, smaller imperials. It was one of the primary reasons there weren't that many Vatninu in the legion's officer ranks. The Vatninu were incredible warriors, but they lacked discipline or at least discipline in the imperial ranks. They fought well alongside each other but had a challenging time obeying imperials. Though when let loose and unbridled they made wonderful shock troops.

Warrec smiled again and almost laughed out loud. It was no small wonder why. Out of all the human nations only the north and The Lake had been unconquered by the imperials. Legion after legion had fallen to them until finally a peaceful trade negotiation had been reached. That had been a few hundred years ago and ever so slowly they had been assimilated. Technically they weren't officially part of the empire. They still hung on to their old ways and viewed most of the empire as soft.

Stubborn, yep stubborn, Warrec contemplated.

Warrec absently scratched at the back of his hand holding the reins as he thought, not that he could feel it through the gauntlet. It was off the battlefield where he had struggled the most, dealing with the politics of both the military and civilian sides. The diplomacy and cool decorum of a legion officer had always been particularly vexing to him. Without

Addie helping him he didn't think he would have been able to advance as far as he had.

I haven't shifted in a long time now, Warrec thought. *Addie has helped a lot with that too*. An image of her face, long blond hair flowing in the wind flashed across his mind. *By the AllFather she is beautiful*, He thought. *Maybe Jay is right, and I should have brought her*. The idea of his father and Addie being around each other was not a relaxing thought. Addie did have some northern ancestry, which accounted for her hair and height, but she was an imperial and a noble. His father wasn't particularly fond of imperials to begin with.

Yes, it would have been a disaster, He told himself. He snorted. It didn't much matter anyway. He wouldn't be coming back here again. He had a familial obligation for tradition's sake to tell his father and some of the other distant relatives, but that was it. Afterward he would be done and would never have to deal with his father again.

As Warrec rode along lost in contemplation, Joenair began blissfully whistling a tune, completely content to allow his friend to ride and brood. Warrec shot him a sideways glance and sighed. It was obvious that Jay was bored and trying to annoy him. It was one of Joenair's favorite pastimes and something he had perfected over the years. They had started training together and had quickly started a friendly rivalry which still continued to this day, though they had calmed down somewhat. It was mainly due to the fact that for the last six years they had finished their basic training and branched out into their specialties.

Warrec had chosen to become a knight; the cream of the crop of the imperial army, worth a hundred common footmen. They wore heavy plate armor and rode massive warhorses through their enemies like a juggernaut sweeping all aside. The title held no hereditary honors in the imperial army. The only thing that separated him from other heavy horsemen was that the title of knight carried the rank of an officer.

Joenair had chosen instead to become a stealth agent more commonly known as an assassin, though Jay disliked the term. As Joenair liked to put it; killing was only a small part of his talents after all and he much preferred to call himself an information gather. *Never mind that the futten man can seem to disappear in a crowded room and can do acrobatics that would give a monkey pause.* Warrec thought to himself. Joenair had always been quick and light on his feet and he had such a smooth way of talking to people. Joenair's career path had seemed like a natural choice, just as Warrec's choice was for him.

"Skret, how much farther?" Joenair complained.

The sound of Joenair's voice snapped Warrec out of his daydream. "We're almost there," he answered. "Normally it takes longer to reach Thornglade, but I guess with the weather being so good" -Warrec absently waved a hand at the clear blue sky- "we were able to make better time."

"Thank the River Mother. That's good. I'm not very fond of long trips myself. Rather hurry up and get there you know." As he said this, a dark shadow blocked out the sun. A Great White Eagle swept down just barely above their heads and startled the horses. "Futuo! Look out!" Joenair shouted as his horse reared up.

The snow-white bird let out a screech that almost sounded like bird laughter. Warrec could tell it was a female by the lack of black markings the male's bore around their eyes. With a powerful pump of her six-foot wingspan, she soared off.

Warrec let out a deep belly laugh at his friend and the eagle. "Didn't I tell you everything up here was a little wilder than down south?" Warrec reached over and grabbed Joenair's reigns to help steady the horse. "She was just curious, no real threat to us."

Still flustered, Joenair let out a few more curse words, some Warrec had never heard before as he got the horse settled back down. With a deep breath, Joenair wiped his face with his free hand and reset himself as though nothing had happened. Once again, the world was a brilliant and wonderful place for being smart enough to have Joenair in it. Warrec laughed again and shook his head. It amazed him how easily his friend did that.

"Yes, well I knew that," Joenair said with a sniff. "Just startled me is all, skretbird," he added the last under his breath.

"I'm sorry, what was that last part?" Warrec said with a wide grin.

"I said meh," Joenair trailed off as he grumbled, but he was smiling as he did so.

Warrec chuckled at his friend. He absently patted at his horse's neck, but then his face quickly grew somber. "I wanted to thank you for coming with me back home. This trip would have been…. difficult by myself."

"Eh don't worry about it buddy, I was getting bored at the capital anyway. I mean loose women and beer fests at the tavern every night are only fun for so long. Out here there's trees and rocks, lots of those, and crazy birds trying to kill young men in their prime. Oh, and sore backsides from sitting in a saddle all day. Yeah, I love it up here," Joenair said with a sarcastic laugh as Warrec glared at him. "Though seriously I'm happy to come, I get to see where the great Warrec grew up. Besides how many city rats like myself get to see a Vatninu village? Huh?"

Warrec gave a half-hearted laugh at his friend. "Well don't get your hopes up too much, it's not that big. There are a few houses, the storehouse, a merchant store, one tavern and the smithy, in the village proper. Most of the homes are scattered out in the forest and surrounding farms."

"Only...only one tavern" -Joenair clutched at his chest- "by Grendir's Beard you people are barbarians," he stammered out in fabricated shock.

"Ha...yeah that's us. Well, it is a small village after all. Oh, there is also the temple."

"The temple? What temple?"

"Yeah, the temple. My father's temple, ancient going back farther than anyone can remember." Warrec hesitated before speaking again. "It's kinda complicated a family secret and all."

"Secret you say? Oh, I do love secrets." Joenair clapped his hands together in mock excitement. "Makes life so much more interesting."

Warrec rolled his eyes at his friend. He then rode for a few minutes in silence as he debated with himself how much he wanted to tell Joenair. It wasn't that he didn't trust him. It was more of how much he really wanted to talk about it. Joenair rode along, though he did cock his head at Warrec waiting for him to speak. He knew that sometimes the best way to get someone to talk was to just be silent.

Finally, Warrec sighed and shrugged his massive shoulders. "Well, to be honest I don't know much about it. All I know is that there is some sort of ancient artifact in there and my father is the guardian of it. I've never seen it though. I used to play in there as a child. I climbed over every nook and cranny in that old building and if there is something hidden in there I haven't a clue where. My brother Everett was supposed to take my father's place as guardian and keeper of the temple, as he was the first born, but now that he is dead…" Warrec trailed off and looked skyward.

"What's wrong?"

"I was eleven when he died." Warrec sighed again. "It's just that ever since Everett died my father has, well, given up. He drinks all the time, like he is trying to drown himself. He acts like he has failed and that his entire life has been meaningless. All the joy drained out of him. He was never cruel or anything, he just...ceased to be, waiting for the end, to die. I think he took Everett's death worse than when my mother died."

"Why is that?" Joenair sounded eager for more. In the many years that Warrec had known him, Joenair had asked a few times about Warrec's family. He knew a few things, like Everett's death, but it wasn't something Warrec liked to talk about. Joenair had learned to let it be. This was one of the few times Warrec had spoken openly of his family and Joenair was overcome with curiosity.

Warrec really didn't want to talk about it still. Though

after a moment decided that he needed to and forced the words out of his mouth. "Well, apparently my family has been the guardian of this temple and whatever is in it for close to four thousand years. It's a small temple dedicated to the AllFather. Our family maintains it and takes care of it, or we used to anyway. Pilgrims and others seeking blessings would visit. They would leave offerings and donations. That's how we fed ourselves mostly.

"And in that time the line has not been broken once, passing from father to first born child. I apparently can't take over for Everett because I'm second born. If Everett had become the next guardian and then died, I could have taken over but not before. Or so Father told me. It was this one damn thing that tore him apart. Though it's not like I even wanted the responsibility; Father couldn't let it go, it broke him."

Warrec started to reach up and rub the back of his head in one of his nervous ticks, before he caught himself and let his hand fall back to the saddle. "It's all just a bunch of stupid legends." He grunted.

Joenair furrowed his brow as he tried to wrap his mind around his friend's words. "What is it? What's the artifact?" he finally asked.

Warrec shrugged and shook his head. "It's some kind of sword. Father only showed it to Everett and no one else. In fact, you're probably the only person outside the family that even knows about it. It's hidden in the temple and only my father and Everett know where. I asked both of them and neither would tell me where or even show the sword to me. Everett said it was a powerful looking sword and that the blade glowed red when held. He called it the Soulblade."

"Really, is it a magic sword?" Joenair cocked an eyebrow in sudden interest. "That would be very valuable to the right person."

Warrec gave Joenair a menacing look that could freeze water. "Don't even think about pilfering it, Father would hunt you till the end of the earth and so would I for betraying my confidence."

Joenair held up his hands in defense. Without meaning to he had struck a deep nerve. "No, no I would never. I was just saying… sorry ok forget I said it, bad joke and all." Joenair stared at the back of his horse's neck for a few seconds before asking. "Do you know anything else about it? It's an interesting story at least."

Warrec stroked his beard as he thought. "Hmm, not much else, oh other than it's cursed."

"Cursed?" Joenair leaned away in his saddle from Warrec.

"Well like I said the blade glowed. Everett told me that it contained all the souls of the previous guardians. And no, I don't know what that means or how they are in there." Warrec dropped his reins and splayed his fingers out as if even he did not quite believe what he was saying. Warrec's destrier snorted and shook her head as if agreeing with her rider. "This is what my father told Everett and what Everett told me."

The two warriors crested the next hill and looked out over the valley and saw the village of Thornglade. A field of blue and yellow wildflowers greeted them. The field extended for half a mile ahead of them before slowly fading into dense woods. A cluster of plowed and planted fields surrounded the fallow one overtaken by wildflowers. While it was mid-afternoon with several hours of daylight left the fields were surprisingly empty of field workers. Above the wood line an ominous cloud of black smoke rose from the vicinity of the village. They pulled their mounts to a stop and gazed in the direction of the hidden village behind the trees for a moment dumb founded.

"Maybe they are having a roast? Cooking up a pig or a calf for us," Joenair said with a slight hint of fear in his voice.

Warrec gritted his teeth and rolled his massive shoulders. "Maybe, except they're not expecting us until tomorrow." Warrec's words were tense, and the anger could be heard, bubbling just below the surface.

Calm yourself Warrec, He thought to himself. *A warrior must remain calm at all times to be in command.* He recited the academy training to himself.

Warrec grabbed his greathelm, donning it and slamming the faceplate down. He reached over and pulled the security rope holding his warlance in place and brought the great weapon up to point forward. "Whatever it is we had better get there fast," he said, his voice slightly echoing from inside the helm. He sounded much calmer and Joenair knew that Warrec was fighting himself to remain in control. They kicked their horses into full gallop and headed into the valley.

Chapter Two

Thornglade was ablaze. The Goblins had poured through the hamlet burning and killing all in their path. The people of the village screamed as they ran for their lives, desperately searching for shelter or at the very least a weapon. The terrified wailing of children could be heard rising above the sounds of fire and steel clashing. Most of the villages' warriors and hunters were away on the monthly mastodon hunt. Those that remained had either already been killed as they were caught unaware in the sudden attack or were trying their best to buy time for the women and children to escape. Despite their prowess they were quickly being overwhelmed by the sheer numbers of Goblins.

A team of ten Goblins moved down the main street toward the market square. They were filthy, ugly creatures that looked like someone had taken a monkey and shaved it down to bare skin. They were slightly shorter than the height of a Dwarve and their bodies were disproportionate and stretched out in the wrong ways. Their arms were too long for their bodies and hung down below the knees, ending in three long bony fingers tipped with stubby black claws. They moved with an odd waddling, half hopping gait.

Their heads were twisted with large pointy ears and huge yellow eyes, slit vertically like a cat. Lipless mouths gave them a permanent, jagged toothy grin. Goblin skin was a sickly mottled yellow-green and they hopped along as they ran. They wore piecemeal armor and carried weapons from whatever they could scavenge. They never slept or rested, they were always moving, constantly twitching.

The Goblin team flittered down the street bouncing along and crawling across the buildings. Two of them wielded torches and happily set the roofs and anything else that would light to burning. Frightened old women herded children along to the outskirts of the small town as quickly as they could away from the encroaching Goblins. The Goblins chattered and clicked their amusement at the suffering they were causing as the villagers fled before them. As they drew towards the town square they stopped and beheld a massive lone figure standing in the center. He was a giant of a man and looked like he could crush a mountain.

Duncan stood at the town center and held fast as the villagers streamed past. Old men well past their prime escorted, grandmothers and mothers along with their crying children to make sure they escaped. A few patted him on the shoulder and smiled a thank you as they fled. Duncan was only dressed in his plain brown homespun robes. He gripped the well-worn handle of his great bardiche and took a step forward.

The bardiche was a fearsome weapon. It was a massive polearm scaled up to Duncan's towering proportions. It was eight feet overall. The shaft of the weapon was six feet long and made of iron wood. The curved blade was a massive two feet long, forged from valentium and as wide as an axe head. The blade came to a thick point for impaling. The giant poleaxe was designed to maim, dismember, and crush enemies with brutal efficiency. If the blade was unable to cut through the target, the weight of the blade and shaft would shatter the bone underneath, but there was very little the powerful weapon could not cleave through. The bastard offspring of hammer and axe, Duncan's bardiche was larger and heavier than normal, unwieldable by a normal man. Only he possessed the strength necessary to be able to wield it quickly and with precision.

An hour earlier he had been in a drunken stupor, but the din of battle had awoken something in him that he thought had long ago died. Adrenaline and a quick dunk of his bald head in a bucket of water had helped sober him a little, but the fog of intoxication still clung to his head. His heart beat heavily and his muscles were loose and ready. The old giant swayed slightly as he now stood in the town center. Mentally he chastised himself. He should have been ready not passed out drunk. He shook his head to clear his vision. Duncan pulled himself to his full height. Most Vatninu stood a head taller than the average imperial and Duncan stood a head taller than most Vatninu. "I am Duncan Vornirulf Bjornson. This is my village. You all will die today!" He snarled with a slight slur.

The Goblins facing him were taken aback at first and shifted nervously in place. Goblins were a cowardly lot and would never fight one on one, but they had this fool human outnumbered. They obviously had expected they would meet no or little resistance, nothing more than a few warriors long in the tooth and a few shield maidens. *How long have they been planning this? Someone is leading them,* Duncan thought. *Goblins aren't smart enough or brave enough to attack a village.*

A few breathes passed and time seemed to slow to a crawl. None of the Goblins wanted to attack first. Duncan waited, smiling a wicked grin through his long snow-white beard. He traced a thumb along the scar across his cheek, which ran from his left eye to the jawbone.

Duncan wasn't quite sure how many Goblins stood before him, he was still seeing double and swayed slightly in the town square. Ten or twenty didn't really matter. He was going to kill them all. He was ready.

Finally, one of the Goblins, who looked to be in charge, gathered enough courage and with a scream it charged. As soon as the scream broke the silence the others moved, leaping over one another. The first Goblin leaped through the air bringing its short rusty sword up to stab down into this foolish man's head.

Spittle streamed from its jagged tooth filled mouth as it fell downward. Duncan snarled as he slashed up with his weapon. Green blood splashed onto his face and chest as the two halves of the Goblin fell past him. He had cleanly split the creature in half from the crotch to the shoulder.

The next few seconds were a blur of slashing blades and sprays of green blood as the great axe cut a path of death through the team of Goblins. As he finished the upward stroke that killed the first, Duncan quickly reversed the blade and brought it down on the next one's head, crushing its skull and splitting it open in a shower of blood and brains. The blade passed through the helmet like a hot knife through butter. A horizontal slash back to the right separated one Goblin's head from his shoulders and opened the next one's belly like an over ripe melon.

The fifth one closed in on Duncan's left side and raised its blade to strike. Before the blade could land Duncan landed a solid kick to its midsection which sent the foul creature sailing back into its comrades bowling them all over. Only three now still remained on their feet.

Duncan snapped the butt of the bardiche up into the chin of number eight shattering its jaw. Number nine was cleaved in two from its left shoulder down to the right hip. Five, six, and seven were struggling to their feet as ten was gutted, stabbed clean through. Ten gurgled and coughed up a goblet of blood as it feebly scratched at the steel blade piercing its gut.

Duncan kicked the impaled Goblin off his weapon and turned toward the last three, his pale blue eyes blazing with murderous intensity. Duncan's mind cleared as power thrummed through his veins washing away the last vestiges of inebriation and fatigue. By the AllFather he felt strong.

The last three stood on shaky knees with their weapons held in front in a pitiful attempt to ward off this crazy monstrosity of a man. Their numbers had dropped by seven in as many seconds. The last three chittered to each other as their eyes darted back and forth. Though dull and witless, they could process that they were far outclassed here.

Duncan drew his nearly seven-foot frame completely up and towered over these pathetic creatures. He flexed his massive shoulder and arm muscles as he brought his bardiche up to strike and roared like a bear brought to bay. The Goblins had finally had enough. They dropped their weapons, turned, and ran.

Number eight still rolled on the ground, abandoned, and

forgotten by his comrades. With one hand it clutched at its shattered jaw and teeth. With the other it pitifully tried to drag and scramble away to safety from the terrifying giant. Duncan brought his foot down on the neck of number eight snapping it with a sickening crunch.

The Goblins made it to the end of the square and disappeared around the corner of a building. The old giant lurched after them in pursuit. A few heartbeats passed as Duncan crossed the square. He was breathing hard, more from excitement than fatigue. An unconscious smile spread across his face, a predator's smile.

"You're old and out of shape old man," he grumbled to himself. "A few Goblins shouldn't even make you break a sweat."

Suddenly, the Goblins skittered back into the square laughing in that odd high pitch squeal of theirs. Duncan stopped dead in his tracks. Coming up the street were two more teams of Goblins and in their middle was a Savan warrior.

The Savan are an ancient race of lizard men, reptilian and alien in both form and culture. Few in the empire had seen one and fewer still had lived to tell the tale. In the times of primordial past, long forgotten they had ruled the world, while men still cowered in caves trying to solve the riddle of fire. Time had displaced them and pushed them to the far edges and deep places of the known world. It was there the last of their kind remained in forgotten and crumbling temples, bitterly remembering a time of glory long past.

Taller and more robust than an average man they ranged in height from six and a half feet tall up to ten in some of the warrior castes. Divided into castes they varied in appearance; some resemble snakes, others massive crocodiles, and some lizards. Their form was molded from the cruelest reptilian features nature could provide.

This one advancing toward Duncan was nine feet tall and must have weighed well over a thousand pounds. Dark green scales and scutes covered its hide. The scales draped down across its back and limbs forming living armor as hard as steel. Cold red eyes glared out from under a heavy ridge of boney scutes. Foot long jaws lined with an army of white teeth parted in an angry hiss. It was bare-chested and wore only a leather loincloth. It carried a long spear and a large square shield, the standard weapons of the warrior caste. The Goblins accompanying it all danced around it with malicious glee and swarmed at its feet.

The Savan hissed again, the sound dropping in pitch before ending in a deep throated bellow. It clacked its jaws shut and banged the spear on the shield with a loud clang. The Savan's attempt at intimidation failed. Duncan simply grinned wolfishly as the enemy closed around him.

Warrec rode hard down the hillside with Joenair following at his heels. The knight aimed his mount at a small footpath through the large grove of trees that lined the village and recklessly plunged through the growth. A path that he had run down countless times as a child playing with his brother, Aluna, and the other children of the village in happier times.

"No, no, no, no, no, no," Warrec hissed under his breath.

The smell of burnt timber and blood wafted through the air. Shouting and the occasional scream of fear and pain mixed with the clang of steel through the smoky air. Warrec set his heels to his horse's side spurring it along faster and ignored the limbs and branches that whipped by his head.

As Warrec and Joenair burst through the wood line and approached the village, they saw that it was burning. A high palisade of cut timber ringed the village proper. The wall was old but well maintained, oiled, and tarred to prevent rot. It was unmanned, its gates broken and torn open. They could see Goblins running through the streets looting whatever they could carry.

Warrec let out a low growl and tightened his grip on his warlance. The lance ended in two points stacked vertically. The top point was longer and thinner ending in a thick spike. The bottom point bulged out forming a long sweeping blade that swept back to almost the middle of the shaft. The double pointed spear tip was designed to give maximum penetration while at the same time slicing through the target cleaving it apart. It was an odd combination of spear and scimitar. The weapon allowed the knights to charge forward but also allowed for sweeping slashes when wielded with two hands.

Warrec set his heels and charged forward through the broken gate. His war steed sped toward two Goblins fighting over a blue dress. One had its back toward the charging knight and wondered why its ally had suddenly let go and ran away. The stupid creature turned around with a jagged toothy grin of victory, holding the blue dress in its hands just as the lance punctured its chest. The tip ripped through the Goblin as Warrec rode past.

The Goblin was spun around on its heels but remained on its feet. It spit up a blob of green blood as it looked down and saw that everything on its right side from its armpit to the hip was gone. The creature gingerly touched where its right lung had been as it fell forward dead. Warrec didn't slow as he urged his mount onward after the fleeing Goblin.

Joenair yelled something that sounded like split up, but Warrec couldn't be sure. The clack of steel shod hooves drowned out his friend's words as Warrec drove his mount up through the cobblestone streets. For a moment, the clacking stopped and was replaced with a slickening wet thumping as Warrec rode over the fleeing Goblin. Its head exploded in a shower of gore as a hoof set down directly on it. Warrec smiled at that.

He slowed as he reached a bend in the street that pulled off to his right before splitting to the left and right. Warrec pulled hard on the reins bringing the horse to a skittering stop. The massive animal shook its head and let out a snort of frustration. A bewildered Warrec looked to his left and right.

This was all new he suddenly realized. He had just charged up a cobblestone street lined with shops and houses. When had they built cobblestone streets? There were so many more buildings.

He remembered a few streets that ran ninety degrees to each other that bisected the village into quadrants. There had only been a few buildings and homes divided up across the village proper. They had been round houses with low thatch roofs or long a-framed longhouses with sod roofs.

Now it looked like ten times more buildings and structures had been crammed into the same space. The streets curved and snaked through the maze of wattle and daub buildings. The shops and houses rose up around him, most two or three stories. Their higher stories hanging out over the streets and alleys gave a tunnel or cave feel to the town. The empire had finally come to his boyhood home, and it had grown out into a thorny maze of disorder.

Smoke billowed down the street and through the air making it hard to see and breathe. The sounds of screaming, crackling wood and chittering laughter seemed to be coming from every direction at once. Warrec whirled his horse in a circle as he tried to orient himself and decide which way to go.

Something slammed into him knocking him from the saddle and to the ground with a loud clank of crashing steel. Warrec groaned and rolled to his back to see what had happened. A large beam that had run from one building across the street to another connecting their second stories had broken free from one side. The large beam had swung down crashing into him.

Warrec sat up looking at the beam. "Why the hell would they do that?" Warrec cursed under his breath and looked for his horse. The beast had whinnied in shock and bolted down the street when he had been knocked out of the saddle. Now it stood about fifty yards away calmly waiting for him.

"Ginger wouldn't have done that to me!" Warrec yelled at the horse. It seemed oblivious to his words. "She is a good girl and doesn't panic," He grumbled to himself.

Warrec hauled himself back to his feet looking for his lance. Suddenly in a chorus of chattering yells several Goblins burst out of the buildings on both sides of the street. Within a few seconds they swarmed over Warrec knocking him to the ground again.

"Oye you futten ratkies!" Warrec bellowed as a fury of blows rained down harmlessly on him. They couldn't hurt him, not unless one managed to slip a knife through the eye slit, still even that would have to be a very thin blade to fit through the cross bars that lined the visor. Their blades clanked and clipped across the plate, more annoying than anything.

Warrec punched the closest Goblin in the face and was rewarded with a satisfying crunch of bone and teeth. It howled in pain as it scrambled backward. He then grabbed another in a headlock and rolled with it onto his stomach. With a savage twist he snapped its neck. Warrec brought his knee up and rose to his feet, casually backhanding another Goblin.

"Right, you damn ratkies here we go." The Goblins surrounded him, eyeing him warily. Warrec didn't even bother drawing his sword. He knew Goblins were stupid, but attacking a knight in full plate? That was baffling even for them.

A Goblin lunged forward stabbing at Warrec's gut. The short sword blade harmlessly skidded across the fauld cross plates. Warrec grabbed the Goblin's wrist with his right hand and brought his steel fist down on its shoulder and collar bone with his left, snapping bone. It gulped air trying to scream but was unable to as a wave of pain washed over it.

Warrec whipped the tiny monster around and swung it up through the air, smashing it down on another of its friends. He spent the next several seconds punching and kicking any green flesh he could find. Leaving a pile of pulpy smashed heap of bodies at his feet he turned to the last one.

This one was particularly brave or incredibly stupid. Warrec couldn't quite decide which. Despite seeing what had happened to its allies it still stood defiantly brandishing a spear at the large knight. With a snarl it savagely stabbed forward again and again unleashing a flurry of stabs against the knight.

Warrec sighed. He looked down at the spear tip as it bounced off the plate again and again. It didn't even have a steel tip. It was just a sharpened stick. Warrec looked back at the face of the Goblin.

Warrec cocked his head and sighed in annoyance again. "Really?" he asked. The Goblin thrust several more times with each thrust slower than the last. It looked at him and then at its spear point again and again. Warrec could see the mental gymnastics it was going through trying to figure out what was happening. Slowly the Goblin tapped the point against his breast plate, once then twice and finally three times.

The Goblin's eyes went wide as he looked back at Warrec again. Very slowly it lowered the spear and gingerly placed it on the ground. It gave the stick a little pat and at a snail's pace turned and started to walk away.

"Are you kidding me?" Warrec snarled. The Goblin froze mid-step and could be seen visibly swallowing. Very slowly it turned to look back at him. Then it smiled, it actually smiled. Warrec couldn't believe what he was seeing. With one smooth motion he drew his sword and took its head off. It was still smiling as the head bounced across the cobblestones.

Now that the Goblins in the immediate area were dealt with Warrec let out a half grunt, half sigh. He then turned to stalk back to where his horse still stood, waiting patiently. Warrec reached up and grabbed the bridle to pull the horse's face towards his. Warrec held up a finger and pointed sternly at the horse. "You and I need to have a long talk."

Joenair watched as Warrec barreled up the street charging ahead without thinking, like usual. "Wait!" He yelled after the advancing knight. "We shouldn't split up!" *And he's gone,* he thought. Joenair raised both arms above his head in frustration and let them fall back down slapping against his thighs.

He looked down at his horse, back after Warrec, then glanced around at the roof tops. "Well...I guess I should make myself useful," he said to his horse, not that she really cared. She didn't seem particularly bright, for a horse.

Joenair gathered his legs underneath him, crouching in the saddle and leapt from his horse onto one of the few houses that remained unburned. He had neither the weapons and armor nor the horse to charge in like Warrec. No, he would deal with these vile creatures a bit more discreetly.

Goblins, now that did seem to be odd when he thought about it. Small, stupid, and cowardly the thought of a gang, group or cluster of Goblins attacking a town seemed very odd indeed. *What is a group of Goblins called?* Joenair thought absently as he crept along a roof, trying very hard not to put his foot through it. *Gang seems right. A gang of Goblins sure let's go with that.* His mind had a tendency to wander.

Well not so much wander as you just tend to talk to yourself, * A separate mental voice seemed to answer from the dark corner of his mind. There were, after all, several voices in his head. They were all his voices; he wasn't crazy he knew that. It was just that being a spy he had to do quite a bit of acting, adopting different personas. After a while those personas had seemed to slightly separate from him and yet they were him.

What does Warrec call Goblins? Ratkies! Yes, that's it, rat monkeys. Joenair supposed that was somewhat accurate. They did sort of look like shaved monkeys.

You know I don't think I have ever seen a live one before. He had read about them, studied, and been taught how to deal with them, even had to dissect one, but he had never seen a live one before. They were increasingly rare in the Glorious Heart region of the empire. The central part of the eastern side of the empire; the region of the capital that encompassed Eldurond (most blessed and high among cities, though still not as good as Artania) and then dipped down to the coast at the twin cities, Artania and Snetha.

Several houses and buildings were clustered around the town square which allowed Joenair to creep along the few unburned rooftops. He spotted a lone Goblin below him. The creature was rummaging around in a bin in one of the alleys oblivious to its surroundings.

Joenair pulled out his length of wire and made a quick loop. Oh, how he missed Artania. His home city really was the best. Eldurond got all the attention and glory being the capital and all. Artania though, well Artania was fun. He then let out a short whistle, mimicking a small songbird. The short bird whistle caused the Goblin to stop and lift its head to look around. Joenair deftly dropped the loop around its neck and pulled tight.

The women, oh the women, Joenair thought fondly as the

Goblin gurgled and danced on the end of the wire. He then paused with frightening realization it had been too long since he had been with a woman. *I'm going to have to remedy that tonight. Surely there will have to be a grateful damsel willing to do anything to thank a dashing hero such as myself.*

Well, there had been that washer widow in the last river port they had stopped at before they had gotten the horses. Though she had been a hedge whore and only given him a jolly fellow, so he didn't really count that.

The wire bit into the Goblin's skin and it squirmed around, frantically clawing at its neck. Its bugged-out eyes bulged out even farther as it desperately gasped for air. Within a few moments the Goblin quit struggling and went limp. Joenair released an end of the wire and dropped the Goblin to the ground in a crumbled heap.

Vatninu women are supposed to be quite buxom. I'll have to take a survey, hmmm probably need a sample size of twenty or so. Joenair pulled the wire back up and stuffed it back into a pocket. The Goblin was still twitching on the ground. Joenair frowned and crinkled his nose.

Surely, it's dead, he thought.

*Gross, * his mind added.

Why is it still moving? "I say Goblin, are you dead?" Joenair flicked his hand at the Goblin below. It was still moving slightly. Joenair opened and closed his mouth several times as if tasting something foul.

"Well, I'm not coming down there and I'm not going to waste a perfectly good knife on you. So, hurry up already." Joenair glanced around the roof top, maybe there was a board or loose shingle he could throw at it.

He found two shingles that had come loose in a storm; he guessed and hadn't been replaced. He pulled them up and returned to the roof edge overlooking the alley with the still twitching Goblin. He threw the first one down and missed.

Joenair sighed and cursed to himself. Of course, he missed. He was only a master assassin after all and able to put out a sparrow's eye with a crossbow bolt from three hundred feet or hit a running target with a knife while flipping through the air, graceful as you please. Though apparently dropping a roof shingle onto a prone Goblin in an alley way from three stories up was outside his wheelhouse.

Very, very carefully he held the second shingle up and tried to line it up with the Goblin below. He glanced several times at the shingle and back down at the Goblin before dropping it. It fell and smacked the head of the Goblin with a wet thud.

Joenair let out a whoop of triumph and clapped his hands together. The Goblin yelped and clutched at its head. Joenair's shoulders slumped, and he stared off into the sky wondering why the universe wanted to mock him. He then spent the next five minutes trying to fish the wire down and back around the Goblin's neck. After several failed attempts he gave up and tried hooking a foot or leg.

That didn't seem to take nearly as long and on his fourth attempt he managed to slip the wire noose around the Goblin's right leg. He then began pulling hand over hand hauling it up to the roof. "You're heavier than you look." He quipped. The Goblin groaned in answer and hung limply from the wire.

Finally, he pulled it up onto the roof. The Goblin gurgled and kicked feebly. It looked pitiful. Well, he couldn't just leave it. Joenair drew a knife from a hidden sheath and stabbed it through the armpit. It spasmed and went limp. Joenair toed it back off the roof edge and grimaced as it thwacked against the ground.

He started creeping along the rooftops again and came to an edge a few buildings away that overlooked the town square. From this vantage point he could see over the entire square and a large part of the town. He saw Warrec running down Goblins a few streets over. In the square to his amazement Joenair saw a huge man fighting a large Savan and several Goblins.

This struck Joenair as odd for two reasons. One - the Savan despised the wretched creatures almost as much as humans did. Two - the mere presence of the Savan was peculiar. While they were not unknown in the empire, they tended to avoid humans as much as possible.

Someone brought it here, Joenair thought. As he mulled further on it the entire attack on the village was odd. Goblins, while dangerous in large groups, would not be bold enough to mount an attack on a town by themselves. Also, if he remembered correctly from the maps, he had studied on the trip up, there was an imperial garrison not half a day's ride away. The Goblins would have had to pass it to get here. *This many couldn't have snuck by.* The lack of imperial reinforcements did not bode well, and an icy feeling began growing in his gut.

He turned his attention back to the town square and thought about helping the giant old man. As he looked, he could see all the Goblin bodies strewn about the square and at the old man's feet. The man was drenched in green blood. He faced off against the Savan and a few understandably hesitant Goblins. With a whirl and flash of steel the man took the Savan's left arm off just below the shoulder.

"Well, I suppose he has that covered," Joenair said to himself. He glanced back and saw that Warrec had begun moving down a street and would reach the square in seconds, much faster than he could hope too. "Yes, if the two of them can't handle that I don't know what I could do."

Maybe you could try throwing another roof shingle. *

Joenair tried to glare at himself and failed. He decided to be the bigger man and simply ignore the comment. Instead, he would find something useful to do.

Joenair began scanning the rest of the town. It looked like the attack was coming to an end. Most of the townsfolk had either fled, were barricaded safely away or had been killed. Then he spied a beautiful young woman, holding off four Goblins at a stable on the outside of town. She was either exhausted or hurt and wouldn't last much longer. "Ah, a damsel in distress, Joenair my boy you may not be sleeping alone tonight," he quipped to himself.

Boobs, his mind added a second later.

He sprang into action jumping from rooftop to rooftop. Joenair dove out into open air grabbing a pole. Swinging across the pole like an expert gymnast he landed lightly on his feet with barely a sound.

He was only a few hundred feet from her now and sprinted toward her in a mad dash. The Goblins' backs were to him, which allowed him to get the jump on them. While on the run he whipped a throwing knife at the middle one without breaking stride.

The woman held her sword feebly in front of her trying to keep the Goblins away. He could see there were a few children that had hidden in the stable when the battle began. It looked like the Goblins had just discovered them. The woman was obviously now exhausted and could barely lift the sword to put up a last defense.

The tallest Goblin, which seemed to be in charge smiled at her, his teeth broken and jagged in a ghoulish grin. He took a step forward and stopped. The smile slowly disappeared from his face and was replaced by a look of bewilderment. A heartbeat passed and he fell forward with the handle of a large knife jutting out of the back of his neck in the small hollow right below the skull. The other three Goblins looked stupidly at each other and began to turn around.

At that moment Joenair reached them. His knife lashed out as fast as a viper striking the one on his right in the throat. The Goblin convulsed sending a stream of blood arcing high through the air. The Goblin clutched at the near surgically precise wound and fell dead.

Joenair then quickly turned to the one on his left kicking it in the back of the knee. The creature, still confused at this sudden turn of events, dropped down on the struck leg with a howl of pain. Joenair then brought his right knee up into the Goblin's face as he moved forward, smashing bone and teeth with a crunch. He finished it off with a quick stab downwards into the hollow between neck and shoulder.

As he moved to the last one, he saw that the girl had already stabbed it through the gut. *Maybe she isn't so helpless after all,* he thought. The woman smiled. Her face was a mixture of exhaustion and relief as she passed out. Joenair quickly stepped to catch her before she hit the ground.

It began to rain. Joenair lifted her limp form and gazed upward. The heavens opened up and a deluge of icy water fell. Joenair gave a quick command to the children to stay hidden and turned to walk back to the village clutching the young woman to his chest.

Chapter Three

Warrec had easily dispatched the remaining Goblins he could find throughout the town and now moved inward toward the square. He had remounted and fought his way back out the tangle of streets back to the perimeter and then back towards the town center. The site of an armor-clad knight mounted on a war steed bearing down on them had sent the majority of the vile creatures running. When he reached the square, he saw his father was battling a Savan warrior and a few remaining Goblins.

Multiple Goblin parts and bodies lay strewn and scattered around the square. The small village square had been paved with cobblestones, cobblestones that now were slick with the blackish green blood of over a dozen cooling Goblin corpses. The scent of death hung heavy in the air permeating every inch of the market.

The Savan was missing its left arm. Crimson blood flowed freely from the open wound, but the scaly monstrosity seemed to give little concern for it. The Savan's tail lashed and thumped against the stones in fury as its spear wove through the air seeking an opening. Warrec kicked his horse into a charge and bore down toward the great lizard.

Duncan was circling the giant lizard trying to gain an advantage and finish the brute off. The human and reptilian warrior whirled around each other in a deadly dance as each sought to find an opening.

Duncan was hampered in trying to keep the Goblins away at the same time. They circled and skittered around the Savan's clawed feet. One got too close and was sent flying by a powerful smack of the Savan's tail. Its body sailed through the air and landed in a broken heap.

Duncan sought to press the momentarily distraction and lunged at the Savan's exposed leg. The old giant's foot found no purchase on the blood slick stones and he slipped, barely recovering his balance. The Savan snarled and thrust its spear towards the old man's heart. Duncan only just parried the blow sending the spear point whistling past his ear.

He countered and slapped the butt of his great waraxe up into the Savan's chin. The hulking lizard grunted in pain as it spat a few broken teeth onto the ground and stumbled back. It roared in savage rage, masking the sound of approaching hoof beats.

Duncan saw a knight barreling down on the Savan's back and dropped his guard letting the poleaxe sink towards the ground for a moment. He was out of range of the lizard's reach and let out a small sigh of relief. The battle had taken its toll on him, and the old man looked visibly exhausted, not that he would ever have admitted it. Casually he pointed behind the Savan with a confidant grin. The lizard cocked its head at Duncan in confusion.

It then heard the clacking hooves of the war steed and whirled to see what it was. Warrec was rapidly approaching but still halfway across the market square. Duncan seized the opportunity and surged forward. He swung the bardiche around in a great arc and struck the Savan with a terrible force beyond the capability of normal men. Before the Savan could dodge the attack, it was cleaved in half, separating its top from the bottom.

The Savan's sundered legs and tail thrashed and flopped madly on the ground. A torrent of blood and organs flooded across the square stones. Yet, the creature did not die. It continued to crawl toward Duncan with its one good arm, dragging a long rope of intestines behind it. The Savan feebly snapped its jaws in futile fury.

Warrec saw his father strike down the Savan and veered toward the last two Goblins. The two turned in panic flight to run for their miserable lives. He rode over one; the destrier trampling the filthy creature beneath its hooves. He impaled the last on his warlance, skewering it right below the right shoulder blade and through the lung. With a twist of the lance, he flicked the dying Goblin off the end leaving it in a crumpled heap.

Warrec turned back to his father and saw the Savan still crawling, reaching for Duncan. As the mangled lizard reached out to grab Duncan's ankle the old giant casually stabbed the Savan through the skull with a meaty crunch, finally killing it.

Warrec trotted over to his father. "Looks like I got here just in time."

Duncan spat and with a jerk pulled the axe point free. "Appreciate the distraction, but I had it under control knight."

Warrec cocked his head at Duncan. He rolled his eyes behind his visor as he realized. Duncan was relieved that the knight had showed up when he had, though he would be damned if he would show it to one of the imperial dogs.

Warrec lifted his visor so his father could see him. "Father it's me. You're welcome by the way."

"Warrec?" Duncan squinted and blinked several times as he stroked his beard. "My boy it is you."

Warrec looked around the town square. The square was littered with Goblin bodies and parts, several buildings were still on fire. The screams of terror had all but stopped only to be replaced with shouts as people rushed to put out the flames.

"Not exactly the welcome I expected," he sighed.

"We're not big on parades up here. Welcome home lad." Duncan finally said with a bitter laugh. His father was laughing. The sound was alien as he realized he couldn't remember the last time he had heard his father laughing. Water began pouring from the sky as it started to rain.

Argis sat on his ebony mare atop a hill overlooking the village. Black steel plate seemly forged of the carapace of some ancient monstrosity and a long sable cloak that appeared tailored from liquid shadow enveloped the lone figure. In sharp contrast to the dark form was his bleached white helm. The helmet had been shaped and polished in morbid fashion to resemble a human skull. Two large, curved horns jutted out on either side forming the helm into a nightmarish mask.

The lurid visage surveyed the smoking village and waited. Other than the basic form and shape there was little to indicate that the mounted motionless figure was human. The cloak swallowed and concealed his neck and mouth. No flesh showed on the dark figure and the skull appeared to float on a mass of inky blackness. Even his eyes couldn't be seen; only two red glowing points that occasionally burned and glinted out of the dark empty eye sockets.

Futuo my head itches, he thought for probably the hundredth time this morning. Argis caught his hand as he involuntarily began to raise it to scratch at that damnable itch right above his ear. *It was a nibblefly, I know it was. Had to be, it's their season anyway.*

He hated wearing the armor and helmet, but he had to keep up appearances. *Have to play the part, especially here,* he thought. Despite the discomfort the plan was going quite well.

He had watched as the village burned and his Goblins ransacked the place. He had seen the old man strike down his Goblins like so much chaff. That was to be expected. They were no big loss; there were plenty more where those had come from after all. The verminous things bred like rabbits.

Had to keep him busy and distracted, that was the key after all, he thought. A slight smile managed to manifest on his face, hidden beneath his helm.

However, the Savan was an unfortunate and costly loss. It took nearly a century for one of the warrior caste to grow that large. Still, that was why he had brought it. He knew the old man would make short work of the Goblins so something more formidable had been needed. He had not foreseen the arrival of the knight and his companion, but it was no matter. He would still have his prize on this day. He grinned to himself again.

After a few more minutes his Goblin captain came running

up. This one had been specially bred for intelligence to serve as an officer, though that wasn't saying much. *At least it can talk in full sentences.* Argis thought as he lowered his menacing gaze toward the Goblin captain.

"They have it milord," the filthy creature croaked.

Argis looked at his servant and nodded. *Excellent. This is coming together quite well, quite well indeed,* he thought.

He then turned his attention back to the old man and knight. The battle was over and the two were talking to each other. The Savan had served its purpose and bought the time needed.

Two more Goblins came trotting up the hill huffing under the weight they bore between them. They carried a long cylinder wrapped in ancient moldy leather. They rushed to their master's side and knelt lifting the cylinder as high as their apelike arms could reach. In a blur of motion Argis leaned down and snatched the object from them. He tore off the leather covering revealing a sword and scabbard from some archaic and bygone age. With grim satisfaction he unsheathed it and marveled at its dreadful beauty.

The sword was long and single edged, with a sharpness that cleaved the very air around it. It was carried in a leathery scabbard that seemed to be bound of human skin. The hilt was formed of bleached bone, wrapped in the same cadaverous leather.

A small shrunken skull forged out of silver with ruby eyes formed the pommel. Vertebrae ran the length of the blade framing its spine. The blade itself forged of nightmare given form in blackened steel slowly pulsed a dull red with stolen heartbeats. Argis' dread countenance seemed to form into a macabre smile as it began to rain. *The Soulblade is mine, now for the chase,* he thought.

Warrec dismounted and removed his helmet. He looked skyward and ran his armored hand across his face and through his sweaty hair. He then opened his mouth to catch a few rain drops in his mouth. He relished the sweet pure taste as it washed the dryness from his mouth. The rain began to ease up from a torrent to a mild shower. The sudden deluge had extinguished the fires. Though much of the village was charred on the whole it remained intact.

Warrec turned to look at his father and started to speak but stopped. Father and son stared at each other, both disliking the silence but neither willing to break it. After a few awkward moments they saw Joenair walking into the square carrying a young woman.

Warrec shook his head in mild amusement and rolled his

eyes. "Of course, he found a pretty young woman to rescue," he muttered to himself. As his friend approached the sudden rain shower stopped altogether vanishing just as quickly as it had begun.

Warrec and Duncan jogged over toward them. Duncan took the girl from Joenair and gently laid her on the ground. He took a small flask from his pocket and pulled the cork out with his teeth.

Warrec's eyes narrowed at the sight of the flask. "What's that, more booze?" Warrec asked bitterly.

"No boy, it's healing elixirs," Duncan replied with indignation in his voice. He brought the flask to the girl's lips and poured some in her mouth. She sputtered as the sickly-sweet liquid washed through her mouth. The healing power of the magical concoction began coursing through her and within a few seconds she would be back on her feet.

Warrec could practically taste the elixir as the sight stirred old memories. They tasted both sweet and bitter at the same time. It was a vile concoction but a lifesaver, nonetheless. A few mouthfuls would wash away all fatigue and close up minor wounds. A whole bottle could save someone from a fatal injury, but it did have limits. It couldn't regrow flesh or cure disease.

Duncan wiped the fiery orange hair from her eyes and gently

stroked her head. *She is beautiful,* Warrec thought absently. Her dress had been torn open at the midriff. He watched as a shallow cut closed up and scabbed over leaving only a lean muscled stomach.

The girl blinked rapidly trying to clear her vision. "Duncan?" she asked, confused.

"Aye Aluna it's me. Are you alright?"

Warrec's eyes bulged. "Aluna? Little Aluna?" Warrec asked in astonishment. It was now that Warrec took a second long look at her. This was not the little girl he had last seen, all knees and elbows. This was a fine example of womanhood.

Aluna's hair was a fiery orange-red and her skin a freckled tan. Her lips jumped out from her face in a natural bright red. She was dressed in a plain blue woolen dress with gold trim that fastened with two silver brooches. A bright green sash was tied around her middle in a loose belt that matched the emerald in her eyes.

The dress was very tight and conformed to her body, giving a good picture of its outline. Her body was tall and leanly muscled. The shape reminded him of the bodies of the female athletes he had seen at the coliseums. The dress was also very reveling as it was split up one side showing a tan well-muscled thigh. Warrec could hardly see an ounce of fat on her other than the swell at her chest common to most northern women. Aluna filled out the dress nicely and Warrec found his cheeks burning as his face grew red.

Aluna glanced around at the three men around her. Duncan knelt beside her, and she reached over and squeezed his arm. Her eyes flicked over to Joenair, and she gave him a quick nod of thanks. Then her eyes scanned over Warrec. He could feel her emerald eyes probing across him, taking in the armor, his height, his looks, and everything about him. *Does she recognize me?* he wondered.

"What the hell are you looking at?" she asked. She then propped herself up on an elbow and spat off to the side.

Warrec had forgotten how little most of The Lake cared about the empire. She saw the armor and nothing else. He started to say something, but his father beat him to it.

"Aluna it's Warrec. It's him," Duncan spoke softly.

Her eyes flashed in realization. She sucked in a deep breath. Her eyes danced up and down as she examined him again. Warrec could see her nostrils flare as she seemed to be glaring at him, but there was something else as she locked eyes with him. He cocked his head in confusion. She sighed and looked away for a few seconds almost seeming to dismiss him.

Aluna grunted and sat all the way up. She rolled her head back and forth and Warrec could hear her neck popping. She looked out across the town square. The rain had washed most of the blood and bile away, but there was still a large assortment of Goblin corpses and body parts littered about. Along with a very large bisected Savan. "I'm not cleaning this up," she grunted.

She waved Duncan away as she stood. "I'm fine. I'm fine. Stop fussing, you're getting as bad as an old hen." They both stood together, and she punched the old giant lightly on the shoulder. Aluna took a deep breath before she turned her attention back to Warrec.

"What's the matter big boy don't you recognize your old chum?" Aluna said dripping with sarcasm. "Hmmm let's see" -she spread her arms out wide- "it's only been what ten years since you last saw me. What? I guess you've been too busy to come back home, off saving the world?" Aluna spread the fingers of both hands and flicked them toward Warrec before dropping them back to the ground in dismissal.

In two long strides she quickly reached Joenair and seized him by the front of the shirt. Aluna jerked him towards her, nearly lifting him off his feet and kissed him hard. Then just as quickly she shoved him back, leaving a very confused look on the spymaster's face.

"That's for saving me," she said. "I was about spent. If you hadn't shown up when you did, I don't know if I could have held those futten ratkies off."

Warrec gave a slight shudder at the thought. Goblins tended to do horrible things to women when they could catch them. It was usually better to go down fighting than let them carry you off to one of their burrows. Warrec suddenly felt his blood begin to boil at the thought of those disgusting things touching her. He sucked in a deep breath and mentally took back control of his body.

Aluna's eyes darted over towards him, and she halfcocked an eyebrow as Warrec's face flushed. Aluna fixed him with a glare and with a sniff she turned her attention back to Joenair. Aluna stepped in close and ran her hand across Joenair's chest. "So, what's your name handsome?" she asked.

With a start, Joenair seemed to realize that Aluna was every bit his height and looked like she might even have a few pounds of lean muscle on him. Warrec could see confusion, then panic, and then consideration wash across Joenair's face.

"Joenair and the pleasure was all mine my lady." A confidant smirk crept across his face as he wrapped an arm around Aluna's waist. Joenair was always ready to jump at an opportunity and Warrec felt an odd surge of jealousy. He didn't like it. Joenair leaned in towards Aluna's ear and seemed to whisper. "And perhaps we could make the pleasure yours as well later tonight."

Aluna gave the smaller man a half smile. She somewhat

gently shoved Joenair back. "Sorry, you're cute but a little short for me." Her eyes darted back towards Warrec. She drew a finger up and down Joenair's chest and said with a sly smile "But perhaps we'll see my brave man. We'll see."

Warrec had not heard exactly what Joenair had whispered but knowing his friend he had a good idea. He couldn't help but feel a twinge of jealousy. Though he didn't know quite why he was feeling this way, Aluna had always been a friend. Now though it seemed different, she was different, no longer a child. She had become a woman yes, and there was something else, an inner strength and confidence that had not been there before. He knew that her father had been training her to become the village's shaman, but surely, she had not completed it yet.

Warrec slightly shook his head trying to clear it. Seeing Aluna again made his head feel fuzzy, almost like his brain was itching and he didn't like it. Then Warrec realized that he had not seen the shaman yet, he should have been out here fighting with the rest of the villagers.

"Aluna where is your father? Athern should be here helping," Warrec said looking around. Duncan sighed and stepped back. The old giant looked back at Warrec and then again at Aluna.

Duncan seemed to shake his head at the idiocy of youth. "Fool boy never knew when to keep his mouth shut," Duncan muttered to himself. Duncan's face contorted in a mask of pain as an old memory seemed to flare up in his mind. "Everett," he whispered. The old giant stared off at nothing for several seconds. He tried his best to keep it from his face but couldn't completely and turned away.

As Duncan was fighting his inner demons, Aluna turned toward Warrec and let hers loose. "My father, my father the village shaman, right? Oh, he is dead." Tears began to well up in her eyes as she spoke. "He died two years ago Warrec. Two years! You would have known that if you had come home." -Aluna slapped at Warrec's chest- "You abandoned us." She pushed at Warrec's chest and reflexively he stepped back.

"Aluna that's not true… I…" Warrec stammered unsure of what to say. He suddenly had no idea what to do with his hands and froze in place, immobile as a piece of granite. Only his jaw worked furiously as he desperately tried to summon something to say, but his tongue refused to obey him.

"Bullskret Warrec, bullskret. You could have come home if you had wanted to. You didn't even bother to write." Then she slapped him across the face and turned away in a furious huff.

Warrec stared at her back still frozen. When she spoke again her voice was quieter now, with almost a slight tremble. "Things have changed Warrec, not many for the better either. I'm the village shaman now. I had to finish my training on my own. I was the one who brought the rain. That's why I was so weak when Joenair found me. If it hadn't been for him, I don't think I would still be alive." Aluna wrapped her arms around her body, hugging herself. "I always thought you would be the one to save me Warrec, to come riding in on your horse your armor gleaming…I guess I was wrong." With that she walked away to see to the wounded.

Warrec was left speechless. He never knew that she had felt that way about him. He had been oblivious to it and now it had created a rift between them; a rift that he didn't have a clue how to mend. He felt like kicking himself.

He looked around the market square and at the charred buildings. "Some homecoming," he whispered to himself miserably. The village would survive. The dead would be exalted and mourned. The buildings would be rebuilt. With the battle now over, it didn't appear that there were many casualties, a few wounded, mostly damage to the buildings, but nothing that time couldn't cure. Warrec almost wished there were a few more Goblins to take his frustration out on.

Joenair's eyes darted back and forth between Warrec and Aluna as they finished speaking. *Ok,* Joenair thought. *That was a little weird.* The conference in his mind began speaking all at once.

*Her lips tasted like strawberries. *

*Nice arse too. *

*Addie has a better one, big and plump. *

*Hush, don't think of your best friend's soon to be wife like that. Shame on you. *

*That guy is a giant, has to be War's father. Note to self to not piss him off. *

*Why did she kiss me like that? Is that something the northern giants do? *

*You nitwit pay attention. Read the body language, she is using you. She wants to make him jealous. *

Joenair gave a slow mental nod to himself as he came to an agreement. Then he wanted to kick himself. There he was thinking with his pants instead of his brain again. She had been playing with him to get Warrec jealous.

I better leave this one alone. That girl is deeply in love with my idiot friend, and he can't see it. Did he know?

*Doubt it. He doesn't pick up on that. Addie had to practically throw herself at him. *

Or he couldn't see it before, maybe now it will sink through his thick skull. Not that it matters. Joenair looked over at Warrec then back to Aluna. Warrec was still watching

Aluna and doing his best to pretend that he wasn't. *Or does it?*
Dammit this is too complicated. This was supposed to be an easy
and happy trip.

This whole romance thing was too complicated for him, and
he didn't want anything to do with it. He sighed to himself.
Where is a good barmaid when you need one? With them it's just a
couple of coins and a kiss on the cheek in the morning. No
strings and nobody gets hurt. His mind begun to wander back to
thoughts of sweet, beautiful Zylaa in Artania, now there was a
woman.

"By the way Joenair this is my father Duncan Vornirulf
Bjornson," Warrec said with a wave of his had indicating the
exceptionally large man holding an exceptionally large poleaxe
next to him. The big man's voice snapped Joenair's attention
back to the present. The image of Zylaa's beautiful face smiling
down at him as she bounced on top of him shattered.

*Bounce, bouncy, bouncy, fun. *

"Pleasure to meet you sir," Joenair said bowing with a
flourish of his right arm before the old man. Duncan only
grunted and didn't bother to turn around.

"As you can see, he is a wondrously hospitable man and an
absolute pleasure to be around," Warrec said his voice dripping
with sarcasm and venom.

It was at this point Duncan finally looked over and glanced

back to the area where the temple was. Joenair followed his gaze and could just see the tips of several conical rooftops peeking out from above the trees just outside the main wall surrounding the town. He assumed that was the temple Warrec had mentioned. It certainly didn't fit in with the architecture of the rest of the town.

It looked like the temple was in a glade surrounded by trees. The main wall had been extended out to encircle the grounds. The main building itself was unseen from the square, blocked from view by a row of two-story houses. However, smoke could be seen rising from the general area of the temple. Duncan was staring hard at the smoke. His brow furrowed in deep consternation, and he hefted his bardiche.

"No, no, it's nothing," Duncan spoke to no one in particular and it sounded more like he was trying to convince himself of his words, than anyone else. "There is nothing valuable in there, except" -the old giant rapidly shook his head- "but no one knows it's there."

Joenair cocked his head at the old man. Something was terribly wrong. He could sense waves of dread and despair coming off the old giant. Without another word Duncan bolted, running off towards the temple grounds.

Warrec and Joenair watched the old man run off. "So that's your father huh? He is huge. I mean you are huge, but he is a giant. You told me he was a drunken old man. He looked like a wild dragon the way he cut through those Goblins and took down a Savan warrior by himself. Color me impressed."

"Yes, but that's not how he is normally now," Warrec said as he spat on the ground. "Well, at least that's not how I remember him being," he added.

"You hate him that much?"

"I wouldn't say hate. We just don't get along. Never really have. But it was especially bad ever since Everett died and then mother dying shortly after. He crawled into a bottle and never came out." Warrec looked in the direction his father had run off. "Truth be told this is the first time I've seen him this sober in a long time, though to be fair I haven't seen him in a long time. It was just the two of us left in our family, but he acted like there was nothing left to live for." Warrec shook his head in disgust. "He wouldn't even speak to me at times. He just looked at me, like...like, it was my fault somehow. Like everything was going to end and I was a constant reminder of how he had lost everything. In the end it made leaving much easier."

The two friends stood in silence for a few minutes. People began gathering back into the square. The only sounds that could be heard were the occasional groan from the wounded and low conversations as people discussed the cleanup plans. Aluna was a hundred feet away attending to an old woman who had broken an ankle running away.

Like a sudden crack of thunder, the air was broken by an inhuman bellow of pain and anguish from the temple grounds. The birds that had sought shelter in the temple grove burst into the air as the mournful cry rose in intensity. Warrec and Joenair looked at each other and broke into a run towards the temple grounds. Before they were halfway across the square Aluna was at their side. None of them spoke as they ran, fearing the worst.

As they reached the temple clearing, they saw Duncan staggering out of the temple. His face was pale and was twisted into a mask of utter despair. "It's gone," He groaned

Chapter Four

All three spoke in unison. "What's gone?"

"The sword," Duncan whispered. The old giant could not hold his anguish back anymore and began to cry. His face dropped to his hands and his whole body shook as he sucked in ragged breath after breath. Warrec stood stunned. He didn't know what to say or do. He had never seen his father cry, not even when Everett or his mother had died.

One of the hilltops that had been obscured by a rooftop in the square became visible in the temple grounds. Aluna was the first to see him and she gasped and pointed at him. The other three turned to look where she was pointing and saw him as well.

The Dread Lord sat on his horse on the top of the hill looking down at them. Argis seemed to have been waiting and watching the temple grounds. When they finally were aware of his presence, he held up the sword high over his head. He taunted them, baiting them. When they all had raised their heads in his direction and seen him, he turned and began slowly trotting away down the hill. He appeared to be in no hurry, almost like he was waiting for them to catch up.

At first the group registered nothing but shock, then Duncan's body began to shake with rage, and he let out another roar that shook the temple grounds. Warrec shared his father's anger. One of the few things they still had in common was their hatred for Lord Argis.

They both hated him for different reasons, but they still hated him. Now it seemed he had the sacred sword. Warrec didn't really care much about the sword. This was a chance for revenge. Plus, he felt it was his duty as a knight in the legion to bring Argis to justice. Argis had terrorized the empire as long as there had been an empire. Now he was alone and vulnerable.

"We have to go after him," Warrec said as the resolve gave his voice strength.

"Yes...now. We have to go now!" Duncan's voice was shaky from anger.

"Right, ok we need to go after…wait, what? Are you two crazy?" Joenair stammered in shock. "That's the Dread Lord Argis, ruler of the Black Lands and you want to chase him down like a common Goblin? I don't believe what I'm hearing. I know you two know the legends."

Warrec slowly nodded. He knew the legends. Argis was said to be immortal. He had ruled over all of the Black Lands for as long as the empire had existed. How the empire had barely been able to hold him at bay, to keep him from conquering the entire world. Time again and again the armies of the Black Lands had swooped down and sowed chaos and death, only to be pushed back at the last moment. Each time the empire had survived but only just barely.

For the last few decades, the Dread Lord had withdrawn his forces and the banner of the Black Lands had rarely been seen since. Everyone had thought for sure that when the empire had split thirty years ago, he would swoop down from the far frozen north and crush the world under his heel and yet he hadn't. Everett had been one of the last to fall to the Dread Lord. Argis had not been seen since then.

The Empire had been ruled by the same family for as long back as anyone could remember. The line of Kalindor had managed to bring an age of progress and prosperity to the Maroveyan Empire despite the constant threat of Argis. However, when Emperor Ordias died the Empire had fractured between his two sons.

Both sons had claim to the throne as they were twins and had been born together. Valorn was technically the first born in that he had come out first. The story goes however that Ptharis was holding on to Valorn's leg and had been pulled out with him.

The rumor was that the two brothers had battled constantly in the womb. Their mother queen Mirabella had a terrible pregnancy and died shortly after giving birth. The complete opposite in appearance and manner the brothers had fought and competed the entire time they were growing up.

Valorn grew to be a kind and wise man and a powerful warrior. He was adored by the wealthy and the common folk alike. Handsome with striking features many young noble women had pursued after him.

Ptharis was slight of frame and never particularly strong. His body was small and twisted and he had gone bald early in life. He was crafty and cunning and slier than any fox. His mind was his real weapon and many a fool had lost to him in political battles.

When the Emperor had died the ruling noble houses had formed an imperial senate. When the twins had reached ten years of age the senate had split Marovia in two. Valorn took the eastern half and Ptharis the west. The White Mountains dividing them in the middle. Eastern Marovia extended to the Slothan Mountains that separated the east from the orc lands of Nangonango. The endless Jade Sea grasslands formed the border of Western Marovia, and the desolate White Desert separated it from The Black Lands. For nearly thirty years the senate had been the principle ruling body of the fractured empire, holding both sides together.

The eastern side was rich in woodland and forests. It was

also bordered by the Dwarven lands and was rich in ore and trade with the friendly Dwarves. The great Orcs lived in the jungles of Nangonango in the south to the east of the Slothan Mountains and a strong alliance had been formed between the two races over the last decade, finally cementing thanks to Addie. The eastern half was rich in trade and natural resources. However, there was little farm and grazing land.

The western half had few natural resources but produced almost all of the empire's food supply. Its plains of the Jade Sea grasslands seemed to stretch on forever, perfect for raising crops or livestock. Huge herds of bison, sheep and aurochs roamed the plains, tended loosely by the ranchers. Almost all the horses were raised there as well, from the smaller scout and coach breeds to the giant destrier war horses. Lately a few ranchers had tentatively begun raising stone wyrms for their meat and bones.

The stone wyrms were one of the few remaining species of the giant reptiles left. They were plant eaters and docile as lambs. The huge beasts lumbered across the steppes grazing with little concern for anyone or anything. Safe from all natural predators they plodded along oblivious to the world around them.

Their back, head and tail were all covered in thick bone protecting a soft vulnerable underbelly, even their eyelids were armored. Most had a thick club or spines on the end of their tail. Not even the fearsome Rajanaga, the dragon kings of the Orc jungles could bite through their armor and hurt them. When attacked the beasts sank to the ground impervious as a stone, occasionally taking a swipe at anything foolish enough to attack them with their tail.

The witless wyrms behaved just like dull witted sheep allowing ranchers to casually walk up and cull their herds. Humans were too small to be of any concern. A rancher could calmly walk up and slit a throat before the animal even knew what had happened.

They were better than cattle in that they were much larger, easily twice the size of a normal cow. So, there was more meat and the bony plates on their backs could be fashioned into shields. The shields fashioned from their plates were almost as strong as the Dwarves' valentium shields though unfortunately they proved to be much heavier and could not be carried by one person. Instead, the empire had taken to using the plates to reinforce buildings and fortifications.

Ptharis had been the driving force behind the expansion of the stone wyrm herds. His vision had brought the western empire much wealth. It had also drawn ire from his brother and the eastern side.

The imperial senate had hoped that by dividing the empire like this each side would have a fair share and the two brothers couldn't throw the empire into a civil war for control, because neither had all the resources to wage war. Ptharis had the food and the horses but not the numbers or the resources. Valorn didn't have a large enough stored food supply or mounts to maintain a large army for long.

Every two years the senate switched between the two capitals, Eldurond in the east and its sister city Eldurania in the west. Valorn and Ptharis alternated overseeing the senate in their respective cities. That had been the original plan anyway. Eldurond had always been the capital of the empire and the senate had begun finding more and more reasons to stay longer in the grand human city. They had now been in Eldurond for close to four years. Valorn had of course denied any involvement in keeping the senate in his city. Rumors had begun spreading of Ptharis' jealousy and mounting animosity towards his brother.

There was danger in the western half as the Black Lands lay to the north and roving tribes of centaurs raided the far western side. So, both kings maintained outposts and garrisons on the borders for protection. At the mouth of the great river Zaphan were the twin cities Snetha on the west bank and Artania on the east. Valorn was given control of Artania and Ptharis took Snetha.

"Wait, let's wait a second and talk about this." Joenair's voice snapped Warrec's mind back to the present. "So, it looks like Argis is back. Ok, that's bad but what we" -Joenair pointed back and forth rapidly between himself and Warrec- "need to do is to ride south and inform our commander, remember him? We need to tell Legate Silnis of this change of events."

Warrec looked at his friend, though it was probably more of a glare than he intended. Jay was right after all; still he couldn't let this opportunity get away. Besides, he knew damn well that his father was not going to just sit here and wait.

Joenair looked at the two men and let out a long-drawn-out sigh. "But no there are two very large and angry men looking at me that want me to come with them to chase down The Dread Lord." He glanced over at Aluna searching for help. The look in her eyes showed that he would find none. "You too? Great, futten great. Futuo, who wants to die of old age anyway?"

"Horses, we need horses," Duncan bellowed as he began running back toward the village.

"Me and Joenair have ours," Warrec said. He began running after his father.

"Ok, I know where the others are for Duncan and me," Aluna answered back following after him. In a flurry the group reached the square. Warrec jammed his foot into the stirrup and swung his other leg up and over. He mounted the warhorse in one quick well practiced move and brought it around. Duncan and Aluna kept running toward one of the side stables off the town square.

"Where's your horse?" Warrec asked as he looked back at Joenair.

Joenair glanced around and seemed to realize he had no idea where his mount was. "I don't know. I don't have any bloody idea. I had dismounted at the beginning of the battle and ran along the rooftops." Joenair swept his arms around in a large circle. "But now the bloody nag has wandered off in the confusion."

"Come on then," Warrec grabbed Joenair's arm and pulled him up onto the back of the horse. They rode towards where Aluna and Duncan had gone. Duncan already had his horse mounted and was helping Aluna when Warrec and Joenair rounded the corner. All four of them were breathing heavy from all the exertion as they furiously moved to try and catch up to Argis. Joenair hopped off Warrec's horse and began saddling the last remaining mount.

"Where's your horse?" Aluna asked.

"I don't know. I lost it during the battle." Joenair's face was beginning to turn red. "Normally I'm a very prepared person. It's just this nonsense that has me addled is all." The last remaining horse was an ancient looking old nag. With a huff he began saddling the antique equine. "This will only take a few moments for me to saddle this relic."

Duncan wasn't going to wait on the rest of them. He pulled the cinch strap tight and as soon as Aluna was saddled up, he was gone. Warrec and Aluna quickly followed. Joenair followed after them a few seconds later bringing up the rear. He was trying very hard to catch up with them, cursing under his breath the whole time.

Chapter Five

The group rode at full gallop for hours as they raced to catch the Dread Lord. Warrec and Duncan both knew exactly where Argis was going. There was really only one place he could go and that was the Gap of Adun. The gap was an immense canyon gouged out by the Adun River. Some legends spoke of a great dragon crashing to the earth which had scourged the land, splitting it in half. Still others referred to a comet instead of a dragon. The imperial scientists had long sought to put away such superstitions. According to them the river Adun had flowed southeast down from the White Mountains on the Vatninu's northernmost border and cut the gorge out over millennia.

The canyon was the boundary between the northlands and the eastern tip of the Black Lands. It was the northernmost point of the empire. The Gap was the place where the map ended and where the spot of dragons and monsters lay. The Black lands were named so because they were unexplored, no map existed, at least none that Warrec knew about. No one that had gone more than a few miles beyond The Gap had ever returned.

The gorge was impassable save for one lone rope bridge. Vatninu and imperial legionnaires had both cut down the bridge numerous times, but every time within a few days Argis' forces had it back up. That bridge was where Argis was heading. If he made it across the bridge, he would be in his territory and there would be no way to stop him. They had to catch him before he crossed the bridge.

Warrec glanced to his side at Joenair and then Aluna. *Jay is not happy,* he thought. He looked back up towards his father. Duncan rode a few dozen feet ahead of them pushing hard to catch Argis. *He isn't going to stop.*

After a little over half a day of riding, alternating between cantering and galloping, they had reached the mid-plains. It was a natural line cut across the plains between the immense White Mountains and the northern forests. It marked the side closest to the mountain's shadow. Here the grass was browner and the whole area seemed more devoid of life. The rolling hills stopped and there were numerous places where the earth had cracked, and nothing grew. They were drawing close to the Black Lands.

With no surprise Warrec could now see the smoldering ruins of Fort Adun. One of the northernmost posts in the empire, the fort guarded the imperial side of the gorge and kept the Goblins from raiding into the Vatninu's territory. For Argis' forces to have reached Thornglade then they would have had to get past the fort first. Of the one hundred and twenty men that normally held the fort none had made it to Thornglade to warn of the impending attack.

Argis had been methodical and almost surgical in his attack. The wooden palisade around the fort had begun to be replaced with high stone walls. The upgrades had done little to stop the forces of the Black Lands. The palisade surrounding the fort had been ripped open as if by some giant unseen hand. It looked like Argis had come in the night and caught the garrison completely unaware. A pile of burnt smoldering bodies was piled up outside. Several heads mounted on stakes formed a macabre forest surrounding the fort.

The company slowed to a trot as they entered the field of carnage. Warrec looked at the heads as they rode past. He didn't recognize any of the murdered men and gave a small sigh of relief. Aluna let out a cry of remorse at the sight of the fort. Warrec was reminded that since Thornglade was the closest village Aluna would have known these men. He looked back over his shoulder and gave her a face of sympathy. Aluna forced herself to look at the burnt garrison again and shook her head as they continued on.

"Come on, pick it up. We can't do anything for them except avenge them now," Duncan growled from the front before he kicked his horse back into a gallop.

After about another thirty minutes of hard riding they slowed to stop and rest the horses. Duncan had some jubee root and the group dismounted for a few minutes as he fed this to all the horses. The roots' properties worked similar to the healing elixir, but nowhere near as potent, although jubee root was a main ingredient of the potion. The root kept the horse's strength up and washed away fatigue. Without it the horses would have died from exhaustion. However, jubee root could only do so much, despite their fortitude enhancing properties. Luckily, it appeared that they would reach the gorge by nightfall.

Duncan had said little since they had ridden out from the village. A few almost animalistic growls had escaped his lips as they had ridden by the destroyed fort. Like a kettle set on a flame Warrec could feel the rage bubbling to boiling as it emanated from his father. He was growing fearful of what would happen when it boiled over. As soon as his horse had finished the root Duncan set heels to it and they shot off across the plain.

Warrec had always known that his father held a deep almost mystical power within him. Before Everett had died and when Warrec was still a boy he had asked his brother about it. Everett had told him that Duncan was a guardian. Warrec had pressed his brother for more information, but Everett would never tell him anything more about it.

Looking back, he might not have known anything else. Warrec thought. He knew Duncan would not stop and would chase Argis to the ends of the earth. Warrec recognized that Argis would have laid some kind of trap for them. The Dread Lord was predictable in that way. Though he doubted his father would realize or even care in the state of mind he was in. *Always assume it's a trap,* Silnis' voice echoed in his mind.

Warrec called out to his father. *The old man is going to get himself killed trying to get some rusty family heirloom back.* Duncan either didn't hear him or was ignoring him and thundered on.

"Dammit," Warrec growled. Even if they were able to catch Argis, Warrec knew in the back of his mind they were no match for him. *This was foolish,* he thought. *I let myself get caught up in the moment. Only a fool would chase after Argis alone. I should have listened to Joenair. Not that father would have listened, and I couldn't let him go alone. Dammit all to hell.*

Legends told of Argis personally destroying entire armies and laying waste to towns and villages. Tales that obviously had been exaggerated over time, but still contained a kernel of truth. Warrec did not want the four of them to test how accurate the legends were.

Warrec spurred his horse on. He had to catch up to his

father to keep him from running blindly into the trap. He may not have liked the old man much, but he was all the family Warrec had left.

Dusk was fast approaching when they again drew sight of him. Argis was still far off, but they were quickly gaining ground on him. The few remaining Goblin raiding party that had accompanied him and managed to survive had long since scattered with a few stragglers rode down by the four of them.

"Is he...is he waiting for us?" Joenair asked.

Warrec did not like the implications. As they approached within an arrow shot's length The Dread Lord was moving along at a slow trot. As they neared, he turned in the saddle to look at them and then spurred his horse to gallop away at full speed.

After another ten minutes of this cat and mouse chase they were less than a mile from the bridge. Argis was only a few hundred feet ahead of them, but they could not close the gap any further. The horses were nearing exhaustion and would not be able to go for much longer.

"We have to stop him!" Duncan roared. He looked back at Aluna with a wild fury in his eyes and he nodded at her. She returned the nod and licked her lips.

"I'm so sorry," she whispered, tears in her eyes. She reached forward and placed her hand on her horse's neck. A small red glow began to swell around her hand. Small lines of red light traced up her arm as it flowed out from the horse, growing in brightness and intensity.

Warrec sucked in a deep breath as he realized what she was doing. "Oh, Aluna no," he said.

She ignored him. Aluna thrust her hand out in front of her and screamed a deep primal scream. The ground a few feet in front of Argis exploded upward in a shower of rock and dirt. A huge crashing wave of earth nearly fifty feet high rose up in front of The Dread Lord threatening to engulf him.

Argis pulled hard on the reins as his horse screamed in fear and slid to a stop. With one smooth motion he drew the Soulblade and swept it forward in a slicing arc. The wall of flowing earth split in half, the two sides smashing back to the ground around him.

Aluna's horse collapsed underneath her. She jumped and rolled like an expert rider and managed to land unhurt. The horse let a last rattle of air and lay still. Warrec and Joenair looked back to see if she was ok.

"I'm ok. Go on," she yelled at them. She began running after them.

Warrec slowly shook his head. *Blood magic,* he thought. He knew it was a tool in a shaman's toolkit, but he had never thought he would see Aluna use it. He glanced back at her horse. It was now little more than a dry husk. She had pulled all the life energy out of it. All magic had a price he knew but using another creature's lifeforce was pushing the boundaries of what was acceptable.

Duncan's roar snapped his eyes back forward. The old giant had caught up to Argis and was pressing him hard. Duncan swept the great waraxe back and forth in a whirlwind of spinning steel. Both horses were stomping and furrowing the upturned earth around them as their riders guided them in a deadly circular dance.

Argis leaned back and forth in the saddle, his head barely moving as Duncan's blade swept past. Each attack would miss him by inches, but still Duncan could only cleave the air around The Dread Lord. Occasionally Argis would use the Soulblade to parry or block an attack that was a little too close. Although Warrec could only see the grinning skull helm he could swear Argis looked bored.

Warrec gritted his teeth and leveled his lance at Argis' chest. He spurred his horse forward at a full charge. Argis cocked his head at the charging knight. The Dread Lord parried another strike from Duncan and spun his horse around to face Warrec completely.

At the last second Argis snapped his wrist to the side using the Soulblade to knock the tip of Warrec's lance off target. It passed harmlessly past as Warrec's momentum carried him forward. The blade was stretched out in front of him, and time seemed to slow down.

Warrec watched as that cursed blade hung in the air pulsing a dull eerie red. Slowly it seemed to move toward him, calling to him as Argis swept it forward at his neck. Warrec knew as he stared at its malevolent beauty that armor or not it would take his head off without an ounce of exertion. This was his end.

"Warrec!" Aluna and Joenair both seemed to shout in unison.

"Son, no!" Duncan bellowed and tried to reach out and catch him.

Argis' head gave a slight tilt to the old giant when he shouted. As the Soulblade bore down on Warrec, Argis turned it slapping the flat of the sword across the top of Warrec's chestplate and gorget. The clothesline blow ripped Warrec from the saddle and sent him flying down to the ground as his horse continued running on.

As Warrec was sent sailing backward through the air Joenair rode into the melee and flipped a knife at Argis. The blade spun through the air seeking its mark at Argis' head. In one motion Argis dropped his reins and ripped the knife out of the air with his free hand before sending it spinning back to its master. Joenair yelped as he leaned back to lay back in the saddle, the knife scarcely missing his face as it flew past. The master assassin lost his balance and tumbled out of the saddle planting face first in the dirt.

Duncan once more entered the fight with a roar that would have put any bearcat to shame. He swept the great bardiche up and brought it down to cleave Argis and his horse in half. Again, the Dread Lord somehow effortlessly parried the blow. Finally, it seemed Argis was growing tired of the game.

He swept the Soulblade back up and neatly clipped the head off Duncan's horse. A shower of blood poured out of its neck as the head plopped to the ground. The poor beast never made a sound as it collapsed like a puppet with its strings cut and sent Duncan tumbling to the ground.

With that final move Argis gave a mocking salute with the sword and sped off back toward the bridge. Dazed, Warrec managed to lift his head and watch the quickly retreating rear end of Argis' horse.

Aluna reached Warrec and skidded to a stop on her knees. Gently she cradled his head in her lap as she checked him for injuries. He let his head fall limply back onto her. He hurt everywhere, but he didn't think anything was broken, though there would be a huge bruise across his chest come tomorrow. For now, the fight was over.

Argis had too much of a lead and there was a Goblin village on the other side of the bridge. They kept anyone from entering the Black Lands. The Goblins and the soldiers from the garrison had often lined up on their respective sides to trade insults and take pot shots at each other with bow and arrows. Neither side had dared to cross over, until now.

Aluna finished her check and pulled his faceplate up. "Hi, dummy. You're lucky to be alive." Warrec groaned in answer. Aluna glanced over towards Duncan. "Your father is already on his feet. Are you going to lie here all day?"

Warrec half growled, half groaned as he rolled over to his stomach. He pushed himself off the ground and brought a leg up underneath him. With another long groan he stood back up. Jay lay face down a few feet away.

"Are you dead?" Warrec asked Joenair. The master assassin only responded with a thumbs up, not bothering to lift his head off the ground.

Warrec looked at his father. Duncan was running after Argis. The old giant seemed to be quickly losing all sense of reason and there was a mad crazed look in his eyes. It didn't look like he was able to think clearly anymore and was planning on storming The Black Lands by himself.

Aluna pulled herself up using Warrec, causing him to groan again and glare at her. She winked at him in response. Slowly she shook her head as she watched Duncan running after The Dread Lord.

"I know your father is a great warrior. I remember from

before Everett died. My father used to tell stories of Duncan by the fireside. He was a terror on the battlefield and despite all the years of depression and anger he has suffered he still has that inside him." She paused. "I'm angry and resentful you left" -then she locked eyes with him- "but I have to admit the training you have gotten must have done something to not make you as clumsy as I remember."

She looked back to Joenair still lying on the ground and swept her arm over indicating him. "And he is...capable, I guess. But we four can't go storming over to the other side. So, you should probably go get your father before he gets himself killed."

Warrec slowly nodded and whistled for his horse. She was right of course. He suddenly remembered her being right a lot when they were kids. He didn't like it.

He walked over and grabbed Joenair by the back of the belt. "Get up Jay. We have to go." In one motion Warrec pulled Joenair off the ground and set him on his feet. He then grabbed the reins of his warhorse and swung back up into the saddle.

"Fine, but I was having such a lovely dream." Joenair said in response. He saddled back up on his old nag. Despite the exhausting run the old horse didn't seem none the worse for wear.

"Oh, what was it about?" Warrec asked as he set his heels

and rode off.

"I was dreaming I wasn't here about to die!" Joenair yelled after him before following.

Warrec and Joenair rode side by side as they chased after Duncan, who was still pursuing after the Dread Lord. Duncan was roughly three hundred feet ahead of them, but they quickly closed the distance on horseback. Warrec hated Argis, but he knew that as much as he hated him his father hated him even more. He had no idea how he was going to keep his father from rushing across the bridge after him.

The gorge was about five hundred feet across. Argis was halfway across the old bridge when they reached the gorge. Argis slashed the support ropes with calculated timing as he crossed. The Goblins on the opposite side had seen their master approaching and the riders chasing him.

They began streaming across the bridge past their master and onto the other side. The three of them found their way barred as they reached the bridge by nearly a hundred jibbering Goblins with more swarming across the bridge. Warrec wheeled his horse in front of Duncan to keep the old man from charging through the Goblins and crossing after Argis.

When Argis was twenty feet from the Goblin side he cut the final support and with a loud snap the bridge began to collapse. Shadows swirled and gathered around The Dread Lord. Argis sprang from his horse and landed lightly on the Black Land side. The scream of his horse mixed with the cries of over a hundred Goblins as they all plummeted hundreds of feet to the dried riverbed below.

Duncan watched the bridge fall and saw his last chance to retrieve the sword fall with it. He let out an inhuman roar that echoed across the canyon and raised his bardiche, ready to take out his frustrations on the ugly creatures in front of him. The Goblins were agitated after they saw so many of their brood fall to their doom and now, they were stranded on the wrong side of the gorge facing an enraged giant.

Warrec and Joenair dismounted. With a slap on their rumps Warrec sent the horses running back towards Aluna. Their horses were past the point of exhaustion and needed rest. Also, fighting swarms of Goblins on horseback was also generally not a good idea. The smaller creatures were usually out of range for a fighter on horseback swinging down at them. They also tended to swarm up onto a horse tearing and biting, which caused the animal to panic and throw its rider.

A voice like rolling thunder came at them from across the gorge. "PATHETIC. I GAVE YOU THIS ONE CHANCE, ONE CHANCE TO STOP ME. A FOOLISH NOTION ON MY PART, BUT ONE I FELT NECESSARY. YOU FAILED. YOU RODE SO HARD TO CATCH ME AND YOU HAVE FAILED. NOW THIS WORLD IS LOST. IT WILL BURN. IT WILL BE PURIFIED BY FIRE.

I'M SORRY BUT THIS IS WHAT MUST BE." Then the Dread Lord began laughing. It was a frightful and unnerving sound that sent a chill down Warrec's spine. Argis turned with a flourish of his cape and walked away, disappearing into the fog of his accursed lands.

"Well, now I wish I brought a change of pants," Joenair whispered to himself.

Duncan lost all sense and reason. He began roaring like a wild lion. His voice echoed through the canyon and absolutely terrified the Goblins standing before him. His eyes changed color to a yellow amber and seemed to glow like a hungry predator peering out from the darkness. His whole body seemed to twist and change almost like he was turning into something else but not quite completely.

His muscles bulged under his robes and the veins in his arms seemed to be about to burst. The old giant lifted his head towards the sky and let loose a howl of mourning mixed with a bellow of rage, deep and terrifying. The low guttural sound resonated through the air and caused the hairs on the back of Warrec's neck to stand on end. It was a sound that was felt as much as heard. He had heard a roar similar to it when he had faced down a charging Rajanaga in the Orc jungles of the southlands and it shook him to the bone.

Warrec saw what was happening to his father and grabbed

Joenair's arm. "Back! Back! Back! Get back. He is shifting! Move, come on!" Warrec yelled as he grabbed Joenair's arm and half dragged, half pulled him away.

"What? I've seen you do it before," Joenair said stunned, but not daring to take his eyes off Duncan. Warrec grabbed Joenair's face and made him look away when Joenair refused or was unable to move.

Warrec looked his friend dead in the eye and spoke. "That was only a child's tantrum compared to what you're about to see. We don't want to be anywhere near him. He may not be able to distinguish us from them." Joenair looked at his friend in disbelief but kept running back with him. They ran into Aluna and grabbed her too. When they were finally a good three hundred feet away, they stopped and turned around.

"War I have seen you change or shift whatever you call it. I've seen you fly into a rage, both while sparring and in actual combat. I've seen you perform feats of strength that no human should have been able to," Joenair said. He looked back to Aluna and back to Warrec.

Warrec looked at Aluna and she slowly shook her head. "Are we far enough back?" Warrec asked her.

"I don't know, this is bigger than I have ever seen," she said. She licked her lips and slowly nodded. "I think so, for now. He is focused on them."

"Ok what am I missing?" Joenair asked. "I've heard stories, you" -he pointed at Warrec- "you have told me stories of a handful of Vatninu holding off or defeating entire armies. I always assumed those were exaggerated and embellished." Joenair looked back at Duncan. "Maybe not."

Warrec looked back at Aluna and saw the fear in her eyes, fear he knew was reflected in his own. "No Jay this is...this is something more."

Duncan's rage kept building and the air around him began to hum and crackle at the buildup of energy. Little bolts of electricity began to arc around Duncan. Small pebbles and stones vibrated and moved by some unseen force. Another roar sent a shockwave out that bowled the first two rows of Goblins over. None of the Goblins were able to recover before Duncan attacked.

He leapt high into the air and brought his giant bardiche down bisecting two Goblins in half. The force of the blow was so great that the blade passed through flesh and bone unhindered and buried itself in the ground. When Duncan brought the blade back up, he ripped a large rock out of the ground in a storm of flying dirt. The blade had sunk deep into the stone and was now firmly lodged.

The weapon itself was unharmed. Dwarven weaponsmiths had forged the weapon long ago. They had used a pattern weld of wootz steel and valentium, along with a little magic had gone into its creation. The combination of these metals had made the blade virtually indestructible and able to cut almost anything without dulling. However, the weapon was useless until it was un-lodged, and Duncan simply did not have the time or patience to do so. He tossed the bardiche aside with a snarl.

Duncan's eyes blazed with fiery rage. What his empty hands needed was another weapon. So, he grabbed the nearest Goblin. Duncan seized the creature's wrist and clamped a powerful hand on its shoulder. With a sickening twist and pop, he dislocated the arm. Then he pulled and the sound of tearing flesh and sinews snapping was severely audible through the night air.

Duncan had moved so fast that the poor Goblin had only been able to see a blur before its arm was ripped off. The Goblin's screams of pain were quickly drowned out as Duncan raised his new club. With a meaty wet thunk he brought it down on the Goblin's head again and again.

Duncan, with the fevered look of a wild animal, seized the back of the head of the next Goblin and shoved the splintered bone of his makeshift club down its throat. With a roar the old giant turned on the rest of the Goblins and began ripping them apart.

Even though the Goblins had their weapons, they were powerless against the onslaught. For several minutes, their screams of pain and terror combined with the sounds of flesh being torn apart, echoing across the canyon. They tried to fight back, but every time they slashed or stabbed Duncan had already blurred past the strike. The old giant tore through their ranks like a hurricane, a whirlwind of death and destruction.

The trio watched Duncan from far off. Despite the distance they could still hear the sickening sounds of the battle. Joenair huffed. He looked a little green. "This is a slaughter," he whispered. "I have never seen in all my life anything like this. I see your point now. By Grendir's Beard I'm glad we're over here and not one of those Goblins. Skret, I almost feel sorry for them."

Aluna had to eventually turn away. The horror and violence was becoming too much for her. "He is ripping them apart like they are made of paper."

Duncan was tearing into them like a hungry beast. There was no remorse, no mercy in his movements. "I have seen plenty of predators attacking and killing their prey," Aluna said. "I understood it; it's a part of nature and nature is savage and indifferent." She wiped her mouth. "But this is..." she trailed off unable to find the words.

Warrec slowly shook his head in disbelief as he watched Duncan obliterate the Goblin forces. He shuddered as he watched his father rip one Goblin's throat out with his teeth.

Warrec knew what Aluna meant. This was more than a bear

killing an elk, more than a wolf finding a nest of baby rabbits. This was death and destruction on the level of an earthquake or a flood, a natural disaster manifested into the shape of a man. The wretched things never had a chance. The entire slaughter had only taken a few minutes, a small collection of heartbeats. Time had seemed to slow to a crawl during the old giant's rampage, extending and magnifying the slaughter.

Finally, there were only two Goblins left. The two remaining Goblins stood cowering on the edge of the gorge. Duncan slowly stalked toward them. He had the same glint in his eye that a wolf had looking at a rabbit. One of the Goblins couldn't take it anymore. With a cry it shoved its broodmate towards the insane human and jumped into the canyon.

It was a fate better than being dismembered at the hands of the monster of a man. Duncan seized the last Goblin and lifted it up to his chest. Its bones cracked and snapped as the life was squeezed out of it. Duncan then apathetically tossed the body into the canyon after its comrade.

Joenair started to walk back but was immediately stopped as Warrec thrust an arm out in front of him. Warrec slowly shook his head. Joenair gave a slight nod and swallowed. He looked back at the old giant.

Duncan's rage had been calmed somewhat, but the fire hadn't been quenched. For another half hour he roared and stomped the ground around the gorge. The ground was soaked in blackish green Goblin blood and their bones were pulverized into the earth. Finally, Duncan collapsed from sheer exhaustion. His rage finally sedated for the moment.

Warrec let out a long breath of air. He realized that he had been holding his breath. "It's over" he finally whispered more to himself than to Joenair or Aluna. Warrec felt Aluna's hand in his. Without thinking he gave it a small squeeze.

Chapter Six

Kunthar could not sleep. For the past several nights he had been plagued by nightmares and strange dreams. A low involuntary growl of annoyance escaped his lips as his eyes snapped open. He blinked rapidly as the last wisps of the dream faded into the dark corners of his mind. Kunthar tried to pull the fragments back into a conscience thought, but they had drifted away like cherry blossoms in the wind. All he could remember now was that there had been blood and war.

The venerable general rose from his bed trying his best not to wake his sleeping wife. He fastened his silk sleeping robe around his waist and padded softly towards the large bay window overlooking the sea. He opened the window to get a breath of fresh air and sniffed at the ocean breeze.

The smell of salt and fish wafted through the night air. He could see a storm far out on the ocean. The sporadic flashes of lightning broke the still darkness of the horizon, although it was too far out to hear any thunder. He twitched an ear towards a clinking sound far below in the right side of the courtyard.

It was only a guard on his rounds. Kunthar sniffed the balmy night air again and caught his scent as the wind changed. It was either Daichi or his brother Daiki. Kunthar could never tell their scents apart.

Kunthar drew a paw across his muzzle and tugged at his whiskers. It was a nervous habit he had picked up over the years. He stroked his whiskers between his forefinger and dew thumbclaw as he contemplated his thoughts.

Heavy is the head that wears the crown. The old proverb rang in his mind. *Though having the crown would also make matters simpler.*

The old lion sighed and leaned out onto the balcony railing. He was burdened with all the responsibilities of ruling with little of the absolute authority to do so. The Kathari Empire was at a crossroads. The current emperor was little more than a child, safely locked away in his palace, attended and educated by his monks and eunuchs, awaiting the day that he would be wise enough to rule. A day that was still too far off for Kunthar's liking.

It was the perfect storm of unfortunate events coupled with rising political tensions. It happened at the death of every emperor. Until the emperor was found on his new karmic journey and ready to rule, a shogun was entrusted with the care of the

Kathari people until the emperor was ready to ascend the throne. Sometimes it lasted centuries and sometimes only a few decades.

A long cycle could mean decades of civil war as the warlords fought for dominion. Eventually one would rise to the top becoming a defacto emperor until the true emperor was ready to return to the throne. A short cycle, such as this one, where the reincarnated emperor was located quickly meant a quick election of an interim shogun by the warlords from amongst their number.

Kunthar had never sought the position of Shogun, but it had been thrust upon him. At the death of the old emperor and upon his reincarnation the other feudal lords had pressed Kunthar into service as Shogun. It was a military title not a civil one. He was only just now being to understand what that meant.

At the time he had thought it a great honor, he had been chosen to maintain order and oversee the day-to-day operations of running the empire. Now he realized it was because no one else had wanted the burden.

His soldiers operated efficiently. Orders were given and passed down the chain of command. There was little back and forth, and projects were completed in a timely matter. Civilians wanted to discuss everything.

There were committees to talk about the law. There were committees to talk about the committees that were talking about the law. Then there were committees to talk about who was on the committees to oversee the committees. It devolved down into one huge writhing wasteful mess.

Kunthar had needed a new bridge built over The Greendrop River. During wartime, the project would have taken three months. It was now well over three years and the bridge was still only halfway built.

The ocean storm seemed to reflect his mood as he watched the lighting flashing out on the horizon. Beautiful, lacquered wood splintered in his paws as he squeezed the railing. Carelessly he caught himself digging his claws into the soft wood.

He was little more than a glorified babysitter, constantly dealing with his problem children. That's how he had grown to see the other feudal lords, little more than squabbling children. There was always something that needed his immediate attention, some insult that needed to be addressed, some favor being asked for and now one child had grown increasingly troublesome.

Alazar, the name immediately came to his mind. Young, brash, and ambitious, Alazar was quickly proving to be a thorn in Kunthar's side. Kunthar suspected that Alazar sought to be Shogun. There were fleeting moments when Kunthar was tempted to step down and let him have it.

Kunthar shook his head. As much as he wanted to be rid of the responsibility, letting Alazar take it would be a grave mistake. Alazar was far too foolish and egotistical and would tear the empire apart, destroying everything.

Heavy is the head that wears the crown. The proverb kept running through his mind. If he was emperor, he could simply execute Alazar or more likely imprison him, perhaps seize his lands. Instead, he was forced to diplomatically hold him at bay.

Diplomatic chains only stretched so far and Kunthar feared that Alazar was already straining them to the limits. Soon he would break them completely and there would be a civil war.

An ear twitched back as he heard soft footfalls padding closer behind him. A soft arm snaked around his waist. He tensed at first as old instincts are hard to get rid of, but he knew he was safe in his home and it was only his loving wife, Reyan, coming to check on him.

"Another bad dream?" she purred as she laid her head on the back of his shoulder.

He placed his arm over hers and continued to look outside. After a few moments he replied. "It's not just the dreams. There is something…something looming on the horizon, and I can't put my claw on what it is." The old lion didn't particularly feel like troubling his wife with his worries over Alazar, at least not in the middle of the night.

Reyan was not some glossy eyed female that had no interest in the world beyond what her husband told her. Her wit was sharper than any sword and she had shown herself to be far more cunning than most of the feudal lords. He had spoken to her before, and her council had proved invaluable many times.

Females were often treated as second class citizens at best or simply ignored at worst. Kunthar had exploited that social paradigm many times in dealing with his problem children. Many times, Reyan had served tea during meetings, watching, and listening. She had a knack for picking up the subtle things that Kunthar missed.

She moved to stand beside him and looked out onto the ocean. "You mean the storm?" she said in jest. "Or do you mean that ship, the ooman one?" Reyan paused as she seemed to mull the word over in her mouth. "No, that's not it…the human ship that landed here a few months ago?"

Kunthar snapped himself back into the present. His mind had been wandering and had continually been drifting back to the dark places over Alazar. He hadn't been thinking about the humans at all, but now his mind focused on another problem that had been plaguing him. The humans were a problem that he had been trying to ignore or at least brush aside for now.

Kunthar gave a slight nod in acknowledgement. "Yes, I fear our period of isolation is coming to an end. And I don't know how our society will deal with it. In my long lifetime I have seen our people change so much already. It was only in my father's grandfather's time that we began to revolutionize farming."

Reyan nodded. "The terraced farming was a great boon from Emperor Kwang," she said. "It saved hundreds of thousands from starving during the four-year blight."

Part of the power that the emperors wielded was they were able to bring the knowledge of heaven down to earth. Kwang had completely changed the way the Kathari farmed and had brought crop yields up seven-fold.

"True enough," Kunthar said.

Reyan ran a paw delicately through Kunthar's massive black mane, careful to avoid snagging hair in her retracted claws. "Yes, and just look how it helped our people." His wife's voice pushed his troubled thoughts away. "We are better able to feed all our people now and we aren't as dependent on prey and fishing for our sustenance."

"I like fishing," he interrupted.

Reyan sighed patiently. "Yes, yes you would fish every day if you could. But you know the point I am making. Change isn't necessarily a bad thing. I think it's time we opened our lands again and learned about this wonderful world of ours. There are so many different peoples out in the world. Think what all our band of islands could teach them." Reyan stretched her arm out and pointed toward the ocean.

Kunthar twitched his tail as he contemplated her words; perhaps she was right, as usual. None seemed to be able to remember why they had isolated themselves from the rest of the world to begin with. For over a thousand years the Kathari had kept to their lands and their islands.

They had not crossed the ocean and had killed any outsiders who came into their waters. In five hundred years no foreign devils had crossed into their waters. No Kathari alive had ever seen any of the other fabled races; until last month that is.

A human ship had been caught in a storm and been badly damaged. It had pulled into a bay to make repairs and contact had been made. A remote Kathari fishing village populated by simple bored fishermen had greeted them. Instead of killing the humans the Kathari had been overcome with curiosity of these furless things. They were strong and sturdy but had no claws or fangs and yet they carried themselves with a sense of confidence and sailed as well as any of the Kathari.

At first the humans had been wary of these large bipedal cats. However, it hadn't taken the humans long to overcome their fear. The human sailors and Kathari quickly found they shared many words each speaking a variation of Highcommon, the common tongue. They had quickly started trading and swapping stories with each other. Both groups were thrilled at all of the other's wondrous and exotic goods.

With that small chance encounter, it had begun. His people's self-exile had come to an end. Rumors and gossip had spread like wildfire through the community; traveling from village to village, island to island, and city to city. Kunthar had read the official reports and even he had to admit he was intrigued.

It was reported that the humans chattered and climbed their ship's rigging like the monkeys in the forest trees. They ate fire from small wooden sticks they called pipes and breathed smoke. The tales grew more outlandish as they spread. By the time they reached the capital Kunthar heard that the humans could fly and could read minds.

There were those, mostly the elders, the old grey ones long past their prime, who thought the humans should have been killed and consumed. Their nay saying had been heard. Two committees had been formed to argue over the issue. Their worries had been discussed, contemplated, and ultimately dismissed. It was the fastest Kunthar had ever seen the government reach a decision.

In the end the damage had been done and many Kathari, including a considerable number in the royal court wanted to learn about these humans and where they came from. Reyan had agreed with them and had made her opinion known, frequently, to Kunthar.

The old lion had sat and listened as each side had argued and debated loudly and endlessly. He had sent a request to the divine child emperor for guidance and as usual received none. Ultimately, as Shogun, the decision had fallen to him. Secretly he admitted to himself that he was also a little curious. Finally, he had decided to send a formal request for an envoy back with the humans.

"There is no stopping it now anyway," Kunthar said. "They will return, and the heavens only know what they will bring with them." Kunthar turned fully toward his wife wrapping his arms around her slim waist. "Reyan, I don't know what to do."

"Shhh…all will work out," she whispered. "All will be well." She gently put a fingerpad to his lips. "What will be...will be. All things will be revealed at their proper time." Reyan gently took her husband's paw in hers. "Now come back to bed my love," she said with a tender smile. Kunthar didn't argue as he let her pull him along.

As he lay in bed with his wife's head pillowed on his wide chest he stared absently out at the dark sky. The humans were one more problem to weigh heavily on his shoulders. They would come, but he did not know if they would bring sorrow or joy with them. It was close to morning before he finally slipped back into sleep.

Chapter Seven

Sasha was a big helper. Today she was helping her mommy pick strawberries in their strawberry patch by their house. Today was her birthday. She was ten years old today and her mommy and big sister said they were going to bake a special strawberry cake for her. She giggled as she thought how good it was going to taste.

The bright morning sun illuminated her red locks, turning them a rosy strawberry blond. Sasha hummed an old sea shanty that her father had taught her. He told her he used to sing it all day long as he sailed across the vast southern ocean when he was younger. He had told her that one day when she was older, he would take her south to see the ocean, even though it was a long, long way away. She wanted to see the ocean so badly.

Why can't then be now? She thought absently as she reached out and plucked a nice plump strawberry. Sasha started to drop it down into the pile in her apron when she realized that her apron was already full.

Well, full enough anyway. Sasha popped the berry into her

mouth and smiled. The sweet berry exploded inside her mouth as she bit down. Sasha rolled it around her tongue relishing the flavor before swallowing. She then jumped up with the energy and speed that only children have and ran over to her mother a few feet away. However, she made sure she was extra careful and didn't spill any of the berries she had collected.

"Here Mommy," she said as she dumped her apron full of strawberries into the basket. Sasha's mother looked up from underneath her wide brim straw hat and smiled sweetly.

"Thank you, sweetie, oh such a good big helper," her mother replied. Mommy then grabbed Sasha and patted and rubbed her tummy. Sasha giggled again as her mother rubbed her tummy because it tickled.

Today was going to be so much fun. Her friend Pattie who lived on the next farm was coming over for the party. They rarely got to play or see each other because Pattie lived so far away. They usually only got to see each other once a month at market.

Sasha's eyes bulged wide as she remembered. "Oh, Mommy do you think Pattie will bring one of the new puppies she has?" Sasha practically squealed at the thought of a new puppy.

"Maybe, Pattie's father did say something about they were trying to give most of them out." Sasha's mother answered with a sly smile.

"The dough is almost ready," Manya, Sasha's older sister yelled from the kitchen window.

"Ok honey we're almost done," Sasha's mother yelled back. "Aren't we Blue Bug?" she asked as she turned back to Sasha. Sasha giggled again and stuck her tongue out through the gap in her teeth where she had lost a tooth a few days ago.

She liked that nickname. Her father had started calling her that when she was three because she had jumped into a pile of hay and all the blue bugs in the pile had flown up all around her. Her father had thought it was extremely cute and had been calling her Blue Bug ever since.

Her father and all her brothers were out in the fields working like they always did. Sasha was excited because today he said they would come in early for her party. This made her so happy because most of the time she didn't get to see them. They came home after she went to bed and left before she got up.

Sasha looked out toward the field that they had gone out on today. She couldn't see them of course, they were miles away, but she still kept looking and waiting. She absently twirled a lock of her long strawberry hair around her finger as she watched the horizon for her father. Then she noticed a cloud of dust way far out in the field. She watched as it got bigger and came closer. After a while she could make out the shapes of horses.

"Look Mommy horsies."

"Where baby?" Her mother stopped picking strawberries and looked up to where her daughter was pointing. She saw horse shapes out on the horizon. "Oh, it looks like Gilly has let his herd wander out again. I'm going to give that old geezer a piece of my mind next time I see him. I've told him time and time again to keep his herd off our fields." She sighed and turned back around to picking strawberries, occasionally picking a stray weed.

Sasha continued to watch the horses. She didn't particularly like old man Gilly. He was cranky and grumpy most of the time and his eyebrows looked like fuzzy caterpillars. Her father had told her he had been a soldier long ago and to be respectful to him. Sasha was, but she still didn't like him.

The cloud of dust had shifted in the wind and the horses now turned towards the farmhouse. Sasha didn't think that they looked like Mr. Gilly's horses. They looked funny.

The horses continued to draw closer, and Sasha could now see what looked like riders on their backs. She started to tell her mother but saw that she was busy, so she just kept watching the horses and their riders get closer.

Sasha wasn't particularly worried. She had seen plenty of soldiers and knights riding by. Daddy said it was because the knights had a fort close by and this was the easiest way for them to go back and forth to their fort. Daddy didn't like it that much though, because they usually squashed a lot of crops when they rode through.

The riders got closer and now Sasha saw something that puzzled her. She could now see that the horses and riders were stuck together. She couldn't see the rider's legs or the horse's head. She started to turn around to ask Mommy about it when something whooshed past her face. Mommy let out a small noise. Sasha turned and saw what looked like one of Daddy's arrows sticking out of Mommy's back, except it was much bigger.

"Mommy?" Sasha said, her voice quivering in fear as Mommy slumped over. Little Sasha shook her mother. "Mommy, Mommy get up there are horsemen coming." Sasha couldn't figure out why Mommy was playing this game when these strange horse people were coming towards them. Sasha hoped Mommy was playing a game. She looked at the arrow and the quickly growing pool of blood. "Mommy!" Sasha yelled and shook her mother harder.

Then she heard them. The horsemen yelled and whooped as they rode up. A few ran past her and crashed into the house. She heard Manya scream and then saw her being carried outside by a horseman. He threw her to the ground and began tearing off her pretty red dress that Mommy had made for her.

Sasha had never seen anything like them, and they terrified her. From the waist up they almost looked human, but from their waist down they had the body of a horse. The front legs were wrong though. They bent at an odd angle and instead of hooves they stood on three splayed toes, almost fingerlike. Her brothers had told her stories of the centaurs, half men, and half horse, late at night trying to scare her. Until now she had thought they were just stories.

Sasha saw that the horsemen were wearing leather aprons, studded with iron circles and fur lined domed helmets. Their bare skin was a dark tan and looked like weathered leather. Stringy muscles rippled as they moved. They all carried small bows and had a quiver of arrows at their side. Most of the horsemen had long black mustaches, braided with small knives or rings woven in at the end. Across their backs was a shiny segmented shell like a large beetle. Sasha counted over thirty of the horsemen stamping across her front yard.

Sasha stood frozen in fear as a horseman trotted up to her. He smiled down at her, his mouth full of jagged yellow or blackened teeth and dropped something into her mother's strawberry basket. Sasha looked into the basket and saw Daddy staring wide eyed back at her. His face was locked in an expression of fear and surprise.

Sasha's breath caught in her throat. *What is happening? Daddy, no, Daddy*, her mind screamed. Sasha couldn't move. She couldn't breathe. She tried to scream, but no sound came out.

The next thing she knew the horseman snatched her up and shoved her into a pouch by his side. As she was being picked up, she could see her brothers draped across the backs of some of the horsemen. They weren't moving and there was a lot of blood.

Sasha could see out through a little hole in the bag and could see her sister. Manya was on the ground on her knees and elbows. She was naked, they had stripped her bare. Manya was bleeding around her face and her bottom. The horsemen were dancing and prancing around her and would take turns climbing on her back. The same way their bull would climb up onto the cows. Sasha knew that meant mating; it wasn't something that should be happening to Manya.

Sasha listened to her sister scream every time one of the horsemen got on top of her. Then she would cry and whimper. Sometimes the horsemen would hit her.

After a while her big sister stopped screaming or moving, but the horsemen kept climbing on top of her and laughing and hitting her. After a while they would just stomp on her with their weird feet and kick her. One horseman set Sasha's house on fire. She was very scared, but she never screamed or cried out as the centaurs took her away.

Chapter Eight

Duncan was beyond exhausted. His rage spent he had finally collapsed to his knees roughly an hour ago and had not moved since. He stared vacantly down into the pit before him.

This was the downside to shifting into grimmig. For several hours after the grimmiger would be very weak and almost helpless. The downtime of the grimmig allowed his people to heal faster than normal, shaking off even some mortal wounds. Duncan's power allowed him to recover quicker than most, though even he had his limits. The imperials called it going berserk.

Duncan managed to give a small chuckle at the thought. That was such a poor and lifeless translation of the Wutendsjelesturm, the storm of the enraged soul. To shift into grimmig was to become infused with righteous fury beyond all reason. It was the blessing of the AllFather upon his people, a blessing of the unconquered, where one man became an army unto himself.

It was glorious. Every painful memory, every regret, every fear, everything burned away into a single pure state of joyful rage. It was the moment where everything became crystal clear, a perfect moment of clarity and focus. In that moment all that mattered was destroying and overcoming the obstacle before you.

Every Vatninu had the ability to tap into their soulstorm, to shift into the grimmig in one form or another. For most it was in combat, but it took many forms. Some shifted into grimmig while woodworking or blacksmithing, or any other dozens of crafting arts. For some it was in fishing or hunting. All that really mattered was that there was a challenge to overcome. In that moment of perfect clarity and focus the world slowed into an ideal singularity of purpose.

Duncan had been the guardian of the Soulblade for most of his adult life. His father had told him the sword granted its bearer power. When he had taken the mantle of guardian from his father, he had felt that power and that burden. He had grown far stronger and faster than any man had a right to be. He was the best fighter in the north, maybe even in the empire.

He had been able to use his grimmig to channel his power as guardian and had greatly amplified his capabilities. A normal Vatninu in grimmig was nearly unstoppable, but with Duncan it was more comparable to a lion attacking a deer as opposed to a cat attacking a mouse. In the end all of it hadn't mattered. He had failed.

"I need a drink," he mumbled to himself.

In truth he probably could have gotten up if he had wanted to, but he just couldn't seem to find a point to do so. He had failed. The line of guardians stretched back over four thousand years. Not once had the line been broken, not once had they failed in their sacred mission, until him.

His father had told him the sword granted power and with that power there came a cost. He hadn't emphasized how big a cost. Duncan slowly reached up and fingered the pale, cobalt-blue crystal that hung from his neck.

"If I had known then would it have mattered?" he muttered. No, he would still have made the same choice. What was the worth of one soul against the rest of the world after all? Still, unlike his father he had told Everett everything when his time came. He had prepared his son better. He had failed.

Duncan had known this day would come. He had known that with Everett dead everything was lost. The oath broken, the world ending, death for all, it was only a matter of time. The sword was gone now, lost. He had failed.

Duncan drew in a ragged breath and then another. *They are all going to die,* he thought. Duncan wept openly. He had no idea how long he wept; it had seemed like an eternity. With great mental fortitude he had pulled himself back to the present.

Now there were only two things he was thinking about. He either wanted to reach into his pocket to get his flask or to hurl himself over the cliff edge and end his pain; though he didn't seem to have the energy to do either one. So, he just sat there and waited. He had been crying for a good while, but the tears had finally seemed to dry up. Duncan just sat there breathing one ragged breath after another.

For once in his life Joenair was at a loss for words. This was so far out of his experience that he could only stand transfixed as the old giant tore through a band of monsters. This was old magic, old and terrifying. Warrec was scary when he did his battle thing, but this, this was more on the level of an earthquake or hurricane.

Warrec, Joenair and Aluna had watched Duncan's rampage and his collapse. When he had finally collapsed, Joenair had started forward to help him but had been stopped by Warrec's hand on his shoulder. Both Warrec and Aluna shook their heads at him, and their eyes seemed to say just let him be for now. So, the three of them continued to wait and watch.

Crazy, insane, angry, hairy, big, scary barbarian people, Joenair thought to himself. *I'm glad they like me,* he mentally added.

In the meantime, Aluna retrieved and watered Warrec and Joenair's horses. Warrec's destrier had held up fairly well during the ride to the gorge. The war horse was bred for battle and traveling over rough country at speed. After a little water it milled about, almost bored as it waited to go. The old nag that Joenair had grabbed also seemed to be fine, too stubborn to die it seemed.

Aluna gathered the saddles and bags from the two dead horses. She knelt before each one and said a small prayer over them and thanked them for their sacrifice. After that she walked the two live horses back over handing the reins to each of them.

"The carrion feeders will have a fine meal, but there was no sense in wasting good tack," she said. "Warrec's horse seems more than able to carry the extra load back."

Warrec reached up and patted the massive animal's neck. "Already dry," he said. "You are a fine horse."

"What's his name?" Aluna asked.

Warrec cocked his head at the question. "You know I don't actually remember. It's not actually mine. I picked him up at the trading post stables. Jay, do you remember?

"Gluepot," Joenair answered. "No wait that's this one," he added as he thumbed at the nag beside him. The old horse snorted in response. Aluna punched him in the arm, and it actually hurt, like a lot and he was fairly sure it was supposed to be playful.

"You leave Notlate alone. She is the best horse ever."

Joenair threw his hands up in surrender. If he hadn't been

a well-educated and well-traveled man- *don't forget handsome*- he would have sworn Notlate was grinning at him.

It was well past nightfall when the three approached Duncan. They could see the night fires of the Goblins across the gorge. The filthy creatures danced around, and their chittering could be heard echoing across the gap.

For a good while the three stood around Duncan and simply watched the Goblins; none of them knew what to say. Duncan merely stared down at the ground, his massive shoulders slumped. He looked like all the life had been drained out of him, like a puppet whose strings had been cut.

Finally, Aluna broke the silence. "We should be going. It will be a long walk back home." Duncan gave no reply and made no move to get up. So Warrec and Joenair each grabbed and arm and helped the old giant to his feet.

The walk back home was long and quiet. The night was silent, and nothing stirred across the plain as they trudged along. They didn't stop to rest or camp for the night. They just kept walking. None of them said anything for a long while. They had mounted Duncan on Joenair's horse because he wouldn't walk under his own power.

Duncan never said anything or even lifted his head to look at any of them; only occasionally taking his flask out for a nip. It wasn't long before he had finished the flask's contents.

Joenair handed his flask of dark Artanian whiskey over to Duncan. Duncan didn't bother to look at Joenair as he took the offered flask, promptly drained it, and handed it back.

As Joenair took the flask back he turned it upside down and shook it a few times. Not a single drop fell out. *I have really got to stop being shocked by these people,* he thought.

It was obvious Warrec was worried about his father and hated seeing him like this. The big man was in one of his brooding moods. He kept looking from his father to the ground and back again. Joenair gave him a cheesy grin and a thumbs up when Warrec finally looked over. All Joenair got in response was a long sigh and slight nod.

Ok time for a more forceful approach, he thought. Joenair froze mid-step, hopped backward, and slid up sideways next to Warrec. He then locked steps with the big man, which was difficult as Warrec had a much longer stride. Joenair then began to mimic every movement Warrec made. It took exactly ten paces before the big man let out a half growl, half sigh.

"Fine," Warrec reluctantly said. He glanced over at Duncan and continued on in a whisper, but it was doubtful the old giant was listening.

"This is the worst I've ever seen him," Warrec whispered. I'm afraid that he's going to slip back into a depression that he might not ever recover from. And as bad as that is I feel like there is a more pressing matter. Which makes me feel like an ass, but Argis has returned and that only means doom for the empire."

Joenair nodded. With the empire divided and weakened like it was, the Dread Lord could sweep in and conquer with little resistance. Warrec looked over at Joenair and knew his friend was thinking the same thing. Warrec started to say something but stopped himself.

Joenair nodded again and flicked his chin at Duncan. That was all the verbal communication the two of them needed right now. Not here, not now, not in front of your father while he was like this. They could wait till they reached Thornglade. They would have to spend a day resting and resupplying before they began their ride back to the capital anyway. Joenair had only wanted to make sure that the two of them were on the same page.

The quartet marched on. The next day they again didn't stop to make camp. They had all silently agreed to keep moving. Well, the large brooding man and equally scary and intense large woman had agreed to keep moving. The very large and absolutely terrifying man, which didn't seem as scary now, almost broken even, was listless and seemed to be just as willing to fall to the ground, never to move again. Joenair's feet were killing him, but he decided that was better than the three scary and large people killing him for stopping.

*You're exaggerating. *

Probably, well yes obviously, Warrec wouldn't, Aluna I suppose wouldn't, the old man doesn't seem to care either way.

*Our feet hurt and we're hungry. *

I am well aware, but no, we should keep moving. Frankly, I'd rather be back in the town than camping out here where it's not safe. The boys in the fort thought they were safe and look where that got them.

*Point taken. *

Joenair sighed as he talked amongst himself in his mind. In their mad rush to pursue Argis they hadn't brought any supplies with them other than the few scraps of food that had been in the saddlebags. They ate what little they had as they trudged onward. Aluna had wanted to stop and bury the soldiers at the burnt garrison, but Warrec and Joenair had gently prodded her away. As terrible as it was that was the duty of someone else.

On the third day they began drawing close to Thornglade. They had been gone for close to a week. They were met by a scout party of warriors from the village. The hunters had returned and were in the process of rebuilding and restoring order to the scarred village. They had been refortifying the town and had been sending out scout parties to watch for another attack.

The scouts had two mounts per person so that they could ride one while the other horse rested allowing them to always have a fresh horse on hand. So Warrec and Joenair were able to grab two horses for themselves and the quartet rode the rest of the way in.

It was close to nightfall when they arrived at Duncan's cottage. Warrec crashed into an old chair in a cloud of dust, thankful to be finally able to rest.

He glanced about the main room and hearth. "It's smaller than I remember it," he said. He brooded as he began staring off into space. Joenair made himself useful by starting a fire in the hearth, while Aluna put Duncan to bed.

"This is very bad," Joenair said breaking the uneasy silence.

"I know. Oh, by the AllFather do I know," Warrec replied covering his face with his hands and stroking his temples. "I've begun to develop a headache, although I didn't know if it's from a lack of food or the mounting trouble bubbling to the surface."

Joenair's stomach grumbled at the mention of food. "Both probably," he said.

"I'm going to make some dinner," Aluna stated as she re-entered the room.

"Thank you my dear," Joenair said in his easy-going manner; trying to do his best to hide the growing fear in his gut. His stomach felt like a ball of ice. He really didn't know the significance of Warrec's family sword or why Argis had taken it.

What he did know is that after many years of absence Argis had returned.

And that's bad, very, very bad. Leave it to the Vatninu to screw up a vacation. Joenair pinched the bridge of his nose and crossed his arms as he thought of the impending doom.

A war with the Black Lands now could only end in disaster. Well, it wasn't like there was a particularly suitable time for a war with the Dread Lord. But now was especially bad.

The Empire was split and there were rumors floating around of a civil war brewing between the two brothers. He knew Ptharis was jealous of his brother and would stop at nothing to seize power. Joenair's loyalty lay with King Valorn, and he would die before he saw his good king disposed.

Could Ptharis have allied with the Black Lands? It was a troubling thought and one that Joenair would have to find an answer to. When they returned to Eldurond he was going to have to contact some people he knew and call in some favors owed. Joenair needed more information on King Ptharis if he hoped to aid his king.

Warrec's facial tattoo seemed to glow from the light of the fire. The Orc tattoo stretched across one side of his face like some monstrous spider. He sat watching the flames and brooding. Finally, Warrec broke the silence. "We should leave in the morning," he said to Joenair. "The quicker we reach the capital the better."

"Agreed," Joenair said as he poked at the fire.

Aluna walked over and placed a pot of stew over the fire to warm. "I want to come too," she said looking at Warrec.

"I don't know if that's such a good idea," Warrec answered. "We are going to have a lot to do when we reach Eldurond, and we won't have the time to baby-sit…" Warrec stopped himself in midsentence and looked at Aluna. Her face quickly turned to a scowl. "That is…what I mean is…," Warrec stammered.

Oh, skret now he's done it, Joenair thought. He had to quickly look away to hide a grin.

Aluna stabbed the big man in the chest with a finger. "Warrec Vornirulf Duncanson, how dare you talk to me like I'm some child. I am a grown woman and this village's shaman." Aluna scowled down at him as she tried to tower over him. Even sitting she was only a little taller than he was. "You would have known that if you had bothered to come home." She said the last in an icy tone that could have frozen the Firefalls themselves.

"Which is all the more reason for you to stay. The village needs you right now more than ever," Warrec quickly interjected.

"Why don't you want me around?" Tears were beginning to form around Aluna's eyes as her hands balled up in fists. For a second it looked like she was about to punch Warrec in the face. Instead, she whirled and stomped back into the pantry. A few seconds later she called out. "Asshole!"

"Do you want help prying your foot out of your mouth?" Joenair quipped at Warrec. *You know I like the big guy, but he can be such an idiot sometimes,* he thought to himself.

Warrec looked sheepishly at Joenair and shrugged. "What did I say?" He took a deep breath and scowled. "I don't understand what her problem is. We have to do our duty and report back to the king. It's going to quickly get dangerous for both of us. I don't want to put her into harm's way and besides, she really will be needed here.

"I also want her here to help look after my father. I don't want to have to deal with him"- he shook his head - "no I can't deal with him. Duncan, being as stubborn as he is, might decide to go after the sword and invade the Black Lands by himself. At least with Aluna staying with him she can keep an eye on him."

Joenair rolled his eyes. *You big dummy,* he thought. He wanted to tell Warrec that Aluna's problem was obvious to everyone but him apparently. *She loves you, idiot. And she wants you to take that sword of yours and plunge it into her sheath, a lot, repeatedly.* But Joenair wasn't going to say that. Instead, he decided to change the subject.

"When are you going to tell them?" Joenair asked.

"Tell them what?"

Joenair cocked his head and gave Warrec a look of mild

annoyance. *Oh, now I want to hit you, not that you would feel it,* he thought.

"Warrec, you know what I'm talking about, about back home. The wedding, you know you and Addie? The whole reason we came up here was to tell your father and everyone else." Joenair eyed his friend carefully.

"Oh yeah that. Not now, it's not a good time now." Warrec said as he gazed into the fire. "With everything that has happened in the last few days I had almost forgotten why we had come up here to begin with. I miss her." Warrec spat into the fire and watched it sizzle. "Hell, it might not even happen now."

Joenair opened his mouth to answer then shut it. He saw there was no point in pressing the issue. Warrec was probably right. It could wait. There were far more pressing matters now anyway.

Aluna came back in carrying four bowls and a loaf of rye bread. She gently ladled some stew into a bowl for Joenair and casually handed it to him. She then poured a bowl for herself and put it aside.

"I'm going with you two," she said as she slopped some food into Warrec's bowl and flung it at him. "I have lived in this village my entire life and this last week is the farthest I have ever been from home." Aluna grabbed her bowl and blew on the hot stew. "I want to go and see the capital, to explore and see new things. The village will be ok without a shaman for a while. Besides the next town is only a day's ride away if they need one."

"And there is no way we can talk you out of this?" Warrec asked while wiping his shirt off. The mighty warrior knew he was defeated and resigned himself to his fate.

"No there is not," Aluna said as she began pouring a bowl for Duncan. "I'm coming with you tomorrow. I'm going to go feed this to Duncan and then we are all going to sleep so we can leave bright and early in the morning." Aluna put her fists defiantly on her hips and fixed Warrec with an indomitable stare, daring him to object further. "And that's all there is to that."

Warrec sighed and held up his hands in mock surrender. He then leaned over and whispered in Joenair's ear. "As fierce and stubborn as my kindred are, the women are worse. I've been around the women of the southlands too long and have forgotten how northern women can be." He chuckled to himself but made sure Aluna didn't hear him.

Aluna had already turned away, confident in her victory and was carrying Duncan's supper to his bedroom when a massive form loomed in his doorway.

"I'm coming too," Duncan said as he stood in the doorway,

fire burning in his eyes.

Chapter Nine

Warrec had spent the rest of dinner and that evening trying to think of a way to talk Aluna and his father out of coming along. Duncan had quickly cut him off with a hostile look. Although Aluna was more than happy to argue with him, he realized that it was pointless and resigned himself to his fate. He had given Joenair several dirty looks for his lack of help, to which his friend would only respond with a grin.

They left early the next morning, slightly after dawn. Joenair was in his normal cheery mood, bouncing around and cracking bad jokes. Normally Warrec enjoyed this. Since, normally it helped alleviate tensions. This morning it just grated on his nerves. Duncan hadn't said anything since dinner and seemed to withdraw into himself. Though there seemed to be a small spark in his eyes. Warrec feared it was madness.

They hadn't brought much in the way of supplies. Just enough for the few days ride to the river port. Warrec had stowed his armor on the back of his warhorse. He wore only his black gambeson coat, boots, and leggings, along with his green cloak. His mark of rank, an eagle with wings spread clutching a spear was clearly visible on the shoulder pin.

Aluna had made a simple breakfast of bread, sausage and cheese and they ate while they rode. It was a good five-day ride to Hammerfall Lake and Port Valdrid, but they wouldn't have to go the entire way there. They would shave off two days travel by hitting the smaller trading post of Cuttersbend. The small town was set on a long western bend in the river, putting it much closer to Thornglade.

From there they could take the Zaphan River straight to the capital and the going would be much easier. For now, they rode through the forest and hills that dominated the north lands.

They stopped around dusk and made camp in a clearing surrounded by giant ironwood trees. As soon as camp had been made and the fire embers glowed a warm red, Duncan retreated to the far corner of the light and started drinking. Warrec shook his head at his father but said nothing.

As they sat around the fire everyone slowly began to relax. Grey horned owls could be heard hooting high up in the trees. Joenair began teasing Warrec, trying to rile him up. This an old game they played, and it always ended with Warrec hoisting Joenair up in the air above his head and threatening to drop Joenair on his head. This made Aluna giggle and her laughter seemed to dance through the trees.

Aluna fiddled absently with her necklace. A small lump of silver dangled from a simple leather cord. The silver had been forged into the rough shape of a double-sided hammer, the symbol of the AllFather. Most of the northern folk wore one as a sign of their devotion.

Long ago before time began, before the mountains rose and the stars hung in the sky the AllFather had laid down the foundations of the world. The AllFather had taken his hammer and brought order out of the chaos of the cosmos to form the world. When his task was complete, the AllFather was weary and his hammer had slipped from his finger to fall to the earth and formed Hammerfall Lake, the largest body of fresh water in the known world.

Warrec unconsciously touched the hollow at the base of his throat. It had been a long time since he had worn his hammer. He felt a twinge of guilt. Something about the motion of Aluna's necklace as it danced in her fingers kept drawing his attention. It took him several moments before he realized it was the necklace, he had given her.

He had given her that necklace as a birthday gift years ago on her thirteenth birthday, not long before he had left. It had been one of the last things he had done before he had headed south to enlist in the legions. Aluna had kept it all these years and the significance of that slightly troubled him. Did she see it as a simple gift from a friend or was it something more in her mind?

Warrec didn't want to hurt her feelings, but if his suspicions were correct that might be inevitable. The big man slightly shook his head. He would cross that bridge when and if he needed to. There were more pressing matters that troubled him anyway. He tried to push Aluna from his thoughts, but she kept dancing at the edge of his mind.

Warrec couldn't help but notice how the firelight illuminated the blazing orange and red in her hair. How her green eyes sparkled in the low light, almost glowing. The way her lips set in a slight pout. How her chest swelled up and down as she breathed.

Warrec stabbed a large branch he had been using as a fire poker into the campfire sending up a storm of red sparks. *Dammit man what are you doing,* he thought. He knew he shouldn't be looking at Aluna like that, but he couldn't help it. She was absolutely gorgeous and there was something else that pulled at him with her, something primal.

Warrec shook his head slightly. Addie was even more beautiful, and he knew she was too good for him. Addie was way above his station socially. While he had risen in rank he was after all a barbarian from the north and she was a nobleman's, a senator's daughter. How he had won her over he would never know.

Addie was sweet and kind and when he held her everything just seemed warm and soft. There was nothing soft about Aluna, well two things, but everything else was hard edged. It was different but not in a bad way. It was confusing. Deep down he had to admit it was part of the reason he hadn't wanted her to come along.

He glanced over at Aluna again. *Is she staring at me?*

The glow from the campfire reflected across Warrec's face and his tattoo seemed to come alive and dance across his face. The black lines and spirals looked like some twisted spider had seized half his face. Aluna stared at it and traced the design with her eyes trying to determine the pattern.

Warrec caught her staring at him. "What is it?" he asked.

"Huh...What?" His voice had snapped her out of her daze, and she was lost for a moment.

"You were staring at me."

"I was? Oh...sorry I was looking at your tattoo. I've never seen anything like it. What is it? Does it mean anything?" A proud grin spread across Warrec's face and Joenair smiled as well, because an epic story was coming up.

"Yeah, it does mean something," Warrec said pride filling his voice. "And the reason you have never seen it before is because it's Orcish." Warrec stopped and said no more as he went back to poking the fire, but he kept smiling, grateful for the distraction. He was teasing her, and she knew it.

"Well, what the hell does it mean? Are you gonna tell me or not?" she said. She then threw a clod of dirt at him and missed.

Warrec held his hands up to stop anymore earthen missiles from sailing his way. "Ok...ok easy...easy now. Well about a year and a half ago me and Jay here got assigned to a diplomatic mission to one of the big Orc tribes."

"The Wolfhelm tribe," Joenair interjected.

"Right the Wolfhelms. I was head of the security detail for the ambassador and…"

"I was spying," Joenair interrupted with a grin.

"Yeah, so anyway one day we were out with a group of Orc hunters. They said that there had been sightings of a rajanaga close by and it needed to be brought down or driven off before it got too close to the camp."

"Is that a dragon?" Aluna stared wide eyed, enthralled.

Warrec slowly shook his head. "Yes, but not really. Not a dragon from the old stories. Not one of the ancient ones. In the forests and jungles of the south there are a lot of huge reptile beasts, and they call them all dragons for lack of a better word."

"More commonly called wyrms," Joenair cleverly pointed out.

Warrec shot him a look. "The empire calls them wyrms."

"They are still big and still dangerous, well some of them,

but they can't fly or breathe fire or whatever," Joenair explained.

"Right, are you going to tell the story, or am I?" Warrec asked his friend. Joenair grinned and bowed with a flip of his hand in a mocking salute. "So anyway," Warrec continued on ignoring his friend. "We were out with the Orc hunting party and boom." Warrec clapped his hands together for effect. "The thing ambushed us.

"Now the rajanagas are very dangerous animals, probably the most dangerous animals in the world. They are about twenty-five feet tall and about sixty feet long. They stand on two legs and have huge jaws filled with big, nasty, pointy teeth," Warrec stated.

Joenair held his hands in front of his face and curled his fingers in a mocking representation and gave a feeble growl. Warrec shot him a dirty look in response. Joenair gave a smirk and a half shrug.

Warrec shook his head and continued on. "We had been tracking the beast for a few days. At first the trail had been easy to follow. It had plowed through the jungle, clearing a path almost big enough to send a barge down. Then it just vanished, it was as if the jungle just swallowed it up." Warrec slowly shook his head.

Joenair nodded in agreement. "It's insane, an animal that

big shouldn't be able to just vanish like that."

Warrec then pulled a dagger from his belt and handed it to Aluna. The dagger was about a foot and a half long. The blade was a simple, but finely made, single edge with a few Orcish glyphs engraved on it. The handle was a beautiful ivory with black leather straps wrapped around it in a tight figure eight for grip. The handle came to a point and as Aluna looked at it, it seemed like a tooth, but it was much too big. The handle was longer than her hand.

"That's one of its teeth," Warrec said as he took the knife back. Aluna whistled in awe as he re-sheathed it. "So, as you can see it's a pretty nasty beast."

Joenair nodded in agreement. "There are around sixty or seventy of those in its mouth. Scary horrible beast, but in a way very...majestic, also they are covered in feathers like a bird." As he said the last bit, he made a little bird gesture with his hands.

"The males, like this one was, have a crown of blue and red feathers that stick up from the head," Warrec said. "The arms are short and stubby, but they have these long feathers that come sweeping off them. They are dull green like an olive on the outside." Warrec lifted his arms up over his head. "But when they spread their arms out like this it's a fiery red and orange and sometimes emerald underneath."

"The females are just a dull brown," Joenair said. "But they both have a ghostly white muzzle, which gives their face an almost skeletal look to it. It's not something you want to find peering out at you from the jungle foliage."

Warrec nodded, lowering his arms, and continued on. "So, as it burst out of the jungle it snapped an Orc up and swallowed him in two bites. One second it wasn't there and the next second it was in the middle of us." He pointed his thumb at Joenair. "Jay here responded by diving and hiding behind some bushes," Warrec said with a laugh.

"I did not."

"Yes, you did."

"I most certainly did not. I did jump behind some bushes, but I wasn't hiding."

"Ok then what were you doing?"

"I was brilliantly and tactically formulating a plan of attack and or retreat." Joenair punctuated the sentence with an affirmative nod.

"Yeah, you keep telling yourself that Jay," Warrec chuckled and punched Joenair in the arm.

"Ow." Joenair rubbed his shoulder. "Ok, maybe"- he brought his hands together in a praying gesture and touched his chin- "maybe I was hiding,"- he then snapped his right pointing finger up- "but only a little. You would have too if you had half a brain, you big dumb brute."

"Ok...ok get on with it," Aluna said. She was on the edge of her seat and wanted more.

"Right so the rajanaga eats the Orc. I can't remember his name, poor guy. So, then we all scattered. The other Orcs are trying to regroup and attack the beast, but it was too busy chasing me. And you know how slow I am at running."

"Yeah, you never could beat me at a race when we were kids," Aluna said with a nod.

"Right, well the rajanaga isn't that fast either, doesn't have to be. Most of its prey is slow too, but it's fast enough to be breathing down my neck."

Joenair coughed and said, "quite literally."

Warrec sighed and rolled his eyes before resuming. "I know I'm never going to outrun it. So instead, I stop and turn and run straight toward it. As it lunged down to eat me, I dodged at the last moment."

Warrec stretched his arms out and brought his hands together in a massive clap. "Snap! Its jaws miss me by an inch or so and I run underneath it. It can't grab me because its arms are too small, and I ran between its legs." Warrec's voice was becoming more and more animated as he excitedly flailed his arms around.

"I have my sword out and I swing with all my might at the

back of one of its ankles. Whack! I managed to sever the tendon and the beast comes crashing down. I barely had time to roll out of the way. Now it's flailing and thrashing around, snapping its jaws and roaring.

"Aluna, it roared so loud it shook the ground. I thought my ears would burst." Warrec put his hands over his ears. "But it wasn't just loud; you could feel it, deep down in the bones." He then thumped his chest with his fist twice.

"Then I jumped onto his neck, which I found out later wasn't that smart a thing to do. But I'm on the neck and I stab down into his skull, burying my sword to the hilt. It twitches a few times and dies." Warrec is now sweating as he tells the story.

"The Orcs told me later that stabbing the beast's head is almost always useless," he said. The skull is thick and well armored, and its brain is only about the size of my fist. So, it's quite easy to miss. But I had neatly cleaved the brain in two." Warrec puffed out his chest with pride.

"Well now apparently no Orc had killed a rajanaga in single combat in several decades," Warrec said. "Maybe even a century and I was the first human to do it ever, so it was a very big deal. They gave me this tattoo which symbolizes what I did. It was an incredible honor and my standing with the Orcs rose immensely."

Joenair gently patted Warrec on the head like a child. "Yes, yes it was a great thing you did, killing that poor creature." Joenair laughed and immediately ducked as Warrec took a swing at him.

Joenair laughed again and winked at his old friend before turning back to Aluna. "Yeah, Orcs tattoo themselves when they do something big or complete a huge feat. So that everyone can see what they have done at a glance. And slaying a rajanaga is one of the highest. It's like killing a thousand foes in single combat...very big deal," Joenair explained.

Warrec grunted at Joenair then decided to ignore him. "So now I can walk into any Orc encampment or village and win instant favor and honor and be treated like a king," Warrec said smiling.

"Wow that's pretty incredible," Aluna said. She smiled and her whole face seemed to light up. "Do you have any other tattoos like that?"

Warrec's heart thudded hard in his chest when she smiled like that. He coughed and it took him a second to recover. "Well, no, none that are that important…but"- Warrec held up his left hand and showed Aluna an intricate geometric design of interlocking lines tattooed around his wrist. - "This means I have completed the tenth level of Pa'tho'cha, which is master level. It's an Orc martial art; it loosely translates as bone shattering. Joenair has completed it as well."

Joenair held up his wrist and showed the same tattoo. "I also have this." Joenair pulled his arm up out of his sleeve and showed a strange design, of asymmetrical lines radiating out from a half triangle, on his right shoulder. "This means I am a shadowglider."

"What's that?" Aluna asked.

"Uh...well it basically means I am seen only when I want to be seen." He then let out an obvious evil laugh.

"Wow," Aluna said it deadpan, but she was really growing more impressed by the minute. "How long did you stay with the Orcs?"

"What was it War?" Joenair asked. "It was about a year maybe a little more, right?"

"Yeah, that seems about right." Warrec paused as he thought about it. "It seems so long ago now. We have only been back a little less than a year now." Warrec's face lit up in a mischievous smile as he looked at Joenair. "Hey, you should tell her about the night of the celebration feast after they signed the trade agreement."

Joenair glared at him with enough heat to melt steel. "No let's not, that's a very boring story, wouldn't be an interest to anyone," he said sharply.

"Oh, go on and tell her. She will think it's funny."

"I don't care. It's not funny to me," he said as he continued to glare at Warrec. Warrec simply smiled at him with a huge grin on his face. Jay was trapped now, and they both knew it.

"Tell me what? I want to know," Aluna pleaded as she looked back and forth between them.

"No, I don't want to talk about it," Joenair said with determination.

"Please Joenair," Aluna said. She batted her big green eyes at him.

Joenair spread his hands out. "No, I'm not going to talk about it," he said. Still there was a little less determination in his voice now.

With a little more begging and the use of her feminine charms she broke him, and he finally relented. Her use of feminine charms had also included threatening to split his skull with her hatchet.

Warrec smiled and laughed as Aluna quickly wore down Joenair's resolution. Their eyes met for a brief second and Aluna shot him a quick wink. Warrec blinked twice and slightly cleared his throat, not sure exactly how to respond.

"Ok fine. I am such a sucker for a pretty face," Joenair said with a huff.

"And sometimes not so pretty, huh, that's what got you in

trouble to begin with," Warrec said poking Joenair in the ribs.

"Look, she was incredibly attractive…for an Orc and besides, I was drunk. Oh, shut up Warrec you're making me get ahead of myself."

"Yeah, shut up Warrec. I really want to hear this now," Aluna said. She rested her chin in the palm of her hands, her total attention on Joenair. Warrec just grinned and settled back.

"Ok. So, this is the night of the celebration feast. The Orcs have prepared this huge feast for us…."

Chapter Ten

Duncan lay curled in his sleeping bag. He feigned sleep as he listened to the kids talking. His head still swam from the amount of liquor he had desperately been pouring down his throat, but it wasn't enough. The effects were already melting away. He wished he could sleep. Instead, he watched the three of them from the shadows as they talked and laughed.

The fire popped and crackled as Joenair finished his story. "And the next morning I woke up and she was gone. I had a splitting headache and I hurt every time I sat down for a week."

"That's really gross," Aluna said clearly displaying her disgust. "And all Orc females are like that?"

"Yep, and that's why you never get drunk with a female Orc around," Warrec chuckled as he poked at the fire. "And really, it's not that gross or weird. Well, to a human I suppose it would be, but you have to understand Aluna it's a whole different culture and species. I mean that's just how they are built. It's normal for them."

"I still think it's gross."

"Painful too," Joenair said sheepishly. "But I think that's kinda the point." He stood and stretched trying to loosen sore muscles. "Hey, I'll be back in a sec." He then spun on his heel and disappeared as the blackness of the night swallowed him up. There was no sound of crunching leaves or the snap of a twig. He was there and then he wasn't.

"It's annoying how he does that," Warrec said. He and Aluna then sat in silence staring at the fire. Joenair's abrupt departure left an awkward silence between the two of them in his wake.

"Aluna, I want to apologize," Warrec said breaking the silence.

"For what?" she asked. "Warrec you're not one to apologize easily as I remember."

Warrec poked a stray coal in the fire for almost a minute before he answered her. "For not coming home more often…for not writing," he finally said. He took a deep breath before he continued. "And for not being there…the truth is a lot of times I couldn't come home or even write." He stabbed the fire hard sending up a shower of sparks. "The times I could I just didn't want to."

Duncan shut his eyes tightly. *My fault,* he thought.

"Warrec I… I'm not sure what to say," Aluna said. "Can I ask why? Was it me…was it something I did?"

"No, no it wasn't you. It's just"- he looked over toward his father, who seemed to them to have fallen asleep, - "complicated."

Aluna followed his gaze and gave a slight nod. "I think I understand now. It still really hurts, but I will get over it. After my father died Duncan kind of took me in, though I took care of him more often than not."

"There's something else though," Warrec said with a little cough. "Something big, it was the whole reason I came home to begin with, but now that all this trouble has started." He trailed off seeming unable to find the right words.

Aluna cocked her head at him. "Warrec what is it?"

The big man took a deep breath before he spoke. "Well…I'm getting ma..." Warrec was cut off as a loud roar and a scream cut through the night. Aluna and Warrec were on their feet in an instant. Warrec grabbed his sword and drew it in a smooth practiced motion, dropping to a crouch and facing the direction the sounds had come from.

"Skret, skret, skret," Joenair was yelling to himself as he burst out of the night. He ran past Warrec and grabbed a torch from the fire. He then spun around in a blaze of motion and light.

"What? What is it?" Warrec said peering into the night. His body tense, but ready to move as he scanned the wall of darkness beyond the firelight. Warrec searched for any movement, any shape in the pitch black as he waited for the attack. Time seemed to slow. All that could be heard was the frantic breathing of Joenair and the occasional pop or crackle from the campfire.

"Dunno, but it was big and had nasty pointy teeth, so I didn't ask questions," Joenair managed to gasp out.

Then a mountain of fur, muscle and teeth materialized out of the inky blackness. The bearcat stopped at the edge of the camp. It reared up on its hind legs and roared at these invaders into its domain. The still night was shattered as its fury echoed through the trees.

The great beast was easily twelve feet tall as it stood up. Firelight reflected in its eyes giving them an eerie red glow. Two long black stripes extended up from the iron-grey fur of its stomach. They circled up the beast's chest and back around its massive shoulders before meeting again across its face, giving it a mask of black where two red eyes burned with rage.

It let out a loud huff, shaking its thousand-pound frame. Twin front paws larger than pie plates extended their long claws in a threat display.

The super predator was legendary in the southlands and the Vatninu knew and respected them quite well. The beast was rumored to be highly intelligent, bordering on sentience and had been observed killing grown mammoths with relative ease.

The wild beast roared again as saliva glistening on its' oversized canines and stepped forward. It was still wary of the fire, but anger was quickly overriding its cautiousness. Warrec instinctively stepped-up front blocking the path to the others. He felt a small hand on his shoulder and turned to see Aluna.

"Wait," she said as she stepped past him and held up her hands in a non-threatening manner towards the bearcat.

"Aluna what are you doing?" Warrec said as he reached for her and tried to pull her back.

"Stop Warrec, just wait, we are ok. She isn't going to hurt us." Aluna spoke in a calm tone as she continued to move toward the bearcat. "Are you mama cat? No, you're not going to are you. You're not going to hurt us. You just got startled, that's all. It's ok, you're ok."

"She?" Joenair asked. He held the torch in front of himself in a feeble attempt to create a wall of fire between himself and the huge predator.

Duncan let out a small sigh. He still lay in his bedding pretending to sleep, but he had been ready if the kids had needed him. He relaxed himself now though. Aluna had this under control.

"Yes she," Aluna said answering Joenair. "See, look no mane. So, it's a female. You probably got too close to her cubs without realizing it." She stopped a few feet away from the bearcat. Aluna knew better than to try and touch her. She spoke softly and sweetly, with a hint of melody in her voice to the enraged mother.

"Easy girl...easy there. No one is going to hurt you or your babies, you're alright. It's ok." The bearcat let out a low growl, but she didn't seem as willing to attack now. "Guys lower your weapons." Aluna said it in the same sweet tone, but while still keeping her attention on the mother.

Warrec hesitantly sheathed his sword and Joenair dropped his makeshift torch back into the fire. They watched in awe as Aluna soothed the great beast. The bearcat dropped back down to all fours but continued to growl slightly. After a few more minutes she seemed to lose interest and turned and walked back into the night.

"Whew...close one huh guys," Aluna stated more than asked as she turned around smiling to herself. She seemed a little taken aback as she saw Joenair standing there with his jaw dropped almost to his knees.

"What the hell was that? How the hell did you do that? What the hell happened?" Joenair blurted out in a flurry of words slammed together. Duncan was impressed as well. While he had seen other shamans including her father do similar tasks. He had not seen it done to a bearcat or very often even, but he knew she could handle it.

Aluna put her hands on her hips and puffed out her ample chest. "Impressive huh," she said, clearly pleased with herself.

"Very impressive," Warrec blurted out. Duncan mentally rolled his eyes. The boy was staring at her breasts with all the subtlety of a trumpet crow with a new shiny button.

The boy abruptly seemed to catch himself and coughed twice and looked away. Duncan couldn't tell if she had noticed. "Yeah, that is… was…that was something," Warrec managed to stammer out.

Aluna smiled even bigger. *Yep, she noticed,* Duncan thought.

"Ok, seriously how did you do that?" Joenair asked still enthralled.

"A girl has to have her secrets," she coyly answered with a wink. Aluna was clearly pleased with herself and rightly so, but she seemed even more pleased that Warrec had noticed.

"No seriously?" Joenair said not letting her dismiss it so casually.

"I'm not telling."

"Please?"

"No Joenair."

"Pretty please?"

"I said no Joenair," Aluna said with a huff.

"Pretty please with sugar and a cherry?" he said in a very childish tone, teasing her.

Aluna waved her hand dismissively. "Look, I can't really explain it. It's a mystical nature thing. Let's just say it's magic."

"Yeah…uh huh…ok sure," Joenair said goading her. So, she responded by kicking him in the shin. "Ow, that hurt," he said rubbing his poor shin.

Ugh enough of this. I'm sober and awake. Now's as good a time as any to tell them, Duncan thought.

"Well, that's what you get when you're a jerk," she said. "And that goes for you too." She punctuated her sentence as she poked Warrec in the chest. Warrec tried to hide his smile, but it didn't work, and he burst out laughing instead.

"Hey! Be quiet over there. Can't an old man find some peace to sleep," Duncan grumbled, clearly letting them hear the irritation in his voice.

Warrec spun around at the sound of his father's voice. "What? How could you sleep with everything happening?" Warrec asked confronting his father.

"Exactly, how am I supposed to sleep with all this racket going on?"

Warrec pressed his fingertips to his temples and took a deep breath to calm himself. As he slowly breathed out, he pressed his hands away from his face, mentally pushing the anger away. The mental exercise seemed to help a little. Warrec had appeared about to explode, in a sudden flash of anger, now it just seemed to simmer.

"You are unbelievable," Warrec said. "You heard the bearcat. Why didn't you get up and help?" The anger was still apparent in Warrec's voice as he spoke.

"Ah, I figured you kids could take care of it," Duncan muttered as he stood and stretched. No one saw him re-sheath a large hunting knife in his robes. "Well, I suppose I'll stay awake for a while since I'm already up." He faked a yawn to punctuate the sentence.

Duncan walked over closer to the fire. He grabbed another log in one massive hand and gently tossed it into the fire. He shielded his eyes as embers were caught in the breeze and drifted up into the night sky. "Son, I think we need to talk," he said firmly. He sat down across from the trio as the fire lit his face with an eerie light. "There are some things I need to tell you."

"Yeah…well I don't think it's anything I want to hear." Warrec replied with a slight sneer and spat in the fire watching his spittle pop and fizzle.

"Warrec," Aluna said placing her hand on his shoulder.

He slapped her hand away. "What?" he snapped. Warrec focused on the fire and tried to shut out everyone around him.

Duncan sighed to himself. *I don't know how to fix this.* His son was clearly angry with him, something had set him off. Duncan doubted it was just the events of tonight. No this seemed to be a festering wound flaring up. *The boy has every right to be angry; I was a terrible father to him.*

"Hey, buddy calm down. There's no reason to be like that," Joenair said.

"No, there is plenty of reason to be like this," Warrec snarled with a glare. A burning coal of anger inside him exploded into a roaring blaze. The world took on a red haze. Warrec wanted to smash something, and he wanted blood. He didn't care where it came from. Warrec half turned ready to strike. Duncan could see the grimmig overtaking his son.

"Boy, sit down!" Duncan roared. Warrec froze in place. His father's commanding voice drenched his blazing rage in a freezing flood. Just like that it was gone. Warrec shook his head.

"I'm sorry," Warrec whispered. "I... I lost myself for a second. I feel ashamed" Warrec hesitated half a second before plopping down on a log. He cradled his face in his hands.

Duncan gave out a long sigh as he looked at his son. "Warrec...son I know things have been strained between us. Things have gotten so bad. I haven't been there for you like I should have and for that I'm sorry, but you have to understand what's happened and what will happen now."

"What are you talking about old man?" Warrec said, finally looking up into his father's eyes.

Father and son looked at each other for several seconds without speaking. Neither one said anything, but they each nodded slightly. *We start here* passed unspoken between them.

Duncan smiled a bit at the corners of his mouth. "Well first we should maybe start with a little history lesson. What do you know about the history of the empire?"

"Nothing much," Warrec said. "Just the basic stuff, I guess. They didn't teach us much more than that. A little more military history but that's about all."

"I probably know a bit more," Joenair said piping in. "My history and lessons in politics were a little more extensive than Warrec's. The empire was founded around a thousand years ago by the Marovian dynasty and the Line of Kalindor, the kings and eventually emperors of Marovia. Seven hundred years ago the Dwarves entered into a treaty with us and have been steadfast allies ever since. Then five hundred years ago the Dwarven lands became officially part of the empire but retained their autonomy."

"Right," Warrec said. "Then after that we started fighting with the Orcs more and more. There had always been border skirmishes and raids, but after the Dwarves joined the empire things began escalating. The empire was pushing its borders outward, settling more and more land along the forest edge. This led to the War of the River against the largest Orc tribe, the Ru'thar, around four hundred and fifty years ago."

The boy practically beamed as he applied his knowledge of military history. "The defeat of the Ru'thar tribe during the war left a power vacuum among the other Orc tribes. So around four hundred twenty-five years ago the huge civil war among the tribes started."

"The War of Burning Tears," Joenair said taking back over. "Where Warchief Gru'dar united the tribes together and proclaimed himself Grand Warchief. Then the united Orc tribes marched against us and nearly destroyed the empire."

The topic of military history had gotten Warrec excited and left his momentarily lapse in control forgotten. His hands darted and danced as he took over again. "But luckily Gru'dar was killed and his successor Herzuul was more reasonable. So, the Treaty of Artania was signed and we have lived in relative peace with the Orcs ever since. Every now and then there are the stray Orc raids but nothing approaching all-out war."

"And our trade and diplomatic relations have been flourishing lately," Joenair said with a grin. His eyes darted around, and he leaned in and whispered as if he was revealing some huge secret. "In fact, the word coming down the line is Fenrim; the current Grand Warchief is in talks now of uniting with the empire completely, becoming a satellite state like the Dwarves. Thanks in no small part to me and Warrec's fine diplomatic help last year."

"Yeah, just don't break your arm patting yourselves on the back," Aluna said poking Joenair in the side with a stick.

"Well, when I'm right I'm right," He replied pleased with himself. Though to be fair he always seemed pleased with himself. "And everything has been relatively quiet for the last two hundred years except for the occasional skirmish with a few of the rouge races and the Dwarven civil war a few years back."

"Except for Argis," Warrec said. All the excitement and joy drained from his voice and the words hung dead in the air. Duncan had been smiling and enjoying hearing the boys carry on, but the mention of the Dread Lord's name twisted his face into a mask of hate.

Aluna had sat quietly soaking in all Warrec and Joenair had been talking about. Most of it she had never heard of. She had started to say something to change the subject when Warrec mentioned Argis, but it slipped from her mouth onto the cool night breeze unheard. All four of them sat in silence now.

A few long moments passed till Duncan spoke again. "Son, I'm actually glad you brought that bastard up, because that's what I really need to talk about. I asked what you knew about history to see if you had ever heard of the Great Suffering."

"What was that?" Warrec said looking up again.

"Well, it was a time before the empire, a time before time. Some four thousand years ago," Duncan replied.

"What?" Joenair asked a bit puzzled. "There aren't any records going that far back. The Great Library of Eldurond hardly has anything dating back to before the founding of the empire. And the Dwarves lost most of their ancient texts and records when the earthquake destroyed Dur-Mordurn."

Duncan nodded. "That's true, but still there was history before what is recorded. Back during the time of myth and legend, that's when the Great Suffering occurred. During this time, our world was almost destroyed. For three long years demons and monsters from another realm of existence ravaged the land. They were called the Aetherburners. They killed and devoured all that they could and would have ended all life on Tala if not for the rebellion."

Joenair stroked his chin faintly as he mentally chewed at Duncan's words. "Aetherburners," he half muttered. "I feel like I've heard that word before."

Warrec nodded in response. "The Orcs called them Shadow Eaters, the Dwarves called them the Wind Takers, but I think they are the same thing."

Duncan let them ponder on it for a few seconds before continuing on. "You see all the sentient races had been enslaved. A few allied themselves with their new masters, trying to win favor and preserve themselves. They were the Savan, the Goblins, the Centaurs and a race called the Xellex. However, it was a pointless endeavor. The Aetherburners' only desire was to cleanse the world of life.

"The rebellion started slow at first. The elves had managed to hide themselves away and avoided being enslaved. But as the otherworldly menace spread, they saw they could not hide forever...so they struck back. They managed to free the humans, Dwarves and Orcs. This fledgling confederation fought back as best they could, but there was little they could do against a foe with inexhaustible resources and soldiers.

"The war finally managed to turn in the Confederation's favor when help arrived from across the ocean. The Kathari arrived and their ferocity bought the Confederation much needed time.

"The Elves had devised a plan to seal the gateway that the Aetherburners used to come onto our plane of existence. They created a key and used it to seal the gate. With their Ethereal Lords cut off from them the betraying races were shattered and thrown to the four corners of the world.

"However, the victory was bittersweet. It had taken the elves all that they could give to seal the gateway. Almost all of their people had been sacrificed in creating the key and its use. A few of their people survived but only a few thousand. The once immortal race now was mortal and broken.

"The Confederation also learned that since the immortal elves had forged the key with all their magic it could not be destroyed by mortal hands. With no way to destroy the key the threat of the gate being reopened remained. Immortal hands had forged the key and only immortal hands could destroy it.

"The last few elf survivors decreed that since the key could not be destroyed completely, it was to be divided in two and entrusted with two honorable warriors. The warriors were charged as the key's guardians and they separated the two parts, one of life, the other of death and hid themselves away, passing the responsibility down their line. That is where our family comes in." Duncan finally concluded.

The three sat dazed as they tried to process everything Duncan had just said. "Wait. What?" Warrec finally said bewildered. "That story is crazy."

"What's an elf? Elve?" Aluna said completely confused.

"And how do you know about the Kathari?" Joenair asked. "The empire just made contact with them a few months ago." There was a strong undercurrent of suspicion in his tone that Duncan didn't care for, but he let it pass.

Don't overwhelm them, Duncan thought. He knew it was a lot to take in. Duncan still had quite a bit of ground to cover. *Let them soak it in.*

The old giant decided to let them think and busied himself by taking a nip. The liquor burned as it flowed down his throat, before settling into a nice warm sensation in the pit of his stomach. It was good to feel something other than pain and despair.

"Ok, what does this have to do with anything?" Warrec asked. "And how does this relate to Argis? I thought you wanted to talk about him killing Everett. Not give us some long bedtime story." The boy was clearly frustrated.

Duncan scratched absently across the scar on his face, trying to find the right words. He elected to just say it. "Warrec, I am one of those two guardians. Our family has been guarding part of the key for almost four thousand years now. The sword that was in the temple is called the Soulblade and it is part of the key."

"Say again?" Warrec said trying to blink the confusion from his eyes. Joenair and Aluna sat speechless.

Duncan spoke slowly trying to walk his son through the thought process. "Ever since Argis appeared all those centuries ago he has been gathering the broken races that betrayed our world and building them up into a huge army. Every few decades he attacks testing our strength and gauging his."

"Right, I know that," Warrec replied.

"Son, when he took your brother, he must have tortured him and learned of the Soulblade, which he now has. He may even have the other half, but I hope and pray that he doesn't or even know where it is. Because I believe he is going to reopen the gateway soon."

"Wait you mean that…" Warrec trailed off.

"Yes, he will unleash an unholy army of things from beyond, into the world." Duncan's voice grew wavy as he spoke the next words. "I knew… I knew something like this would happen soon. I knew it when Everett died that this would happen. Prophecy...prophecy said that the sword must pass from father to son over and over. It was our charge, our sacred oath as we took up the mantle of guardian. If the line was broken, if the sword was lost then the gateway would be reopened. That's the way it was since the beginning. In four thousand years the line was never broken, not once, until my turn to pass it on."

Warrec blinked rapidly. "What? How?"-His head dropped to his chest, and he took a deep breath- "how did Everett die? You never would tell me. Tell me now!"

Duncan slowly nodded. Duncan's hands trembled as he drank again from his flask again. He had to tell him. "We were at the cave to begin the Ritual of Transfer. The sword it...well it eats souls. No living thing can wield it without being consumed."

The old giant reached to his neck and pulled the crystal pendant out for them to see. "This is my soul. Every guardian has to infuse their soul into a crystal at the cave. Then the previous guardian is taken by the sword and the cycle continues."

Aluna gasped and covered her mouth with both hands. Then she slowly began to nod as something finally seemed to click into place for her.

Duncan wasn't looking at them anymore. His eyes glazed over as he stared into the fire, his hand clutching the crystal in a death grip. "I was supposed to die that day, not Everett. We had started the process; he said the oath and took a crystal. Everything was going smoothly, until the Goblins attacked."

The old giant shook his head. "They weren't anything to worry about, nothing we couldn't handle. But I didn't see him there in the shadows, watching us. Not until it was too late. I don't know why he was there, but Argis attacked. Everett and I were separated. There was a cave in."

Duncan let out a long shuddering breath. "I couldn't get to him. I couldn't save him. I... I pounded and dug on that rock wall for hours, I would have torn through the entire mountain. By the time I finally broke through they were gone. No trace left."

Duncan's head fell into his hands as he fought to keep from

crying, the swell of emotion overwhelming him. "It was my fault, I couldn't protect Everett, couldn't save him, and now the line is broken. I have failed."

Warrec chewed on his lip. He looked to Aluna then to Joenair before finally settling back on Duncan. "Father why...why didn't you ever tell me or even mention this?" he asked. Warrec set his jaw before speaking again. "I would have done it. I will do it. I'll take your place."

Duncan looked up at Warrec with tears in his eyes. His voice cracked as he spoke. "I know you would have. But it wasn't supposed to be your responsibility; the secret was to stay between me and Everett, our burden to bear. I know your brother told you a little bit, but you were never supposed to know; not all of it anyway. You would have lived a normal happy life, without this huge weight crushing you down. I didn't want you to have to live with this, but it doesn't matter anyway. Your brother and I had already started the process, before it was interrupted. Without Everett there is no way to complete it and now it's stuck. I'm the last guardian, the line is broken, and I failed."

Aluna got up and walked over to sit by the old man. She held him like a small child, wrapping her arms around his wide back as best as she could. They all sat in silence again as the trio let everything sink in. Warrec was bewildered and a little uncomfortable as his father cried. Duncan was not one to be overly emotional.

Finally, Joenair spoke. "I still don't understand. In four thousand years something like this has never happened before? The ritual being interrupted I mean. Seems like they should have built a failsafe into it or something,"- he waved his hand in a circle- "It just seems needlessly complicated."

Aluna answered before Duncan could speak. "No, in a way it makes sense, from a magical standpoint anyway. Yes, it's complicated, ridiculously so, but that's how spells work. Magic bends the rules and makes shortcuts. The more powerful the spell the more complicated it has to be."

Aluna paused as she thought how to explain it better. "Ok, for example take healing elixir potions. They are a magical creation. It's not just a bunch of ingredients thrown into a pot, well it is, but it takes someone with the ability to tap into the magical forces to make one. Most of the ingredients are common herbs, like jubee root. But some of the ingredients seem unnecessary or pointless.

"For instance, you need a single drop of virgin blood. You can't make a healing elixir without it. Doesn't even have to be human blood, but it has to be virgin blood. There isn't anything special about virgin blood, blood is blood. Yet, the potion won't work without it. Without the magic it's just a strong medicine, with it the elixir can heal most fatal wounds if it's applied quickly enough. Needlessly complicated, that's how magic works. At least if you want to lessen the cost that is. I mean you could always just sacrifice life energy and get the same result in a more streamlined approach."

Joenair closed his eyes and scratched his head as he tried to mull over what she had explained. "But he said the Elves sacrificed their life force along with weaving this complicated thing."

"Which means the magic woven into this key piece and its properties is a ridiculously powerful spell," she said.

Joenair shook his head slightly. "Still, that doesn't explain how in four thousand years it never happened before. Between disease and war and all the other countless ways to die there was never a premature death of a guardian?

Aluna slowly nodded her head. "Yes, if it was woven into the spell like that, I guess.

Duncan wiped his face with one large hand and looked up at them. "No, there have been deaths before, it doesn't happen often, but it has happened. The Soulblade takes the guardian into itself on his death. It doesn't matter when. Then the new guardian from our family takes up the mantle. The problem is that Everett and I are both the guardian now. I can't transfer it to anyone else now, it's stuck in some kind of magical loop.

I poured through the ancient scrolls, books, and diaries of the previous guardians in the temple looking for a solution. I found nothing, either the other guardians never encountered this problem before, or they never wrote it down.

"What did you mean by prophecy?" Aluna asked.

"It was part of the oath we took, part of the spell when we preformed the Ritual of Transfer," Duncan said. "I won't tell you the exact words. Basically, we were to keep the blade hidden, keep it safe. If it was lost or taken from us, if one of us failed like I did, then the gateway would eventually be reopened."

Warrec let out a long puff of air. "So, the key couldn't just be thrown in the ocean or buried?"

Duncan nodded. "The blade feeds off souls, it keeps it powered. Every guardian feeds himself to it at death. Without that steady stream of power going into it I don't know what would happen. A few of the ancient guardians theorized on it, that it might explode, open the gate, or partially open it, even destroy the planet, nothing good in any case. I assume that Argis would need the other half of the key to open the gateway permanently, but honestly, I don't know."

Aluna shook her head. "As long as it existed it was a threat. It couldn't be destroyed. Maybe the creators could see certain events in the future and knew certain things. Better to stack the deck and prepare for what they knew would happen then to leave it to chance."

"That seems ridiculously complicated," Joenair said.

"That's magic," Aluna answered with a shrug.

Joenair shook his head. "So, what does this mean now, what are you going to do Duncan? What are we going to do?"

Duncan took a long deep breath and regained his composure. "I may have failed in my duties, but I'm still alive. I'm going to try and find the other part of the key myself and hopefully keep Argis from obtaining it as well. I pray to the AllFather that will be enough to keep him from opening the gateway."

"Jay you and I have to report back to the king." Warrec laid a heavy hand on Joenair's shoulder. "Maybe he will let us take a squad or two towards Argis' lands to see what he is planning and maybe stop him, before he gets too ready," Warrec said with steel in his voice.

"It's a plan, a start at least," Aluna said. "That's all well and good, but we aren't going to be able to do anything if we don't get some sleep."

Warrec's head reeled as he spread out his sleeping bag. He lay there now, his head pillowed on his arms staring up at the stars above peeking through the needles of the iron wood trees overhead. The other three had quickly gathered their sleeping rolls and blankets and settled in. After a few moments both Duncan and Joenair could be heard snoring peacefully.

It was so much to take in, but now things made more sense. He could see some of what his father had been dealing with. He felt terrible; he shouldn't have been so hard on the old man.

Warrec lay awake unable to sleep. Part of him wanted to go with his father, but a bigger part, the part in charge, told him that was impossible. He had duties. He couldn't just abandon his post. It was a death sentence for desertion, something he couldn't just ignore. Still, the stakes seemed high enough that he might have to help his father. Could he just abandon everything and go running off? What about Addie?

Warrec sighed and closed his eyes. I'll talk to the legate, surely after I explain it to him, he will see reason, he thought. His eyes were closed, and he was about to nod off when he felt something moving against his side.

His first reaction was to tense up readying to strike, but he relaxed as soft hands snaked across his chest. He opened his eyes and found himself looking up at one of the most beautiful women he had ever seen. It was Aluna, but she seemed different. Her hair fell around her face and the moon shone behind her head framing her face in a soft white halo. There was also something about her eyes, the way she looked at him, with tenderness.

"Hey soldier boy. It gets cold up here at night in case you forgot. I figured we best share body warmth." She half kidded, but her eyes and body language were clear. A leg snaked its way over his body, and she lay half draped across him.

Warrec tensed again, this was a very awkward situation, and he didn't know what to do. "Aluna, I don't think…"

"Hush," she said as she put a finger to his lips. Then she kissed him. Warrec tried to resist, but his senses were quickly overwhelmed, and he lost himself. A passion stirred in his chest as their lips joined together. He clutched her, pulling her in tight. The scent of her hair and her warm breath in his ear was overwhelming.

He pressed himself toward her as her hands greedily began to unlace his leggings. She let out a small moan into his ear. "My knight," she whispered.

An image of Addie saying those same words, looking up at him, love in her eyes flashed through his mind. *Addie, my Addie,* he thought. Warrec managed to pull himself back and remember. This seemed wrong and he wouldn't let himself give into passion. He gently pushed her away.

"What? What is it?" Aluna said as confusion and hurt set in visibly on her face.

"Aluna we can't do this. Not here. Not now. Not ever...I

can't do this." Warrec started to say more but stopped unsure what he could say that wouldn't hurt her more.

"Umm, ok...how silly of me." A masked smile spread across her face. "Oh, you big dummy. You should see the look on your face right now." She punched him lightly in the chest and laughed. "I got you Warrec. I got you so good. This is too funny." She pushed herself off him still laughing. "Ok, I will...I'll see you in the morning. Night." She quickly turned away and waved casually at him as she walked back to her bedroll.

She had tried to play it off, but he knew. He saw the tears as she had turned away, moonlight and firelight glinting off them. She cried herself to sleep that night. She was quiet, hiding it, but he could see her as she lay with her back to him. Occasionally she would shudder, and her breathing would be ragged and barely audible as a whisper in the night. Warrec spent the next several long minutes listening to Aluna crying, before she finally fell asleep. He knew it was the right thing, but he still felt like an ass.

Chapter Eleven

Aluna awoke at dawn as usual. As the first dawn rays came filtering through the trees her eyes snapped open. It was jarring and annoying, but it was something she had gotten used to, she hadn't had much of a choice as her abilities had grown stronger.

She got up and quickly and silently got herself dressed. There were no village dresses out here in the bush; here it was leather and steel. She threw her long leather poncho over her head, slipped on her pocket vest, and then pulled her leggings and chaps on. She belted her thick walking belt on and checked its contents. Two hatchets rode at her hips and a long-wicked kukri sat sheathed at the small of her back. The raven skull necklace sat nestled between her breasts as it should while the black and white feathers flared out from her neck hiding the small silver hammer.

Bare toes gripped the ground, pulling at the grass. As usual she wore no boots or shoes while out in the wild. She bounced twice to make sure there was no sound. Satisfied, she grabbed twin satchel packs and threw them over her shoulders.

She glanced over at the three men still snoring away. Joenair had a large dangle of drool yo-yoing up and down from his mouth as he breathed. Duncan lay curled in a fetal position. The man mountain managed to look small curled in his blankets. Then there was Warrec.

Stupid fat headed Warrec, she thought. She glared at him for nearly thirty seconds before she whirled and stalked off into the brush. *Stupid Warrec.*

She made no sound as she practically glided through the underbrush. Thorns and sharp stones barely caused her notice. Years and years of walking barefoot had toughened her feet to soft leather.

Absently her hands darted here and there plucking and picking different flora as her mind cataloged them. A red cap mushroom, good for stopping bleeding, went in one pouch. Millwarts Folly, a deadly poison went into another. Forrest tea, that would be good for their breakfast. Oh, good fungus bread, a few slices of that with the tea and a rasher of bacon will make a fine breakfast.

She foraged for about eighty yards before deciding that was far enough away from camp to relieve herself. She unfastened her flap and squatted. *Stupid Warrec,* she thought again. It was becoming a running thought in her mind.

When she was done, she dipped two fingers down and ran them along her slit. She brought the fingers to her face and sniffed. Then her tongue darted out and she tasted the foul liquid before spitting.

Yes, she was still in her fertile time. She stood and grasped her breasts. The soft flesh easily overflowed from her hands. Yes, those were still good.

She knew most males enjoyed them, or rather wanted to enjoy them that is. She had caught many males looking at them, so she knew they were a positive display. Even Duncan had made a pass at her one night not too long ago when he had been deep in his cups.

She had been putting him to bed as usual and had been half tempted to let him mount her. However, he had passed out after a few seconds, which looking back had been for the best.

I'm young, attractive, and fertile, she told herself. So why hadn't Warrec wanted to mount her she wondered. She was still a virgin and knew that was highly prized, so that wasn't the issue. Still, she was almost in her mid-twenties. It was time to start having children. She turned and looked over her shoulder at her backside.

Maybe that was it, she would need to bend over and display her rump in invitation. Aluna caught herself and closed her eyes.

You are not an animal, she thought. *You are a human. People don't act like that.* Except hadn't she been a wolf before? She distinctly had memories of running and hunting with a pack, although maybe that had just been just a dream. Sometimes it was hard to tell, and she had to remind herself that she was a human after all. Well at least she hadn't made a fool of herself.

"No, you just tried to mate,"- Aluna shook her head- "make love to the man you love and got promptly rejected," she muttered. The rational part of her mind told her that she had loved him years ago. She didn't really know the man or who he was now. She promptly told that part of her mind to shut up. *Stupid Warrec.*

Best to forget him for now, she decided. She then began to do her morning stretches and breathing exercises. As she moved through the movements her mind opened up and touched on the life all around her.

She could sense the rhythm of life flowing around her. She quickly tuned out the trees and smaller plants. Theirs was a dull tone that pulsed constantly in the background. They set the beat.

Next were the insects. A troop of ants marched along across a log a few feet to her right. Sixty-seven spiders skittered or hung in their webs within a fifty-foot radius of her. The amount of insect life all around was almost overwhelming. She condensed it and tuned it out, setting the tempo.

Now she moved onto the larger animals. A chipmunk sat on a root forty-seven feet to her left, completely oblivious to the leafback snake slithering up behind it. Seventy-three feet to her right a mother fox slept peacefully in her den, with six kits growing in her belly. All around her squirrels scampered through the trees above, birds sang good morning to the dawn. The ebb and flow of life flowed around her. These were the notes.

The song of life filled her mind. It was and is the most beautiful thing she had ever experienced. Every song was the same and every song was different. It was pure joy.

Aluna reached back and checked on the three notes of the men still sleeping. Each person was a collection of notes as unique as the individual. Joenair was like a flute, light and airy with a quick succession of notes. Stupid Warrec was a trumpet, loud and brazen.

Aluna pursed her lips as she looked to Duncan. As always there was no music from Duncan. He was an absence of sound, a void, except right at his center. If she strained, she could just make out a single sad solitary note. It had bothered her as long as she had been able to sense it. Now she finally had an understanding as to why.

She loved being in the forest. This was her home. She lived

in the village, but her heart belonged out here. She could sit and listen to the song all day and had several times. However, today was not to be one of those days.

Reluctantly, she tuned the song out and it slowly faded into the background of her mind. She sprinted back towards camp, relishing the feel of her muscles propelling her over rock, leaf, bush, and root. At the last few feet she leapt, soaring through the air to land in a crouch between Joenair and Stupid Warrec. She involuntarily let out a low growl.

Joenair slowly opened his eyes and found her face only a few inches from his. Aluna stared at him wild eyed and gave him a toothy grin. Joenair responded by promptly screaming.

Stupid Warrec yelled and tried to spring to his feet only to become tangled in his blankets and trip. Joenair's brain still hadn't woken up yet and his body was trying to inch backwards while still stuck in his sleeping bag. Aluna rolled on the ground laughing.

Duncan slowly got up and shook his head at the sight of the three of them. "She is worse than a rooster," he grunted. The old giant then walked off into the woods to take care of his morning business.

When Aluna was finally able to compose herself, she set about making breakfast. The fire had gone out in the middle of the night. After poking at the ashes for a few minutes she resigned herself to the fact there weren't any good coals left.

She sighed in frustration. It was a minor spell, but it was still going to hurt. She quickly rebuilt the starter branches. Stupid Warrec and Joenair had set about breaking camp. She could feel them watching her now. Magic was not common so watching someone perform it, even a minor heat spell, was extraordinary.

Aluna reached out and touched the twigs in the starter pile with her left hand. Slowly she pulled cold from the twigs, which increased their temperature. She could feel the cold creeping up her own arm. The pain grew steadily stronger, turning into a burning sensation. She gritted her teeth, just a little longer. She hissed out a long breath between clenched teeth, the air visible as if it was a cold wintery morning. All at once the twigs hit their combustion temperature and ignited.

She shook out her arm trying to get the pain to dissipate faster; it would eventually, but the faster the better. Stupid Warrec walked over and put a few larger branches on the fire to really get it going.

"That's really impressive, you're amazing," he said. Aluna smiled at him.

Stupid Warrec thinks I'm amazing, she thought. She nodded and pointed over to the bacon. "Hand me that." *By the AllFather he smells good.* It was one of the better breakfasts she had eaten in a while.

Chapter Twelve

Within an hour they all had eaten, fed and watered the horses, and were back on the road again. There was heavy awkwardness between Aluna and Warrec as they rode. She didn't know what to really do about it. They made small talk, but neither made any mention of the previous night and the unspoken words hung in the air between them. *Stupid Warrec,* she thought.

The travel on the road went slowly. Aluna hated taking the roads. She longed to run wild through the forest, not plod along on the dirt. Joenair told elaborate stories, all of which she had to believe were lies, and Duncan mostly kept quiet, occasionally muttering to himself.

The next two days passed quickly and uneventfully. The same routine over and over again: travel, make camp, sleep, break camp, travel, listen to Joenair tell bad jokes, look at Stupid Beautiful Warrec when he wasn't watching, take care of Duncan and on and on.

By the afternoon of the third day, they began to walk into the outskirts of Cuttersbend. Small hovels dotted both sides of the roadway. The smell of fish and salt hung heavy in the air, although there was no salt water for thousands of miles.

The small river port had turned into a boom town almost overnight when the new salt mine had been opened up a few miles south. Now both fish caught up at The Lake and salt from the mine were run back and forth both day and night between Cuttersbend and Port Valdrid, or shipped further south, trying to keep up with demand.

At the crossroads Aluna dismounted and bent down, scooping up a handful of dirt. She rolled the soil between her fingers, exploring the texture and smell. She then turned and looked north.

Two days travel north or half a day by river runner would take them to Port Valdrid. The port was the capital of The Lake and the largest city by far, not counting the Dwarven cities in the mountains, far, far to the east. She had been to Valdrid twice before. Both times had been a bit overwhelming, there were just too many people.

If they continued on to Valdrid and almost eight hundred miles northeast beyond the port, across The Lake and countless islands, they would reach the Dwarven lands. She had always wanted to see the mountain kingdom. Aluna slowly shook her head.

"Not this trip," she muttered to herself.

Her people owned The Lake. They lived The Lake. Hammerfall

Lake was theirs and theirs alone. Every island, every fish, everything that crossed or swam its watery expanse was theirs. The empire just got the lion's share of the profits now.

The Vatninu had started as raiders. They had sailed across The Lake hunting anything they could find. Unfortunately, in the beginning the only other things they could find were other Vatninu clans carrying the same sealskins, fish, and lumber.

The Dwarves had left The Lake to the Vatninu. Dwarves had a strong dislike for deep water. They couldn't really swim after all, their bodies being too compact and dense to float. This made the thought of traveling by boat particularly unappealing to them. So, they stayed on their shores, raising cattle, farming, and mining their mountains.

The Vatninu had tried raiding the Dwarves on the far shores. That had been pointless. As soon as their longboats had made shore the Dwarves disappeared down into their holes, sealing themselves and their hordes of treasure underground. Eventually, her people had decided that trade was the better and more profitable option.

Within a few centuries they had built a trading empire unrivaled across all of Tala. Then the Maroveyan Empire had come calling eager to take the vast wealth of The Lake for themselves. Her people had laughed as the smaller people had tried to take the river, or take the land, or the lake ports, or any foothold they could get.

Twelve legions had marched north to take the wealth of Hammerfall Lake, and twelve legions had never returned home. Then, like her ancestors, the empire had discovered trade was better than conquest. The Vatninu ruled The Lake and the north, but there was an entire world of other humans eager for her people's goods and craftsmanship.

Now the wealth of The Lake changed hands between the port barons and their imperial lackeys. The rest of her people weren't poor, but they lived simple lives. They did as they had always done, completely unconcerned with the problems of the empire or of the greater world.

"Hey, are you coming or not," Stupid Warrec asked. His voice snapped her out of her daydream. She looked back up and realized they were almost fifty yards ahead of her. She remounted and kicked her horse into a trot to catch up.

"Sorry just lost in thought," she said glancing back north one last time.

Stupid Warrec nodded and gave a half shrug. He then set his foot in the stirrup and gave the great beast of a horse he rode a nudge to move forward. She and Duncan hadn't wanted to take any of the village horses. They hadn't particularly trusted the imperial groomsmen in Cuttersbend to bring them back. But after a round of cajoling and refusal to go at a walk, Annoying Stupid

Warrec and Joenair had convinced them to all ride. They never could find out what had happened to the one Joenair had borrowed from the imperial stables here. Instead, he rode along on Neverlate, cursing the dependable old horse regularly.

"I'm going to ride ahead and go turn this fellow back in," Stupid Warrec said back over his shoulder. He reached down and patted the warhorse's thick neck. The sunlight framed him, and he looked magnificent. "Can the three of you make it to the town's post express on your own?"

Stupid Handsome Warrec, I'm not a child, she thought. "I think we can make it just fine," she answered. The icy undertone to her voice was quite clear.

Stupid Warrec actually blushed as he turned back to her. "Sorry I just, I mean I," he trailed off. He then gave a jerking nod and rode up the road and into the town proper.

"He means well," Joenair said. "Not too bright though. Well, come on, daylights burning." He scratched absentmindedly at his chin before muttering to himself. "Say I wonder if that nice washer widow is still around?"

Aluna gave him a quizzical look then shook her head. She decided she probably didn't want to know. A few more minutes of riding took them through the town gates.

Cuttersbend sat on a peninsula in the river. The only way to access the majority of the trading area and town was by river. The road they were on was the only main one and ran straight to the end of the peninsula. As such the town didn't really have any walls or a proper town gate.

The gate they rode through was more makeshift fencing and cattle guard than serious defense. It was designed to funnel both people and animals through the town to the main port at the end.

While the main port was at the end of the road, all the stables and animal stalls were at the front along the fencing. Every animal at some point was taken through the heart of the town along the main road. Throughout the day a multitude of livestock traveled through the town. Drop pie jumping was a favorite game of the local children.

Four guards sat just outside the gate, while one slumped against a post. They were intently focused on their dice game and didn't bother to look at the three of them as they approached. At the last minute, the lone imperial private, that was halfway working, waved them by before throwing his dice again.

They dropped their horses off at one of the side stables and grabbed their gear, walking into town. Aluna hadn't walked a hundred feet into the town before she realized two things: one she wished she was wearing boots and two both Duncan and Joenair had wandered off.

She quickly backtracked and stuck her head through the swinging doors of the first tavern on the road. Duncan was already perched on a stool at the bar with a line of drinks set up. Joenair was holding court at a side booth and somehow seemed already to be halfway through some ridiculous story. His audience seemed enthralled and hung on to his every word. He shot her a quick wave and turned his attention to the barmaid at his side.

Aluna rolled her eyes and walked back out onto the roadway. As she watched a steady crowd of people walk pass by, she realized she didn't know what she should be doing. Those two in there would be busy for a while and Stupid Warrec was still somewhere in the maze of the imperial stables further down where the warhorses were kept.

"I guess I'll head to the postmaster," she said to herself. She knew they would want to send messages out before they all boarded the boat. Not that she knew what needed to be sent or to whom. She felt out of her element and unsure, it was not something she was accustomed to or cared for.

With a grunt of annoyance, she stepped off the wooden sidewalk and crossed the main road. The postmaster building was the largest building right outside an assortment of stables past the gate.

There were two primary ways of sending mail and

communications in the empire, either by Good News or by Messenger Bird. Good News was a network of horse riders that rode back and forth along the web of roads that crisscrossed the empire. Messenger Birds, while much quicker, were far more expensive.

Unless you're in the military, she thought. Aluna wasn't quite sure why that thought had been so bitter. There was definitely some resentment there. *Stupid Warrec.*

As she started to walk up the steps into the post, she heard someone shout her name. Turning she was not prepared to see him, here or now.

"No, no not Landin," she muttered through gritted teeth.

A young man came sprinting over from the Good News' horse stalls. Only a couple years younger than her, he was dressed handsomely in a freshly laundered Good News uniform. The uniform consisted of a long blue shirt that dropped well below his knees and a red cloak with twin blue stripes down its length. At his waist he had a simple sword belt and short sword. A long blue cap with a bell at the end topped the uniform.

"Aluna, it is you," he said. "I thought it was you, I saw a forest nymph walking through the street and I says to myself Landin that's Aluna. Not too many girls as pretty as she is I says." Landin was grinning from ear to ear and didn't seem to be breathing between sentences.

Aluna forced herself to smile. Landin meant well and he was sweet. She very much regretted making out with him at the harvest festival last fall, he was a very wet kisser. Aluna hadn't expected to see the boy again, at least not this soon. With a start she realized that Landin hadn't stopped talking and was gushing over her.

She held up a hand. "Landin, what a surprise, what are, what are you doing here?"

"Me? Oh, I works here. Been promoted I has to full courier I has. No more mucking stalls and grooming horses for me, no sir. Well, no I still has to do that, but now I'm riding too. Been running all up and down the hills up here I has. Even been to Buckport I has. That's all the way up on the norf side of The Lake that is."

Aluna didn't have anywhere to run or escape. If she went inside Landin would just follow her. *He is sweet and kinda cute in a short imperial kind of way,* she thought. *But by the AllFather he doesn't shut up.* She remembered now that was why she had kissed him, it was to shut him up, that and she had already drunk seven cups of hard cider.

"Shoot, nows they got me running all over this way and that," Landin continued on. "Few more years and I'll be bona fide. Set me up with my own post, has my own runners I will. A girl could do far worse than me I tell you, far worse." Landin actually paused for a second or two. "I've been thinking a lot about you, I've missed you something fierce."

Run, her mind screamed. She couldn't though, couldn't just take off running down the street. *Or could I?*

The bell to the postmaster door tinged behind her. "Who's this then?" Stupid Warrec's voice boomed behind her.

Stupid Life Saving Warrec stepped out of the post building accompanied by a portly older gentleman in a more elaborate and expensive looking version of the Good News uniform. On his arm sat a menacing looking Messenger Bird.

"Ello friend, names Landin. Me and the lady here was having a nice quiet chat we was." Landin finished the sentence before Warrec had stepped all the way out the door. As the Major Postmaster stepped out Landin snapped to attention. With a quick salute he slapped the back of his hand to his forehead.

"Idiot," the large scary looking parrot squawked. Aluna couldn't help but giggle at the bird. She had always wondered just how smart the parrots were.

Messenger Birds were wicked looking and practically worth their weight in gold. Highly intelligent, the birds could be taught simple phrases and words, which combined with a written message tied to their legs and an uncanny ability to home in to almost any location made them greatly prized. However, they did tend to repeat certain words more often than others, especially if they were offensive.

"Hey, here now Tripps, that's not nice," Landin said.

Cold avian eyes turned and considered Landin. The bird was pitch black except for a collar of blood red feathers. Tripps clacked the wickedly sharp hooked beak on its bare face twice. The bird cocked its head from side to side.

"Run," it said.

"Landin, boy are the horses done brushed out and your kit saddled up?" The Major Postmaster asked, completely ignoring the ominous looking bird on his arm.

Landin snapped another salute. "Yes sir, right and ready they is."

The Major Postmaster handed Landin two sealed envelopes. "Good, here take these messages and relay them down south to Falls Gap. It's got to get to the capital double time, very urgent, military matter."

Landin took the envelopes and looked back to Stupid Warrec and then at his rank. Landin swallowed and nodded. He started to turn and walk away but suddenly whirled and grabbed Aluna by the hand.

"I'll be back in a few days. Will you wait here for me? I want to take you to see the hoppers out on the marshwalk. They are right amazing when they sing at night, they is."

"Landin, no I can't," she said. She glanced over at Stupid

Warrec who was grinning at her. "I'm leaving probably today, and I have no idea when I will return. It could be a long, long time."

"I can wait! I can, I could wait forever for you I could." Landin looked to be on the edge of tears.

"You could do worse than him," Stupid Warrec had to chime in. Aluna wanted to stab him.

Slowly, she shook her head. "No, Landin, no. You're sweet, but I couldn't do that to you. That's not fair to you." She then gave him a quick kiss on the cheek.

Landin slowly nodded clearly crestfallen. Without another word he walked away, shoulders slumped, back to the stables.

"Good lad, bit impulsive though," the Major Postmaster said. "Anyway, I have the message all attached here"- he pointed to the leather tube tied to the bird's leg- "Tripps here will get the message to Eldurond within a couple days. My other bird is out, but when he gets back, I'll send him on up to Valdrid along with another runner. Not to worry."

Stupid Warrec thanked him and turned to walk away. He wrapped his arm around her shoulder. "Any other business you need to attend to while we are here? If you need a few more minutes with Landin I can wait," he said grinning at her like an idiot.

She elbowed him hard. "Don't be an ass."

"Fine, sorry, sorry," he said laughing. "Where are the other two?

"Where else," Aluna answered and pointed across the street back to the tavern.

"Of course, they are. That was a stupid question." Warrec sighed. "Ok, let's grab them and go find a boat. The sooner we leave the better."

Chapter Thirteen

Warrec didn't particularly like boats. This was an odd thing when he really sat down and thought about it. Sailing was after all in his blood. Most of his people spent a good deal of their lives either on The Lake or one of the several tributaries running out of it. It was probably the rolling deck; he preferred to have solid ground underneath his feet. Still, like it or not, this was the fastest way to get back to Eldurond.

Traveling overland would have taken weeks and over very rough country. Good News couriers covered the ground so quickly because they never slept. That is, they relayed, one rider would ride hard from one point to the next before handing the mail over to the next rider and so on down the chain. Good News ran twenty-four hours a day, seven days a week. That wasn't an option for the four of them.

From Cuttersbend it was a long slow tedious boat ride down the river. It was ten long boring days on the river where they had to stop at every single port along the way. Of course, the trip up here had taken the same amount of time, but he hadn't been in a hurry then.

Still, the several days with nothing to do gave him ample time to talk with his father. Before the events of the last few days, the thought of doing that had filled him with dread. He would have rather been facing down a thousand enemy soldiers. Now, well now he understood a little more. He was still mad at his father for a lot of things, but he didn't resent him anymore.

Midday on the tenth day they finally drew sight of the capital. Warrec was amazed every time he returned home. He thought it was odd that he now considered the capital his home and not the tiny village of Thornglade. He wasn't quite sure when that change had occurred.

Eldurond was the jewel of the empire. Nowhere else in the world was a city as beautiful and as magnificent. It always amused him as he looked on the great metropolis how this glorious city began as a simple fishing village over a thousand years ago.

"Wow." Aluna's voice broke him out of his contemplation.

"What?" Warrec smiled as she gazed wide eyed at his home.

"It's so…it's so big," she managed to stammer out. "I thought Port Valdrid was big, but this, this is on a whole other scale."

"Yeah, ain't it something kid," Joenair said. As he walked

up behind them and threw his arms around their shoulders, although he had to stand on his tiptoes to do so. "Home sweet home."

Within a few minutes the merchant barge passed under the Northwall Bridge. The Northwall Bridge spanned the great width of the Zaphan high enough to easily let a three-mast ship pass underneath. Aluna looked up and gazed wide eyed at the giant portcullis above them. The barnacle encrusted portcullis loomed above them like the jaws of some monstrous thing, threatening to snap shut down on them.

Green Face gulls squawked loudly at each passing boat. There were easily a hundred of the noisy birds perched in the teeth of the portcullis. The birds spent most of their day up there yelling, waiting for the occasional fishing ship or food barge to come through. Then the flock would dive bomb the hapless boat trying to steal a fish or three.

"Those things are really annoying," Warrec said looking up at them.

"They're just birds; they do the same thing up north. They got to eat as well," Aluna said. Then she poked Warrec in the chest.

"Yes, well you never have been up on those walls and have them swoop down on you," he answered. "Nearly knocked me off," he said the last muttering under his breath.

To say that the city of Eldurond was a huge city was an exercise in understatement. Over the centuries the city had sprawled out over both banks of the river and far outside the high walls that contained the original city proper.

The bustling trade district was on the west bank, while most of the living quarters and houses were on the east bank. The main legion garrison and stables were also on the east bank. Nine bridges spread across the length of the city connected the two riverbanks.

A fifty foot, almost as thick as it was tall, stonewall constructed of granite and limestone surrounded the city proper. When the sun hit the wall just right the pink in some of the granite stone would shine, casting a red haze across its surface. The Northwall Bridge and the Southwall Bridge sealed the city off from attacks from the river if the need ever arose. The two bridges were flanked by their massive drum towers stretching up well over two hundred and fifty feet, which seemed to catch the bridge arching between them.

Eldurond's walls had never been breached from the outside. The city itself hadn't been attacked since Gru'dar had laid siege to the capital for one hundred and forty-three days back during The War of Burning Tears, over four hundred years ago.

"Look there," Joenair said as he pointed. "You can see the spires of the Imperial Palace on the island."

The city had been built at a wide point in the long river. Here, the Zaphan moved lazily along with little current. In the center of the river a long narrow island divided it. The island was close to two miles in length and a quarter mile wide at its widest point. The island was the center point of the city and the location of the original fishing village.

Now, the Imperial Palace with its twin spires and its gardens covered the island. Four bridges connected the two riverbanks to the island and to each other. It was from this tiny island that the Maroveyan Empire had been run since its founding, the very heart of the empire. It was arguably the most valuable piece of real estate in the whole world.

Inside the capital walls the buildings seemed to gleam white as the sun struck them. Older marble and stone buildings were slowly being replaced with newer concrete. Large spiraling towers and domes jutted up here and there throughout the city. The streets were filled with well over a million hustling people going about their day. Warrec smiled to himself.

The barge pulled in to dock on the west bank. Its crew immediately set about unloading the boat's cargo to the dock hands. Practiced hands smoothly traded cargo from barge to dock. They broke out into song as they worked. A quick and merry tune of being drunk in an alley and missing their wedding day.

"Ok, so where to first?" Aluna asked. Her head constantly

swiveled back and forth as she tried to take everything in.

"Well, me and Jay need to go report in, to Legate Silnis. But the military ward is on the southeast bank. So, I guess we will have to go through the city." Warrec said as he smiled at her.

Aluna let out a little yip of glee. "I've never seen so many people at once or a city this big. There are too many people, too much noise. It's almost overwhelming, but I still want see it all."

"I'm going to head to the library," Duncan said. His booming voice and the fact they had no idea he was standing right behind them made them all jump. None of them had heard him approach and even Joenair was caught unaware when the old giant had seemed to materialize out of nowhere.

"Ok, The Great Library is…" Warrec started to point vaguely in the direction of the grand structure.

"I know where it is," Duncan said cutting Warrec off.

"But how do you know…" Warrec stopped his question midsentence. He wasn't sure he wanted to know the answer. "Well, ok where do you want to meet us later?"

"I'll find you," Duncan said. He then hoisted his massive polearm to his shoulder and turned to leave, stepping down onto the dock.

"Um, ok then." Warrec didn't know what else to say as his

giant father disappeared into a sea of people. Warrec blinked twice and shook his head. His father was easily head and shoulders taller than most people, even more so down here. He stood out in a crowd, but after a hundred feet or so, the old giant just wasn't there anymore. Warrec whirled toward Joenair. "Did you teach him that?"

Joenair pointed at himself. "What? Me,"-he turned and followed where Warrec had been looking-"oh that, no, no, he must have just turned a corner or something." He dismissed the idea with a flip of his hand.

"Somehow I don't believe you."

Joenair shrugged in response. "Well, we should get going too." He stooped down grabbing his bag and lightly leapt down to the dock.

Warrec frowned but let the matter drop. He knew he wasn't going to get a straight answer. He turned and spoke to the boat captain and the Dockmaster standing nearby about his armor. One of the privileges of being an officer, even a low rank like him, was he didn't have to lug all that gear through the city.

He tipped the two men a few silver heads each out of courtesy and had the gear shipped back to his quarters. However, he still threw on his black gambeson and green cloak over his tunic. They were part of the uniform after all. He buckled on his sword belt and checked the rank belt buckle and the pin insignia on his left shoulder. Satisfied, he stepped down to where Joenair and Aluna waited patiently, well Jay did anyway.

Joenair was dressed simply as always and gave no indication of his rank, title or who he was, which was normal. His wide floppy hat was pulled down low covering most of his face. The man probably had over a dozen different knives or similar weapons hidden on his person, but you could never tell by looking at him. And, as always, his, the world is a brilliant place for having me in it, grin was plastered on his face.

Aluna appeared to be fidgeting; barely able to contain herself. She was absently drumming her fingers across the raven skull that hung from her neck. Aluna still only wore her poncho, leggings, and chaps. She looked wild and very out of place in the cosmopolitan setting. She had woven her hair into an intricate seven braid pattern, with bits of straw and a few feathers here and there. Crisscrossed across her shoulders, her twin satchel bags covered the hatchets at her hips and the kukri in the small of her back. She had added a simple leather vest full of pockets to carry her small assortment of herbs and accoutrements.

Warrec slowly shook his head and wondered if he should say anything. *Did she bring any other clothes,* he wondered. He wasn't sure. Now that he thought about it, he hadn't seen her in a dress since that first day they had set out heading south.

This outfit looked more natural on her.

He then glanced down at her bare feet and decided that did need to be addressed. "Aluna you're going to have to get some shoes."

Aluna looked down at her feet and wiggled her toes. "What, why, what's wrong with my feet?"

At that moment, a carriage happened by and one of the horses took the opportune moment to relieve itself in front of them. "That's why," Joenair said. "It's a pretty clean city as cities go but still. Though not as bad as the main road through Cuttersbend I suppose."

Aluna shrugged. "It's just dung."

"Didn't you mention wanting boots as we were walking through Cuttersbend?" Warrec asked.

Aluna frowned. "Nope, don't think so."

Yes, you did. You even stopped and looked in the window of the cobbler," Warrec said.

"No, I didn't," she said. Warrec narrowed his eyes at her. Aluna smiled sweetly at him. "You're just remembering wrong." Joenair laughed and looked away.

Warrec let out a long breath as his nostrils flared. "Well, not all of it is animal though," Warrec said.

At that Aluna frowned and nodded. "I probably need some boots then." With that they began to weave themselves through the crowd and into the market proper.

The marketplace was a hive of activity as the trio passed through. Venders shouted and hawked their wares to anyone and everyone passing by. The clang of hammers could be heard as blacksmiths and weaponsmiths crafted their items for sale. An overzealous vender shoved a large smelly fish at Aluna.

"Fresh fish!" he shouted, startling her. She politely said no and stuck her tongue out in disgust as she turned around. She leaned over to whisper to the two of them. "I have serious doubts about the freshness of that so called fresh fish." Warrec and Joenair both laughed at her.

Joenair tapped the side of his nose. "Well, considering that particular species of fish is a saltwater fish normally caught off the coast of Artania and we are just about a thousand miles from the coastline, you're probably on to something there." This prompted another round of laughter from all three of them.

"Oh hey, I need to stop in here," Warrec said as they passed by a weaponsmith shop. The sign above the door read _Three Dwarves from Vell-adair_ and underneath the large bold words someone had scribbled _Swords Shields and other Skret_. Aluna giggled at the joke. The shop name was written in Highcommon, the bastardized trade language that had become the dominant language throughout the empire. Underneath the main Highcommon letters the shop name was repeated in Dwarvish and Orcish, but the joke graffiti was only written in Dwarvish runes.

Joenair cocked an eyebrow. "You can read Dwarvish?"

Aluna shrugged. "Read it yes; speak it, not so well. Why, can't everyone?"

"No," Joenair said. "Most people can't even read Highcommon, let alone another language."

"You kind of have to up north," Warrec answered. "Most of us uncivilized barbarians can read, write and speak in both."

A bell rang as Warrec opened the door and he had to stoop to go through the doorway. A Dwarve sitting behind the counter looked up from his book and peered at them over his spectacles. He was old and it showed. His long snow-white beard was braided down to his stomach and his massive hands had liver spots on them. His spectacles were perched precariously on one of the many wrinkles that crossed the bridge of his large blunt nose.

"Who's der?" he grumbled squinting at them.

"Hey Kel, it's me, Warrec."

"Oh Warrec, good to see ya lad," Kel said. "Where haf you been hiding yer self?" The old Dwarve scooted himself off his stool and landed with a thud. There were several loud audible cracks and pops from his joints as he came around the counter.

He was barely four and a half feet tall and almost as wide. His shirt sleeves seemed about to burst as the muscles flexed underneath despite his age. His long beard draped over his big belly, matching the shock of white hair on top of his head.

"Oh, I've just been out of town for a while," Warrec said as he stepped over to shake Kel's hand. The Dwarve's hand completely engulfed Warrec's.

"Right...right. Oh, and who might ye be ye pretty wee thing?" Kel said, turning toward Aluna. Kel licked the palm of his hand and tried to slick back what little hair he had left.

Warrec rolled his eyes at Aluna. She caught his eye and rolled her eyes back at him with a half grin. Old Dwarves were all the same she seemed to say. Warrec shook his head as Kel did his best to make googley eyes at her.

"Hail to thee...Mr. Kel, I am Aluna Dimmaloper Atherndotter. The winds bring me to you." Aluna finished by crossing both hands and pressing her palms towards Kel.

Warrec cocked an eyebrow. The full Dwarven name declaration seemed to be a bit too formal of a greeting here. Kel flustered for a second and gave a loud snort. *Oh, that's right, it'll keep him acting a little less salacious, well at least for a few minutes anyway, clever.*

"And may the winds bring you back to safe places. I am Keltec Forgefoot." Kel finished by crossing his hands and pressing his palms towards his own chest, as he was the receiver of the greeting. He then quickly fluttered a hand at her. "Bah, no need to stand on ceremony here and ye didna have to call me mister lass. Kel will do fine please and thank you."

"Now Kel, she isn't even a quarter of your age, and besides what would your wife say?" Warrec said teasing the old Dwarve.

"Ah ye cannae blame an old Dwarve fer trying. And I dornt care what tha old bat says," Kel said after he quickly looked around to make sure she wasn't in earshot. "So's anyway what can I do fer ya today?"

"I wanted to see if my shield was ready yet," Warrec said. He casually started to pace and look around the room at all the equipment. The walls of the small shop were lined with all manner of weapons and armor. Warrec absently picked up a Dwarven war hammer and studied the intricate scroll work on the head.

"Ah, I'm not sure tae be honest." Kel took a quick look behind the counter. "And I dornt see it up here. Lemme go see if Glem has it innae back." Kel walked over to the back door. As he opened it a blast of heat came in from the furnace and loud hammering could be heard. "Glem, Hey Glem," Kel shouted.

The hammering just kept going. "Glem, ye deaf bastard answer me!" Kel cursed and grumbled under his breath when he got no reply. He kept cursing to himself as he disappeared into the forge. The hammering kept on for another few seconds before falling silent. After a few minutes Kel came back still cursing and muttering to himself.

"Ah yeah...seems Glem finished yer shield yesterday, but fer some reason he went ahead and shipped it to yer place," Kel said rubbing his balding head.

"Oh, well ok, that's not a problem, actually that's better," Warrec said. "I have a few errands to run today so I won't have to carry it then. When do you want me to pay you? I don't have the money on me now."

"Och that's nae a problem fer you lad. Ah, why don't ye leave a draft at tha bank and I'll go pick it up there so's ye don't have to come all tha way down here again."

"Are you sure? It shouldn't be a problem for me to come back tomorrow."

"Ah, well, it might be lad." Kel narrowed his eyes and looked around the shop to make sure no one else was listening, despite the fact that only the four of them were there. "See tha word on the street is that you boys might be heading out soon."

"Say what?" Joenair said putting down the knife he had vaguely been looking at. "I hadn't heard anything about that."

Warrec started to ask Joenair when he would have heard anything as they had only arrived today, but then thought better of it. The man had an uncanny talent for knowing things that shouldn't be known.

Aluna cocked her head and muttered to herself giving a

quiet voice to Warrec's silent thoughts. "We have been in the forest and on a boat for the last few weeks. Where would you have heard it?" No one seemed to have heard her or at least they ignored it.

"Yeah, news come in the other day," Kel continued. "Lot of bad things happening over in the west, people starting tae talk about war." Kel shook his head, clearly worried.

Warrec gritted his teeth. "This couldn't have come at a worse time. Kel, we need to be going. You take care of yourself." Warrec turned to leave and gave the old Dwarve a quick wave.

"Dornt ye worry about me lad, ye watch out fer yer self. Wind be with ya boys." Kel waved as the trio left. "Wind be with ye." He said again to himself as they walked out the door.

The trio weaved their way through the throng of people till they came to Ambassador Row. One of the main roads that ran through the city, Ambassador Row, was flat paved concrete instead of the normal cobblestone of the side streets.

Aluna paused and then slapped her barefoot down on the roadway. "What is this? It's like smooth stone except not."

"It's called concrete," Joenair answered. "It's some kind of rock powder that they mix with water. When it dries it hardens into this. They have been paving and rebuilding all the main roads in the empire with it, much easier to travel on."

"Come on let's grab a palanquin. I'm tired of walking," Warrec said. He then half stepped into the roadway and waved down one of the numerous hand drawn vehicles sitting in the edgeway waiting on passengers. Two lean men in linen shorts and half vests jumped up and pulled their cart over.

Warrec piled everyone into the palanquin and told the drivers to head down the row to the end at the bridge. He would have rather liked to ride all the way to the military ward, but this was a green roof palanquin. They weren't allowed to cross the bridges to the west side. He quickly checked to see if a blue roof was around and of course there wasn't one. The nobles generally kept those around the imperial island since they could run anywhere in the city.

Ambassador Row was one of the eight main roads that bisected the city horizontally. The Row ran all the way from Hopper's Gate across Drowned Maiden's Bridge to Woodlawn Gate. The Row was the widest road and had the second most northern bridge in the city, after the Northwall Bridge. Drowned Maiden Bridge was almost a city unto itself, with shops and apartments running the length and stretching four or five stories at the middle.

Warrec closed his eyes and managed to catch five minutes of sleep before the palanquin pulled sharply to a halt. "Dallep Plaza," one of the drivers said. He wasn't even breathing hard despite the long run. "Far as we go, eh capo, mighty quick it was."

The three of them climbed out and Warrec handed the man two silver heads and twenty copper pennies. "Very quick," he said. He hadn't really meant it as a compliment, he could have used a few more minutes of sleep, but the man took it as one.

"Much thanks capo," the man replied grinning at the generous tip as Warrec handed him the money. The two men then pulled their cart over to the edgeway by the plaza and waited for their next customer.

Dallep's Plaza was where most of the nobles shopped on the north side of the city. A whole host of street performers, everything from jugglers to fire eaters, plied their various entertainments for the delight of the shopping crowd. A huge half circle lined with a mix of bourgeois and gentry shops; the plaza was dominated by the fountain in the middle. The fountain depicted the ancient general Dallep sitting proud on the back of his warhorse, arm and sword outstretched towards the sky.

Warrec shook his head and chuckled. The fountain always made him laugh. It was several hundred years old and showed Dallep in the uniform and armor of the time, even though Dallep had lived back at the beginning of the empire, before there really had been an empire. That breed of horse hadn't even existed then. While it wasn't very historically accurate, it was pretty, and that was the point after all, he mused.

As they were passing one of the last buildings before crossing the bridge, they heard a soft feminine voice shout. "Warrec!" They all three turned and saw a blond woman running down the steps of one of the fancier looking shops toward them. Three ladies-in-waiting tried desperately to keep up as the blonde woman sprinted toward them.

"Oh boy here we go," Joenair said softly to himself. Aluna gave him a puzzled look and cocked her head at Warrec who had a big sheepish grin on his face.

By the AllFather she is beautiful, Warrec thought. A wellspring of joy sprang up in his chest as he watched her run gracefully toward them. He couldn't help but admire her elegant beauty. Her long straw-colored hair floated in the breeze behind her. She was dressed extravagantly in a green and silver silk dress that she pulled up with both hands to keep from tripping over the hem. An ample bustle on the back bounced wildly as it matched her nimble strides. She was the most beautiful woman he had ever seen, maybe the most beautiful in all the empire. *One of the best rears too,* he couldn't help thinking as she leapt into his arms. She practically melted into him as she wrapped her arms around his neck and pressed ruby red lips to his.

"My lady," one of the girls running after her shouted.

"My lady please this is not appropriate," another said.

Aluna's eyes went icy for a second and she let out a loud cough when the two kept kissing. Warrec gently broke the kiss and pulled away. He had a huge grin on his face.

"Hey Addie," he said oblivious to everyone around him.

"Hey you," Addie said.

Addie barely came up to his chest. The two of them stared at each other for a second before Warrec wrapped his arms around her again and lifted her to eye level. Addie grabbed his face and kissed him again, and again.

"My lady!" the first girl said again, more forcefully this time.

"Oh, Miriam stop, can't you see my knight is home," Addie said finishing the sentence in a half purr.

"Aah, aah hem," Aluna coughed again as obnoxiously as she could.

"Oh...uh...right, uh," Warrec stammered. He gently lowered Addie back to the ground.

Addie looked over at Joenair and Aluna and smiled. "Hello Joenair, long time no see." Her smile seemed to make the whole day brighter.

"Ambassador Adelia Flavius, lovely to see you as always," Joenair said. He swept his arm in front of himself in an elegant courtly bow, which was so low the brim of his hat almost brushed the ground.

"Oh, stop it. How many times do I have to tell you to call me Addie," she said as she rolled her eyes at him. Addie spread her arms and flexed her hands telling Joenair to come give her a hug, which he did with a small peck on the cheek. "Oh, and I see we have need for introductions," she said looking over at Aluna.

"Uh, Addie this is...Aluna. Aluna this is...uh...my fiancée Addie," Warrec said sheepishly.

"Aluna? Oh yes, your little friend from back home. Oh, how lovely. Warrec has told me so much about you," Addie said beaming her smile at Aluna.

"He did? I'm sorry he never mentioned you," Aluna said staring daggers of ice at Warrec.

"Really, did you at least tell your father about me?" Addie said as she playfully elbowed Warrec. "I did want to meet him though at some point. Well,"- Addie stepped back and swept her arm before the three young women behind her- "These are my ladies-in-waiting. Warrec, you know Miriam of course," she said pointing to the raven-haired oldest woman. "Loreia is new," she said pointing at a young brunette woman in her early twenties. "She is from an up-and-coming house, the Fetorlams. I'm not sure if you've heard of them." Addie wrapped a protective arm around the youngest girl, a small petite girl that couldn't have been more than ten and had hair to match Addie. "And this is my cousin Tettia."

Joenair slyly caught Warrec's eye. The jaunty fellow raised both eyebrows and gave a slight head tilt toward Loreia, he then cocked one eyebrow. Warrec rolled his eyes and gave a half shrug. He then closed his eyes for half a second and nodded. Joenair grinned wickedly and turned his full attention toward Loreia. The young woman blushed when she caught him grinning at her.

If Addie caught the exchange, she paid it no mind. Warrec sighed to himself. Asking Jay not to chase available women was like asking the sun not to rise in the morning. He just wished he wouldn't do that with his fiancée's attendees. The last one had to return home in disgrace.

Addie then looked Aluna up and down. "Oh, but darling whatever are you wearing?"

"What? This?" Aluna said as she touched her leather poncho and pocket vest. "What's wrong with it?"

Addie pursed her lips. "Leather isn't, well it isn't exactly fashionable for a proper young woman to be wearing, at least not in public. Don't you keep up with the fashions from Artania?"

"Not exactly, we don't get much fashion news up north," Aluna said. There was a strong current of ice in her tone.

Addie seemed oblivious to the tone in Aluna's voice. Instead, her face lit up in an explosion of delight and she clapped her hands together. "Yes, I know what we will do. Let me take you shopping. I saw a dress earlier today that would be perfect on you."

"I'm not sure that's...that's a good idea," Warrec said panic spreading across his face.

"She needs shoes," Joenair piped in, although his attention still seemed to be solely fixated on Loreia who herself was giggling and covering her mouth.

"That's not helping," Warrec said glaring at Joenair. Loreia giggled again at something Joenair whispered to her. "Besides I'm sure Addie has a million things to do," he continued on ignoring them.

"Nonsense, we girls are going to go shopping and you boys run along and play or whatever you do," Addie said as she gently pushed Warrec along. "Let's all meet for dinner. Where do you want to eat?"

Warrec seemed to be unable to form a complete sentence and only managed to stutter out a grunt.

"Let's eat at Gor'thak's," Joenair said jumping into the conversation again.

Addie let out a sigh. "That dump? I don't see why you boys like that Orc dive," Addie said making a disgusted face.

"Well, the beers some of the best in town and besides, we get to eat for free if Warrec's there," Joenair said finally pulling his attention away from Loreia.

"Fine," Addie said. She rolled her eyes at the two men.

"The wings are good," Warrec said his mind jumping to food.

"What are wings?" Aluna asked not quite sure she wanted to know.

Warrec grinned as he spoke. "Chicken wings, the Orcs roll them in flour and spices and fry them. They are wonderful."

"Pish posh, but whatever if that's what you want," Addie rolled her eyes again. "Ok, let's go spend some money Aluna and you can tell me all about your home." Addie wrapped her arm through Aluna's arm and dragged her away back towards a line of shops. Aluna glanced back at Warrec with death in her eyes. Miriam narrowed her eyes at Warrec before turning to follow after them. Loreia gave Joenair a half smirk and a wink as she left. Little Tettia curtsied and practically ran to catch up.

"Man, you are so dead," Joenair said patting his friend on the shoulder.

"Yeah, I know," Warrec sighed. "I should have told her."

"Yes, you should have."

"Why didn't I tell her?"

"Because you're an idiot," Joenair answered before Warrec finished his last question.

Warrec shook his head and stared at the ground. "But, hey on the bright side at least I get a good last meal," he finally said with a laugh.

"See, that's the spirit. Hey, why don't we stop at the stables before we report in. Seeing your puppy will cheer you up.

"Yeah," Warrec said smiling as they walked off.

Chapter Fourteen

Duncan quickly made his way through the grand city. Despite it being over thirty years since he had been here last, he still found it easy to navigate. The shops were different, a few street names had changed and there were a few new buildings, but the layout of the city was the same. It was basically a large circle split in two by the river and divided by the main roads that ran east and west. The Great Library was at the southern tip of the market district, so all he had to do was keep heading south and crossing the main roads as they came.

The people he could have done without. Most gave him a wide berth, which he appreciated greatly; he really did not want to interact with anyone. Unfortunately, the ones that didn't leave him alone, the ones he couldn't ignore, were a problem. There were just so many more here in the city. He tried hard to ignore them, the crying, the screaming, the wailing, pleas for help, but there were just so many.

Duncan cut down an alleyway and around a corner. As he turned the corner he skidded to a halt. *No, no, no,* he thought as he saw her.

A little girl, maybe six or seven, stood standing in the middle of the alley. She clutched tightly to a ragdoll as if it was a life preserver. Her face was a deep blue and there were dark bruises around her eyes and neck. When she saw Duncan, her eyes lit up.

"Mister, please I need help. There were bad men. I don't know where I am. Help me please. Where is my mommy? Please don't let them hurt me again." The words flowed out of her in a torrent, unstopping and repeating.

Duncan sucked in a ragged breath as he stared at the child ghost. Sadness mixed with rage as he looked at her. Something bad, unbelievably bad had happened to her. Someone, some sick monster had done horrible things to her and strangled her, leaving her corpse here in the alley.

He looked around but didn't see a body. There was no telling how long she had been trapped here since she died, unable to find peace, unable to move on. The ghost child continued to wail and beg for help.

Cities were always bad. There were just so many lost souls wandering around. He couldn't do anything for them. He couldn't talk to them or at least they didn't seem to hear him, but they could see him, and he could hear them. Duncan clutched at the crystal around his neck. Ever since he had taken up this mantle and injected his soul into this damned cursed crystal, he had been able to sense them.

It was maddening. It was one of the reasons he drank so much. *I failed,* echoed in his mind, reminding him of the other reason. Duncan reached into his robes and took a long pull from his flask.

"I'm sorry," he whispered to the ghost child. "I'm sorry this happened to you, I'm sorry I couldn't stop it. I'm sorry you can't find peace. I'm sorry you can't hear me. I'm sorry. I'm sorry. I'm sorry." The old giant blinked away tears and forced himself to walk past her. As he exited the alleyway, he could still hear her crying. *That one is going to stay with me a long, long time,* he thought.

Duncan exited the alleyway and found he had walked out into an open tent market. He quickly scanned the area and found a wine seller. With a few quick strides he barreled his way to the greasy looking man.

Duncan slapped his meaty palm down on the makeshift counter. "What is the strongest thing you have?"

The small man was portly and looked like he had dunked his head in a vat of grease. His black hair was slicked back and shone with oil. A long thin moustache stuck out and curled at the sides of his mouth, it twitched violently as the old giant bellowed.

The wine merchant quickly recovered, however, as he realized a sale could be made. "Sir if you please, we have many bottles to select from. Some of the best vintages from Artania, or perhaps the noble spirits from our sister city Eldurania. Perhaps, you prefer the fire spirits of the Dwarves, no?" The merchant leaned in closer and whispered. "I even have a few bottles of that swill the Orcs drink, though I would not recommend it. Whatever sir desires, Antione the Honest is here at your service."

Duncan was not in a mood for a sales pitch. "Whatever is cheapest and strongest."

Antione let out a small sigh. "That would be the Orc swill, fifty-six copper."

Duncan tossed him a silver as Antione pulled the bottle from underneath the counter and placed it on top. "Keep the change." Duncan then grabbed the bottle and pulled the cork with his teeth.

Antione's moustache twitched as he put the bottle opener back away and grabbed the silver coin. "Sir, is most kind and generous. Would you like a glass?"

Duncan shook his head and tilted the bottle up chugging down almost half of it. It burned going down and slammed into his stomach like a kick from a mule. He sighed in relief. *That'll help,* he thought. He wiped his mouth with his sleeve.

"Been any murders in that alleyway back there lately?" he asked, pointing a thumb back at the alleyway he had come out of.

Antione barely blinked at the question. He was obviously used to people asking him all manner of random strange questions. "Sir, I do not believe so." Antione tapped a finger against his lips as he thought. "Yes, now that I think of it, not for quite some time, years I believe. A little girl was found there, bloody and bruised many years ago, terrible business." Antione clucked his tongue.

"They ever catch the murderer?" Duncan asked.

"Sir, is not familiar with the local city guard, I think. Most of these guards walking around, they are legion green, barely out of training, babies in armor. Much more likely to catch a cold than a murderer Antione says this."

Duncan took another much smaller drink. He just wanted to be numb for a few minutes. He chastised himself for pitying himself; he still had to get to the library.

"What do you mean by that, green untrained guards?"

Antione nodded. "Yes, that is the way of it. They take the legion soldiers and put them into the city as guards for a year or two after they finish their basic training. Very good for keeping the peace for the most part, little fear of being robbed or some such thing. But the sinister things, not so much. The child she was murdered somewhere else and left there. Who is to know? Some of the guards they stay on in the city permanently, but only those with coin to spend can find justice. The child she have no one."

"That's terrible," Duncan said. "There is no way for common folk to find justice?"

"This I did not say." Antione grabbed a rag and began wiping a glass before he poured himself a small glass of dark red wine. He sniffed the wine and took a slight sip. "For the common man there is the Friendly Fellows, their rates are much cheaper than official guards, mostly."

"The Friendly Fellows?"

"Yes, a local crime syndicate. They control most things in the underground. Protection money is demanded, even from Antione the Honest. But it is a small price to pay. I pay them and no one else bothers me. If I am robbed, they take care of the robber, simple yes."

"I suppose. So, they took care of the murderer then?"

Antione shook his head sadly. "No, as I say, the girl she have no one. No one to pay the Friendly Fellows, her murder goes ignored and unavenged until a new guard come along."

"New guard?" Duncan cocked an eyebrow. Getting information out of Antione was slow, but at least he didn't have to pay for it. The portly man genuinely appeared happy to be talking to someone.

Antione leaned over onto the counter. "Yes, a new guard he come, assigned to the area, took special interest in case. He ask around, follow up, gather evidence and eventually he find the killer. But the killer, he was some minor noble, rich enough though to pay off the right people. The noble he walk free, the little girl still she no have justice." Antione sighed sadly. "Such a shame, but what is to be done about such things."

Well, I spoke to soon, he buttered me up good, Duncan thought. Slowly, he slid another silver across the rough wooden countertop.

Antione grinned and quickly snatched up the coin. He then lightly touched his nose with his forefinger and winked. "But justice she come in the middle of the night. A few days later they find the noble swinging from a tree in his garden. The man he was beaten savagely, his tongue cut out and his privates severed and stuffed into his mouth."

"The new guard," Duncan said.

Antione shrugged. "Who is to say? The noble's family they quiet it up, pay no investigation, bury him, and move on. Antione suspects that the family, they know about what this man liked to do in the dark." He then spit on the ground. "Despicable."

Duncan nodded. "So, what happened to the new guard, where is he now?"

Antione shrugged again. "He leave, his tour of duty here finished, who is to say." He furrowed his brow trying to remember. "A big, big man, like you he come from the north. His name was Erick, no Eren, no that is not it. Everton, no these are not right.

"Everett?" Duncan asked.

Antione snapped his fingers. "Yes, this is the name, Everett. Do you know this man?"

Duncan slowly nodded. "I did." He then turned and walked away.

It took him much longer than earlier, but Duncan managed to stumble his way through the rest of the twisting streets to the Great Library of Eldurond. He had only run across a dozen or so suffering lost souls on his way and thankfully there were no more children. As he made his way up the stairs to the entrance of the library two guards moved to block his path.

"Halt!" the first guard said in a slightly squeaky voice.

These weren't from the city garrison. The uniforms were all wrong and sloppy. Neither man appeared to be in any condition to do any actual fighting. The first man that had spoken was rail thin and looked like a stiff breeze could knock him over. The second man was far older than Duncan and even looked to be half asleep. They must have been some kind of private security the library hired to keep street people from wandering in.

Duncan glared down at the two guards as he towered over them. He sifted the grip on his bardiche. The first guard gulped and looked like he was about to wet himself. The second guard barely paid any attention to Duncan. He was paid to stand there, and it seemed as far as he was concerned that was the full extent of his job. "What's the problem?" Duncan growled at them.

"Uh...no problem, sir...it's just, that civilians are not permitted to carry arms into the library. You, you'll...you have to leave it here at the guard station," The first guard managed to stammer out.

Duncan had been using the great waraxe as a walking stick and he didn't want to admit to himself how much he needed it to steady himself. He glared at the two men for a few seconds. *This is petty and stupid,* he thought. *They can't stop me, but is it really worth the trouble?*

The second guard snorted. "Now Zeb, we can't go depriving a man of his walking stick." He leaned toward Duncan and winked showing off a hundred wrinkles around his eyes. "Us old folk need to stick together."

Duncan gave a slight nod. He was old, well past when he should have passed on now, but this man was ancient.

Zeb turned and looked at the old guard. "But Morn, we're not supposed to let anyone in carrying a weapon." Zeb looked back at the sheathed blade, a blade that was as long as his torso and head and gulped again. "And that's not a walking stick."

Morn looked at the bardiche and blinked twice trying to open his eyes as wide as he could, which did not appear to be much. He then sucked on his teeth for a good ten seconds before he spoke. "Well, I reckon it's not. Mister, I'm sorry, but the youngster here is right, can't have folk walking into the library carrying things like that. The librarians are a jumpy lot, get scared real easy, not used to being around actual people. They stay up in there, reading all the time and don't much talk to folk."

"You two couldn't stop me if I decided to go on in," Duncan said. Zeb let out a squeak.

Morn let out a little chuckle. "No, no I don't suppose we could. If you wanted to go in there and kill the lot of them nothing we could do. I'd just walk on down to the guard post a bit that ways and let them know. You'd probably be done and gone by the time I got there, and they got back here."

"So, this whole thing is an exercise in futility and stupidity," Duncan said.

Morn shrugged. "Only if you're wanting to go in there and kill a mess of folks. Most people just want to look at the paintings or a book or two. Not any money stored in there and most folk can't even read. Only people that use it often are the scholars."

Duncan found that he was liking the old man. Morn had a practicality that was hard to find in the heart of the empire. Probably, as his dark skin indicated because he was from the Shattered Isles. "Fine, but it had better not walk off," He finally said. Duncan handed the colossal polearm to the first guard. Zeb reached out gingerly to take it, but as soon as Duncan let go the weight of it pulled the guard off his feet.

"Be careful with it," Duncan growled. Mentally he began laughing as he walked inside. There wasn't anything that they could do to damage that weapon, but they didn't know that. He smiled as the two guards struggled to move it over to the guard hut.

Duncan walked into an immense lobby; his footsteps echoed loudly through the high domed chamber. The floor was made of exquisitely crafted marble, checkered red and blue. A stunning mural of all kinds of animals covered the ceiling, though whoever had painted it had a poor understanding of anatomy and obviously had never seen some of the animals depicted. Fine white marble statues of heroes and exquisite women dotted the floor. Duncan ignored it all and walked straight up to the librarian's desk. The librarian was peacefully reading a book. He looked up as Duncan approached and almost fell out of his chair.

"Ah what...ah yes...hello. What...what can I do for you?" The little man stuttered out. He fidgeted and readjusted the spectacles perched on his thin nose. He was bald and looked both skinny and fat at the same time.

"Where is your ancient history section?"

"Ah, down that hall. At the fork turn right, it's right past the section on biology," the librarian said. He pointed a shaking finger to a hall on the right. Duncan nodded curtly and turned to walk away.

"Do you need for me to send for a reader, for you?" he asked to Duncan's back. Duncan gave no reply as he walked down the hall, his footsteps still thundering through the cavernous building.

The halls weren't as long and as massive as Duncan remembered them. But they were still very ornate. The Great Library was a monument unto itself. Marvelous paintings and tapestries lined the wall, some hundreds of hundreds of years old. Duncan paid them no mind as he made his way down the hall.

The building itself was lit by a combination of reflective mirrors, which caught the sunlight from windows in the roof and glowstones. The glowstones were Dwarven make. It was a craft that they alone had the monopoly on. Once enchanted, the stones would glow softly in an assortment of different colors, depending on which length of time was selected. These lining the hallway glowed with a soft blue light and looked to be ten-day stones.

They were one of the cheaper ones available, but much more economically feasible for a large building like this. Glowstones were far from cheap, however. The stones could vary in price from ten to a thousand gold sovereigns each. Relighting one alone would probably cost fifty or so silver heads. Whoever had the illumination contract for this building was making a killing.

Duncan reached a door with a sign above that read _Ancient History and Antiquities_. He opened the large oaken door and stepped into a massive room with a high vaulted ceiling. The ceiling was several stories above his head. Thousands upon thousands of books and scrolls lined all the walls. A younger plump bald-headed man sat at a desk in the middle of the room. He was pouring over some scrolls that he had laid out on his desk. He looked up as Duncan closed the large door behind him.

"Ah, hello sir, what can I do for you on this wonderful day?" he said cheerily. The man did not seem at all perturbed that a giant had just entered into his personal kingdom. Duncan walked over to the desk and peered down at the man. On closer inspection the man wasn't naturally bald, but had shaved his head, all except a piece on the back that extended in a long braid.

Had the first one had a braid? Duncan tried to recall but found he couldn't really remember. *Sloppy, you're better than that. You're not that drunk,* Duncan chided himself mentally. "I'm looking for a book," he said deadpan.

"Well, of course you are sir. Why else would anyone come here?" The man said with cheerfulness still filling his voice.

Duncan glared at him. "I need the Chronicle on Elvish History." The little man blinked twice before answering.

"How odd, how very odd indeed, no one ever asks for that particular volume, and you are the second in two days. Did the other man send you?"

"What are you talking about?" Menace gleamed in Duncan's eyes. Someone else had wanted to see the book. Dark thoughts flowed through his mind. Did someone find the same thing he was looking for? Was someone else searching as well? *What are the odds someone else would want to look at that ancient tome,* he thought. *It can't be coincidence. You old fool of course Argis has agents out looking. I'm moving too slow, can't let someone else beat me. Not again!*

"Ah, well sir, a man came in the other day asking for that same book. I was unable to locate it at the time, so I told him to return in a few days. When you asked for it, I thought perhaps he had sent you in his stead."

"No...no one sent me. Who was it that came before?"

"Ah, I didn't catch his name I'm afraid, sharp dressed fellow though. Looked to be a noble or perhaps someone from the royal court."

"I see. Do you have the book now?" Duncan was unhappy at this news of someone else looking for the book. He shook his head slightly; it was probably just a coincidence. *You're just being paranoid,* he told himself. He didn't believe that no matter how hard he tried to convince himself.

"Yes, yes, I was able to find it just this morning as it were. But I'm afraid it won't do you any good. The entire volume is written in Elvish, and we have no means of deciphering its contents. Dead language and all, you know."

"Just show me the damn book." Duncan's patience was running thin.

"Of course, right this way sir." The cheery little man led Duncan across the vast room and through aisle after aisle of books. Towards the back of the room the man turned and walked down an aisle filled with ancient looking books and scrolls, some looked several thousand years old and about to disintegrate at the slightest touch.

"Ah, here it is," the man said as he selected a text. The leather cover looked almost new and oddly out of place amongst the other relics. He handed the book to Duncan. "Remarkable condition that, despite being thousands of years old. Amazing craftsmanship, but as I said it is useless because we have no way of translating it as no one can speak or write Elvish anymore."

Duncan took the book and opened it to a page randomly. He read a few passages aloud the beautiful ancient language flowing off his tongue like a clear waterfall cascading off a mountain side. He looked up as the man's jaw hit the floor, his eyes bugging out in astonishment.

"Thank you for your help," Duncan said. "I need to look over this, you may go now." The little man rubbed his shaved head and merely nodded as he turned around and walked off, still in shock. Duncan found a reading alcove and settled in.

Chapter Fifteen

Aluna pouted as she sat on a lavishly stuffed bench in the middle of the dress shop, while murderous thoughts floated through her mind. *I'll kill lady prissypants first, then the other two. I guess I'll let the young one go. Hmmm she might tell though, better to be safe and off her too. Then I'll hunt Stupid Warrec down and murder him. Yes, that is an excellent plan.*

"Aluna?" Addie repeated.

Aluna gave a start. "What, yes, what, I guess." *Hatchet right to the face.*

"Dear, I asked which one you preferred," Addie said.

The other woman was standing before a bank of mirrors. Mirrors weren't exactly cheap, and Aluna's head hurt thinking about the astronomical cost for such a luxuriant display. Addie's three hand maidens each wore a slightly different cut of the same-colored gown. They were pink, a pink that made Aluna want to gouge her eyes out.

"I liked the blue ones better," Aluna said. *Stupid Warrec.*

If there was a more awkward situation, she couldn't think of one. There were several things she could think of that would be better than dress shopping with the love of her life's fiancée; like wrestling a bearcat, walking over broken glass, or playing Drop Pie Jump while blindfolded, on her hands and knees.

To make things even worse Addie was wonderful. Aluna had never met a kinder or sweeter woman in her life. Addie threw money around like it was dirt, but not in a pretentious way. She genuinely liked giving her money to people.

Her ass is fat though, Aluna thought. It seemed to be anyway, it was hard to tell in that stupid dress and bustle. *Short, skinny, sweet, with a big butt, that's what Stupid Warrec likes. Not you.* Aluna growled at her brain mentally and told it to shut up.

Addie sighed. "I knew it; pink is definitely not your color." Addie turned to the couturier standing beside her. "You see Yvette, Aluna is a woman of refined tastes, she knows what she is about."

Yvette was a slim woman in her mid-thirties and obviously had a taste for the finer things. It appeared that she had spent so much time around the nobility patronizing her shop that she had started to consider herself part of the aristocracy. Aluna hated her; her aura notes were sour, like an out-of-tune oboe.

"My lady is right again of course," Yvette said. "I will

have them change back into the blues. Come girls."

Loreia let out a low groan. "Again, we have tried on twenty different dresses." Tettia clapped her hands and let out a squeal of delight. The younger girl was obviously enjoying herself immensely. Aluna liked her, she had the aura notes of a piccolo and a piano mixed together.

"Do you like the boots?" Addie asked. Aluna glanced down at her feet again. The brand-new boots were calf length, cut from soft deer leather. The leather molded itself to her feet, not so thick that she couldn't still feel the ground beneath her, but just enough to protect her feet from the hazards of city life. They were absolutely perfect, and Aluna loved them.

Aluna gave a half shrug. "They're ok I guess, functional I suppose.

Addie gave a slight frown. "Oh dear, they're not good enough are they. Ok, after we get you a gown here, we will march right back across the plaza to that cobblers and get you a good pair, the best pair."

Aluna's eyes went wide, and she held her hands up to ward off any further argument. "No, no, that's really ok, it's not that it's." Aluna trailed off for a second tilting her head back and forth. "It's just, I'm not used to having someone buy me things like this. Plus, we just met, I don't know you and you don't know me. It's a little weird."

"Oh, pish posh," Addie said. She started to wave her hand dismissively but stopped. Addie pursed her lips as she thought about what Aluna had just said. "Well, perhaps you're right. I don't mean to be like that. Please don't take it as me trying to make you feel bad or trying to lord money over you. It's just; well, it's just nice to have another girl to talk to, a friend. Warrec has told me about his childhood and how you two were thick as thieves, so naturally I want you and I to be the best of friends as well."

"What about your lady attendants or whatever?"

"Oh, that's not quite the same. I mean they are sweet, and we do pal around as it were, but they do work for me after all. Miriam is one of my closest confidants and Loreia is fun, although she is trying to better her station through me. Tettia is still a child. I don't have any female friends, not any real ones anyway." Addie's eyes grew a bit misty.

"Oh no, no, no, I didn't mean it like that," Aluna said. *Please, please don't start crying,* she thought. *Great now I feel like skret.*

Addie quickly dabbed at her eyes. "Sorry, there I go, look at me getting all emotional. I really didn't mean to dump all that on you. You must think I'm a horrible person. I tend to throw money at people I like. Unfortunately, it's one of the ways my family shows affection."

Aluna smiled, happy for the opening to change the conversation. "Tell me about your family. I've never actually met nobility and I have to say you're much more personable than I thought."

Addie dabbed her eyes again and smiled back. "That's sweet of you to say. No, I'm a bit of an oddball to them, been hanging around a rough and tumble lot." Addie smiled bigger. "That's Warrec and Joenair by the way. I have to say after meeting those two; I had to reevaluate my world view, especially thanks to Warrec."

"How did, how did you two...get together. Warrec isn't exactly highborn; I figured there were rules or something about that."

Addie nodded in agreement. "Yes, he doesn't quite fit in with the upper crust of society." Her eyes glazed over for a second and Aluna could see the love and lust flash across her face. "But it's really like right out of a storybook. Honestly, I owe everything to him."

"What do you mean? You're an ambassador, how did Warrec help with that?"

"Well, if it wasn't for Warrec and Joenair too, I wouldn't be. Honestly, I probably would have been eaten by the Orcs, or worse." Addie shuddered. "But I'm getting ahead of myself. Would you fetch us a glass of that wine over there and I'll tell you."

Aluna walked over and grabbed the bottle of red and poured them both a glass. *Remember you hate her,* she had to remind herself. "Here," she said as she handed Addie the filled wine glass. "Warrec told me a little about the Orc trip. He was running security for you I wager."

"Thank you dear, my throat gets parched." Addie took a large sip, a little bigger than Aluna would have guessed from such a delicate thing. "That's better. Yes, he was, but he probably didn't tell you that our mission was doomed to fail. Aluna, I am no ambassador, I have never done anything of that nature in all my life."

"That doesn't make any sense," Aluna said.

"That's what I said when the imperial senate picked me," Addie said. She took another gulp. There was clearly something that angered her about the story. "My father is a senator; he owns the shipping docks for the entire city and most of the ports running up and down the river. We are very well to do. I don't mean to say this to be pretentious, but yes we are one of the richest and most powerful families in the empire."

Aluna snapped her fingers. "Of course, why didn't I put that together. Flavius, Ulbright Flavius. Yeah, everyone in The Lake knows that name. He has been feeding off the wealth of the North for years. Still, he isn't as bad as some of his predecessors."

Addie nodded. "Yes, Father can be a bit overzealous with his business dealings. I hope that hasn't caused you or your people hardship, I really do."

Aluna shrugged. "It's just a point of contention in the region. People like to complain and blaming your father is as good as anything else. Don't worry about that, but anyway please continue."

"Right, thank you," Addie said reaching out to give Aluna's hand a squeeze. "As I was saying Father controls practically all the shipping for the empire, at least the east and north. A while back a few of his fellow senators wanted to get a little of that pie as it were. Father did not take kindly to them trying to move into his domain and without going into all the political infighting and backstabbing, some of it literal, Father put a stop to their plans."

Aluna slowly nodded as she realized what the young woman was getting at. "And so, when it came time to mount a dangerous expedition to make contact and peace with our enemies, an enemy that was well known for its savagery…"

"I was chosen as the sacrificial lamb," Addie finished the thought. "Yes, to get back at my father, they sent me, a woman who while intelligent, had no training in the diplomatic arts and was in way over her head. They sent me with two security personnel, two, to meet with the Orcs, two. I completely believe they expected all of us to die out there in the jungle the gods forgot."

"And then Warrec came along and screwed up all their plans," Aluna said.

"Yes, yes he did," Addie said. She smiled and sighed. "May the Rivermother and your AllFather bless that man."

Aluna's shoulders slumped slightly, and she mentally sighed to herself. "So, it was love at first sight?"

Addie let out a most unladylike guffaw. "Oh, my no, no I couldn't stand him at first. He was the most obnoxious, rude, pigheaded, uncouth, stubborn man I had ever met."

Aluna smiled then frowned. "Yeah, that sounds like him. So, what happened?" Yvette and the trio returned at that moment. Tettia bounced across the room and twirled.

"Aluna, you have to pick this one," Tettia said. "It looks so good. Hey, what are you two talking about?"

"Tettia dear, don't pry into conversations you aren't privy to, it isn't ladylike." Addie leaned over and whispered to Aluna. "We'll talk more later." She then turned back to Tettia. "Tett that is a most exquisite dress, and it looks amazing on you. But dear, I don't think it's right for Aluna. The cut is all wrong, it wouldn't fit or look right."

Tettia looked down at the dress and whirled again looking at herself in the mirror. "Why? What's wrong with the cut"-

Tettia gasped and covered her mouth as she started to giggle - "oh her boobies won't fit." Aluna felt her face flush red.

"Tettia do grow up," Loreia said. "Besides it's those huge man shoulders and arms that won't fit." Aluna stifled a snarl and caught herself involuntarily reaching for an axe.

"Loreia!" Addie snapped. "You will not say such things. Her people may have a bit more robust physique, than you or I. That's to be expected in that type of rough and tumble world, but she is a fine example of feminine beauty. Any man would be proud to have her on his arm."

Aluna wasn't exactly sure how to take that. She was sure Addie had meant it as a complement, somehow, but she didn't really need someone else's opinion to prove her worth. *You say that but if it was Stupid Warrec's arm you were on, you would melt all over it,* she scolded herself.

"Besides Loreia, you could do with a little more physical exercise yourself," Miriam said. The older woman then grabbed Loreia by the waist pinching two rolls of fat. "You're getting a little soft and too well fed."

Loreia turned beet red and slapped Miriam's hands away. "How dare you. I'll have you know men like their women to be soft and not some scrawny twig."

"Soft yes, but not some cow lying around the house all day," Miriam replied. The older woman began laughing as Loreia turned even redder.

"Ladies please, enough," Addie said raising both her arms. "Be civil, you will give Aluna the wrong impression." She then turned back to Aluna and squeezed her hand again. "Dear I'm sorry, sometimes the girls can be a bit catty. Please don't think less of us."

Aluna nodded and turned to look at Loreia, giving her a smile that was all teeth. "It's fine, no worries, although in my homeland I've seen people get stabbed in the face for less." Aluna reached over and casually picked up the fruit knife off the fruit and cheese platter. "But after all this is the more civilized part of the empire, right? Oh, and I pick that one." Aluna pointed with the fruit knife at Loreia. The redness drained from Loreia's face, and she put a hand to her throat. She quickly nodded.

Addie beamed, Aluna couldn't tell if she had caught the undertone or not. "Excellent, let's all get dressed and then we can go across the way for our hair. Tettia keep that one you're wearing, it's yours now. Loreia find something appropriate for tonight. Yvette, Aluna will take that style, but please make sure there is ample room in the bust."

Aluna grabbed an apple and sliced off a piece. "Good apple." Loreia glanced back at Aluna as the trio hustled back to the changing room. Addie and Aluna rose to follow them back. As

Loreia made eye contact Aluna gave her a wink. She mentally laughed as the young woman went wide eyed for a second before disappearing into her changing alcove.

After a few minutes Loreia draped the dress over the door and Yvette retrieved it, handing it to Aluna. Aluna took her dress and went into her own changing room. She let out a low whistle as she opened the door and walked in. The changing room was bigger than some of the homes she had seen in the north.

Three mirrors sat along a wall forming a half circle. Across from the mirrors was an opulent fainting couch, with plush cushions stacked against the high wall that looked like they would envelope someone as soon as they lay down. Across from the door on the far wall was a mosaic of ducks. Aluna thought they were ducks, though they didn't really look like ducks. The artist was definitely trying for some type of waterfowl. The room itself was lit by a soft white light that had to come from a hundred-day glowstone, the way it was perfectly lit.

As Aluna looked around the room at the overt display of wealth, she shook her head. Then she glanced down at the dress she was holding and reverently draped it across the couch. If the entire shop was decorated like this Aluna did not want to know how expensive this dress was. She stared at the blue silk and ran her hand along it.

It's so soft and beautiful, she thought. This dress was probably worth more than all the money she had ever had. She probably could have bought every shop in Thornglade for the price of this dress and Addie was just giving it to her. Aluna wasn't sure how she felt about this. It was too generous a gift, too extravagant. *She just met me and yet she doesn't think twice about buying this for me, or the boots. I don't deserve this.*

She stripped out of her travel clothes, gear, and new boots then placed them in a bag that had been provided by the door. She smelled herself. She had bathed in the river yesterday, so she wasn't too bad, normal musk. Still, she would have liked a bath before getting dressed again. Aluna shrugged, nothing to be done about it. She bet Addie always smelled nice for Stupid Warrec.

She frowned and grabbed the bottle of rose water and lavender oil off the side table by the couch. She sniffed it and recoiled back. It was strong, stronger than any perfume she had worn before. *Except most of what you use to cover your scent is the opposite of perfume,* she realized. Aluna told her brain to shut up. This wasn't the bush, and she didn't need to rub fox urine on herself here. She quickly dabbed a bit of the perfume under each arm, under each breast, and right below her belly button.

Aluna took the dress and slipped it on. It was simple and

functional, which she liked as well as being ornate. The dress dropped down to her calves and was slit up one side almost to her hip, which allowed her to move freely. Any higher though and she would have had to remove her undergarments and the thought of going out in public like that made her blush.

The dress buttoned up the side, with what looked like whalebone buttons. As she finished fastening it, she realized that it was tight, in the chest, across her shoulders, and along her arms, very tight. Yvette obviously didn't know what ample meant. Aluna breathed deeply and slowly. She felt the dress was going to burst apart as she did, but it held. Aluna flexed her right arm and winced as the silk stretched, it too held, if just barely. Loreia had made the comment to be mean, but there was a little truth in what she had said, which made Aluna frown. *Well, I'll bet miss soft gut has never wrestled a hammerbadger either.* She slipped on the matching shoes and turned to look at herself in the mirrors.

"Is that me?" she asked herself as she stared into the mirrors.

Aluna didn't recognize the woman in the mirrors. The woman looking back at her from the mirrors was refined and elegant, not a bush woman, a witch, a shaman, one of the wild ones. Aluna reached up and touched one of the few dreads that were woven into her ponytail. It was still there, she was still her, but she felt different. Aluna smiled at herself.

"I like it," she finally said. She nodded twice more and grabbed her bag with all her belongings. Aluna made her way back out from the back rooms and into the lobby of the shop. Yvette was standing behind the counter, clearly pleased with the money she had just made.

"The others are still getting dressed," Yvette said. "Your carriage and coachmen are outside waiting for you." Aluna thanked her, but the slim older couturier was clearly done with her and dismissed her with a wave of the hand.

Aluna decided to let it go and not smash her skull across the marble countertop. Besides, the blood would ruin her dress and Addie wouldn't approve. *Wait we still hate Addie remember;* Aluna reminded herself.

She made her way out to the waiting carriage. A four-horse coach sat parked in front of the shop, obviously the no horse rule in the plaza did not apply to nobility. The carriage itself was sturdy, black and undecorated. Aluna realized that the nobility probably didn't want to advertise their movements through the city.

A burly looking coachman sat on the driver's seat, clearly bored. A sharply dressed footman stood by the door waiting. Both men wore a half helm and a gladius at their side.

Aluna squinted at the footman as something seemed slightly

off about the man. With a start she realized that he had no eyebrows. She started to ask when Addie came bouncing down the steps.

"How do I look?" she asked Aluna. Addie twirled, her floor length white gown billowing out from her feet. The dress had a high collar but a plunging backline, while hugging her sides. Aluna could now get a good look at the shorter woman's figure without all the extra dress padding and bustle. Addie was quite petite up top, but her hips were wide giving her a thick pear shape.

Wide hips and a fat ass, Aluna thought. Aluna mentally frowned and pouted. *That must be what Stupid Warrec likes.* She thought of her own backside and felt inadequate by comparison. It was a new sensation and not something she could ever recall feeling before. Addie was also far, far prettier than her as well. *No wonder Stupid Warrec picked her.*

"You look," Aluna trailed off trying to think of what to say. Looking at Addie made her feel worse, but that wasn't the shorter woman's fault. She wasn't trying to make Aluna feel this way and probably would have felt bad if she did. Somehow, that thought made it feel worse. Aluna decided that here again she wasn't going to let someone else determine her worth. She was going to be who she was and if Stupid Warrec didn't like it then it was his loss. "You look amazing," Aluna finally said with a slight nod.

Addie smiled deeply. "My dear, you are too kind. I only look presentable. You look amazing. The way that hugs your body, oh I wish I had your breasts."

The two women stood for a moment admiring each other. *She is making it really hard to hate her,* Aluna thought. Before it grew too awkward, she pointed a thumb at the footman. "Ok, I hate to ask, but I was going to anyway before you walked out. Why does he have no eyebrows?"

Addie turned and looked at the footman. "Oh, Niko, he is a slave, well technically a bond servant due to his debts. Come, I'll introduce you."

The two women walked down the walkway to the plaza edge where the carriage sat waiting. This wasn't the first time Aluna had walked in heels, but it definitely wasn't something she was used to. It took all her focus to keep from rolling an ankle and despite that she stumbled twice. Addie of course moved effortlessly and as gracefully as a doe.

"Domina Flavius," Niko said greeting them.

Addie rolled her eyes. "Niko, I've told you a hundred times, you don't have to address me like that. Aluna this is Niko, and that sourpuss up there is Orban." Orban grunted in acknowledgement.

"Yes Domina, forgive me but I will continue," Niko said.

"If you must," Addie sighed. Aluna could tell this was an ongoing thing. "This is Aluna. She is from Warrec's hometown and my personal guest."

Niko quickly nodded. "Yes, the big lieutenant. I like him, he no good at table dice. Niko win big off him."

"Now Niko, that's how you found yourself here in the first place," Addie said as she crossed her arms.

"Sorry Domina, the dice they call to me. I must answer."

Addie sighed again. "Speaking of which Aluna was asking about your eyebrows and how you became a slave."

Niko nodded. "Yes, yes, is very sad. Niko plays dice all the time and for too long he lose. Niko can no pay back gambling debts so he sell himself into slavery to pay debt."

"Unfortunately," Addie said. "His new masters decided that Niko would be better off working in the salt mines, very hard labor you know. Luckily, I came across him and was able to snatch him up from the market."

Niko nodded enthusiastically. "Yes, Domina Flavius save Niko from years of rough, hard work. Now he live in big mansion, have own room and eat well every day. All Niko have do is ride coach and keep it fixed and protect family. Niko love this job, he live better now than before. Does"- Niko paused as he seemed to try and decide how to address Aluna, finally he decided to be safe and do the same as with Addie- "Domina Aluna not have slaves in big north country at Lake?"

"Oh, I'm no Domina. I don't have a title or anything," Aluna said. "But yes, we do have slaves, I suppose, but they're different. We call them thralls."

Niko looked puzzled. "What mean this, thrall?"

Aluna pursed her lips thinking of how to explain. "Well, thralls come from fighting and war. They are the left-over losers of a battle and their families. It's the duty of the conquers to look after the conquered after a battle. They take them in, and they become part of the clan but of the lowest rank. Eventually though they can work their way up the clan social ladder."

"Warrec told me a little about that," Addie said. "It keeps your people from having to wipe out whole families or towns after a battle." Addie looked down at the ground. "That's much better than what some of the Orc tribes have been known to do." Aluna cocked her head at Addie. Addie leaned over and half whispered. "They have been known to eat their enemies."

"Niko is glad he is not an Orc. Hey Orban, you hear that? Orc take long time to eat you, eh?" Niko burst out laughing.

"Quit your mouthing ya hangdog," Orban half growled back. "I ain't no slave. I'm a free man and have a vote. I'm your better in every sense, so don't you go forgetting it."

Niko laughed harder. "Orban you are grumpy man. Niko thinks

is because Miss Berta is away upriver with the master."

Aluna looked questionably at Addie who mouthed back the cook. Niko and Orban continued to trade insults for a few more minutes until finally the trio of Addie's hand maidens came out of the dress shop and joined them.

Addie clapped her hands together. "Excellent, everyone into the carriage," she said. "Orban my dear, we are to go to Madam Nicolette's and get our hair and makeup done. Then it's on to Gor'thak's." She turned back to the rest of them. "Ladies tonight is going to be a fun night."

Addie flashed Aluna a wide smile as the smaller woman climbed into the carriage. Aluna returned the smile and finally gave herself permission to listen. She finally listened to Addie's aura notes, the notes of a full symphony playing a sweet and soft melody. It was beautiful.

Chapter Sixteen

"**W**hat's the worst that could happen?" Warrec asked.

"You mean other than Aluna stabbing Addie?" Joenair answered.

"Aluna is not some feral animal. She can act normal around people," Warrec said. "At least I think she can." Joenair simply shrugged.

They made their way across the western bridge and onto one of the public streets bisecting the royal island. From there they crossed the eastern bridge to the military sector of the city. Once on the eastern bank they grabbed another palanquin and made their way to the main stables. Upon reaching the main military stables and continuing on foot Warrec was forced to return salutes almost every five seconds as soldiers passed by. Joenair walked along beside him, whistling, and completely ignored by everyone.

As they walked across one of the courtyards adjacent to the main stables, Warrec glanced up at the immense flag flying in the wind. Staring at the symbol of the empire filled him with a profound sense of pride. A solid red circle stood on a saltire field of black and gold. The flag of Marovia flew across almost all human communities bringing peace and unity to its people.

"That is a beautiful sight," Warrec said. Joenair nodded in agreement.

Warrec walked through the large oaken exterior doors of the massive imperial stables and the smell of horse smacked him in the face. He breathed deeply; it was a scent he greatly enjoyed. The Stablemaster on duty was busy with his account log as they approached. He looked up as Warrec and Joenair walked up and immediately snapped to attention.

"Morning sir," he said as he saluted.

"At ease sergeant," Warrec said returning the salute. "Just came to check on my puppy," he said with a grin.

The sergeant let out a long sigh of relief. "Sir, that is not a puppy...Sir and I'm glad you're here. She has been hell to deal with since you left. Sir." The sergeant collapsed back into his chair and waved them by. Warrec just grinned again.

As they walked through the massive stables, they could hear horses whinnying and an out of place low growl coming from the very back. Two privates who were mucking out a stall breathed a sigh of relief as Warrec walked by towards the very end of the stables. In the very last stall as far away from the other horses as was possible was a gigantic wolf.

The huge beast was as tall as any warhorse and well over a thousand pounds. A huge two-foot-long skull with jaws easily capable of crushing the massive thigh bones of an auroch swung toward him. Icy blue eyes fixated on Warrec revealing keen predatory intelligence. The massive hump of muscle across the shoulders twitched in anticipation.

"Hey baby girl," Warrec said in a soft voice as he walked up to the huge predator. Instantly, her lips pulled back as he approached revealing four-inch canines. But this was no snarl. The huge beast seemed to be smiling at Warrec in a sort of odd doggie grin. He reached out without hesitation and began petting her massive head. Warrec petted her and she stomped her front paws in a little dance of excitement to see him. She licked his face as he gently stroked her immense head and down her brown and red brindle coated body.

"Hey Ginger. How's my sweet girl," Warrec said in a childish voice as he petted her. She almost bowled him over as she lovingly body bumped him against the gate. Ginger was so excited and happy to see him. Her tail beat a fast rhythm against the stall wall sending out echoes into the stables. Ginger whined and grunted as she tried to push her head into Warrec's chest. "I know, I know, I missed you too."

Joenair smiled at them. "I think she missed you."

"You think?" Warrec laughed. Warrec had gotten Ginger when

she was just a pup. She had been a gift from Fenrim, the Chief of the Wolfhelm Orc tribe. Warrec was the only soldier in the entire army that rode the same mounts as the Orcs.

The Orcs called them wuru. Over several generations they had bred the huge wolves into something capable of carrying a rider. The huge beasts now looked like a cross between a bear, a wolf, and a nightmare. Long legs built for speed supported a massive muscular body. Wuru riders had been the terror of the imperial army as far back as anyone could remember. Warrec was one of the few humans to ever ride one, though in truth Ginger acted more like a puppy around him than the beast of war that she was.

He partially hadn't taken her on their trip because she spooked any horse that wasn't used to her presence. Most of the disciplined army mounts were fine around her. Although, being kept in the same stables could be taxing on the horse's nerves. A horse neighed to punctuate the point. Still, there hadn't been anywhere else to keep her, and Ginger was happy to share the space to the other horse's displeasure.

"I know, I know, I'm sorry but there was water and boats this trip," Warrec whispered to her. The wuru cocked her head at him as if understanding and let out a loud canine sigh. That had been the main reason. Wuru and boats did not mix well. The huge canines couldn't stand being trapped on a deck in a body of water, at least not for very long.

Warrec hadn't wanted to risk anything happening up in Thornglade, so he had left her. Neither Warrec nor the wolf had been happy about it, but it had seemed necessary at the time. Looking back now he wished he had taken her. With her speed and ferocity, he might have been able to overtake Argis and beat him.

Probably, he thought. *Maybe, well a better chance anyway.*

That fight had been playing over and over in his mind in almost every idle moment. Was there something he could have done different? He didn't know. The simple fact was the Dread Lord had beaten him, and easily. *So why didn't he kill me?*

Warrec spent the next twenty minutes petting and playing with Ginger as he brooded. Eventually he and Jay had to leave. Ginger whined at them and wanted to come with them, but Warrec told her to stay. So, she sulked in circles for a bit then lay back down, resting her head on her paws and pouted.

The two of them exited the stables and headed towards the parade grounds. A quick race across the parade grounds left Warrec breathing hard as Joenair had beaten him in the race yet again. The slim man stood leaning on a rail buffing his nails on his chest as Warrec came puffing up.

"That makes what thirty-seven times now," Joenair asked. The bastard wasn't even breathing heavily.

"Thirty-eight," Warrec said grudgingly. "And you damn well, know it. One of, these days, I'm going to beat you, just you wait." He managed to pant out.

Joenair rolled his eyes. "If you say so, I honestly don't know why you keep trying. You don't have to be the best at everything you know."

Warrec bent over and ducked his head between his knees, resting his arms on his legs. "Shut...up," he forced out between heavy breaths.

"You are ridiculous and stand up. You can't breathe bent over like that. Honestly, why do you think I don't challenge you to swordsmanship or lifting heavy things?"

Warrec stood up and put his hands on top of his head sucking in huge lungfuls of air. "Because you're a fazart and can't stand getting beat."

Joenair waved his hand dismissively. "You're calling me a dickless rooster? How rude, but no, it's because I know my limits, something you should learn. And you're the one that can't stand being beaten. Now, if you are done sucking all the air out of the city, the legate is waiting."

Warrec nodded with a grin and the two walked into the Command Post. After a few minutes they found themselves waiting outside the legate's office door as a very scared looking private peeped into the office to announce them.

Legate Silnis looked up from his paperwork as a knock sounded on his door. "What is it?" the old veteran snapped. His aide cautiously stuck his head in the door, preparing to duck if something came flying at him.

"Sir...uh...Lieutenant Vornirulf and Mister Joenair are here, and they wish to speak with you, sir."

"Fine, fine, send them in." The old, grizzled veteran leaned back in his chair. He ran his hand through the short brush of stubble of his graying hair and absently scratched at the eye patch covering his left eye.

He had lost the eye some twenty years ago in a skirmish with centaur raiders. The story floating amongst the soldiers was that he had been shot in the eye with a stray arrow. As the story went Silnis had ripped the arrow from his head, taking the eye with it. He had then eaten his own eye because he wouldn't allow the vile creatures to take it from him and had continued on with the fight, ultimately emerging victorious. It was a rumor that the old commander didn't affirm, but one he didn't deny either. Warrec had to force himself every time he was with the Legate not to stare at the eyepatch.

Warrec pushed the door open wide with a bang as he stepped past the private, causing the tiny man to jump, and he and Jay walked in. "Why the hell is it, that I give the two of you leave and you two both end up tangling with the futten Dread Lord of

The Black Lands?" Silnis growled at them. "I've got reports coming in from the west that Ptharis' fat ass is prepping for war, the king breathing down my neck to get our own troops ready, complaints stacked up to my eyeballs from merchants and nobles about why this shipment didn't come in or why that one didn't go out. And now you two send me a bird saying Argis has raided some remote town in the bloody, frozen, wild, and uncooperative northlands."

Joenair thumped down into one of the two chairs in front of the legate's desk. "Ah boss, don't act like you didn't miss us. It's not like we went looking for trouble."

Warrec eased himself down into the other chair. It didn't look very sturdy and wasn't quite big enough. "Besides," he said. "You always taught us to go big or go home. Well, we went big, clashed swords with the Dread Lord and everything."

"Well, Warrec did, got knocked on his ass too," Joenair said.

Silnis pinched the bridge of his nose and closed his eye. "I'm going to murder you both," he said. "I knew when you two were assigned to me a few years ago you would be the death of me. I knew it, a heart attack or a stroke, something." With a loud sigh he opened his eye and looked at them again.

"Sir, we have a huge problem on our hands," Warrec said. "As the message said Argis is back."

"I was really hoping this was some stupid joke you two decided to play. I was going to have you both flogged of course, but it would have been a nice distraction."

"Nope, sorry boss, this is serious," Joenair said. The tone in his voice made the legate sit up.

Silnis' brow furrowed and he ground his teeth. Almost a minute passed before he said anything as it sank in. "Ok, give me the full futten report," he finally said.

The two men began their tale. Duncan had told them to make no mention of the sword and they had both agreed. They told the legate of the attack on Thornglade and the race to the gorge and the fight. They also told of The Dread Lord's apocalyptic words. After they were done Silnis sat and stared at them trying to digest this information. Finally, he rubbed his face and stood.

"You're sure it was him? You're absolutely sure?" he said.

"Yes sir. We saw him with our own eyes. There was no mistaking him," Warrec replied.

"Dammit! Dammit to hell. This couldn't have come at a worse time," Silnis exclaimed as he began pacing the room. After a few seconds he stopped and paused. "Why the hell did he attack your town? He never attacks the north, can't get troops in there."

Warrec and Joenair shot each other a look. Warrec just shrugged. Silnis grunted and started pacing again. "Maybe probing, new strategy, doesn't make sense. I don't have the manpower to send reinforcements up there. Bridge was destroyed good, that was his only access. Or was it? Attacking The Lake is suicide. Why then? Doesn't make sense." Silnis muttered as he paced. After a few seconds he stopped pacing and looked at them. "What was the final casualty report?"

Warrec blew out a breath of air before answering. "Fifteen people were killed, eight of which were very old or sick, three children, twenty-seven wounded greatly, forty-six minor wounds, a few dead animals, and several buildings suffered fire damage with three totally lost.

"And how many Goblins did he lose?" Silnis asked.

"They counted four hundred and sixty whole Goblin bodies with a few left-over parts and one Savan warrior," Warrec said.

Silnis grabbed a paperweight off his desk and hurled it against the wall, embedding it into the mortar. "That doesn't make any damn sense!" Silnis bellowed. "Why the bloody hell would he attack the north, that was a total loss for him. And for absolutely nothing gained." Silnis cursed to himself a few more times.

"Boss, you look a little red, more than usual," Joenair said.

"It's these futten reports," Silnis said. "We have been getting reports in from the west that King Ptharis is moving to war. At first it was just rumors. But then trade caravans started getting hit hard. And just a few days ago a report came in of a fort being attacked with no survivors and several farm families were murdered as well." The legate appeared deeply disturbed as he spoke.

"So, then the rumors are true?" Warrec asked.

"Yes, it's looking that way," Silnis said. "At this point have to assume so. Dammit!" Silnis growled as he crashed back into his chair.

"Boss, that can't be true," Joenair said. "King Ptharis has always coveted the imperial throne, but even he wouldn't throw the empire into a civil war. I could maybe see him trying to have his brother assassinated but not open war. Besides, he doesn't have the troops or resources to win a war.... unless." Joenair paused, staring down at the desk.

Warrec could see the mental wheels in Jay's head start to spin. Joenair had a quick wit and a mind made for scheming and plotting. Warrec had known him long enough to guess where his mind was going. The scary part was as he thought about it, he could see that his friend might be right.

"Unless what?" Silnis asked. Silnis seemed to have picked up the train of thought as well and did not like where Joenair was heading with his thoughts.

"Unless he had backing," Joenair said. "Someone powerful, someone that would tip the scales in his favor." Joenair stroked his chin as his mind raced. "But that would make sense, with his reappearance. It can't be coincidence."

"Son, surely you're not suggesting what I think you are," Silnis said. "That Ptharis is in league with that…that monster. He is a fat piece of skret granted, but he would never align himself with Argis."

"Wouldn't he?" Warrec said. The words hung heavy in the air.

"Boss, we have to at least consider the possibility," Joenair said.

The legate rubbed at his mouth and scratched at his empty socket again. "You two are giving me a headache." Silnis leaned back in his chair and closed his eye.

Warrec and Joenair watched in silence as the old veteran processed the information. Warrec watched as plots and schemes, tactics and logistics, and everything in between flowed behind that single closed steel grey eye. Thousands of men and horses, baggage trains and siege weapons, were mentally deployed across the empire towards the western side, across mountains and hills and across rivers and lakes and through deep forests as the legate quietly tapped his fingers on his chin.

After a few moments, the legate shook his head. "All that can wait," he muttered to himself before turning back to them. "I suppose it is a possibility, but for now let's make no mention of it to anyone. We need to play it close for now, don't want to get the bloody nobles and senate all in an uproar. However, we need to speak with King Valorn now though. He needs to be informed of this latest news of the Dread Lord."

Silnis stood again and shouted for his aide to fetch his coach. He started to walk out of the room. He stopped, turned, and beckoned for them to follow. "Oh no, you two are coming along. You get to tell his majesty the bad news."

The three men swiftly exited the Command Post and loaded into the waiting carriage. The three of them sat in grim silence as the carriage bounced along the main bridge towards the imperial island. Silnis glowered at them the entire way and Jay sat quietly beaming a smile back. The fact that the smaller man wasn't joking or trying to further agitate the legate relayed the seriousness of the situation. After a few minutes, the coach pulled into a side entrance of the palace complex used by the staff and kept open to allow kitchen deliveries. The legate did not appear to be in a mood to wait for the tedious delay of formalities by using and announcing at the main entrance.

The three of them walked through the kitchens ignoring the stares from the staff and down the hall to a large junction. From there they cut through a grand but empty ballroom and turned back onto the main hall. Their steps echoed across the tile as they walked down the grand hall toward the throne room.

Warrec could never help but feel in awe when he walked through the palace. He had meet with King Valorn a few times before and each time he had walked away feeling like he was a better man for it. This time was different, however. He couldn't shake the feeling that something was off, just off, that was the best way he could think of to describe it.

There seemed to be a dark cloud hovering about the palace, but no one but Warrec seemed to take notice of it. There was an energy in the palace that made the hairs on the back of his neck stand up. He glanced over at Jay, but he didn't seem to notice it. Warrec shook his head, there was something definitely eerie here, but he just couldn't figure out what.

As they approached the huge, closed oaken doors that led into the imperial throne room Silnis pointed at a grouping of chairs indicating for them to sit. The legate then walked over and whispered a few words to a steward standing outside the doors. The steward nodded and disappeared through a smaller door set in the larger ones.

Silnis shook his head and walked back to sit down. "Now we play the waiting game," he said.

Warrec tilted his chin up at the imperial throne room doors. Valorn held court in the imperial throne room, the same room that every emperor had held since the founding of the empire. A sore point that had often been brought up by the delegation from Ptharis' own court. "Why are the doors closed?" he asked.

Silnis cocked his head back at the doors and nodded. "Dunno, they shouldn't be, emperors always kept them open while they were awake, symbol of their open court. Anyone could be granted access to see and speak with the emperor. Valorn had been keeping the practice, till now it seems. Very odd."

Joenair leaned over and whispered to the two of them. "So, what changed?" No one seemed to be able answer that. The three men sat in silence as they waited.

Silnis, Joenair and Warrec had been waiting outside the throne room for what seemed to be hours. Finally, an aide came out and told them the king would see them now.

"Bout damn time," Joenair whispered to Warrec.

The three men walked into the throne room. It was a massive cathedral of a room with columns on both sides of the central division and high vaulted ceilings. Benches, able to sit several hundred lined the room between the columns. An ornately carved and gilded throne of dark stained wood sat on a raised dais at the back. A massive imperial flag draping down from the ceiling hung behind the dais framing the imperial throne.

On the dais a few steps down from the throne was the emperor's desk. Carved from the same wood as the throne, but less decorative, more designed for function, sat the desk where the true heart of the empire lay. From that desk law and authority flowed down to the senate and from there to the people. At that desk, every emperor had spent the majority of their time in the actual business of ruling. It was the true symbol of the wisdom and grand design of the Maroveyan Empire. It currently sat empty.

The king lounged on his throne in the middle of the room flanked by an army of advisors, aides, and sycophants. He had a sybaritic air about himself that hadn't been there before. At least Warrec hadn't seemed to notice the attitude of self-indulgence and self-aggrandizing before. The king watched them as they walked across the opulent room and knelt before him.

Warrec noticed that the room appeared to have been redecorated since last he saw it. Several new tapestries with Valorn leading armies to victory in imaginary battles hung from the walls. The throne was newer as well. Emperor Ordias had sat upon a simple and plainly carved throne. Valorn now sprawled on an elaborately carved and gilded throne of freshly stained ebony mahogany. Warrec also noticed that Valorn had put on quite a bit of weight.

"Yes, Legate Silnis?" the beloved king asked.

"Your Majesty, I bring distressing news," Silnis said. The king motioned for them to rise and continue. "Your Majesty, it has just been reported to me by these men that The Dread Lord

Argis has returned.

The king made a poofing sound before speaking. "Legate Silnis that is preposterous. The Dread Lord hasn't been seen or heard from since my father sat here. We all know he only comes once or twice a century. Our blessed Emperor Ordias drove him back again just as my great-grandfather did. It simply isn't time for another attack." Valorn spoke with a dismissive air and started to wave them away.

Silnis gritted his teeth before answering. "Your Majesty, with all due respect these men have firsthand accounts of him, and they are to be trusted. And yes, The Dread Lord usually doesn't appear more than twice a century now, however, he has done more so in the distant past."

Valorn wrinkled his nose as if smelling something foul. "And just who are these men that you believe with nary a shred of proof?"

"Your Majesty, they are Lieutenant Warrec Vornirulf Duncanson and Joenair..."

"Ah yes, yes, I recognize them now," King Valorn said interrupting. "They played a major part in the Orc peace accords a year or so ago. And you say they saw the Dread Lord firsthand and lived to tell the tale? That is impressive, most impressive. Why if they keep going at this rate before you know it, they will be legends in their own time." Valorn absently stroked the bottom of his lip.

Warrec watched as the king spoke. There was a casual air and aloofness to his mannerisms. The king had fawned over a tray of cheese while he spoke, half ignoring the legate, until Silnis had introduced them. Warrec caught it. The king smiled and was genteel, but the eyes, the eyes had changed. The smile didn't go up to the eyes and there was a coldness there now.

"Well, then tell me what happened," Valorn said. The king sat and listened intently as Warrec and Joenair retold their account of the attack again. When they were done their noble king stroked his neatly trimmed and manicured beard, pondering their words.

"This is grave news," the king said. "Grave news indeed, what would you have me do lieutenant?" Valorn addressed Warrec directly. Silnis gave no indication of the snub his king had just given him.

"Your Majesty, I humbly ask permission to lead a platoon to investigate the threat. And hopefully learn what the Dread Lord plans."

Valorn sighed. "No Lieutenant. I'm not entirely convinced that there is any threat at all. And I have more worrisome concerns at the moment. My evil brother is preparing to try and seize control of the empire. I simply cannot spare twenty-five legionnaires on some fool errand to chase down the boogieman."

"Your Majesty please, just let me take a few men then, a squad perhaps. Just ten men please. We must look into this…" Warrec pleaded.

"No Lieutenant. Actually, now that I think on it, I have other plans for you two, the heroes of that Orc business. As you may or may not well know, three weeks ago a group of sailors came back and reported making contact with a race of giant cat people. Because of your splendid handling of the Orc affair, I'm sending you two to investigate the sailors' claims. They may prove valuable allies in dealing with the troubles my brother is stirring. We must secure relations with them with all due haste, or Ptharis may beat us to the punch as it were."

"But, Your Majesty, I'm not a diplomat I was only handling security for the ambassador. I…" Warrec tried to explain but was cut off by a wave of Valorn's hand.

"No, lieutenant. This won't be a diplomatic mission in the normal sense, not yet anyway. The report is that these cat people or tiger people or whatever they are, they are a savage warrior race. And since you were able to induct yourselves so fluidly into the Orcs you are the perfect ones for this mission. I want both of you to leave in the morning."

"But Your Majesty, Argis…"

"Enough Lieutenant." The king tapped his lips as he looked at them in thought. Finally, he smiled at the three men. "But because you are so adamant about the Dread Lord matter, I will do this, and you will have to accept it as the wish of your king." Valorn turned his attention back toward Silnis. "Legate Silnis, you will gather a small group of trusted men and head west to investigate any signs that the Dread Lord is planning to move."

"Yes, Your Majesty," The grizzled veteran said as he bowed. Out of the corner of his eye he glared at Warrec. Silnis, with a simple catch of the eye told Warrec to shut up and calm down. Warrec fumed but gave a slight nod. Warrec gritted his teeth and did his best not to show how pissed off he was.

"That is all. You have your orders. Dismissed," the king said with a wave of his hand. The three men turned as one and strode out of the throne room. Warrec managed to make it halfway back to the legate's office before he started cursing.

Chapter Seventeen

Several hours later Warrec still found himself in a foul temperament. Shipping out tomorrow was annoying, he wanted to spend at least a few days here with Addie, but it wasn't the first time he had gotten orders like that. The life of a soldier ran on someone else's clock after all. It wasn't just having everything he said to the king dismissed out of hand, although that was a huge contribution to his mood. It was the feeling that something was very wrong, and he had no idea what. He felt like there were enemies all around, they were walking into an ambush and there was no way to stop it.

"Still mad?" Joenair asked. The smaller man had grabbed a change of clothes at the barracks. Warrec wasn't actually sure from where, as Jay never slept there or kept any belongings there, at least none he was aware of. Joenair was now dressed in a smart looking maroon suit with matching coat that swept back down to his knees. He could easily pass for an upper-class merchant, just shy of a nobleman.

"Very," Warrec answered. He fiddled with a pin on his

uniform. It wasn't quite a full-dress uniform, but still a little more than a travel kit. He had replaced his cloak with a green coat in a similar fashion as Jay's but longer in the back with large gold embroidered cuffs. A large spatha sword hung on his left hip.

"Well," Jay said looking back at the tavern. Loud music and raucous laughter leaked out from the door and side windows. "You may get a chance to hit something or someone. They sound pretty wild in there tonight."

Warrec glanced back at the door. The two men leaned against a low stone wall that enclosed a small patio from the street. Warrec shook his head. "Doubtful, not with the Orcs anyway," he said and tapped the tattoo on the side of his face. "They won't challenge me without a blood duel and it's dishonorable for me to pick a fight with someone lower than me. Plus, if a non-Orc did try to pick a fight with us, they would have to deal with all of them."

Jay rolled his eyes. "You kill one little lizard and for the rest of your life you get to walk around the Orcs as king My Farts Don't Stink."

Warrec let out a deep belly laugh. "Yeah basically," he said wiping an eye.

Warrec looked up as a carriage came rattling up to them. Orban gave a slight nod to them, which was about all the greeting they could hope to get out of the man. Niko came bounding from around the back of the carriage and up to the side door.

"Ah, Lieutenant Warrec, Mister Joenair, Niko is happy to see you and greets you. Eh Lieutenant, you throw dice with Niko again soon, yes? Niko needs a bit of walking around coin." The skinny footman grinned and rubbed two fingers together, before letting out a laugh. "But not tonight, no tonight Niko bring you the best women in all of Eldurond, maybe all of empire." In one smooth practiced movement Niko swept his arm up and opened the carriage door while bowing deeply at the waist.

As Aluna stepped down out of the carriage Warrec felt the air in his lungs being sucked out. He had gotten used to seeing her in her scruffy poncho, usually with a bit of mud smeared on her face and the occasional leaf or two stuck in her hair. This was something else. Aluna reached a hand back and helped Addie down. She seemed to radiate light as her golden hair caught the last few rays of sunlight.

The two women looked stunning in their new clothes. They had their hair up and their make-up was impeccable. Adelia was wearing a gorgeous white gown that hugged her body, perfectly accentuating her feminine curves and was far too fancy for Gor'thak's restaurant. Aluna wore a blue silk dress that contrasted nicely with her flaming hair. The two women were a contrast in ideas, but both seemed to compliment the other. Aluna was tall and broad while Addie was short and petite. Both women smiled and waved before turning to help the handmaids out.

Joenair elbowed Warrec sharply in the side. "Ow, hey, what was that for?" Warrec grunted.

"You zoned out there for a second," Joenair said.

"Oh, you've just never been in love," Warrec said. He gave Joenair a small shove while simultaneously pushing himself off the wall and to his feet. Warrec let out a whistle as he walked up to the carriage.

"Which one though?" Jay whispered just loud enough so only Warrec heard. Warrec turned back sharply and shot the smaller man a glare but said nothing.

Adelia sauntered over to Warrec. With a sly smile she reached up and gently tugged on his beard to bring his face down to hers, before giving him a small kiss. Warrec couldn't help but smile stupidly. Aluna forced a smile and looked away. Addie stepped back and twirled.

"So how do I look?" she said with a knowing smile

"You look fantastic as always. You both look fantastic." Warrec said as he glanced over at Aluna again. The three handmaids stood idly waiting. "Everyone looks fantastic," he said trying not to sound impolite.

Joenair strolled over and swept his eyes across the lot of

them. "We are all far too overdressed for this place," he said.

"Oh, pish posh," Addie said. She waved her hand dismissively at him. "Orcs respect strength. Taking pride in one's appearance and projecting one's beauty is one way for a woman to display her strength."

Warrec nodded. "Did you to have fun shopping today?" he asked.

"Why of course we did," Addie said. She reached over and gave Aluna's hand a squeeze. "Aluna is a pleasure to be around, she is like the sister I never had. We had a wonderful time. Isn't that right girls?"

"Yes," Miriam said. "It was refreshing having someone that could talk about something other than the available bachelors in court," The older woman looked directly at Loreia as she spoke.

Loreia let out a huff and walked over to Joenair, entwining her arm in his. "Some of us are still in our prime and not all dried up and dusty."

Adelia quickly cut off Miriam's retort with an upraised hand. Tettia let out a giggle. "Enough you two," Addie said. She looked up at Warrec and seemed to say with her eyes they have been like this all day.

Warrec smiled back at her. *You enjoy it and you know it,* he thought.

As if reading his mind Addie flashed him a wicked grin,

before continuing on. "As I was saying, it was absolutely wonderful showing her around the city. We bought her this stunning dress, doesn't she look amazing, and of course new traveling boots. Isn't that right dear?" Addie wrapped her arms around Warrec's neck and stood on her tip toes to give him another quick kiss.

"Oh...yeah," Aluna said nodding.

"Although, I think she likes the boots more than the dress," Addie whispered. "And I bought something for you too, but you can't see it till tonight." She gave him a quick wink and slight finger touch to his nose.

Warrec grinned as his mind started racing, thinking about it. Joenair had to cough to break him out of the wonderful daydream he was having.

"We should go on in," Joenair said. He offered his other arm to Aluna who took it with a smile.

The party slowly made their way over to the door which Warrec opened and swept his arm forward for the ladies to enter first. Addie walked in first followed by Aluna. Jay cocked an eyebrow and grinned at Warrec, seeming to say I caught you looking. Warrec shrugged before Joenair did the exact same thing as Loreia and even for Miriam as they walked in.

Tettia stopped and looked up at the two of them as they watched the women walk in. "You two are bad," she said. She then stroked both index fingers on top of each other at them. "Shame on the both of you."

Joenair cocked his head at her. "And you are too young to be noticing such things," He then ruffed the top of her head.

Tettia let out a squeal. "Do not touch my hair, it took two hours," she yelped throwing both hands over her head to protect the precariously stacked bun. Then she kicked the both of them in the shin before striding in to join the other women.

The place was lit by several candles and a couple glowstones stationed to maximize their light. In the center of the main room a large fireplace ran through half the main dining hall. The fireplace had a huge pig slowly roasting on a spit. A small Orc child was busy turning the spit and basting the pig in some unknown marinade. The place was far from crowded, but there were several Orcs and humans laughing, drinking, and eating. Some tables were mixed, others were not.

The place reeked of spilled beer, smoke, and roasted pork. Warrec inhaled deeply, a look of bliss creeping across his face. By the AllFather he had missed this place.

Addie gently patted and rubbed his arm. "Happy?" she asked and smiled sweetly at him.

"Yes, I know you wouldn't have picked here. Thank you," he said. He then kissed her forehead.

"What the hell do you want?" A deep female voice asked from

behind the bar. Aluna stepped back while the color drained from Loreia's face. A large female Orc came out from behind the counter and waddled toward them.

She was almost as tall as Aluna and very muscular. Her skin was a dull red-brown almost the color of rust. Her face had lines of age and the tips of her tusks could just barely be seen through her thick lips. Her face was narrower and more human like, as were most female Orcs, but she still had the open nose similar to a pig, common to her people. Her head was shaved save for a large bush of purple hair, streaked with grey, that was pulled into a ponytail. She wore a traditional female Orc skirt, several thick leather straps ending in steel rings coming off a leather loin cloth. She also wore a large leather apron that barely contained her massive bosom.

She walked up to Joenair and Warrec, eyes narrowing as she looked them up and down, sizing them up. Then her face broke into a huge grin. She grabbed both of them in a huge bear hug that threatened to squeeze the air out of them. Then she planted a huge wet kiss on each of their cheeks.

"Ah, it's good to see you boys again. Come sit, sit. Me have the best table in the house for you. Oh, and Madam Ambassador you grace our humble place here." The Orc then turned and walked a few steps before throwing a front kick that sent a passed-out Orc sleeping at a nearby table flying across the room. The Orc landed with a thump, raised his head, and grunted before passing back out.

"I thought we were going to die," Loreia whispered.

"Pish posh," Adelia said. "There is absolutely nothing to worry about."

"That was awesome," Tettia said. She tried to mimic the kick but couldn't lift her leg high enough in her dress.

"How's it going Zu'na?" Joenair said smiling. "Glad to see you're finally wearing a top."

"Ah, well me got tired of silly guards coming by with fines." She quickly wiped down the table and began arranging chairs for them. "So, me figure wear apron while restaurant is open." Zu'na let out a quick burst of barks, which was unmistakable as Orcish laughter. "Sorry Joenair, you no get to see anymore." She thrust out her chest proudly and cupped both breasts, which Warrec thought only watermelons were comparable to in size, lifting them to Jay's face before letting them drop. "Me know how you love us Orc women." Joenair grimaced as she teased him. Zu'na laughed again and slapped his ass before he could sit down.

Zu'na whipped a white rag out from under her apron and wiped up a pool of spilled beer, as the party finished sitting down. Warrec found himself seated with Addie to his right and Aluna on his left. Joenair sat across from him, between Loreia and Miriam. Loreia looked incredibly uncomfortable as Zu'na teased Joenair. Tettia was given the seat at the head of the table.

Warrec caught Aluna giving him a puzzled look. He leaned over and whispered to her. "Orc women don't normally wear clothing to cover their breasts. But when they move to human lands, they have to adapt to our culture somewhat. However, they still hate wearing clothing, so they wear as little as possible."

"Gor'thak get your green arse out here!" Zu'na bellowed. "Warrec and his friends are here!" She took their drink orders and left to fetch them. From out of the kitchen a huge Orc came out wiping his hands on his stained apron.

He was about just a bit shorter than Warrec but much thicker and broader. He looked like he weighed four hundred pounds, but other than his gut there was no fat on him. The muscles on his arms stood out like steel cables and the veins looked like they were about to burst through the skin. His massive barrel chest was bare and decorated in several tattoos and brands. His broad flat face was grinning from ear to pointy ear. One of his large tusks was broken at the tip and had been capped with gold. He had no hair on his head or his face. He was the epitome of a typical male Orc and one of the nicest people Warrec had ever met.

"Ello, ello Warrec and friends," Gor'thak said. "So nice of you to come here to me lowly place. Me make best food for you, meat, meat, good meat, pig, and bock bock. You special guests, course all on house, order whatever you want. Just yell at me wife, she get what you need." The massive Orc sounded like a child meeting his hero. Gor'thak didn't stop grinning as he clapped Warrec and Joenair on the shoulders and vigorously shook their hands. He even turned to the girls and after a moment's pause bowed deeply.

"Thank you Gor'thak. It's always a pleasure coming here," Warrec said smiling at his strange host. That was one of the reasons he liked Gor'thak so much. Most male Orcs wouldn't have bothered to greet or even acknowledge the women. An unbonded female had no rank or say in Orcish society. Gor'thak made the extra effort.

"No, no, pleasure mine, pleasure be mine," Gor'thak said as he bowed again and returned to the kitchen. As he left Aluna leaned over and whispered a question.

"Why are we getting everything for free?"

"This is why," Addie answered as she tapped the tattoo on Warrec's face. Warrec just shrugged and grinned.

Zu'na came bouncing back carrying two pitchers of beer in one large hand and five glasses in the other. A young Orc child, who couldn't have been over five, brought Tettia and Miriam each a glass of spiced fruit juice. Tettia was too young for beer and Miriam didn't drink.

Zu'na poured the rest of them all a glass and made sure she bent over extra in front of Joenair making him look at her ample cleavage. This of course made him go red in the face and look away. Zu'na laughed at his uncomfortable state. This was an old game they played. Ever since she had found out one night when they had gotten too drunk and Warrec had let slip out what had happened between Joenair and an Orc girl on their last mission. Zu'na had been teasing Joenair ever since.

"Zu'na your husband's getting much better at speaking Highcommon," Adelia said politely.

"Yeah, him getting better, but Highcommon is bad language to speak. Not as good as descriptive or elegant as Orcish is."

They all ordered their food and Warrec ordered his typical fifty wings to start with. He really liked his wings. It wasn't long before everyone was mellowing as the alcohol flowed and the food was eaten.

"Well, we went and spoke with the king today," Warrec said around a mouthful of food.

"Oh, about what, that Argis thing?" Addie asked.

"Hey, how did you know about that?" Joenair asked as he finished his beer.

"Oh, Aluna mentioned it at some point today. She didn't

tell me everything just that you all had seen him and that he is supposed to be planning an attack or something."

"You don't seem that concerned about it," Aluna said.

"Well, no I suppose I don't. I mean I am. It just doesn't seem like an immediate threat. What with talks breaking down between the two kings and the rumors of a civil war." Addie wrapped her arms around Warrec's arm and leaned into him. "Plus, I have a wedding to plan." Aluna choked a little on her beer.

"We did more than just see Argis up north," Warrec said around a mouthful of food.

"What do you mean?" Addie sat back looking hard at Warrec, then Joenair, finally Aluna. "What didn't you tell me?" she said looking at the other woman. Aluna stuffed a fork full of food in her mouth so she wouldn't have to answer.

Warrec rubbed at the back of his neck. "We kind of chased him back to The Gap and might have fought him, just a bit."

"You did what!" Addie's unladylike bellow caused the entire tavern to stop for a moment. Her eyes were wide as she looked at Warrec. "No, no. Are you ok? What?" She became frantic as she began checking Warrec for wounds despite him seeming to be fine.

"Adelia calm down," Joenair said. "He is fine. Stupid but fine. And ok yes, Argis almost killed him."

Warrec shot him a glare. "You are not helping." Gently he took Addie's hands in his. "Really, I'm ok. I was wearing the armor you bought me, nothing could get through that." He wasn't about to tell her how close he had come and how he was only alive because Argis had chosen not to kill him. A fact that still disturbed him greatly.

Addie shook her head at him and clutched at his arm hugging him tightly. "Worth every copper penny. You foolish man. Don't you dare die on me. I won't allow it."

Warrec sighed and put a comforting arm around her. "I won't. I promise. We spoke to the king about going after him, but Valorn shot that down."

"Going after him, why?" Loreia asked. "It's not like he can attack the heart of the empire."

"He has done it before," Joenair said.

"Yeah, but not in like five hundred years," Loreia said. "I just don't see the fuss."

Warrec's face clouded over. "Maybe you should ask the people of Onalas Province what the fuss was about." The table sat silent for a moment. The slaughter at Onalas in the west had been the worst attack by Argis in the last two hundred years, five thousand men, women and children had been impaled and staked to the ground.

"Dear, she didn't mean anything by it," Addie said.

"No, she's just an idiot," Miriam said. Loreia looked down and picked at her food.

"So, uh, what did the king say?" Aluna sputtered out, changing the subject. "Are we going after Argis like you had planned?"

Addie's eyes flared wide for a second. Warrec gently patted her hand before turning to answer Aluna. "No, the king saw fit to send me and Joenair on another diplomatic mission instead, this time to see the Kathari. Wait what do you mean we?"

"Well, I can't go back home yet," Aluna said firmly. "And I don't even know where your father is. I don't have any money to stay in an inn and I don't know anyone here."

"You know Addie, you could stay with her," Joenair chimed in. Warrec kicked him under the table, hard.

"Yes, Aluna dear, you're more than welcome to stay with me. But honey what's this about the Kathari?" Addie asked Warrec. She had a worried tone in her voice.

"Well, you probably know more about them than we do. But that's where we are going and I'm really not happy about it." Warrec grumbled.

"Yes, I have heard about it, but what I meant was why is he only sending you two? Why not an ambassador? The king has made no mention of formalizing a team to go," Addie asked concerned. She tapped a long delicate finger on her cheek and slightly bit her lip as she thought.

Damn, she is cute when she does that, Warrec thought. He

mentally shook his head as he realized what she had just said. The king was sending them out with no support and the diplomatic offices had no clue about it. There it was again that ominous feeling of dread.

"We really don't know. I guess he wanted...he just wanted a military presence at the first official meeting," Joenair said.

"That is odd. When do you two leave?" Addie asked.

"First thing in the morning," Joenair answered reaching for another wing.

"You're joking," Addie said unhappily.

"No, he is serious," Warrec said as he rubbed Addie's shoulder.

"But you just got back," she said to no one in particular. "Aluna, I hope you don't think me a rude host, but would you mind staying with Joenair tonight. Warrec and I need time alone, we have some things to discuss."

"Um, ok, sure, yeah no problem." Aluna was clearly uncomfortable about the whole situation, but she tried not to show it on her face or in her voice. Warrec still caught the undertone in her voice.

"Hey, don't I get a say in this? What if I want some alone time with someone tonight?" Joenair asked looking at Loreia.

"What, are you and Zu'na meeting later?" Loreia said and pushed his arm off her shoulder.

Warrec and Aluna erupted in laughter and even Addie couldn't help but snicker. Then they all started laughing except for Joenair, who just grumbled under his breath.

Chapter Eighteen

The next morning Warrec woke as the first rays of sunlight began peeking in through the huge bay windows. Addie's head lay pillowed on his shoulder, and she was snoring softly. Technically they shouldn't be sleeping together. They weren't married yet and it could cause quite a scandal. That is if every other young couple wasn't doing the exact same thing. It was one of those cultural norms that everyone talked about, but also looked the other way when the reality of life set in. Besides, the ceremony was only a formality at this point anyway. At least that's what Warrec told himself.

Gently he untangled himself from her arms and padded across the large bedroom to the watercloset to relieve himself. When he returned the sunlight was now splashed across her face illuminating it. One leg and bare white hip hung out from under the covers. Warrec looked out the window again estimating the time.

Yeah, there still is time, he thought. With a wicked grin he crawled back into bed and kissed Addie softly on the cheek.

She stirred, reaching for him. *Yep, plenty of time still.*

A couple of hours later he kissed Adelia goodbye and grabbed his gear to meet Joenair at the docks. Last night with her had been special. They had to make the most of what little time they had together, but they had grown accustomed to the short bouts of time together. He was going to miss her terribly, but he knew it would only be for a few months, hopefully.

He made his way to the imperial stables to select a steed. He petted Ginger and told her to behave and that he would be back soon. She was almost as upset to see him leave as Addie had been, actually probably more. He wished he could take the big wuru, but she hated boats. She did not do well on sea voyages, so he had to leave her behind again. She whined when he left.

As he was walking out of the stables an ear-piercing howl rose up from the back of the stables. The sound was high and sad and echoed through the building and across the parade grounds. It nearly killed him, but he forced himself to keep walking. He could still hear her as he crossed both bridges to the west bank.

He and Joenair had a long journey ahead of them. It would take about four days to sail down the river to the coast. After that it was a long sea voyage southwards across the Meridiem Ocean of at least a month if not longer.

When Warrec finally reached the dock where their transport

was berthed, he found that Joenair was already waiting for him and so was Aluna.

"Morning," he said.

"Morning War, here got ya a cup of coffee. Your armor is already loaded," Joenair said handing the mug to Warrec. "I don't know how you drink that stuff. You know the Orcs let the beans pass through the long-neck's guts before they grind them.

Warrec shrugged as he took the mug. "They wash the beans first. Hey, Aluna, did you come to see us off? Jay told you how to get to Addie's estate right?" Warrec asked as he blew on the hot liquid. "They're expecting you this afternoon for tea."

"Well, actually big guy, I'm coming with you two," she said with a big smirk. Warrec had been trying to sip his coffee and spilled some of it when she told him.

"Oh, no you're not," he said wiping his mouth.

"Oh, yes, I am. Warrec, I have never been away from home. Now that I'm here I want to see more. I want to see the world and I want to meet these Kathari people."

Warrec savagely shook his head. "Ok, be that as it may and yes, I do understand that, but I also don't care, you still can't come. We are on official imperial business and you're not a member of the military or an ambassador. So no," Warrec said forcefully.

Joenair lightly sucked in air through his teeth. "Uh...well

actually Warrec she can." Joenair said as he rubbed the back of his head.

"What?" Warrec said. The big man turned slowly glaring at Joenair.

Joenair began fiddling with his fingers as he spoke, refusing to meet Warrec's eyes. "Yeah…see after we left last night, she told me about her intentions and... I was like you, imperial business, and all that. I said she couldn't, but she can be…forceful to put it mildly. And so, we ended up going to see Silnis in the middle of the night. After hearing her arguments, he made her a field medic. I mean she is your village's shaman after all; she has all the proper training plus some. So, long story short, she then convinced him to allow her to accompany us as our medic and…"

Warrec cut him off by balling up a fist and then shaking his index finger. "You're kidding; I mean this has to be a joke." Warrec said looking down at Aluna, who just smiled back at him, clearly pleased with herself. Warrec couldn't get the image of a fox licking its lips after raiding a chicken coop out of his head.

"Nope it's for real," Aluna said. "I'm coming with you two and there isn't a damn thing you can do about it Warrec." She punched him in the shoulder. "Orders are orders after all."

Warrec didn't flinch; instead, he stood there for several

seconds blinking before turning back on Joenair. "And you couldn't talk her out of it?"

Jay didn't answer; instead, he stood still before pointing with both hands at Aluna. He raised them up and down, indicating all of her, before he just threw his hands up in the air. The message was clear, have you met her, what was I supposed to do?

Warrec was not very happy at this news and Aluna seemed to realize she may have pushed things a little too far, so she tried to change the subject. "Have you heard from Duncan?" she asked.

Warrec shook his head to try and clear his thoughts. "Uh, yeah actually…well kinda sort of," he said. "When I woke up this morning there was a note on the table. He said that he had found a clue and was heading to Hammerfall to see if anything could be salvaged from the old museum. He wished us luck and would see me when we got back."

Joenair cocked his head. "How did..."

Warrec raised his hand and cut him off. "If you're going to ask how a nearly seven-foot-tall giant snuck into a nobleman's estate, unseen, and left the note I can't answer that. I have no idea when he came in, how he knew where I was or even that I was leaving. I'm beginning to learn that I really have no idea what my father is actually capable of doing and should just stop questioning it."

"That's…well man, that's just weird," Joenair said shaking his head. "I'm going to go check with the harbor master about when we leave. I'll be right back." He turned whistling and walked down the pier leaving Warrec and Aluna alone again. A few awkward seconds passed before one of them spoke; neither of them knew exactly what to say. Ultimately fate broke their silence for them.

"Look out!" Warrec yelled as he grabbed Aluna and pulled her off her feet out of the way of one of the ogre dock workers. Aluna stared wide eyed at the massive creature as it lumbered past.

The ogre was easily twelve feet tall and monstrously heavy. The boards of the pier creaked under his heavy steps, each foot broad and round. He was bare chested revealing a pale white stomach, contrasted against the mottled grey of the wrinkled skin covering the back and arms.

One of his two heads looked down at the two of them. Its gaze was vacant, and drool was congealing at the corner of its mouth. The other head paid them no attention as it set about its work. Both heads had a massive underbite and a pair of large tusks extending about a foot from the mouth.

The ogre reached down and lifted a pallet of cargo off the pier. The cargo was stacked about four feet high, but the ogre's massive hands easily covered half the sides of the pallet. The pallet was fully loaded and looked to weigh over a ton. The ogre lifted it and moved back down the pier as if it was as light as a feather.

Warrec could feel the softness of Aluna's breasts pressing against his chest. "Are you ok?" Warrec said as he quickly released her.

Aluna turned away, partly to watch the ogre move down the pier and partly to hide her blushing cheeks from Warrec. "Yeah, I'm fine…I…just startled, I guess. What…what was that thing?"

"That was one of the ogre dockworkers. The empire hires them to load cargo. They are quicker and more efficient than a crane and they work for next to nothing."

Aluna nodded to herself. "That's what that drum beat I've been feeling has been since we got to the docks, just a steady thumping." She shook her head and looked back at Warrec. "Is that safe? I mean he almost stepped on me."

"Well, normally yes, these are a little more civilized than their wild cousins and they train fairly well. I think he was just grumpy because he is pregnant."

Aluna did a double take and cocked her head at him. "Say again? He is pregnant? How is that… possible?"

Warrec grinned at her. "Well yeah, see he had two heads. Ogres reproduce differently than everything else. I'm not a scientist but they somehow…split. When they become pregnant, they grow another head and after a few months the ogre forms some type of cocoon and out pops two of them." He shrugged at the absurdity of it.

"That's the stupidest thing I have ever heard. You're making that up."

Warrec smiled and shrugged. "Well, no one has ever seen a female ogre." Aluna laughed and that made him smile more. They looked at each other for a second and the smile dropped from his face as he grew serious again.

"Aluna I'm sorry about all this. I should have told you about me and Addie sooner. I mean I tried but…"

"Warrec let's just drop it ok. You're right, you should have told me. And I guess you did try, but you should have tried harder. That was a very awkward situation you put me in yesterday and I didn't appreciate it one damn bit." Aluna stared down at the waters lapping at the pier for a moment. "Luckily, Adelia is such a sweet person, a little ditzy perhaps, but she is great. I can see why you would want to marry her. I realize now that you never owed me anything and that I had let a childhood crush grow out of hand. I wish you two the best of luck, I really do. But let's forget this for now and not bring it back up. We have a mission to complete so let's get on with it."

"Ok, friends then?"

Aluna raised her eyes and looked deeply into Warrec's eyes before she spoke. "Warrec we will always be friends." Warrec started to say something, but let it drop as Joenair bounded back down the pier towards them.

"Hey, let's move you two. The boat is about to leave!" Joenair yelled at the two of them from down the pier. Warrec grabbed his gear and trotted off down toward the pier.

"Yeah friends," Aluna said. Warrec wasn't sure, but he thought he saw her wipe away a small tear before she picked up her gear and followed after him.

Chapter Nineteen

The gates of Hammerfall loomed up before Duncan. The huge iron doors stood as a monument to Dwarven engineering. Rising up before him the gates were easily five times his height. Solid and impenetrable, they had only been closed a half dozen times in all of Dwarvish history. No army in the entire world, living or dead, could break them from their hinges.

Despite the cool air, Duncan found himself sweating. He paused to wipe his brow with a sleeve. The hike up the ever-steepening terrain from Hammerfall Lake had been more tiring than he had imagined and had taken the better part of the day. He let his rucksack slip to the ground as he caught his breath.

With an easy practiced motion, he slipped a hand into the folds of his robes and retrieved his flask. He took a quick nip and craned his head up as he gazed up at the snowy peaks of the western edge of the Black Mountains. Mountains were an inadequate term, as the peaks of some stretched high into the sky hidden behind clouds. Mount Turmo, the highest peak in the chain, had never been summited. The great peaks formed high valleys with lush although cold farmland for the Dwarves. The north side of the chain running along the northern edge of Hammerfall Lake were little more than hills and forest land with a group of several individual mountains with large families of hills spreading out and connecting all of them. Here though, here the majesty of the mountains was unrivaled. Duncan let out a low whistle.

Looking back down the trail he could see a steady plume of smoke and steam rising up from the iron works. The heart of the Dwarven economy beat steadily day and night processing raw ore into workable ingots. Iron, coal, copper and valentium, along with a bit of precious metals flowed down from the few large mountains in the chain to the various ore processing and smelting facilities built up along the lakeside.

A Dwarve sitting on the bench of a heavy-laden flatbed wagon drawn by two dull-eyed yaks passed Duncan as the Dwarve made his way down to The Lake.

Duncan gave a wave in greeting. "May the wind greet you," Duncan said.

"Aye, and may it find you in deep tunnels," the Dwarve said. He returned the wave and favored Duncan with a gap-toothed grin splitting his black beard. He nodded once more before turning back to the yaks and urging them along with a stream of curses. The shaggy, dull beasts seemed oblivious to their master's cantankerous shouts and proceeded at the same slow pace.

With a deep sigh Duncan bent down to retrieve his pack and set off again up the trail. A few minutes more and he would be inside the city. He could finally get a good meal and sleep in a comfortable bed. Sleeping on the decks of the various river barges as he made his way north from Eldurond had left his back feeling stiff and disagreeable. However, tonight at least he could sleep well and get a fair sampling of the various brews the Dwarves were so famous for. The fact that he had seen very few lost souls while making his way up here had been a welcome bonus and relief.

While not the capital of the Dwarven nation, Hammerfall was the largest Dwarven city and the closest to the empire. The city was a trader's paradise. Practically anything and everything could be bought or sold inside the mountain city, for the right price. Most of it was legal, some of it was not. That was only partly the reason for this trip. Duncan could easily have outfitted himself in Eldurond. No, the real reason was the Grand Dwarven Museum of Relics, Artifacts and Antiquities.

The museum contained the artifact that he would need to continue this quest. He had known that it was here, he just hadn't known exactly what it was. That had been the reason for traveling with Warrec to Eldurond. He had found the right passage in the ancient elvish book at the library, and it described in great detail the artifact.

He had been so energized when he had found that passage in the ancient Elven book. Thinking back, he probably could have stayed the night in the city and talked to the boy in person. However, at the time he had been too excited and in a rush.

Duncan had gone to the military ward looking for Warrec, but of course the boy wouldn't be where Duncan needed him to be. Still, finding out where he was staying hadn't been hard. Warrec was apparently very well-known and his relationship with a noblewoman was common knowledge.

Finding the estate hadn't been too difficult either once he got a general direction from several of the soldiers. By the time he finally reached the estate it had been very late and if Duncan wanted to catch the first river runner heading north, he didn't have time to stay. So, he had quickly scribbled a note and gave it to one of the night guards, a Niko or Niail, it had definitely started with an n.

He had left Eldurond that same night, barely making time to acquire travel supplies. "The boy will be alright," he said to himself as he took another swig. Warrec never would have come with him. He had his own responsibilities to deal with. Besides, this was something Duncan needed to do alone. Maybe in some small way this might make a little amends for losing the sword, that and dooming all of humanity. "Right, that too," Duncan mumbled.

As he neared the gates, he noticed the two Dwarven guards outside. They sat on stools leaning against one of the outer doors. Their crossbows were within easy reach as they watched the flow of traffic. They wore steel cap conical helmets, with a thick nose guard. Steel hauberks that dropped down to their knees and greaves seemed to encase the bored Dwarves in a steel shell. A broad leaf headed spear easily twice their heights rested comfortably in a crook of each of their arms. Their demeanor spoke of boredom, but ready to deal with trouble should it arise.

The guards were obviously used to a steady stream of traffic coming to and from the city. Duncan nodded a greeting at them as he strode over to the stone desk used for processing new arrivals. One of the guards returned the nod and let out a low whistle. Duncan could hear rustling coming from the guard shack behind the desk. The shack door creaked open and an ancient looking Dwarve appeared.

The Dwarve was dressed in a simple white shirt under a purple velvet vest. A plaid chuba robe of yellow and green dropped down to his ankles, barely covering thick leather boots. His beard was slate gray with a few stray red hairs streaked through it. The chest length beard was cut square and was braided with copper and silver beads. He held a mass of papers under one arm and had a writing quill stuck behind his right ink-stained ear. On his head he wore a tall orange conical cap tilted to the left, designating his status as a clerk.

The Dwarve paused to adjust the spectacles perched precariously on his blunt broad nose, before seating himself behind the desk. The clerk systematically began to spread the papers across the desk. He then took the pen from behind his ear, licked it once and dipped it into the ink well built into the desk and prepared to write, all before so much as glancing up at Duncan.

Duncan sighed to himself. The Dwarven people blew new life into the definitions of methodical and precise. Trying to hurry one along was as effective as trying to make the sun rise faster. It happened when it happened.

A more impatient man might have become irritated at the slow proceedings, but Duncan had dealt several times with Dwarves in the past and knew they rarely did anything swiftly. He instead had taken the time to lower his pack and the sling holding his massive bardiche to the ground and took a drink of water from his canteen.

The Dwarve finished his preparations and finally looked up at him. "My you're stretched out ain't ya," he grunted in Dwarvish. "My name is Clerk Garven, third rank," he said switching over to Highcommon. "For the record, state your name and business in Hammerfall." Garven spoke with little accent indicating that he had probably been raised amongst humans or at least had a very formal education.

"My name is Duncan Vornirulf Bjornson. My business is to see the museum and rest a few days in one of Hammerfall's famous taverns. Do you have any recommendations?" Duncan answered and then added in Dwarvish "Oh aye, I am possessing quite ah large frame, more benefitting ah bearcat than one ah the wee imperials."

Garven cocked an eyebrow at him. "Ah, I see you have a grasp of the proper tongue. To answer your question about our taverns you really have only two choices if you want the absolute best. If you want only a drink and a bed, the Black Mushroom is the place to be. If you want a drink, a bed, and some company, the House of the Rising Sun is it. I don't know where your tastes lie, but I am sure they can accommodate you. But a word of warning, it's the best and been the ruin of many a lad, many have gone bankrupt or been ruined by it throughout the years. They even have a few female Orcs in their employment...if you like that sort of thing," he added with a nod and a wink.

"Now, to address the first part of your business. I'm afraid that the museum is closed at this time. One of the main corridors leading down to it collapsed a few days ago. At this time there is no estimation as to when it will reopen." Garven reached into the drawer in the desk and brought out a simple visitation badge. He then stamped the date onto the back.

"This is good for twenty days. If after that time you find yourself needing to stay longer in our grand city, you will have to visit the main government hall and apply for an extended residence pass. Those found to have an expired visitation pass are subject to fines and/or jail time... and as always please enjoy your stay." He finished and handed the badge to Duncan.

Duncan tried to hide his disappointment as he took the badge. He couldn't afford to stay more than a few days. He had planned to visit the museum tomorrow, but with its closure he had no idea how he was going to gain access to the artifact. He trudged solemnly through the massive gates of the city. His mind was heavy with thought.

"Oh, and spin the prayer mantras on the cylinders there as you walk in," Garven called out after him. "They're good luck."

Duncan walked through the massive gates and looked around the bailey that led into the city proper. Along the tunnel walls sat banks of huge metal cylinders, each covered in a set of Dwarven runes.

A gust of wind blew in from the gate rattling an army of wind chimes. Duncan looked up and saw that a multitude of chimes hung from the ceiling and walls. They looked to be constructed of various materials, from bamboo to brass or copper. As the wind rattled them a chorus of different notes chimed together.

A large blast of trumpets sounded adding to the chimes. Duncan jumped for a second then realized what had happened. As the wind flowed through the bailey it was forced down and through chambers imbedded into the walls, producing the trumpet blast.

"Not too bad a welcome," he said. Duncan looked back at the prayer wheels and shrugged. "What could it hurt?" He ran his hand along one of the cylinders and found they spun easily. As he finished walking into the city, he dragged his hand across each one on the right side of the tunnel spinning them each in turn.

He found the House of the Rising Sun fairly quickly as it was located close to the city entrance to greet weary travelers. A rather attractive blonde woman waved at him from the second story balcony. He thought about it hard before pressing on. He hadn't been with anyone since his wife had died. The loneliness had been crippling, but it was something he had grown used to in a way. Though he was still a man and could still see.

"Ah I probably couldn't afford her anyway," he mumbled as he took one last long look at her. He dismissed the idea with a shrug before pressing on.

His poor memory didn't do the complexity of the underground

kingdom justice. Hammerfall sprawled out from the main entrance in a huge labyrinth of tunnels. At first to a newcomer, it could be confusing as the tunnels twisted and turned back on each other. However, there was a method to the madness as each tunnel eventually would lead to one of several massive subterranean caverns.

Duncan stopped to look at one of the several maps drawn on each tunnel. Duncan noticed that the city was decorated more as a temple than an urban landscape. Every tunnel was decorated in some way or fashion, with barely a hint of bare rock. Most had elaborate frescos painted on the walls. Some had intricate geometric mandalas carved and painted into the rock. With all the designs it was sometimes easy to miss the maps.

Most amazing was the sheer volume of color in the underground city. The Dwarves obviously had a love of colorful things from their clothing to the frescos on the city walls. The colors were brought out even further by strategically placed glowstones of various lights.

He could see why there were city maps somewhere on every tunnel wall. With the constant light and dazzling colors mixed with twisting tunnels it was easy to get turned around. Looking at the map he could see the city from the top down.

Hammerfall was laid out in somewhat of a wheel pattern, although it was a broken and mangled wheel with several layers.

Each layer had tunnels shooting off from a central hub that connected to different caverns or districts. Each map had a large marker indicating its location in the city. After a few minutes scanning Duncan was able to find a marker for the Black Mushroom and it didn't look too far off.

Despite the necessary help of the maps, it took the remainder of the day for Duncan to navigate the city of Hammerfall. Most of his time was spent between walking down corridors so wide a three-mast ship could have sailed down them comfortably and tunnels so tight that even a Dwarve would have had to squeeze through them. He had gotten lost four times and had to ask twice for directions from one of the guard patrols before finally arriving at the Black Mushroom.

It was growing late as he pushed the large oaken door leading into the Black Mushroom open. Duncan had been able to keep track of the time with the clocks embedded periodically in the walls throughout the city. Every hour they had chimed out in perfect unison. It boggled his mind at the level of precision and engineering needed to keep each clock synchronized.

It was now close to seven as he made his way inside. The tavern was filled and busy with the evening dinner crowd. Every table was filled with various groups of Dwarves, from one or two individuals to whole families. There were also several humans, mostly Vatninu, sprinkled throughout the company and Duncan thought he spied an Orc over in a dark corner.

Walking in he had to stoop low as his head bumped up against the ceiling. He made his way carefully to the bar, doing his best not to step on anyone and managed to find an empty stool. A bald red bearded Dwarve snored loudly as his head laid blissfully pillowed in a puddle of beer suds next to Duncan. The Dwarve behind the bar set a large tankard brimming with beer in front of Duncan before he had dropped his pack and sat down.

"Welcome to the Black Mushroom stranger. What can I do fer ya?" the Dwarve said as he wiped his hands on a rag.

"Thank you," Duncan said as he took a sip of beer. It was good, wonderfully good, rich, and dark. "I would like dinner and lodging."

"That will be sixty-seven silver iffen you please. Six drinks are included with your meal," he said holding out a palm the size of a small dinner plate. Duncan dug the money out of his pouch and handed the coins over. The Dwarve shook the coins once in his fist. He then took one and placed it in his pouch, dropped two coins in the tip jar on the bar and put the rest in the cash box behind the bar. Duncan nodded to himself pleased. He had expected to pay almost a full gold sovereign, at these prices he might be able to stay long enough to see the museum, but it would be stretching it.

The barkeep then rang the gong hanging behind the bar. A

small teenage Dwarve appeared at Duncan's side. The boy's beard was just starting to come in and Duncan guessed his age to be about thirty.

"Please, your pack sir. I'll be taking it up to your room and your weapon iffen you dornt mind," he squeaked. Duncan nodded and handed his gear over.

The boy grunted as he took the load. For a moment it appeared that he wouldn't be able to bear the weight, but he then shifted everything around and turned to walk slowly up the stairs to the private rooms. Duncan was still surprised at just how strong the Dwarven people were, even as children.

He sat there for a few minutes drinking his beer and eyeing the crowd. After a few minutes, a stout Dwarven woman walked over carrying a massive food tray, precariously balanced on one hand. "Ready for yer supper lad?" she asked.

Duncan nodded a bit taken aback, but then he realized even though he was an old man she probably had a few decades on him easily. By the look of her she was still in her prime and quite attractive. She would have been stunning to another Dwarve.

Duncan caught himself staring at her as her twin braids of golden hair danced across her ample cleavage. She sliced into the large slab of mutton aggressively which made the jiggling of her breasts almost hypnotic. Duncan realized he had been too long without female companionship as she slapped several slices of mutton onto his plate along with a large helping of mashed potatoes. She then dripped a ladle of some type of brown mushroom sauce over it all. It smelled delicious. A few drops had fallen onto her cleavage, which Duncan thought was probably on purpose as she wiped it away with a finger and licked it clean.

Duncan had already dropped ten silver heads on the tray before he even realized what he was doing. *I just over tipped her. That show probably rakes in the tips for her,* he thought. He then mentally shrugged. There was nothing to be done about it now, but he would have to be more careful, or he would blow through his funds quickly, cheap lodging or not.

"Enjoy," she winked at him as she picked the tray back up. "And ye...wake up ye old drunk," she said smacking the bald head of the Dwarve that had been passed out seated next to Duncan.

The bald Dwarve woke with a snort. "Ore beer," he grunted at the bartender. The Dwarve lazily stretched and smacked his lips a few times. "Ello there," he said turning to Duncan. "Names Barix Hammerstone, but mah friends call me Wildbeard." He spoke with a brogue accent, magnified by inebriation. Wildbeard smiled broadly showing perfect if slightly yellow teeth.

Duncan nodded. "Wind greet you friend, I'm Duncan Vornirulf."

Wildbeard was completely bald. He seemed to compensate for

the lack of hair on his head by having a thick, unkempt beard the color of fire. The beard sprang out from his face to both shoulders and down to his stomach. Duncan would not have been surprised if half a forest of small woodland creatures hid somewhere in the depths of the aptly named Wildbeard's facial hair.

He wore a simple brown tunic, belted at the waist, which was half untucked and a plain black kilt. His boots, unlike the rest of his outfit, appeared to be expensive black leather with a steel toe. It looked like he had grabbed whatever clothing, clean or not, he could find before he left his home. Duncan immediately liked him.

A few hours passed as the two old drunks, a giant and a Dwarve, sat telling stories to each other and anyone else that would listen. Duncan and Wildbeard had found a kindred spirit with each other and had quickly become comrades in cups.

Wildbeard sputtered as he tried to mop the beer out of his long flame red beard. Duncan had timed the punch line of the joke he had been telling perfectly as the Dwarve had taken a long pull of brew. The Dwarve had laughed so hard that the suds had come back out his broad bent nose. This in turn had caused Duncan to roar with laughter.

"Err now, ya got me boyo. Ya got me good," Wildbeard chuckled as he finished wiping himself off. Duncan gave him a toothy grin before taking another sip. His head was starting to buzz from the vast amount of beer the two had drunk. The beer and the Dwarve's good company had momentarily lifted his spirits and the weight of the world had seemingly been lifted from his shoulders.

"So, other than making a Dwarve look foolish..." Wildbeard started to ask before being interrupted by the bar maid.

"You don't need any help with that," she quipped as she walked past.

"...what are you doing in Hammerfall?" Wildbeard continued on while shooting her a wink and a kiss. She snorted at him and turned her nose up as she left to wipe down some empty tables.

She mumbled something under her breath as she walked away which sounded to Duncan like "Not again in this lifetime." Though he couldn't help but notice that she seemed to throw an extra swing in her hips as she walked away. Wildbeard was staring at her as she left and had leaned over so far that Duncan had to catch him to keep him from falling off his stool.

Wildbeard looked up at his new friend grinning from ear to ear and they both started laughing again. Wildbeard took another long pull of his beer before continuing on. "Any who, ya was saying about being err."

Duncan nodded as he took a sip and wiped his mouth on his sleeve. "Right, well I had planned on going to the museum, I have some business to attend to, which included looking at one of the artifacts there. But I was told at the gate that the bloody thing is closed due to some tunnel collapse."

"Ah hell, what a coincidence, I work there. You should have said something sooner," Wildbeard said smacking himself on the forehead. "Aye, but you're right it is closed," he added somberly. "We think someone was trying to break in and collapsed the tunnel behind them tae cover their tracks. Happened about a week ago."

Duncan cocked an eyebrow at the news. "Did they take anything? I take it they weren't caught."

The Dwarve waved his hand dismissively and took another swig before answering. "Nah, they were good. I'll give um that. But there are a few extra security measures we employ at night that they hadn't ah counted on."

"Such as?" Duncan asked.

Wildbeard wagged a thick sausage like finger at him. "No…no me new friend, trade secret and all that," he said with a wink. The pair sat in silence for a moment drinking. Finally, Duncan broke the easy silence.

"Say, Wildbeard, since you work at the museum. I don't suppose..." Wildbeard cut him off with a clap of his ham hock sized hands.

"Stop right there. I know what you're gonna ask already and

I canna do it. I canna go pulling favors like that for simple sightseeing. I....." He trailed off for a moment. "Ya said ya needed to see something specific. What…what exactly was it ya was needing to see?"

"Well, it's a puzzle box about this big." Duncan held out his arms to indicate roughly two feet. "It's detailed in elvish and forms a map of sorts." Duncan stopped himself. The color had drained from Wildbeard's face. He could have sworn the Dwarve had started to reach for a hidden dagger but had stopped himself. Wildbeard eyed him warily.

"And what would your interest be in that particular piece? It seems that item has grown particularly popular recently." Wildbeard narrowed his eyes. "Let me see your visitation badge." The Dwarve said thrusting out his hand. Duncan slowly handed him the badge.

"They were trying to steal the box, weren't they," Duncan stated as fact.

"Aye, all the evidence seems to point to it," Wildbeard said eyeing the current date on the badge before handing it back. "But you couldn't ave been the thief in question. I know that, but ya coulda hired them." The Dwarve stated as he handed the badge back.

"Oh, how so?" Duncan asked.

"The thief or thieves would have tae have been either a

very short skinny human or a Dwarve tae fit through the ventilation shaft they escaped through. And you dunna have the right frame for it, if ya catch my meaning. But ya still haven't answered me as tae why ya needs tae see it."

Duncan let out a long sigh. "I really can't go into that."

"Ya going tae have tae, iffen ya want me tae help. And I still ain't sure ya dinna have something tae do with the burglary."

Duncan sighed again. This was going to take a while. He resigned himself to telling the same tale to the Dwarve he had told the kids, minus a few personal details. He ordered them both another round and began at the beginning. The evening crowd had thinned considerably by the time Duncan had finished.

"Aye, that's a whopper of a story," Wildbeard sighed as he rubbed his eyes. "It's almost completely unbelievable, but there be enough truth there tae keep me from dismissing it outta hand. Some o' the facts and details aren't well known to the public, just us historians. So, there's that." His bushy red eyebrows furrowed in deep thought as he rubbed the back of his bald head.

"So, you believe me?" Duncan asked. The Dwarve sat in silence mulling everything over in his mind. Finally, he let out a low grunt and slapped the bar to get the bartender's attention.

"It's a lot tae consider. I'll have tae sleep on it, me

heads not fully clear. But ya did help pass the evening and for that I'll buy yar brews."

Wildbeard handed two gold over to the bartender who gave him back a handful of silver heads in change. Wildbeard dropped the change in the tip jar before clapping a hand on Duncan's shoulder.

"I will see ya around my friend and don't let the mountain drop on ya while ya sleep." With that the Dwarve stumbled out the door leaving Duncan with an empty mug of brew and a disheartened feeling. He decided he had drunk enough beer for the night and began downing shots of Dwarven fire water.

After a few more hours he stumbled his way through the tavern towards his room. The old wooden stairs creaked as they bore his weight. At the top he nearly lost his balance and tumbled backwards but was saved at the last second by the barmaid.

She quickly grabbed his beard and pulled him back to his feet. Instead, he stumbled forward and planted his face into her immense cleavage. The barmaid gave an exasperated sigh and half carried the old giant to his room. She dumped him like a pile of laundry on the bed and blew out the candle as she left with another shake of her head. "Old drunks," she muttered as she closed the door. He was asleep as soon as his head hit the pillow.

Chapter Twenty

Duncan had been passed out asleep only a few hours when he was quickly snapped back to consciousness by a torrent of ice-cold water.

"What?" he sputtered as he bolted upright in bed.

"Mornin, Sunshine," Wildbeard said grinning as he stood over the bed, holding a now empty bucket. The Dwarve did not seem to be suffering any of the effects of consumption from the night before.

Duncan rubbed at his eyes. His head was still swimming with inebriation. He was still very drunk and felt like he would be sick at any moment. Duncan bent over as he sat on the bed and put his head between his knees. That seemed to help a little.

"Err now," Wildbeard said as he handed Duncan a small herb pouch and a glass of water. "Bite it in half and swallow."

Duncan pulled a brown lump from the pouch. It smelled like it came out of the wrong end of a long dead goat. Duncan could feel the bile rising in his throat. "What is it?" he asked, not sure if he wanted an answer.

"Merry Man's Miracle. Lump o' herbs one o' the local apothecaries sells for a hangover cure. It works miracles, hence the name, just take it."

Duncan held his nose as he bit into the putrid mass. The disgusting wet lump tasted worse than it smelled. Somehow, he was able to swallow the two halves with the help of the water. He seriously thought this was the perfect example of the cure being worse than the symptoms. However, after a few seconds he could begin to feel it working. Within a few minutes his head was completely cleared, and he felt a thousand times better.

"Feel better?" Wildbeard asked with a knowing grin.

"Yes, actually I feel great."

"Heh, half the time it works every time. Tha stuff is horrid but well worth it."

"Thanks, and thanks for the bath," Duncan said glaring at the Dwarve, who was still grinning at him.

"Think nothing of it lad. Ya smelled like ya needed one and I was happy tae oblige ya. Now get dressed. We ain't got all day."

"What are you talking about?" Duncan asked as he got up and started to dress into dryer clothes.

"Ya wanna see the museum or not?" the Dwarve asked as he grabbed Duncan's pack. Wildbeard easily hefted the hundred-pound rucksack and handed it to Duncan. He was slightly surprised when

Duncan easily took the sack and casually threw it over one shoulder. The surprise quickly turned to respect as he handed Duncan the bardiche. Any human that could wield a weapon as heavy as that demanded it. Duncan smiled to himself, he was old, but he was far from frail.

"So, I guess you believed my story?" Duncan asked.

Wildbeard turned and started downstairs with Duncan in tow. "Let's just say ya peaked me curiosity. We'll ah sees what ya make of the artifact." He answered with a wink.

The clocks showed a quarter past eight as the two set out into the huge warrens of the city. As they moved through the city Duncan realized something he had been too preoccupied about yesterday to notice. He hadn't seen one wandering Dwarve soul in the city.

"Wildbeard how does your people dispose of their dead?" he asked.

Wildbeard gave a loud sniff. "Sky burial. We take them up above the terrace farms on the mountain and leave them. The mountain and the winds takes them back tae Father Sky." The Dwarve leaned a little closer and whispered. "Though tae be honest it's mostly the buzzards and critters that have them. Why do you ask?"

Duncan nodded. "That's what I thought." *I can't tell him because I haven't seen any souls wandering around; he would think me a loon. Still, that does explain it, not enough of a body left to anchor the soul too.* "Oh, I was just curious, that's what I had heard but wasn't sure."

When they came to the collapsed tunnel, Wildbeard flashed a badge and the guards at the entrance stepped aside without a word. The tunnel was in various states of repair as they made their way through.

All around them the walls echoed with the sounds of Dwarves busily repairing the tunnel. Dwarves armed with pickaxes, mattocks, hammers, and shovels hewed relentlessly at the rock. Several stands for powerful white glowstones had been set up around the work area. Despite this, each Dwarve also wore a helmet with a glowstone fixed in the center. The sounds of picks and hammers striking stone mixed with merry singing and several good-natured curses.

After about a quarter of a mile they came to a section completely blocked off. Duncan had to crawl on his hands and knees to squeeze through the access tunnel the repair teams had made to bypass the blockage. Luckily for him it was only for a few hundred feet. After about another quarter of a mile they reached the door to the museum warrens.

As they entered the deserted lobby Duncan gazed at an immense diamond easily as tall as he was mounted on the central podium. A beam of sunlight shone down through a ventilation shaft cut through the mountain. The sunlight struck the gem causing refracted light to illuminate the room in sparkling radiance.

"I guess you're not too worried about anyone stealing it?" Duncan said. He started to touch it but stopped himself.

"Go ahead. The children climb all over it. And no, we aren't worried. Blasted thing weighs several tons. If anyone could get it out of the city without being seen, we figured they deserve it more than us." Wildbeard said with a grunt as he was leading them over to a side door.

Wildbeard grabbed several torches from a bin just on the other side of the door. He tucked two into his belt before lighting one with a striker mounted on the bin. "Ere the glowstones haven't been recharged," the Dwarve said handing Duncan the lit torch and lit the second one for himself.

The two made their way down a spiral staircase into the warehouses and work rooms under the museum. "This is where I work," Wildbeard said. "This is the part of the museum the public don't see, where all the real work is done. My office is down there," he said absently pointing down a torch lit corridor.

As they entered a subbasement, they had to carefully weave their way through a multitude of a variety of artifacts in various states of packing and unpacking. The room was the size of a town square, but it seemed almost every inch was crammed with something. Several animal skeletons in various stages of assembly took the center of the room. Most of the beasts were things Duncan had only heard about. Chief among them was a complete skeleton of a rajanaga. The five-foot skull leered at him; its jaws poised to snap up anything that came within reach. The tiny arms looked ridiculous on the massive body, and he mentioned it to Wildbeard as they passed it.

"Aye, the bones dunna do it much justice. Ya have to keep in mind that the arms were covered in these long, brilliant feathers," he said as he picked up an emerald, green feather longer than he was. On the reverse side it was a dull olive drab.

"They use this side tae attract females," Wildbeard said as he spread his arms out to show the bright side. "It's actually very pretty when they do that and fluff out the feather mane and crown."

As they came to the end of the vast room Duncan stopped to stare at the statue of a large imperial soldier. There was something oddly familiar about it. Suddenly he realized who the statue was.

"That's my son!" he exclaimed.

"Err now, what?" Wildbeard asked. He then smacked his bald head as the realization sank in. "Of course, I dunna why I didn't think of it before. Vornirulf...hmmm...so Warrec's your boy huh?"

Duncan slowly nodded as he stared at the statue of his son. His son stood proudly incased in marble. He wore full plate and rested his hands on the pommel of a long sword. The face wasn't quite right or at least a little different to Duncan as it was clean shaven.

"Yes, but why is there a statue of him here?" Duncan leaned down and read the plaque at the base.

Sergeant Warrec Vornirulf

Hero of the Battle of the Long Bridge

Friend to the Dwarven people for eternity.

"Aye, Warrec is a hero to us all," Wildbeard said. "Him and ah handful of survivors held the Long Bridge long enough for reinforcements to arrive."

"He never told me any of this," Duncan said mournfully.

"Truly?" Wildbeard asked. At Duncan's nod he began the tale of the Battle for the Long Bridge.

"Warrec was still green at the time, fresh outta guard duty at the capital. He had been promoted tae sergeant and was in charge of nine others. Their squad was part of the ill-fated 23 Centuri. This was durin' the brief civil uprising in the Dwarven nation.

"The Cult of the Black Hand had been growing in strength for decades and had finally grown powerful enough tae attempt a coup. The 23rd had been assigned tae lend aid and support as the Dwarves quelled the rebellion. We had assigned them tae guard the entrance tae the supply line tunnel. The only outside access was at the Long Bridge across Felware Chasm.

"It was supposed tae ave been a cake walk assignment. Most of the 23rd, including Warrec, were fresh from training and had not seen combat. The main force of the Black Hand was supposed tae have been far enough away that the Long Bridge should not have been in any danger." Wildbeard gave a half shrug. "Chalk it up tae bad intel, deception, or bad luck, but somehows they had tricked the majority of the Dwarven forces tae come out and meet them. What the Dwarves found was a handful of cultists and hundreds o' fake ones, straw dummies as it were."

"Right, right I remember a bit about them," Duncan said. "They had tried to start recruiting and preaching around The Lake as well."

"Aye and what happened to them?"

"We killed them, burned most of them. They wanted to eat babies after all."

Wildbeard spat. "Yer people were smarter than mine. Religious freedom is all well and good, but a line has to be drawn somewhere." He absently mumbled to himself. "Cheap fatherless sons o' whores."

Wildbeard pointed with the torch backup at the statue. "Any who, the Black Hand had managed tae slip behind and scaled a sheer cliff tae reach the Long Bridge. The 23rd now found themselves under attack and outnumbered fifteen tae one, by insane cultists. They were slaughtered. But somehow Warrec's squad was able tae hold them long enough so that the bridge could be collapsed. He held his position, fighting alone; long enough for the rest o' his squad tae collapse the bridge.

"If the Black Hand had secured those supplies and cut the supple line, they woulda ave been able tae capture the capital and the Dwarves woulda ave been thrown into chaos. Your son is a hero and brother to every Dwarve, and none will forget his name.

"And that statue was supposed tae go on display last week, but with the closing we had tae put it down here," Wildbeard said with a reflective sigh. "Ya must be very proud."

Duncan breathed deeply as his chest threatened to burst with pride. "I am."

The two stood in quiet reflection for a moment before heading through the door and down another long winding tunnel. The tunnel terminated at a single vault door. Wildbeard slid a key into the door with a loud click. The sound of several locking mechanisms sliding into place echoed down the tunnel.

The Dwarve spun the large door seal and pulled the heavy door open. As the door slowly opened, a deafening screech rang out from inside.

"Down ya stupid beasts," Wildbeard bellowed. "It's only me." He lit a wall lantern beside the vault door. Several more lanterns lit in succession around the room bathing the vault in light. Wildbeard didn't hesitate as he entered, but Duncan warily stood in the doorway as he looked to see what had made the noise.

As the room filled with light, he saw them. Two large raptors crowded in a corner, ready to pounce. Wildbeard calmly walked over and patted them on the muzzle. They relaxed as their master patted them, chirping with happiness to see him.

They both were taller than the Dwarve but not by much. The larger of the two was covered in a mix of bright crimson and blue feathers. A large crest of orange and yellow feathers adorned its head. The smaller one's feathers were a plain drab brown. The brightly colored one cocked his head at Duncan and slowly stalked toward him.

"Easy boy, he is a friend," Wildbeard said. The raptor seemed to understand and let out a pleasant chirp followed by a series of clicks as it tapped the huge, curved killing claw on its right foot on the stone floor. The plain one answered with a different set of claw clicks and swatted its long lizard-like tail against the floor.

"The big ones' named Red and the other is Sweettooth. And ya I know, I didna name them. We got them as hatchlings from the Daggerfoot Orcs."

"Aren't they dangerous?" Duncan asked. As he asked Red nuzzled his hand wanting to be petted. Red seemed to grin showing a mouth full of razor-sharp teeth.

"Aye, of course they are dangerous, that's why we got them, but only if they don't know ya. If you can get them fresh outta the egg they are pretty docile, the Daggerfoots ave it down tae an art. They're great for guarding the place at night. Just some of the surprises I was telling ya about." Wildbeard finished with a toothy grin. He then grabbed a couple of dead rats from a locked bin and tossed them to the raptors, who greedily gobbled them up. Red held a rat in his clawed hands and savagely tore the foot long rat in half with two bites.

They then went back to their corner of the vault and laid down in the pile of vegetation they had built into a nest. Red then began to chirp a merry little tune punctuated by the taps of his claws.

Wildbeard grunted at him as he turned away. "Stupid things canna make up their minds if their birds or lizards," he said to no one in particular.

Duncan shook his head at the absurdity of it. Here was a

predator that could probably disembowel a horse with one kick, singing along like a tiny sparrow in a tree.

"Dunna let Red fool ya though. He can be downright vicious if he doesn't know ya and ya enter his territory. Ya probably would ave been dead before ya hit the ground iffen ya came in here alone," Wildbeard said with a wink.

Duncan grunted in response. "I can imagine." Sweettooth was still licking blood off her jaws.

"Now, which one was it?" Wildbeard muttered to himself as he scanned a wall full of drawers. "Ah here it is," he said as he selected a drawer from a bank of them along the wall. He quickly unlocked it and pulled it free. He then placed the drawer on the only table in the room. Wildbeard beckoned Duncan over. "This is it lad. Whatcha came all this way to see." The Dwarve removed a two-foot square box from the drawer and pushed the empty drawer away.

"May I?" Duncan asked. Wildbeard stepped aside so that the big man could examine the box. Duncan gingerly unlocked the clasp and it opened with a creak.

The inside was a large map of the known world and some bits that weren't known. The map itself was made up of hundreds of moveable type, precisely arranged to form the layout of the world. Each piece was intricately detailed down to the smallest geographic feature. Several of the pieces had ancient Elven hieroglyphs arranged on them. No other language was present.

The Dwarves had neatly arranged the type to form the map. The map showed several places not shown on any other map, including several chains of islands to the south across the Meridiem Ocean and a large stretch of desert to the far southeast. In the top right corner, the pieces had aligned to show several lines of elvish.

"As ya can see, it's just a map o' the world," Wildbeard said. "We dunna know what those hieroglyphs say. But even without them we were able tae piece it together." He pulled out his pipe and lit it. The Dwarve took a few satisfied puffs as Duncan examined the map. Wildbeard sputtered as the big man began moving pieces around. "Err now, what're ya doing?" he asked.

"It's you that can't read elvish. I can and this map was put together wrong." Duncan answered

"Whata ya mean?"

"See this, it basically translates as: If you can read this the map is wrong," Duncan said pointing to the first line in the right corner. "The rest of the glyphs up here are directions to arrange the pieces so that the rest of these random hieroglyphs scattered about make sense. The map was not meant to be an actual representation of the world but a list of landmarks and directions."

"Directions to what?" Wildbeard rapidly puffed on his pipe and stared at the type trying to will them to reveal their secrets.

"I don't know yet. It's not just these glyphs. The elves relied heavily on arrangement and symbols. Trying to read without the hieroglyphs arranged properly is like trying to read with every other letter missing."

Wildbeard looked on fascinated as Duncan slid the map pieces around. After almost an hour Duncan announced he was finished. Wildbeard peered at the map. It was now a jumble of random pieces scattered about with no apparent reason. The only bit of order now was that the glyphs that had been previously scattered about were now joined with the others.

"What's it say now?" Wildbeard asked. The tension in the Dwarve's voice was clear. He had spent the better part of the hour pacing and smoking and asking if Duncan was finished yet.

"Well, now we can figure that out. You saw the borders of the map are lined up with numbers?"

"Aye, map coordinates or so we thought."

"Well, they are, and they aren't. When it's a map they are the correct coordinates for that location, latitude, and longitude. When it was a map you had these pictures scattered about birds, animals, representatives of the different races and various objects. Now with the glyphs we can use the coordinates to locate the right picture and it forms a complete sentence." Duncan furrowed his brow as he stared at the puzzle box. "Interesting...the starting location is listed as Hammerfall Lake." Duncan began translating and copying the directions down. When he finished, he let out a low whistle.

"What is it?" Wildbeard asked exasperated. He couldn't read the puzzle box himself and it was obvious it annoyed him greatly.

"It leads to the last Elven city."

Wildbeard sucked in a loud breath. "The lost city of Naacada Niwt?"

Duncan slowly nodded as he stared at the type. "Yes, the same."

Wildbeard stood stunned for a second before answering. "That place is more myth and legend than location." The Dwarve stood for several minutes stroking his massive red beard and smoking his pipe as he stared at the puzzle box. "Well, how's about we leave in the morning," he finally said.

Duncan cocked an eyebrow at the Dwarve. "We?"

"Aye, we. I'll be damned iffen ya think I'm gonna miss this."

"What about your work here? Will the curator just let you pick up and leave?" Duncan asked.

"I dunna know. I'll ask him." The Dwarve turned and faced a

wall. "Curator Wildbeard?" he said.

"Yes, Curator Wildbeard?" Wildbeard answered himself in a slightly more formal tone.

"Iffen it please ya I would like to accompany dis here human to the lost Elven city. Ya knows the one we ave been looking for information about most of our lives." The Dwarve said switching back to his normal voice.

"That will be fine Curator Wildbeard."

"Thank you, Curator Wildbeard," he said with a mischievous grin. "Well, I gots permission tae go."

"You never said you were curator," Duncan stated.

"And ya never bothered tae ask what I do 'err either." Wildbeard said with a wink.

Duncan let out a deep laugh. "Fair enough, I suppose. Now how about a beer? I'm feeling a bit parched."

"Aye lad, yer singing me song. Come on. I'm buying."

Chapter Twenty-one

By the AllFather I hate boats, Warrec thought to himself.

It seemed for almost half a year now he had been stuck on a boat. First, it was on a barge heading up to Thornglade, then heading back down to Eldurond. Then he was on a little river runner for almost ten days traveling down to the coast even though the captain had assured them it would only be four. Then it was on this leaking hulk for the past two weeks. Ever since they had set out on the Meridiem Ocean, he had felt like he had been seasick.

He had hated the confinement of the river runner. Those tiny barges were barely two hundred feet long and forty wide. Heading down river from the capital they were heavily laden with goods packed and stacked everywhere and anywhere space was available. He had to walk sideways to squeeze through the tight packed artificial corridors. It was almost like walking through a maze.

Heading upstream the barges were usually pulled from shore by teams of oxen or horses. Occasionally sails could be used on a blustery day, but the current north of Eldurond was usually fairly strong, strong enough to overcome a little wind. So mostly they were pulled. It was slow but steady.

Heading south was worse. South of Eldurond the Zaphan spread wide across the land creating the wide Zaphan Delta before turning into the Zaptira Mire further south and east. There on the western edge of the delta the current was almost nonexistent. In the delta the sailors had to use long poles to help push the boats along as what little current there was barely kept the boats meandering along.

Warrec had felt trapped on the boat. Unable to move about and stretch he had sweltered in the delta heat. Swarms of biting flies and mosquitoes feasted on them as they crawled down the river. The sailors kept huge jip leaf fronds around the boat and jars of gum-gum oil opened to help keep the flies away. They worked a little, except against the most persistent ones. For most of the trip they had lain in their hammocks encased in mosquito netting.

He had brought a few books to read on the trip, a book on the finer points of swordsmanship, a collection of humorous Dwarven stories, and a discussion on the social characteristics of the different races. He had finished the Dwarven book before they had reached Snetha, even reading several stories twice to find the hidden meaning those Dwarven writers were so fond of adding. However, since they had transferred to the carrack and hit the open ocean, he had spent too much time leaning over the side to do much reading.

The Silver Cloud was a heavy four mast carrack, square-rigged, with a smaller lateen-rig sail behind the mizzenmast and was built for gliding seamlessly across open ocean. At least that's what Captain Kral Obar had said. Warrec was beginning to suspect that the good-natured captain was a liar, what with the way the ship pitched and rolled.

Oh, how he missed the river runner now. He couldn't turn around without bumping into someone or something, but at least then the bloody boat didn't jump or threaten to capsize every two minutes.

"Warrec, hey Warrec," Aluna called as she walked up beside him. Warrec merely grunted an acknowledgement at her as he leaned over the railing. "Still not feeling any better?"

Warrec ran the back of his hand across his mouth. "Well, if you mean, have I stopped trying to puke up everything I've eaten in the last ten years then yeah, I feel better."

"Oh, you poor thing," she said as she rubbed his back. "Were you able to keep the soup down?"

"Yeah, for the moment. I'm still queasy though."

"Well, that's good." Aluna suddenly squealed in excitement. "Oh look, look dolphins. Look Warrec, look. Wow, look at them jump. They seem so happy and carefree. Not a care in the world." Aluna clapped her hands together in glee as she watched the pod jump and dance in the wake of the ship.

Warrec didn't bother to look. "Good for the bloody dol…" Warrec started to mumble but was cut off as a bout of nausea hit him. Through sheer force of will he kept himself from throwing up again. Now, he did look, as a large dolphin leapt and flipped through the air. "I want to stab it," he growled. Right now, he pretty much hated everything and everyone.

Aluna lightly slapped his shoulder. "Oh hush, you're just being grumpy now."

"Hey, what's all the hubbub bub?" Joenair said as he came sauntering up, bare feet slapping against the deck. He was chewing on a piece of jerky and washing it down with a bottle of rum. He wore a loose pair of black pantaloons and an unbuttoned grey shirt. Given a parrot and an eyepatch and the master spy could pass easily as a stereotypical pirate.

"I just don't see how you can eat and drink like that," Warrec said as he wiped his mouth again.

"Just a matter of getting your sea legs Warrec me boy," he said as he did a couple of quick squats.

Warrec growled at him. "Well, it would be easier to get my sea legs, if the bloody boat would quit rocking back and forth."

"Ship," Joenair said as he took another sip of rum.

"What?" Warrec asked in a cynical tone.

"Ship, it's a ship," Joenair replied. "Boats travel on freshwater like rivers and such. Ships travel on saltwater like the ocean here,"

"Jay sometimes I really, really, really hate you," Warrec said glaring at his friend. Joenair just grinned.

"I don't think that's right," Aluna said. "Boats are just smaller. A ship can carry a boat but not the other way around," Aluna corrected Joenair.

Joenair cocked an eyebrow at her in surprise, but then nodded his head ever slightly towards her. He then just shrugged dismissing the whole thing. "Well, I guess it really isn't fair. I did grow up on the coast in Artania. Been sailing since I was a kid," Joenair said still grinning at Warrec.

"I didn't know you were from Artania. Was your father a fisherman?" Aluna asked.

Joenair laughed. "No, if he had been a fisherman we would have lived in Snetha. Artania is a bit ritzy for a fisherman. No, my father was an architect, and my mother was a singer. Well, they were my adopted parents."

"Oh. What happened to your real parents? If...if you don't mind me asking?" Aluna asked.

Joenair took a bite of jerky and chewed for a moment before answering. "Well, I was adopted when I was a baby, still in diapers. My folks said that my birth mother had been a maid in the royal palace. My real father had supposedly been a member of the Senate, a lower noble or some such and had gotten her pregnant.

"She had been forced to flee to avoid a scandal and couldn't take care of me. I never met her; they said she died shortly after. My adopted father always suspected that she was murdered though. I'm just one of hundreds of bastards scattered across the empire, the product of aristocracy dalliances."

Aluna placed her hand over her mouth afraid that she had overstepped some boundary. "Oh, I'm so sorry. I didn't mean to…"

Joenair waved a hand dismissing the thought. "No...no it's ok. Like I said I was a baby. I don't remember any of it, so it doesn't bother me to talk about it. Though it's not a particularly interesting story, like I said there are probably hundreds of others who have the same one." Joenair smiled at her and waved the bottle dismissively again before taking another swig.

"Did they ever tell you who your father was?" she asked. Now that she knew Joenair would talk about it she tried to probe for more information.

Joenair stared off at the horizon slowly chewing on the last bite of jerky. "No, they didn't know, and I never really cared to find out. I figured it was best just to leave it alone.

My parents are wonderful and the only ones as far as I'm concerned," he said smiling.

"I'm going to go lay down," Warrec grunted. The big man took two steps away from the rail and staggered one to the side before freezing in place. He doubled over and through sheer force of will kept from dry heaving. A low grunt, half growl escaped his lips before he continued on and slowly made his way back to his hammock below deck. Tiredness overtook him and he managed to fall asleep within minutes.

Joenair shook his head and quietly laughed to himself as he watched his friend disappear into the bowels of the ship. He then looked over at Aluna. With a flip of his wrist and if by magic he produced a shiny green apple. Aluna huffed and rolled her eyes not at all impressed. Joenair laughed again and shrugged. He then sliced off a piece and offered it to her before cutting one for himself.

No point delaying this any longer, he thought. This was a conversation that needed to be said and things needed to be addressed. There hadn't really been any chance to talk to her alone without the big guy within earshot until now. Joenair doubled checked to make sure she wasn't armed.

*I mean you could delay it, she isn't going anywhere, *

another mental voice chimed in.

Let it play out, it will be interesting

No, I couldn't do that to War; he would do the same for me.

*You wouldn't get yourself in this position to begin with. We don't get tied down, that's the rule remember. *

*Maybe you should sleep with her instead. * Joenair paused. Now there was a thought. If he slept with Aluna that might break her out of her infatuation. It was tempting, even if she could and probably would break him in half.

She had gone back to wearing her travel poncho and chaps as soon as they had left Eldurond, something that he couldn't help but notice. Granted it was a more durable and practical outfit for travel than a lady's dress. But he also couldn't help but notice her breasts threatened to spill out the sides.

*No, that might make things worse. That'll just make things much messier. Don't skret where you eat, remember. *

*She wants Warrec to see her boobies, not you. *

And I don't think that guy fell down the stairs

Agreed, Aluna is off limits. Now that the mental conference had come to an agreement it was time to have a talk with the barbarous beauty and hope she actually listened and didn't just throw him overboard.

Joenair turned and leaned back against the rail, casually watching the crew go about their duties. Aluna continued to stare out at the endless ocean. They both chewed in silence for a moment. When he finally spoke, his demeanor was much more somber and serious. "Aluna why are you here?"

Aluna gave a start at the question and swallowed the remains of the apple slice. "What...what do you mean?" she choked out.

Joenair sliced the apple again before answering. "You know exactly what I mean. Why are you here?" He emphasized her with the point of the knife, but not in a threatening manner.

Aluna turned away and rubbed at her arm. The dolphins had disappeared back into the brine, and she suddenly didn't seem to feel as comfortable and content as she had a moment ago.

"I still don't understand what you mean," she said. "I'm here to help you two...on your...on your mission."

She is going to make this difficult, typical woman won't ever just come out and say what they mean. Joenair sighed as he realized he was going to have to pry the statement out of her. "Look I didn't argue too much back in Eldurond, though of course you did pull a knife on me."

"I was coming with you two no matter what," she said. "I... wasn't going to use the knife though. It was...it was just for show." Aluna gave him a half smile.

Joenair shook his head at her. "I knew you weren't." He gave a half laugh. "At least I hoped you weren't. You northerners can be pretty stubborn. But that's exactly my point. Why were you so hell bent on coming along?"

Aluna answered with a half shrug. "I thought I could help."

"How exactly? Sure, you can wield magic and all, but you are untrained in this sort of thing. Hell, you had never even left The Lake before. You have no place on a mission like this."

Joenair pointed the tip of the knife at the hatch Warrec had disappeared into. "That man is one of the most dangerous men alive in the empire today. Doubtful he realizes it himself, but I have personally seen him perform feats bordering on the extraordinary to the miraculous, to the downright impossible. After seeing his father in action, I have to think it's a family trait, which scares me even more."

Joenair paused for a second and sighed, his voice dropping to a near whisper, carrying just far enough for her alone to hear. "And I may not look it, but I'm no slouch myself. My point being he doesn't need a babysitter and neither do I." Joenair tossed another slice of apple into his mouth chewing loudly.

Aluna glared in defiance at him. "What are you trying to say? I can be of great help. Warrec needs me."

"Ah, there now we come to it." Joenair grinned at her, but it wasn't a pleasant smile. He had spent a long time perfecting that smile; the, you just fell into my trap smile. "I know exactly why you came, and it was for him." Joenair traced a circle with the knifepoint a few times in the air in front of her before jabbing it at the hatch again. "I make my living reading people and you dear Aluna are as plain as day."

Aluna's lip started to curl up into a snarl and for half a moment Joenair thought he had pressed too hard, that she was about to seize him and throw him overboard.

His body slightly tensed, but he couldn't show it, he had to maintain his cool, this was the make it or break it moment. He could see the rage burning behind those green eyes, but then her shoulders slumped, and she let out a long-exasperated sigh. Joenair cocked an eyebrow at her, ready to spring away, if need be, but mentally he let out a sigh of relief, he had won.

Defeated Aluna gave her statement that he had been trying to pry from her. "I love him. Ok, I said it. I love that big, stubborn, annoying, wonderful man. I... I lost him for so many years and... I won't lose him again." Aluna hugged herself and stared down at the deck. "Happy now?"

He felt like a jackass. That what he wanted, for her to admit it. The tiny victory tasted bitter in his mouth and suddenly he wasn't hungry anymore. Joenair tossed the rest of the apple into the water.

"No, I'm not happy, but it needed to be said by you and heard I guess by me. Not like you were going to tell Warrec anyway."

Aluna sighed. "Was it that obvious?"

Joenair nodded. "To me yes. To anyone else probably. To Warrec? More than likely not. The big guy doesn't really pick up on that sort of thing. Hell, it took Addie months of dropping hints before he even noticed. Then she still had to make the first move."

Aluna leaned back on the rails still holding herself. "Addie. Adelia. Ambassador Adelia Flavius. Warrec's fiancée. Perfect Addie." Aluna spoke slowly and deliberately, mulling the words over in her mouth as she spoke. "She is...nice. I like her. As much as I wanted to and tried, I couldn't dislike the woman."

Joenair turned and gripped the rails. "Addie, Warrec's fiancée, everyone likes her. She is one of the kindest, sweetest, most caring people you could ever meet...and one of the most naive. After you strong-armed your way onto the mission, I told her. And do you know what she said?" Aluna shook her head but didn't want to ask.

Joenair continued on not giving her a chance to speak. "She said oh good. Warrec will have an old friend along with you to help watch out for him. I like Aluna and even though I just meet her I feel like I can trust her." Joenair shook his head. "Trust her. Most women would have been jealous and probably rightfully so, but not Addie. She trusts everyone. I had my suspicions about you; maybe I should have said something then."

He shot a sideways glance at her. Aluna looked like she felt awful and was unsure what to say. He waited, letting the guilt eat at her. Finally, she asked. "What are you going to do? Are you going to tell Warrec?"

Joenair pushed back upright from the rail and turned to walk away. "Me? No, I'm not going to say anything, and neither are you. This conversation never happened. We keep on like normal. You love him? Good and fine. Love him like a brother like I do. We're just one big happy family." Joenair turned and pointed a finger in her face, his voice dropping into a harsh whisper again. "Because he is like a brother to me and no one and I mean no one is going to hurt him. He loves Addie and she loves him, so unless some act of fate or the gods steps in that's going to be the end of it."

Aluna started to speak, but Joenair cut her off. "Don't mistake my bumbling carefree attitude for incompetence. It's all an act. I am very, very, good at what I do. I like you Aluna, I really do. I want us to be good friends. But you will not break his heart. Am I clear?"

The northern fire sparked in her eyes again for a moment, northerners always had that defiant kneejerk. Then just as quickly it died out. She knew he was right and getting angry and trying to bluff him wouldn't do her any good. He made sure there was an icy coldness in his eyes that she had never seen before. Most people that did see it didn't continue to breathe for much longer after seeing it.

Aluna slowly nodded in agreement. Joenair smiled and just like that he was back to normal. "Good. I'm glad we never had this conversation. I'm going to go grab a nap. I'll see you at dinner." With that he half bounded like a child across the deck and disappeared into the hold.

Chapter Twenty-two

Aluna drooped over the port railing bored out of her mind.

The monotony of ocean travel was beginning to wear heavily on her. The first few days and even weeks had been wonderful. The ocean reminded her of Hammerfall Lake with its expanse and waves and the wind coming over the water, but the smell was much nicer, cleaner. Except on The Lake, you never really got out of sight of land, between the shoreline and the thousands of islands spread across it. In fact, there were only a few spots on The Lake where you could sail more than a day without seeing at least a rock jutting out of the water.

They had been on the ocean for almost six and a half weeks now and there was nothing, nothing but blue sky, blue water, a hot burning sun and an occasional white cloud. Day in and day out, it was the same thing over and over. The waves rolled against the ship pitching it back and forth. The sun beat down mercilessly with the only reprieve granted by the steady salt infused wind.

There had been a bit of occasional wildlife and that had

helped break up the repetitiveness. They had spotted a couple different pods of various whales. At one point Captain Obar had dropped the whaling boats and they had taken one of them, a smaller one of twenty feet. The captain had explained it helped stretch out the rations.

Aluna hadn't wanted to complain, she was tired of eating hardtack and pemmican. Fresh meat was a welcome addition, though she hadn't quite cared for the oily taste. It was a weird combination of red meat and fish tastes, like an oily, fishy steak.

Stupid Warrec had finally stopped getting seasick about four weeks in, which was also about the time the crew had killed the whale. She was convinced the fresh meat and fat had finally settled his stomach. Stupid Warrec had still complained though and had kept in a state of various grumpiness.

Aluna smiled to herself. *He is cute when he is grumpy,* she thought. *I wonder if Perfect Addie thinks he is cute when he is grumpy.* As the idle thought slipped through her brain, she snapped her head up looking around. She wasn't one to frighten easily, if at all, but Joenair had managed to do it.

He had scared the skret out of her; she would never forget those eyes. This seemed odd to her, because since then he had been as nice as ever. *Which probably makes him even scarier. Scary Joenair, that doesn't really fit, he isn't scary, but that's what makes him scary.* She shivered slightly, there was Joenair and then there was Scary Joenair. It was almost like they were two different people.

She shook her head. She was a predator. She stalked the forest and night was her domain. Which was probably why Scary Joenair now bothered her so much. She had seen into him for a moment and had seen a fellow predator, one that was better at stalking and killing than her.

"Land ho," the crewman in the crow's nest shouted. Aluna snapped her head up to look at him and then tried to follow his gaze out. She still couldn't see anything. She turned and made her way up the deck to the stern. Looking up she saw Stupid Warrec and Joenair were talking with Captain Obar, and she moved to join them.

Captain Obar stood tall and lanky, projecting absolute authority over his floating kingdom. He was a dictator but a carefree and good natured one. She had only seen him have to discipline one of the crew once. One of the sailors had tried to sneak a couple extra rations of grog and been caught. Obar had spent a good twenty minutes explaining why this wasn't good for the sailor, the crew, or the ship, before handing out the standard ten lashings. The sailor had even thanked the captain afterward.

Obar crossed his arms and chewed on a cobaco stem. His coal

black skin glistened with sweat. The captain didn't seem to be bothered by the sun at all and often went about shirtless as he was now. Only a small cloak of command covered his left shoulder. Other than a pair of linen trousers and a red kerchief tied around his bald head it was the only clothing he normally wore.

He was a Corithan, natural sailors like her people, but from the Scattered Isles off the southeastern coast. There were a few other Corithans mixed amongst the crew, and they all seemed to share the same carefree disposition. They were a bit odd and smelled funny, but nice enough for the most part, except for Denvar.

He had shown himself to be a problem fairly quickly when a few days in he had decided that Aluna would be the perfect woman to share his hammock. At first, she had tried to turn him down gently, but he had been insistent and grabby. Luckily, she had stopped herself before she had hurt him too much. Denvar got to keep living with only a broken arm and two missing teeth.

He had told everyone he had fallen going down into the hold. Aluna hadn't bothered to correct him. She hadn't wanted to make it a big deal for one and she was fairly certain that either Stupid Warrec or Scary Joenair would have killed the man, which could have caused problems on the ship.

"So, what's the plan captain," Stupid Warrec said.

Obar chewed on his stem for a moment before shooting a stream of brown spittle into a nearby brass spittoon. "Seems to me, the best course of action is to sail a bit closer in and then cut sails and wait for them to come out to us. We don't want to be rude and show up unannounced." The captain punctuated the sentence with another stream of spittle. "Ah, Lady Aluna greetings to you," Obar said with a bow as she joined them. The others nodded to her.

"How long do you think we will have to wait," she asked.

Obar shrugged. "Seems to me it's hard to say miss, could be hours, could be days. These are the approximate coordinates they told us to return to. Here we are, now we wait for them."

It was early morning of the next day before the Kathari came out to greet them. Six weeks and five days after leaving the port of Snetha the Silver Cloud finished her voyage across the Meridiem and pulled into the harbor of the capital city of the Kathari Empire. This morning three large Kathari junks had met their carrack and guided them into port. As the ship's crew began unloading the trade goods it had brought; Stupid Warrec, Aluna and Joenair stood at the rail of the ship and marveled.

"This isn't exactly what our reports said," Stupid Warrec said.

Joenair nodded in agreement. "When that merchant ship that first made contact several months ago returned, they had given reports of a primitive fishing village. The Kathari had been dressed simply and their ships were small fishing boats and out rigger canoes. The reports had given the impression that the Kathari were a primitive race with poor technology and no large cities. The reports were wrong, very wrong."

"It looks as big as Eldurond," Aluna said.

"Bigger," Joenair said. He gazed at the bustling port looking up and down the waterline. "I can hardly believe it, but I think this port is even bigger than the harbor in Snetha." It was filled with ships of all shapes and sizes from small two-man fishing boats to two and three mast ships. "There are so many you could practically walk across the harbor."

As their ship was guided into its berth by a large tug, teaming with so many oars it looked like an odd aquatic porcupine, Aluna could see the docks were swarming with the cat like people. The docks were filled with the Kathari moving about loading and unloading cargo. The noise and rapid pace of the dock began to die down as word spread of the human ship amongst them.

Stupid Warrec let out a low whistle as he looked over the city. "Definitely bigger than Eldurond. Just look at it stretch out as far as you can see." Most of the city appeared to be constructed of one- or two-story buildings. The buildings had high arched roofs that looked to be covered in green or grey tile with eaves that sloped out far over the streets. Several pagodas rose up throughout the city dominating the skyline. The city looked almost to be on fire as the cherry blossoms were in full bloom throughout the capital.

Aluna smiled at the grand beauty of it all. Eldurond had been impressive, but she wouldn't have called it beautiful. Eldurond favored utility and function over form. There were of course some magnificent artwork and architecture scattered throughout, but it wasn't common and was proudly displayed. Here the Kathari seemed to celebrate the form of everything. Every building, every tree, the dock warehouses, roadways, everything she could see was built to be its own piece of art.

As she took in the grandeur of the city, she noticed what appeared to be a group of Kathari soldiers making their way through the crowd towards them. She elbowed Stupid Warrec at the same time Joenair did. He grunted glaring at them both but then nodded.

The soldiers were like nothing Aluna had ever seen before. They wore armor, but it was different than the plate and chainmail she was used to. It did not have the metallic glint of steel plate or the blue-white tinge of valentium. The armor was a deep burgundy and at first glance appeared to be leather.

The soldiers carried long spears with what looked like short swords fixed on the end. On their side they carried two swords beside each other, one short and looked like a leaner version of her kukri. The other was called a katana, a long single edged and curved blade. They wore high domed helmets with a skirt of chainmail that covered their faces. Their armor gave the impression of being sturdy but also light.

"I suppose that's our welcome party," Joenair said. The three of them grabbed their belongings and made their way down the gangplank. At the bottom they were met by the soldiers.

Aluna could now see that the armor was made of several pieces of small metal plates coated in lacquer and woven in strips onto a jacket similar in design to the scale mail that most of the imperial foot soldiers wore. There were larger segmented pieces covering the limbs. The armor looked extremely flexible and did not seem to hinder the movement of its wearer in the slightest. With the color and segmented plates, it reminded Aluna a little of a crab.

A lone Kathari was leading in front of the soldiers. His fur was snow white with black stripes that crossed down his neck, disappearing into his clothing. His whiskers grew long and wispy drooping down the sides of his face like a long moustache. He wore no armor, only what appeared to be layered crimson and blue jackets that were bound by a large black silk belt. His pants were dark ebony, large and billowy and hid his feet. In his belt were two swords like the soldiers carried but these seemed more elaborate, more personal.

Aluna now noticed that the entire dock had grown silent and hundreds of inhuman eyes were watching them. It was a bit unnerving, but she steeled herself and forced herself to lock eyes with as many as she could. To her surprise several of the Kathari averted their gaze from her.

She was surprised by the size of the Kathari. Somehow, she had expected them to be taller, but most appeared to be shorter than her.

Aluna came from the Vatninu, from The Lake. Her people were known for their height and were considerably taller than the rest of the people of the empire. She was like her kin a tall woman herself. She was a little bit taller than Joenair who seemed to be of average height for a southern imperial male. Stupid Warrec stood a good head and a half above him and was much broader and heavier. Duncan was almost half a foot taller than Stupid Warrec and towered like a giant over all men. It seemed the Kathari, like almost everyone else would be dwarfed by her people. As the thousands of cat eyes watched her, this comforted her.

Most of the Kathari dockworkers that she could see looked like ordinary house cats. There were a few giants scattered out amongst them, several of them resembled the tigers and cave lions she had seen in the wilds close to her home. Some resembled cats she had only seen in drawings in books.

The one that was leading the soldiers looked like an elderly, though still well-muscled white tiger. His dark amber eyes traveled over the three of them and then settled back on Stupid Warrec. He strode forward with a swift easy confidence and stood eye to chin with the big man. He stopped a few feet from Stupid Warrec and placed his right clenched fist in his left hand and bowed. Stupid Warrec returned the gesture.

This seemed to please the tiger and he spoke something to all the Kathari around. His words seemed like the grunts and growls of a wild animal and not a civilized people. Aluna could sense the energy of the crowd shift from trepidation to curiosity.

The white tiger then turned back to them. "Welcome to the city of Olasanaka. I am Zareem. Please follow me to the palace, honored guests." He spoke with a well-articulated accent rarely heard outside the royal court of the Maroveyan Empire.

Before they could respond he turned and walked away. His soldiers parted before him waiting on the humans to follow.

Joenair leaned in close and whispered into Aluna's ear. "And away we go." The three of them quickly fell in step behind their escort and began making their way through the bustling streets of Olasanaka.

Aluna nodded and whispered to herself. "Definitely not at

The Lake anymore."

Chapter Twenty-three

Legate Silnis twisted the reins in his hand, wishing it was a neck. The black plume of horsehair from his helmet waved slightly in the cool breeze. Silnis wasn't quite sure whose neck he wanted to strangle, but he definitely believed there was someone that needed a good throttling. So far, this mission had been nothing but a wild goose chase.

Silnis had been dispatched a few days after Warrec and Joenair had set sail. King Valorn had graciously allowed Silnis to ride northwest to sniff around. He had believed them and had wanted someone to go, but now this whole thing was starting to stink.

Those two are going to be the death of me, I can feel it, he thought. They had been right of course, as bloody usual. If Argis was planning another attack they needed to know about it. Still, things weren't sitting well with him.

One thing was why, he himself, was he here. He commanded four legions, two primary and two support after all. When the king had denied Warrec and Joenair from coming up here, Silnis had been slightly surprised. This type of mission was right up their alley. He had been even more surprised when the king had been serious in sending him. Frankly, this mission was for someone beneath him and a waste of resources. He didn't know if the king had meant it as an insult, but it certainly felt like one.

The second thing was who had been dispatched along with him. The king and a few of his close advisors had personally handpicked the men for this mission. They had chosen a mix of some of Silnis' most trusted officers and raw green recruits, fifty men in all. None of them should have been here either, again a waste of resources.

Commander Ranir Saximius rode quietly beside him. The commander's brown eyes glared out from under his galea helm. Saximius was in charge of the fifth legion and wore the yellow plume proudly. He had no business being out here either.

"We shouldn't be out here," the commander said echoing Silnis' thoughts.

Silnis grunted in acknowledgement. "Do you mean you and I or all of us together," he asked.

Saximius paused a second before answering, considering the question. "Both. Between us and the other officers and" - Saximius swept his free hand over at the marching men- "and these children, the king couldn't have picked a more inappropriate group of soldiers." Saximius sighed as the green soldiers lost step and fell out of rhythm again. "They haven't even learned to march properly."

"I noticed," Silnis said. He sighed as Master Sergeant Garsham bellowed and yelled at the men to get back in step. There was another man that had more important things to do than trying to get raw recruits to fall in formation while out in the field.

"The king said to ease my mind he would send me out with some of my best men," Silnis continued. "He also said this was the perfect opportunity to help train these new soldiers, help break them into legion life. He had said since there was obviously no threat of Argis returning right now it was the perfect way to quickly train these men up as they would be needed quickly to fight for the glory of the empire against his evil brother."

Saximius spit. "That's a load of skret if ever I heard one."

"Exactly. Still, we have been in the western kingdom for a couple weeks now and so far, there hasn't been any sign of The Dread Lord."

They had seen several signs of large volumes of traffic, mostly farmers and their families fleeing. They had seen many farms burned and several bodies of innocent people. For all intents and purposes all the signs pointed to King Ptharis' own men, which in itself seemed a little odd to Silnis.

Ptharis had a reputation for shrewdness. The western king was intelligent, far more so than any other person, but with his strange personality quirks it was always thought that the king was bordering on madness.

Silnis had only met the man a handful of times, but the reports of the king's eccentricities had been quite thorough. Ptharis had peculiar speech patterns and would often jump from one topic of conversation to another and back again. He abhorred being dirty and washed himself at least twice a day. He would only eat certain foods and with only certain dinnerware. One of the oddest things was the king would not sleep until he had climbed to the top of the tower keep and touched a certain merlon twenty-three times, exactly twenty-three.

Had he finally snapped, had Ptharis finally gone mad? Was he sending his troops to slaughter his own people and burn his own farms? Everything seemed to point to that. Yes, it appeared that he had gone insane and was killing and pillaging his people for some twisted reason and that's what bothered Silnis.

There seemed to be almost too much evidence, almost as if he was being baited into believing it. There were too many tracks in some places, pieces of equipment specific to the western army left behind, things that no soldier would leave…

unless it was supposed to be found.

He shook his head. "Perhaps I'm just being paranoid," he mumbled to himself. Still, he couldn't shake the feeling that something was off and then there was the other thing.

Right before they had left King Valorn decided that several members of his personal royal guard would accompany them. Silnis had no objections to this at the time. He could always use more men if they did encounter anything, especially with the men he had been given, but it just seemed odd. The king had never sent his guard out like this before.

His royal guards also made no attempt to integrate themselves into the unit either. They were polite of course, when given a task they set to it with a cheerful and helpful disposition almost to the point of a sycophant. Still, they kept to themselves and whispered amongst themselves, whispers that would quickly cease whenever he or one of his men drew near.

He shook his head again. "I am... I am definitely being paranoid. I have no reason to distrust them." Silnis spoke as if he was trying to convince himself, but he just couldn't shake his gut feeling. He had survived too many battles to not trust his instincts and right now his instincts told him something wasn't right. He just couldn't figure out what it was.

"All right!" he bellowed. "Let's set down and make camp for the night." He pulled his horse to a stop and his men followed suit. Fenix Actoris, the Legate of the royal guards came riding up to his side and raised his faceplate. That was another thing that Silnis didn't like. Fenix didn't have any business being here as far as he was concerned.

Fenix had spent his entire career safe behind the capital's walls. Over the last few years, he had passed on field duty time and time again, but still had managed to climb the ranks in the city guards. Now he was at an equivalent rank to Silnis. While he seemed capable at his job, Silnis didn't have much use for the man and yet here he was a thorn in his side.

Fenix was pretty, far too pretty to be a soldier. Brown hair and blue eyes combined with his clean shaven and chiseled face allowed Fenix to dance through life completely oblivious to the difficulties life presented for most people. Both charismatic and amiable Fenix generally found most people agreeing with him. It was a face that had known little difficulty or strife. It was the type of face Silnis wanted to punch the teeth in.

Fenix, like the rest of the royal guard, wore full plate. Similar to the suits the knights and heavy shock troops wore. A deep purple crescent plume rose from Fenix's full helm, matching the purple cloaks of the royal guard. Plate was expensive and the fact that they all had full suits grated on Silnis' nerves.

Silnis still wore his old segmentata. The bands of

horizontal and vertical steel had been more than enough to keep him alive all these years. Equipping all the royal guard in full plate was a display of ostentation that just ate at him. He could have fully outfitted an entire squad for the same price as one of those suits and here were fifteen of them that normally set around doing nothing in the royal palace.

"We should move on just a little further to make camp," Fenix said. He smiled pleasantly, he always smiled pleasantly.

"Why the hell, do you think we should do that?" Commander Saximius said. The commander glowered with steely eyes. Silnis probably should have chastised Saximius for the tone, Fenix did technically out rank the commander, but he felt the same way. Silnis was tired and didn't feel like trying to explain himself or hide his dislike of the man.

Fenix sniffed but ignored the harshness in the commander's tone. "My uncle had a small hunting lodge out here some many years ago. When I was younger, he took me hunting out here. I know that there is a small outcropping of rocks up ahead. It would provide a more defendable place and would shield us from the night wind."

"You sure about that Legate Actoris," Silnis asked. He overemphasized Fenix's rank, pronouncing it almost as an insult, but then sighed as he realized he was being childish and petty.

Fenix smiled pleasantly. Either he had completely missed

the insult or was taking the high road and ignoring it. "Yes, I'm positive."

Silnis scratched absently at the weeks' worth of growth on his chin. Why *did Fenix even bother to shave every day out in the field*, he thought. "Fine, we'll move on up," he said.

Silnis didn't want to admit it, but logically it made sense. The rocks would make a better campsite than out on the open plain. *And it would be nice to have shelter; blocking the wind from freezing off my bollocks,* he added mentally.

He raised his voice for everyone to hear. "Alright boys change of plans. We're going to move on up a bit. Head up." The men pulled back into formation and continued marching.

About three miles later Silnis saw the outcropping of rocks that the captain had told him about. As they approached it the feeling in his gut had gotten worse, but he ignored it. Another odd thing the royal guards had taken up a defensive perimeter around the rest of the men.

He hadn't ordered them to do so, and he hadn't heard the master sergeant give the order either. Fenix had ridden with him to the rocks and hadn't given the order to his men. Though it did make sense he supposed the royal guard wore much heavier and stronger armor than the regular soldiers and would act as shields for the rest of the men. Perhaps they were trained to do so without command. Perhaps Fenix wasn't completely useless in the field after all.

His gut feeling got worse and warning bells started going off in his head. There was something about the rocks he didn't like. It was too fine a place for an ambush. They were now less than five hundred yards from the rocks. *Dammit I should have listened to my gut.* Silnis started to give the order to halt and form up into defensive formation, but the words froze in his throat.

Fire lanced through his side from his armpit. He twisted and saw Fenix pulling a dagger back wet with blood. Silnis tried to draw his sword, but Fenix swung the blade in a backhanded blow knocking Silnis from his saddle. His helmet had caught the strike, but he couldn't keep his balance and hit the ground hard. As he fell the words "always assume it's a trap" rang over and over in his mind. He had drilled that into countless soldiers over the years.

From out behind the rocks several Savan warriors came charging out accompanied by several dozen Goblins. There was no time to retreat. Silnis groaned and tried to prop himself up on his good arm. "You stupid old bastard, should have listened to your own futten advice," he groaned to himself.

"Shield wall!" Saximius bellowed the order as he drew his sword and the men crudely formed a defensive line, spears and shields out, to meet the oncoming enemy. Silnis rolled on the ground trying to get his legs to work properly. He turned as he heard approaching horses. Two dozen centaur cavalry were charging him from behind. The Royal Guard slammed into his men from the sides. It was too late he had walked straight into an ambush, and they were now trapped.

Chapter Twenty-four

Sasha had no idea how long the horsemen had run after destroying her home. How long it had been since her parents died? How long since her sister had died or how long since her brothers had died? How long since her home had burned? How long since her world had ended?

I'm going to die, she thought. It wasn't a thought her little ten-year-old mind had ever thought before or one that she thought could actually happen. She had seen death before. She had even helped Daddy when he butchered one of the goats one time. But the thought she or Daddy or Mommy or her brothers or Manya could die, didn't seem possible. *Then, in a couple of minutes, it had.*

She sat curled in the dusty, dirty sack bouncing against the horseman's side as he ran for hours upon hours. She hadn't cried, couldn't cry, but she shook and trembled. She didn't even really feel scared anymore, she just felt numb.

She could hear them as they ran. They spoke in a harsh guttural language, punctuated by a series of clicks. She had no idea what they said, but it didn't sound nice. Every now and then, the one carrying her would say something and slap the bag she was in a few times. This always seemed to make the other horsemen laugh.

She hated their laughter, hated them. That was something new as well. She had never hated anyone before. She had gotten mad a bunch of times especially when one of her brothers had dumped one of the water buckets on her head. They had liked to do that. Though that wasn't something that would ever make her mad again now.

Sasha sucked in a ragged breath. She wished she wasn't so little, wished she was big, wished she could fight. Daddy had been big though and they had killed him just the same. She hugged her knees and squeezed her eyes shut hard, trying to push the image of her father's face looking up at her from the strawberry basket out of her mind. Blood, there had been so much blood.

"Please," she whispered. "Please help me." Sasha didn't really know how to pray or who to pray to.

Mommy had come from the south and had lots of gods. She had a little shrine in her bedroom with little wooden dolls in it. Sasha had gotten in big bad trouble the one time she had been playing with the dolls. Mommy had been very mad about that. Sasha couldn't remember any of the names of the little god dolls though.

Daddy had come from the big, big lake far to the east and over the mountains. He used to tell her stories of The Lake and she had always wanted to see it. He had promised that someday he was going to take her there. That was never going to happen now.

Daddy had said there were lots of little gods, but really there was just one big god that had made everything and was in charge, all the other gods worked for him. Daddy had said that the big god was the father of everything and that's why he was called the AllFather.

"If you're going to pray, you might as well pray to the boss," Sasha whispered what her father had always said.

She started to pray again but then stopped. She hated the horsemen, hated them. As much as she wanted to get away, she wanted them to hurt. Like she had hurt, she wanted them to hurt more, she wanted them dead. "Please," she prayed. "Please make them pay." She wasn't sure if her prayer worked, or if anyone heard. The horsemen just kept running.

It was well past dark when they finally stopped. Sasha felt her bag being picked up and then she was tossed to the ground. She landed with a thump and let out a whimper, which brought forth a chorus of rough laughter.

A cruel hand reached into the bag and seized her by the hair. The horseman dragged her out of the sack and pulled her off the ground towards his face. Sasha grabbed at his hand, but more to help hold herself up than get away. Her hair hurt so badly as he picked her up, it felt like her scalp was going to come off.

He pulled her close to his face and barked a few words before holding up a crude-looking knife to her face. Her eyes grew wide as she looked at the foot long blade. She could see his face well now and noticed it didn't look as normal as she had thought.

The horseman's eyes were big, shiny, and black. They weren't people eyes. The thin moustaches at the corners of his mouth wiggled back and forth. One lifted up and brushed against her face. The worst thing though was his mouth. The teeth were sharp and black, and his mouth seemed to open both sideways and up and down, splitting in half.

The horseman turned her to look at the bonfire in the middle of their camp. It looked like they were getting a spit and roast ready for cooking. The horseman holding her laughed again and tossed her back to the dirt.

They're going to eat me, she thought. Sasha sat on the ground and hugged her knees, rocking slightly back and forth.

She looked around but couldn't see anything beyond the glow of firelight. They were on a flat grassy plain with nothing around. Once he had tossed her away, the horseman and the others seemed to ignore her and busied themselves with drinking a foul-smelling drink. *I can't run. Where would I run to? They would catch me again before I even got away from the fire.*

Wait. The word suddenly appeared in her mind. Had she thought it? She wasn't sure, but now a sense of calm seemed to wash over her.

A burst of angry shouting made her freeze. Carefully she turned to look at where the noise had come from. Two of the horsemen had started fighting.

They bounced back and forth, slamming their backs together against the glossy blue, black plates there. Each time they did there was a high-pitched squeal as the plates rubbed against each other. Finally, one of them reared up on his hind legs and kicked with both front legs.

As the kick connected, the other horseman's head just seemed to pop. His head exploded in a shower of fleshy bits and green goo. It was disgusting and vile but watching him die made her smile.

The other horsemen stopped for a second before they all cheered. They seized the body of their fallen comrade and began tearing it apart. Once they had torn the body into chunks, they began searing it in the fire and then eating it.

The horsemen gorged on their friend and drank their drink. They completely ignored her as they feasted and drank and drank and drank some more. After a while they seemed to grow more and more sluggish. Then one by one they began to drop, falling asleep where they lay.

The one that had been carrying her dropped about ten feet away from her. He grunted and then he too fell asleep, snoring loudly. Sasha sat there watching him. She watched them all as they began snoring. She watched the knife he had shown her rising up and down in its sheath as he breathed.

Sasha chewed on her lip as she watched him. She wasn't sure how long she sat there trying to work up her nerve. Then something snapped inside her.

Slowly, she stood up. Her blood felt like it was on fire. The world itself seemed more detailed. She could see more clearly and hear everything around her. The putrid stench of the horsemen filled her nose, but it didn't make her feel sick. She smiled.

Without hesitation she walked over to the horseman and pulled his knife free. The big knife felt good in her hands and felt even better as it cut through the horseman's neck.

He grunted and gasped as a fountain of red blood and green ooze flowed out of his neck. His eyes briefly fluttered open as he clutched at his neck. After a few seconds he shuddered and lay still.

Sasha stared wide eyed at him watching him die. He saw her

before he went still. She made sure he saw her, made sure he knew it was her. As he rattled out his last wet breath, she kicked him in the face.

She stood over him for a few seconds, slowly breathing. Her body seemed to hum. She wanted to hurt them, wanted to lash out, smash them, kill them. "Kill them," she whispered. "Kill them all."

The light steadily grew as the rising sun crept over the eastern horizon. Sasha sat cross-legged on the ground in the horseman camp. Her back was to the dying bonfire, which was little more than a few smoldering embers now. The large knife sat cradled in her lap.

She watched wide eyed as the dawn sun rose. The sky and the clouds took on an orange, red and yellow glow. The grey evening sky seemed to retreat before the advancing dawn. It was the most beautiful sunrise she had ever seen.

All around her the corpses of the horsemen lay, dying in the same place they had fallen asleep. Not one of them had stirred as she had made her way through their ranks, slitting each throat one by one. The ground was now soaked in that putrid mix of their blood and the green ooze.

Sasha had felt like one of those wraiths in the ghost stories Daddy would sometimes tell late at night. A monster that caught unwary travelers, unlucky enough to be out after dark, when the mists would come rolling up from The Lake. It made her feel good, made her feel strong. She had been helpless, now she wasn't. The horsemen had been helpless as she killed them, she had enjoyed it.

"Am I a monster now?" She didn't really know. Now she didn't really feel anything. Killing them had been right; she knew that they had deserved it. It was satisfying watching the panic and surprise in their eyes as their blood drained out. They had taken everything from her, and she had returned their actions back to them. "I'd rather have my family back," she quietly whispered.

Tears welled up in the corners of her eyes. "No, don't cry," she told herself. "Gotta be tough, be strong, don't...don't." Sasha broke.

Her body shuddered as she sucked in ragged breath after ragged breath. This wasn't crying like she had done before, when she had hurt herself or gotten really mad. This came from deep inside. She wailed. She screamed at the rising sun. Why, why had this happened? Why was she alive? Why, why, why. She screamed and wailed and cried till she passed out from sheer exhaustion.

When she opened her eyes again, she could see from the position of the sun that it was well past noon. A kettle of vultures circled lazily overhead. A sudden caw made her bolt upright.

A raven sat nearby on one of the bodies of the horsemen. It yelled at her again before going back and pecking at the body. It tore out a chunk and greedily swallowed it down. Sasha smiled.

"You're welcome, by the way." Sasha slowly stood up and gave a slight curtsy. As the provider of the feast, it was her job to be a gracious host. The raven cawed again as a large vulture landed nearby and started to hop walk his way over.

"I hope they taste good," Sasha said to the birds. "They don't look like they do though." A sudden rumble in her tummy made her realize she hadn't eaten anything since breakfast yesterday.

She checked a few of the bags the horsemen had been carrying. More and more carrion birds were starting to show up and she had to shoo a few of them out of the way as she checked. She didn't find any food other than some dubious jerky that she wasn't keen on trying; frankly, she didn't want to know where the jerky had come from.

The camp was beginning to reek, and more and more scavengers looked to be showing up. Sasha decided that she needed to be going, especially before something bigger than vultures and ravens showed up. Something showing up that might prefer fresh little girl to rotting horsemen.

Sasha grabbed the leather sheath and belt from the first

horseman and sheathed her new weapon. The belt was too big to wear around her waist, so she draped it across her shoulder and chest, letting the knife ride down by her hip. On her the big knife looked almost like a small sword. Satisfied she picked a direction and started walking.

As she cleared the ring of the camp she stopped. She had no idea where she was. She couldn't go home. Even if she knew which direction it was in, there was nothing there now. She didn't know any towns. She had no idea where to go.

Sasha glanced up at the sun and mentally tracked it like Daddy had taught her. She turned looking to her right, that way was west, more or less. Sasha scrunched up her face and thought. She didn't know anything west. Daddy had always said there was nothing but grassy plains that way.

Sasha tried to remember some of Daddy's maps. South was the city of Eldurania and Crescent Lake, then eventually the coast, but both were probably a million miles away. Sasha looked north, Daddy never said what was north other than to never go there.

Sasha turned east. East seemed good. The Lake was east, just over the mountains and then a little north, north past the mountains was good she remembered. Daddy's people came from The Lake, her people. Maybe she even had family that way. She nodded to herself twice. Her mind made up Sasha started marching.

After a couple of hours Sasha decided that she was not a

fan of marching. She didn't know how soldier guys did it, march here, march there, march, march, march. Sasha sighed. She was getting tired, her feet hurt, and she was thirsty and hungry.

She saw a small rock nearby and decided it was time for a break. She plopped down on the grayish brown rock and sighed, happy to be off her feet. Her butt, however, was not happy. This was the most uncomfortable rock she had ever sat on. It was knobby, with lots of weird bumps and a few sharp bits. She squirmed around trying to get comfortable. Then her rock moved.

Sasha let out a squeak and jumped off the rock and ran a few steps away before turning back. The rock rose up on four stumpy legs from the ground and gave itself a shake tossing dirt off its sides.

A long tail ending in a thick bony lump extended out from one end. A short blunt head peered around from the other side looking back at her. The dull brown eyes suddenly went wide as they locked onto her and it let out a loud bleating trumpet, almost like a goat.

Sasha stared wide eyed back. She had never seen a stone wyrm this close before. This one was also nowhere near as big as the ones at the fair, she had seen. This one was only about six feet long. It also didn't have any of the sharp spines that jutted off from the sides and backs of the bigger ones. Sasha could see though the knobs where the spines would grow from and the two big ones at the shoulders that the boy wyrms had.

"Oh, you're just a baby," she said. The wyrm made a grunting sound and smacked its tail on the ground making a loud whumph each time. The baby wyrm was trying to look fierce and dangerous; all it did was make her giggle.

Sasha glanced around trying to find the rest of the herd. She couldn't see anything on the plains other than those weird muddy rock towers that seemed to be scattered around. They were about four times as tall as she was and only a few feet around. She was pretty sure they were some kind of ant city. She couldn't see any other stone wyrms though, or any rocks that might be wyrms.

She looked back at the baby. It bleated again and thumped its tail three times on the ground.

"You like hitting your tail on the ground don't ya," she said. The wyrm answered with several more thumps. "Where's your mommy and daddy?" The wyrm seemed to pause for a second and then made a soft honking noise.

"Oh, you're all alone like me. I lost my family too." The wyrm made another honk. "I'm sorry I sat on you. I thought you were a rock."

The baby stone wyrm seemed to narrow its eyes at her and thumped his tail several more times. Sasha rolled her eyes at it. The wyrm seemed to smile as its mouth opened up revealing a mass of blunt and wide teeth before it bent down and chomped off a mouthful of grass.

Sasha gave a huff. "It's rude to start eating when someone is talking to you." The wyrm, deciding she wasn't a threat, went back to chewing. "Especially when the other person doesn't have anything to eat," she finished.

The baby wyrm thumped its tail once and took another bite. Its mouth ended in a sharp looking beak that almost made it look like a turtle. Until it opened its mouth in that weird goofy grin, before shearing off another mouthful of grass.

"What am I going to call you," she said. The wyrm looked up at her and thumped its tail again. Sasha rolled her eyes. "Ok Thump it is." Thump thumped his tail again.

Sasha slowly walked over and placed a hand on the bony shell covering Thump's back. Now that Thump had decided she wasn't a threat he became rather indifferent to her. Sasha was just glad to have someone to talk to, even if it was a big bony lizard thing. Thump was kinda cute she decided.

"You're lucky Thump," she said. "You can just eat grass whenever you're hungry. I don't have anything to eat and I'm starving."

Thump took a few more mouthfuls of grass before giving a grunt and thumping his tail again. The wyrm seemed rather oblivious to her now and took another bite. Sasha sighed again and started looking around again.

Thump made a much louder honking noise and started to shuffle off. "Hey, where are you going?" Sasha followed after the blundering baby wyrm as he lazily plodded over to one of the ant tower-mounds.

Thump let out another bleat and smashed the tower in half with a swipe of his tail. A swarm of red ants boiled up out of the mound. Thump seemed to not care in the least as they swarmed across his body. He just stood there slowly lapping up the big white ones and the eggs, occasionally licking around his face to keep the angry ones off his eyes.

Sasha watched fascinated. The ants couldn't do anything to deter Thump as he ate his fill. Curious, she walked over to the far side of the mound away from Thump and the angry swarm. She reached down and grabbed one of the fat white ones.

It wasn't a queen she knew that, but she wasn't really sure what it was. She knew the angry ones were the soldiers and maybe workers too. This one didn't really seem to do anything it was about the size of her thumb and didn't really seem to be able to move on its tiny legs.

Sasha was hungry, but was she that hungry? She stared at the fat ant for a minute or so, trying to decide. Finally, she shrugged and tossed it in her mouth.

She bit down on it, and it popped in her mouth spraying a

cool liquid all over the inside of her mouth. Sasha made a face, it was a slightly unpleasant feeling, but it didn't taste bad. In fact, as she chewed it didn't taste at all, there wasn't any flavor. It was like a little pastry puff that had been filled with water. She decided that no flavor was much better than bad flavor.

She grabbed a handful and began eating them. Each time they popped it was like getting a mouthful of water. It took numerous handfuls, but after a while she didn't feel quite as thirsty or as hungry.

"Thump you're pretty smart," she said. Thump wacked his tail on the ground but didn't look up as he greedily ate up the hive. Eventually though he too had his fill and started to shamble off. "Now where," she asked.

Thump of course didn't make any reply not even thumping the ground. He just tromped along either oblivious or unconcerned with the world around him. After about an hour and a little after dark he just stopped and dropped to the ground.

"I guess this is where we're stopping for the night," she sighed. Sasha didn't have anything to make a fire and she knew how cold it could get at night on the plains. Cautiously she walked over and sat on the ground next to Thump.

He gave a slight grunt as she leaned against him, but he didn't stir. Thump was warm and blocked the wind a bit. "Ok," she said. "You get some sleep ok." Sasha barely finished the sentence before she too was asleep.

The next couple of days passed the same as the first day she had met the baby wyrm. Thump would eventually wake up, usually well past midmorning. He snuffled around for a few minutes eating a bit of grass and relieving himself.

Sasha found it hilarious. She had been around all sorts of animals and watched them all go to the bathroom. It wasn't that big a deal, but Thump raised his tail and would spray out a stream behind him as he walked, everything going out all at once. She had almost been caught by the blast the first time. Now it made her giggle.

At least once or sometimes twice a day Thump would smash open an ant mound. Sasha still wasn't sure if he did it after she asked him to or just whenever he felt like it. Thump seemed to acknowledge her, but he also didn't seem to acknowledge anything either.

The ants helped her hunger and thirst, but it wasn't quite enough. Sasha didn't complain though. Right now, she was just happy to follow Thump as he slowly made his way across the plain. Even though he moved slowly and seemed pretty lazy, he never really stopped moving except at night to sleep. She was also happy because he was heading east.

After three days Sasha finally saw something other than

grass and ant mounds. She saw a large outcropping of rock jutting up from the ground. These weren't fake rocks like Thump had been either. These were a jumble of sharp jagged rocks protruding from the ground like some giant hand.

Thump seemed to be heading straight for the rock formation. As they got closer Sasha could hear the squawking of a great host of birds. Thump let out a bellowing trumpet and charged into the midst of the carrion birds.

Thump gleefully hooted and trumpeted as he sent the vultures, ravens and smaller ones sky high. He turned back to her panting, his long tongue drooping out the side of his mouth. He was standing in the middle of a battlefield.

Sasha smiled. Despite the carnage around him Thump still looked silly standing there, clearly pleased with himself. Sasha looked around at the bodies. It didn't really seem to bother her anymore. They were dead, she wasn't.

She could see they were soldiers. They all wore armor and had carried weapons. She slowly walked around the sea of bodies; there were easily fifty or so men. It looked like they had tried to put up a fight, but she couldn't see any bodies of the bad guys. All these soldiers wore the same uniforms and emblems, so she assumed they were all on the same team.

A low groan caught her attention. Thump came over to her side but didn't make a sound. Slowly she followed the sound to one of the soldiers.

He had dragged himself across the ground before stopping at a smaller rock. He now leaned back against the rock watching her with one eye. The other was covered with a black patch. His armor was stained with blood, and he looked to be slowly dying. Slowly, he raised one arm; the other hung uselessly at his side and beckoned her closer.

"Come closer child," he said. "I need." He stopped as he was wracked with a fit of coughing, bloody sputum splattered on his chest. "I need to tell you what happened."

Chapter Twenty-five

Argis stood on the balcony of The Citadel of An Sioc Dubh, his fortress overlooking the Firefalls in the Black Lands. From this vantage point he could see the flow from the volcano as it crashed over the breach like a cascading waterfall into the Pit. The balcony was his one refuge in this dark and desolate land. This little balcony was the one place where he could relax and simply enjoy the natural beauty of the falls. The one place he could be himself and not The Dread Lord.

Wrapped in ebony cloak and armor he was little more than a silhouette against the light from the falls. The Firefalls fell for several hundred feet before entering into the Pit, where the glow from the molten rock could be seen far below before vanishing into the darkness. They were magnificent and he was one of the few people that had ever gotten to see them. He had stood here for hours the first time he had been brought here.

The falls were a beautiful natural creation. The volcano continuously erupted spewing its magma out in a river of fire. The river steadily flowed over a cliff on the mountain and crashed into the Pit below. The volcano brought warmth and life to the cold surrounding area and also death to anyone foolish enough to disturb it. He found it a fitting analogy for his kingdom.

He leaned over the rail looking down into the yawning cavity below. The Pit was a vast hole in the earth, and no one knew exactly how deep it went. The light from the lava flowing into it could be seen for several miles in depth before the darkness of the earth swallowed it up.

Maybe I should start the experiments again, he mused. He had tried to figure out just how deep the hole went. He had started by tossing a few Goblins in and counting till they disappeared from site. Thirty-five or thirty-six seconds seemed to be about average before the darkness swallowed them. They had tried building scaffolding down to increase the distance, but the heat had been too great to go very far. Then he had gotten bored and abandoned the project.

That was one of the major problems with being the Dread Lord; there wasn't much too actually do. Other than keeping tabs on a few of his projects and issuing the occasional order he didn't really have much to put his hands on. Mostly he just puttered around the fortress, putting on airs and keeping the minions in check.

Argis' fortress, The Black Frost in the Highcommon tongue,

had been built across the Pit from the falls long before recorded history. It was a monstrous building with spiraling towers and seemed to absorb all light. It was also drafty and quite uncomfortable to live in.

The fortress was also pretty much empty. He had his personal quarters, laboratory, and training rooms, but other than that and a few servant quarters the monstrous building was empty. He didn't have a staff, not a normal castle staff anyway. "Nooo, the great and terrible lord of the Black Lands can't have someone to tidy up his bedroom," he grumbled. An Sioc Dubh really had only one purpose and one purpose only, to look intimidating.

The citadel had been breached only twice in the history of the empire. Both times none had returned to the empire to boast of it. This was the capital of the Black Lands and Lord Argis was its master. "Yay me," he groused. He twirled his finger sarcastically in the air.

Argis had this balcony built specifically for him. It jutted out from the highest tower, his personal tower. From here he could gaze out and see the falls. They were the only beautiful thing in this dark and broken land. He often came here to plan and to meditate. The balcony gave him a good vantage point to observe his kingdom.

To the southwest he could see out into the White Desert. It

was a cold desolate region that separated the Black Lands from the Jade Sea grasslands of western Marovia. The White Desert was his little buffer zone from the empire.

A glacial desert, it locked up most water in half a dozen glaciers that slowly ground down the tundra beneath them. It deterred all but the most foolhardy from trying to cross into his kingdom. The climate combined with the denizens of the deep desert kept the fools that entered from leaving again.

He shuddered as he thought of those vile things out there, hibernating in their massive hives. Goblins were bad enough, but those things just gave him the creepies. "Xellex," he spoke the word in disgust. He sighed. "I'm probably going to have to use some of those nasty bugs soon though."

He turned back to the east, below the fortress stretched the Savan colony. The Dread Lord had granted them asylum long, long ago. Their once great empire had been shattered millennia ago and the Savan had been driven from their homelands before most recorded history, long before the empire. Now, they had built themselves a small city on his lands as they eked out a living in the cold lands.

Honestly, he had no idea how they managed the cold. He had seen a few of them just lock up and freeze after an arctic wind blast, unable to move. Yet, somehow, they survived, herding the vast hordes of reindeer and tundra camels that roamed the tundra. Some had moved north to the Frozen Sea, fishing its waters, and hunting the seals there.

Farther east he could see small fires lit by Goblins trying to keep warm in the cold. Their breeding pits were now constantly churning out warriors for Argis' army. The little ratkies didn't really have any form of civilization. They ate what they could find, and they bred, and they defecated, sometimes all three at once. The Goblins were barely more than animals, but they did have their uses. It was one of the reasons he didn't mind sacrificing them, there were always more.

Argis lands were sealed from the rest of the world now. Since he had destroyed the bridge over the Gap of Adun there were only two ways into the Black Lands; a small gap in the mountains between the Pit and the Gap of Adun or across the desolate wastes of the White Desert. He controlled the gap; it was guarded by the Savan, and the White Desert was impassable except for his forces and for the creatures that dwelled there.

His plan was quickly coming to fruition and soon this world could be reset, could heal. His army grew daily and soon he would invade the weakened empire and conquer it. Of course, having one of the kings in his pocket certainly would make his conquest easier. A little gold and a promise of power and even the most righteous could be swayed, though this king was far from righteousness.

That made him sick. Pulling the king had been so easy, too easy. After his agents made contact with the king, he had practically leapt at the chance to betray his brother and the empire. All for power, power, and the sick perverted games he liked to play. It disgusted Argis, and he was looking forward to brutally executing the wretched man when his use was finished.

He sighed. That had helped steel his nerves to go through with this plan, the corruption had to be purged. The king would get what was coming to him. When things settled, he would take personal satisfaction in taking that bloody piece of skret's head off.

He absently stroked the hilt of the Soulblade. Its scabbard glistened wetly from the light of the Firefalls. It appeared to be made of freshly exposed muscle fiber. The hilt had the look of bone wrapped in tanned human skin. The pommel was a shrunken skull frozen mid-scream. Its blade was forged from some poor soul's vertebra, sharpened to a single edge that still pulsed with the spent life of its creator's heartbeat and the heartbeats of all those that had carried it. The weapon was created to be an embodiment of death and took the form completely.

This was the key to his plan, this sword. He could feel the power emanating from it. He had only just begun to tap the potential power residing in it. Once he located the Aegis of

Life, the other half of the key, he would be able to open the portal and use the army of Aetherburners to burn this world away and remake it according to his design, free and good once again. A slight smile hidden by the gleaming skull of his helm crossed his lips. "Soon," he whispered.

Then doubt crept back up into his mind. He reached up and pulled the helm of The Dread Lord off and placed it on the nearby table. Sometimes it was hard to think wearing that cursed thing. It could get difficult to separate himself from his role. He still wasn't sure if the helm actually was cursed, but he did feel a little different when he wore it. "Maybe it's just playing the role."

He took a deep breath, enjoying the cold breeze mixing with the heat from the falls. It was refreshing and helped clear his mind. If he went through with this plan a lot of innocent people were going to die, good people, people that didn't deserve to have their lives ripped apart.

"It's for the greater good," he told himself again. The greater good, that had been his mantra pretty much the entire time he had been here. It was the mantra of the Dread Lord, but now he was preparing to take it to a level far, far beyond what had been done in the past. "To save the world you have to destroy it first." He shook his head, that couldn't be right, but the more he thought on it the more it had to be.

He pulled the Soulblade clear and held it up to his eyes. The old man had been right. This thing was an object of power on a scale only measured by gods. It was his and rightly so. He had taken it and hadn't had to spill blood to take it. "Well, not the blood of the one I was worried about anyway," he still felt bad for the villagers that had died, but it was for the greater good. He had taken the blade and saved the old man from dying. It was a win, win as far as he was concerned. For the greater good.

He re-sheathed the sword and ran a hand across his short sandy blond hair. He would need to shave it down again soon; it was just too hot wearing that helm with long hair. "The Dread Lord can't show weakness or be seen sweating, boy," he quoted. He leaned heavily on the railing with both hands again.

Had that knight that had shown up been Warrec? "Of course, it was," he told himself. "Why else had they shouted his name, the old man called him son." His little brother had gotten big, very big. He hadn't recognized him. "Of course, he obviously hadn't recognized you either. Why would he?" He scoffed. "Plus, it's hard to see your face behind the grinning skull, that's kinda the point."

Everett burst out laughing. It was a deep belly laugh, the kind that only the truly disturbed ever get to enjoy. *You're mad*, he quietly told himself. Though why shouldn't he be mad, he had been broken and rebuilt in this sinister place. Forced into isolation, cut off from everyone he cared about, and the weight of the world placed on his shoulders. It was all for the greater good.

The door to the balcony opened and the sound of rasping scales across the bare stone could be heard as the Savan priest slithered towards his master. The Savan priests were easily distinguished from the warrior caste by their snake like appearance. They had no lower limbs, only a tail which propelled them like a writhing snake across the ground. Long slender arms protruded from their torso and their forked tongue was constantly darting in and out of their mouth.

Everett didn't turn around, but resolutely reached over and redonned his mantle. "What is it?" The Dread Lord spoke barely above a whisper, but his voice rolled like deep thunder echoing across the Pit as the helm projected his voice. A voice that could make even the bravest of men cower in fear.

"My lord I bring good newsss." The priest's voice was a raspy hiss punctuated by its tongue. "The production of warriorsss hasss increasssed greatly. We have alssso been able to breed even more Goblinsss than exxxpected. The hill tribesss of man join usss and the glitter of promisssed gold bringsss in battle hardened mercenariesss to you." The Savan priest clapped his hands together and bowed his head before his master.

Argis lovingly fingered the skull pommel of the Soulblade. "Good," Argis said dialing his voice back down to a normal level. And how are the centaur raids coming along?"

"They continue to raissse fear in the sssouth landsss. The wessstern half of the empire isss under sssiege, though the foolisssh humansss do not sssee the threat yet. The centaursss were able to dessstroy a large garrissson of sssoldiersss recently."

Argis clasped his hands behind his back and peered out towards the vast unbroken horizon of the desert. "How is our little brotherly rivalry coming along?"

"Thingsss are uneasssy between the two kingsss. Our sssspiesss have planted rumorsss that war isss inevitable."

"Good. I will send word to the king to go ahead with the war, but for the time being make no mention of my involvement. We will let him use his forces first, as I doubt his soldiers would follow him if they knew who was backing him in his bid for Emperor. Has there been any information gathered yet of the location of the shield?"

"Not yet my lord, but we have our sssspiesss out looking and it isss only a matter of time until we locate it. We have attempted to find the trail at Hammerfall, but our agentsss were thwarted. The old giant one isss searching and we ssshall follow."

Argis gave a slight nod. "Good, but he is not to be harmed. That is my will. Fine then, you are dismissed." Argis finally turned to look at the priest. It was Jasat.

Dammit why did it have to be Jasat, he thought. He liked Jasat, but he had given the order. As much as he wanted to, he couldn't show leniency, not on this. *You old fool, why didn't you listen. Damn you for making me do this.*

"Yesss my lord," the priest bowed again and turned to slither away.

"Wait a moment...tell me...what were my orders when I was out on this balcony?" Argis stood unmoving, a frozen statue of darkness as he looked at Jasat. His skull helm seemed to grin menacingly. The priest was now looking quite fearful, and his eyes began darting around looking for a place to hide.

"You sssaid that...that you were not to be disssturbed, but I thought you would want to hear thisss report right away massster." The Savan lowered his head and curled his tail around himself defensively. "Pleassse forgive me my lord."

Maybe, just this once. It's Jasat after all. He bound my wounds, cared for me. Argis bit his lip hard enough to draw blood. *The Dread Lord cannot afford to show weakness boy.* It had been drilled into his head countless times. *It's for the greater good.* He swallowed and hardened himself.

Argis looked down at the cowering creature, he towered

easily a head taller than Jasat. With a flash of steel, the Soulblade cut through the air. The Savan priest's head sailed up and over the balcony rail into the pit below. His tongue continued to dart in and out as his jaws opened and closed, silently begging for mercy. The Soulblade soaked up the blood on it and gleamed bright red then slowly faded back to a dull pulsating glow.

Argis smoothly re-sheathed the sword and with a wave of his hand the headless body was flung into the Pit following after its head. "You are forgiven." He took a slow breath and whispered, "I'm sorry, it's for the greater good."

Chapter Twenty-six

A few weeks of hard travel through rough terrain after leaving Hammerfall had Duncan and Wildbeard finding themselves in the sweltering jungles of Nangonango in the Orc's territory. The hot sticky heat hung on them like a cloak. Their clothes sticking to them like wet sack cloth. Even breathing seemed difficult in the oppressive heat and humidity.

Duncan let out a long sigh as he leaned on the haft of his bardiche. He reached up and pulled the rag he had tied around his head off and began wringing it out. He sneered in disgust as a torrent of sweat came pouring out of the soaked rag. He snapped it a couple times to knock the excess moisture off and retied it around his head.

Neither of the two was prepared for the climate of the Orc lands. They had both spent the majority of their lives in the cool expanse of the north. More and more frequently they found themselves stopping to rest. It was just past midday when the Dwarve dropped his heavy pack to the ground and plopped onto a large flat rock.

"I hate this place," he stated. Duncan nodded in agreement as he too dropped his pack to the ground. "How much further?" Wildbeard asked.

Duncan leaned the bardiche against a tree, he had been using the massive weapon as a walking stick and despite himself his arms were getting a little tired. He too sank down to the ground, thankful for the rest. Duncan reached over and began rummaging through his pack for the puzzle map. After a few seconds of digging, he found it and pulled it free. He opened it and quickly arranged the pieces. After staring at it for a moment he snapped it shut and returned it to the pack.

"About two more days travel, possibly three," he finally answered with a depressed look.

Wildbeard bellowed a curse and fell backward splayed out on the rock. "Only an Orc would be stupid enough tae live in this hot, sticky, and wind cursed place. No one in their right mind would live err," he muttered.

Duncan was about to agree when a cry of terror sounded through the jungle. The two looked at each other and without a word snatched up their weapons and took off toward the sound. Duncan barreled through the undergrowth and left the Dwarve behind. The old warrior broke through the jungle wall into a small clearing.

In the clearing a female Orc stood. She was brandishing a

tree limb as a club trying desperately to fight off a pack of a dozen raptors. One raptor lay thrashing on the ground, a large knife sticking out of the top of its back. It screeched at its pack mates as it clawed furiously at the hilt of the knife. The other raptors were now circling their prey waiting for an opening.

These raptors were smaller than the ones Duncan had seen in Hammerfall. They were barely three feet tall and six feet long from snout to the end of the tail. They were a cobalt blue with bright emerald green feathers. The killing claw on their hind feet was only half the size of the ones Red and Sweettooth had sported. Still the vicious little things would make quick work of the Orc if something wasn't done.

Duncan brought the great poleax down on the prone raptor decapitating it. The raptor's screeches stopped immediately, but its legs continued to kick and thrash. Duncan didn't wait for it to die. With a mighty roar he leapt amongst the remaining raptors. He swung the weapon in a wide arc, cleaving another raptor in half and knocking two more down. The remaining raptors let out a screech of fury and turned to face the new threat.

The Orc seized the advantage and struck with all her might. She brought the makeshift club down hard on the head of the closest one. The beast let out a shriek of pain and staggered back. Still instinct took over despite the pain and it kicked out with a leg. The long-curved claw lashed out and caught the Orc across the belly, just short of causing a death blow and spilling her guts onto the jungle floor. A few inches closer and the claw would have disemboweled her.

Wildbeard burst into the clearing and fired off a quick crossbow bolt into its open mouth. The raptor gagged on the bolt stuck through its jaw and tried to claw the obstruction clear. Wildbeard rushed forward and stabbed his war spade through the creature's heart. The flat shovel blade tore through the raptor's breast, nearly cleaving it in half. It fell thrashing about on the jungle floor.

With a screech a raptor, bigger than the rest, launched itself into the air toward Duncan. Its jaws gaped wide as it brought its arms up to seize him. Duncan battered the beast aside with the blade of the bardiche. It landed with amazing agility and prepared itself to pounce again.

Duncan used the momentum of the blade to spin a quick three hundred and sixty degrees, swinging the great weapon in a large arc. The blade caught a second raptor in the throat and continued on leaving a decapitated body behind it. Duncan twisted the blades arc and brought it down severing the arm of another raptor. The animal cried out in pain and recoiled backward from the attack.

The first raptor cocked its head back and forth as it

slowly circled the big man. Based on its size and brighter colors Duncan guessed it to be the alpha. A quick series of chirps from the alpha brought two raptors attacking from opposite sides on Duncan's left and right. Duncan stabbed out, skewering the one on the right. He slammed the creature down to the ground catching the one on the left in mid-air with the butt of the poleaxe and throwing the raptor past him.

Wildbeard bellowed as he slapped the flat of the spade across the muzzle of a raptor that was getting too close to the prone Orc. Blood and teeth exploded out of the creature's mouth as it shrieked in pain. The Dwarve kicked it aside as he brought the heavy blade up and down on another's back, cleaving the raptor in half.

The alpha used the distraction from the attack on Duncan and again launched itself into the air at Duncan with a screech. The old giant didn't have time to swing the poleaxe back around. In one smooth motion he dropped the massive weapon and drew the machete from his belt and stabbed it upward. The blade made a sickeningly wet schlunking sound as it caught the alpha in the bottom of its jaw and pierced through the base of its brain. The alpha let out a soft gurgle as Duncan dropped it and the machete to the jungle floor.

The remaining raptors began slowly backing away. A series of chirps and whistles passed between them. The remaining pack continued to back away into the jungle undergrowth. A few more chirps and tweeting notes and they vanished into the jungle in search of easier prey.

Duncan let out a sigh of relief. The heat of battle combined with the heat of the jungle had left him feeling exhausted and lightheaded. He stood in the clearing panting with sweat pouring off his face. He reached up and wiped his head with his sleeve.

"Wildbeard?" he asked, turning around. The Dwarve was stooped over the prone figure of the Orc. Her breath was ragged as she clutched at her torn stomach.

"Over err lad. Ye didna happen to have any o' them healing elixirs with ye?" The Dwarve asked as he cradled the Orc's head and gently pulled her hand away to look at the wound.

"How bad is it?" Duncan said as he walked over to them. He pulled a small vial of ruby red liquid from a pocket and handed it to the Dwarve. The Orc had lost conscience, having passed out from the pain and blood loss.

The Dwarve pulled the stopper out with his teeth. He spilled a few drops on the wound and poured a small amount into her mouth. "She'll live, but not without care. Though I don't think she'll be dancing anytime soon. Blast these are cheap," he said and shook the now empty vial. "Infection is the biggest risk now. A few inches deeper and she would o' been dead already."

The Orc let out a sigh as she swallowed the lifesaving liquid. The bleeding from the gash on her stomach slowed, and then stopped altogether. The wound began to close shut. After a few minutes, the gash scabbed over and closed, leaving a small slightly oozing scab. Wildbeard pulled a long strip of linen cloth from his belt and began wrapping the Orc's stomach.

"Within a few weeks even that wee scar will be gone," Wildbeard said. "O' course the good stuff would have her up and doing back flips without a hint that she had just been opened up by the beastie," he added with a wink.

"You bought them," Duncan said. The old giant raised his hands and shrugged.

Wildbeard raised a finger and opened his mouth to answer then shut it like a trap. After a few seconds he had to admit it. "Aye I did didna I." Wildbeard grinned then laughed out loud as Duncan shook his head at the Dwarve.

Duncan turned his attention back to Orc. He looked her over. She was dressed only in a leather loin cloth and a few small strips of leather to serve as a bra, not unusual, typical female Orc clothing. Her skin was a deep olive shade of green. A plume of fiery orange hair sprouted from the top of her head. It was pulled back into a long topknot with the rest of the skull shaved clean. Two small points of white showed from her bottom lip as her lower canines barely poked above her lip. Her nose was small and broad, and her ears came to a small point.

The Orc's body was strong and lean, muscles could be seen rippling under her skin as she groaned and began to move. Her outfit left practically nothing to the imagination. The loin cloth was long reaching down past her knees, but just barely wide enough to keep her feminine qualities from showing to the world.

The leather straps stretched across her broad chest in an x-design. Her breasts weren't overly large for an Orc, but still fairly large for a human. The leather squished them tight against her body, as they were barely contained by the twin straps of leather, making them appear larger. All in all, she seemed quite attractive, even beautiful, for an Orc anyway.

I have been too long without a woman, when an Orc starts to look good, Duncan thought. Still, there was something about her that was alluring, though alien. It was now that Duncan finally noticed that along with her scant outfit, she was wearing an iron collar and manacles.

"She's quite pretty," Wildbeard stated. "For an Orc anyway," he quickly added, echoing Duncan's thoughts.

"I'm pretty regardless...Dwarve," the Orc said as her eyes snapped open, and she shoved Wildbeard away. She slowly sat up groaning in pain and clutching her stomach. Then looked at the two of them. She then spat on the ground. The Orc braced herself on an arm and jumped to her feet. She winced and grabbed at her side as she stood. She had stood too quickly and began to swoon. Her arm shot out as she caught herself by grabbing onto Duncan's chest.

"Easy. That raptor almost took you out," he said placing his arm on hers.

"I'm fine...just got a little lightheaded," she grunted. She snatched a glance towards him and then their arms touching and jerked her arm back. She then took a few steps back. Her eyes darted to the knife still embedded in the raptor's carcass. "Who are you two? What are you doing here?"

"We could ask ye the same thing," Wildbeard said.

"I live here," she snapped back.

"Oh, err in this clearing ya mean. Aye, a fine place ye be having err too." The Dwarve shot back. The Orc glared at him. "Could use a little sprucing up though, some decorations, maybe a rug or two," he droned on as he looked around the clearing placing imaginary furniture in his mind.

"No, I mean I live here in the jungle. You two obviously aren't Orcs and last I checked we didn't have any Dwarves or giants setting up shop down here," she growled.

"Oh obviously," the Dwarve sneered. Wildbeard glared back at her. "And yer welcome by the way."

Duncan sighed. "I'm Duncan Vornirulf and my friend here is Barix Hammerstone or Wildbeard for short."

"How is that short for…" she said and cocked her head at Duncan. "Oh, I get it. Ha, he just made a joke about you runt or was that over your head." The Orc burst out laughing that quickly cut off as she clutched at her bandaged stomach. "Ow," she groaned still giggling slightly. Wildbeard's face shot bright red.

"I didn't mean it like that," Duncan added quickly. The Orc continued to laugh at the Dwarve.

"Err now, see err missy." Wildbeard started taking a step and stabbing a sausage thick finger out at her. The Orc was about average height for a female Orc, taller than an average Imperial human female. She was just shy of six feet by an inch or two; still she towered over the Dwarve. The Orc loomed over the Dwarve and to her delight found that Wildbeard's nose came to the center of her chest.

"Easy Whiskers, you're turning the same shade as that lovely growth you call a beard. Wouldn't want you to blow a vessel, would we," she said teasing. She stepped forward and jammed her fists on her hips. At the same time, she thrust her chest forward. The apex of her cleavage was just barley an inch from the tip of Wildbeard's broad nose. Wildbeard blinked a couple of times and grunted as two large green orbs filled his whole field of vision.

"Err now...um," he stammered.

The Orc gave a wry smile at Wildbeard. "There, that's a good boy," she said with a condescending air as she patted the Dwarve on top of his bald head. She then casually walked over and wretched her knife free from the raptor's back. Then she bent over away from the two of them to wipe the blade clean on the vegetation. By doing so she had given the pair a good view of her ample backside.

The broad strip of leather on the back of her loincloth did little more than cover the dividing line of her cheeks. Like all female Orcs it was rather expansive to say the least and gave even the Dwarven females a run for their money. Duncan and Wildbeard caught themselves staring, a little slack jawed. The Orc then turned back to them oblivious as to what she had done, or perhaps not altogether unaware.

"Now, you still haven't answered my question why you're here," she said lightly fingering the point of the blade.

"And you still haven't told us who you are," Duncan said.

"Or why yer wearing that collar," Wildbeard added.

The Orc sighed and stuck the knife under her belt. "I do suppose I owe you two my life. My name is Akana. As to the collar…I'm a slave...or was anyway."

"Not anymore?" Wildbeard asked suspiciously.

"No, I escaped...was escaping when those raptors found me. I suppose I would have been ripped to shreds and in their bellies by now if the two of you hadn't come along. Though mostly thanks to you big guy," she said winking at Duncan.

"Err now, what about yer former master? Won't he come looking for ye?" Wildbeard said with a huff.

"Well, no. Not unless he finds a way to come back from the dead anyway. He sort of had an accident while I was escaping."

"Such as?" Duncan asked.

"Well, this knife here somehow managed to slit his throat, though I'm not really sure how," she said grinning like a wolf.

"How bloody convenient for ya," Wildbeard said crossing his arms.

"Listen short stuff, I don't suppose we could continue this over supper, could we?" Akana said. "I'm pretty tired and I bet you two are as well. Let's say we make camp for the day and then start back again on our journey tomorrow." She walked over and twisted a bit of Wildbeard's beard around her index finger.

"Err now just a second I...wait what do ye mean our journey?" Wildbeard stammered as he pulled his beard free.

"Well, wherever it is that you two were heading to of course," she said over her shoulder as she turned back to Duncan. "Lead on handsome." Duncan cocked his eyebrow at her before turning back to where they left their gear.

"What makes ye think ye are coming with us?" Wildbeard grunted at Akana.

"Because I am, that's why. Look I'm a slave, was a slave"- she shook her head -"either way you two saved my life, which means that you're now responsible for it. I'm yours now. Besides, someone has to lead the two of you out of this jungle. Otherwise, you might blunder into trouble and get yourselves killed." She followed after Duncan. Akana gave an extra swing to her hip as she shot a look back at Wildbeard. "Especially you Whiskers." The two continued to argue the rest of the way back to the gear and long into the night, though Wildbeard was hopelessly outmatched.

A few hours later after having filled their bellies, Duncan was busy repacking his gear. Or at least he appeared to be, in truth he was just finding something to do with his hands to pass the time. Wildbeard furiously puffed on his pipe staring at the fire. Akana had curled up a few feet from the fire and stolen the Dwarve's pack for a makeshift pillow.

The Dwarve stared at her back. Finally, when he could hear her snoring, he spoke. "I dunna like it," he whispered to Duncan.

Duncan sighed and put his pack down. "I know. I'm not really happy about it either but what can we do now? We can't just leave her out here."

"Can't we?" Wildbeard shot back. He then sighed. "I dunna know. Her story seems fishy. She speaks Highcommon without a hint o' accent."

"Which means she has been around humans a long time," Duncan stated. "During dinner she said her master had been an Orc. A now dead Orc with which we can't verify her story."

"Aye, but what Orc slave have you heard of going to humans and then back to Orcs. I dunna like it," the Dwarve sighed. "We'll have to bust those manacles and collar off; in case someone comes looking for her. Aye, it's very fortuitous for her that we happen tae run into her out here in the middle o' nowhere." The Dwarve puffed on his pipe.

Duncan stroked his beard as he thought. "You're thinking about the botched museum robbery." Wildbeard slowly nodded his head. "Could she have fit in the ventilation shaft the burglar used to escape?"

Wildbeard sucked on his teeth for a few seconds as he thought. "Aye, it would have been a tight squeeze, but she looks lean enough. Might have had tae strap those down though," he added pointing with the stem of the pipe at her chest.

"She probably has been following us since then," Duncan said. "Probably we still wouldn't know about her if those raptors hadn't come along."

"Yer thinking it's best to play it close to the vest, keep

her close, keep an eye on her."

Duncan nodded. "Better to have her close where we can keep an eye on her than her out there watching us." He shook his head and stifled a yawn. "Nothing to be done about it now. We will watch her, but for now we need sleep."

Wildbeard sighed again and blew a smoke ring off into the still night air. He tamped out the pipe and stowed it away in its pocket. "You want first watch or me?"

"You go ahead and get some sleep. I'll take the first watch," Duncan said. Wildbeard nodded and rolled over and quickly fell asleep. After a few minutes, the sound of his snoring mixed with the Orcs. Duncan watched the two of them sleeping. The Dwarve was right; it was very fortunate that they happened to find her out here in the wilderness. Both for saving her life if she was just an innocent Orc and for them if she was following them and spying on them.

Someone else was looking for the Aegis of Life. That thought troubled him deeply. No one should have known about it. He barely knew anything about it, other than it existed, somewhere. Argis had the sword, could he be looking for the shield as well?

Probably, he thought. The stakes couldn't be any higher. If The Dread Lord got both relics, it would spell certain doom for the world. *I failed before.* Duncan gritted his teeth. *I won't fail again.* In the morning, the party of now three set out again.

Chapter Twenty-seven

Kunthar breathed deeply. The old lion sat with eyes closed in lotus position on a padded mat before the shrine to his ancestors. The scent of cherry blossoms and his prize-winning purple orchids wafted through his private garden. He held the breath, letting the energy flow through his body as he released it again. Kunthar's ear flicked back at the slight sound of crunching gravel.

Kunthar smiled to himself. That would be the only alert his former teacher would give him. Zareem walked silently through the garden where his master was meditating. The snow-white tiger picked his way through the sand garden and around the large cherry tree. Kunthar couldn't hear him, or smell him, but had to instead sense the elder tiger's life force as he moved through the garden.

He could cheat of course. All he had to do was turn his head and open his eyes to see Zareem. He had done that once when their roles had been reversed, when Zareem had been the master teaching an impatient young lion the arts of war. Kunthar had peeked and gotten his ears boxed and rightly so.

When Zareem was still a few feet away he stopped and stood silently awaiting his master's acknowledgement. When Zareem stopped, Kunthar tilted his head and lashed his tail towards the elder tiger, acknowledging him. If he hadn't, he probably would have gotten his ears boxed again, shogun or not.

Kunthar was sitting at a small cluster of shrines against the outer wall. Wrapped in the white traditional prayer robe, the old lion had been deep in thought and prayer asking his ancestors for guidance. After a few seconds he opened his eyes and spoke to Zareem.

"What is it Zareem?" he said in a calm and peaceful voice.

"Master the barbarians are here. They are waiting for you in the tearoom," Zareem answered to the hooded visage of his master.

"Thank you Zareem. I will meet with them shortly. Please make them comfortable until I arrive. You may go." Zareem bowed to his master's back and turned to leave. "Zareem wait, tell me what are your impressions of them?"

Zareem stopped and looked to the sky as he thought of his response. "Master they are...foreign."

Kunthar smiled. "Well, yes I suppose they would be, but that's not what I meant."

"I know master, it is hard to explain. They are a strange

delegation to send. The big one has the bearing of a warrior. Battle hardened yes, yet something more weighs on him, I think. A burden...a choice he has not made and does not know of yet, but one that may alter the face of the world. The female is new, untested, and out of her element, but willing to follow the big one wherever he goes. She loves him deeply, but it is a love that is not returned in kind, and it tears at her. Though there is a deep power within her, old magic. The other male...I cannot read him. He hides within himself. Who he is...is not who he shows. I do not know if even the other two truly know him, perhaps he does not know himself but dangerous, very dangerous."

Kunthar nodded. "Thank you Zareem." The elder white tiger bowed again and left his master in peace. Several minutes passed in silence as Kunthar mediated on his trusted friend's words.

Who are these three humans? He wondered. It was no coincidence, no matter of chance, that these three had come to his shores. However, what meaning it had he could not discern. His ancestors sat in stony silence, refusing to grant their wisdom.

The old lion growled in frustration and quickly finished his prayer and rose from the ground. His old bones popped and creaked as he stretched out the kinks. He pulled back his hood and shook his grey streaked, black mane out. The old lion yawned wide showing his large canines that had begun to yellow with age. Kunthar grabbed his sword and stuck it back into his belt as he walked out of the tranquil garden.

He padded quickly across the bamboo floors towards his living quarters in the palace. He slid the paper door to his apartments back and entered. Beside the sleeping mat he found that Reyan had laid his clothing.

Kunthar removed his prayer robes and casually tossed them to the floor. Looking down he quickly thought better of it and neatly folded them before stowing them away in a small chest. Even a shogun does not wish to tempt the wrath of his wife.

Kunthar grabbed his silk kimono and haori robes. He quickly donned the scarlet and purple robes, colors only he and the emperor were allowed to wear. The old lion then put on his black hakama pants with the silver embroidered waves his wife had given to him years ago. They were his favorite pair. As he finished dressing, he quickly grabbed his family sword from its place of honor in the room and stuck it into the belt next to the smaller walking kukri. He checked himself in the large mirror. Grinning to himself, he still looked quite good despite his age and left to greet his guests.

When he entered the tearoom Zareem was seated speaking with the humans. Reyan was quietly preparing tea for their guests as was custom. Reyan was dressed in her finest kimono.

Her dress was an explosion of color with a bright floral

pattern. Kunthar thought she looked absolutely stunning. She peeked up at him from bowed head as he entered. She winked and gave a slight nod before returning to her duties.

Zareem leapt to his feet as Kunthar entered the room and moved toward a corner behind him. The three humans also rose as he entered. Kunthar nodded at his friend as he then looked the humans over. They weren't particularly impressive. There were two males and a female as Zareem had said.

The big one was self-apparent, easily twice the size as the other two. It took Kunthar a moment to discern which of the other two was the female. He had read the reports from the first contact months ago and the briefing for this visit.

According to what he had read human females were quite a bit smaller than their male counterparts; similar to the dimorphism in the Kathari. However, the other two looked to be close to the same height. The redheaded one was thicker and more robust looking with clearly visible muscles. The other one was lanky and lean.

Kunthar mentally shook his head and chastised himself for getting old and missing details. Upon closer inspection it was easy to tell which was which. Human females had a slighter build, longer hair, and breasts at all times. The female must be larger for her gender he quickly concluded.

The two males appeared relaxed, but the female was hiding

tension, her breathe coming short and quick. Both the big male and the female were armed, though he only carried a sword and belt knife, while she seemed bristling with an assortment of axes and knives. Kunthar found it curious that the other male wasn't armed. All three waited patiently for Kunthar to speak as he looked them over.

Kunthar bowed before them as they were after all his guests. Politeness is what separated the Kathari from these barbarians and Kunthar would not break with tradition.

"Greetings humans. I am Lord Kunthar, Shogun, and head of the Two Rivers Clan. Welcome to my home. You must be thirsty and hungry after your long journey." He clapped his hands together twice and two females appeared to assist Reyan in serving the tea.

"Thank you, Lord Kunthar. I am Lieutenant Warrec Vornirulf Duncanson, and these are my compatriots Aluna Dimmaloper Atherndotter and."

Before he could finish, Joenair interrupted him. "Plain simple Joenair. I'm a man of many names but few titles oh great one." Joenair finished with a flourish and deep bow.

"Please, you are my honored guests," Kunthar said. "Let us dispense with titles. You may simply call me Kunthar." Trying to remember these human's names and titles would definitely give him a headache, best to stop that formality now. The old lion tried to smile without showing too many teeth as he had been told it may frighten them.

The big one, Warrec let out a small sigh of relief. "Thank you Kunthar."

"You have already met my aid, Zareem." Kunthar held out his arm and Reyan took her side by her husband. "And this is my wife, Reyan." Reyan bowed deeply.

The four of them sat back down on the floor at the low table. Warrec appeared to be having a tough time getting comfortable until Aluna nudged him and told him to sit cross legged.

"I apologize Kunthar," Warrec said. "I'm not used to sitting on the floor at a table."

"Barbarians," Zareem muttered in Kathariss. Kunthar shot the elder tiger a look but said nothing. Zareem bowed his head slightly in apology. Reyan was still serving the tea when the paper door slid open with a bang.

A huge Kathari came storming in quickly followed by two palace guards who were doing their best to hold him back without actually restraining him. The Kathari was heavily muscled and had a snow-white mane and a black striped neck. He was missing his left eye from a grouping of scars where claws had slashed open his face. His top canines protruded from his jaw by several inches, glistening savagely. The halfbreed lion and tiger glared at everyone in the room.

Zareem thumbed his sword loose, but Kunthar casually waved him off. Zareem moved to stand behind his master, frowning at the intruder. *If it wouldn't cause a war, I'd let Zareem cut him down here and now, Kunthar thought.*

"Lord Alazar what is the meaning of this intrusion?" Kunthar asked in the same calm tone in which he had greeted the humans.

"You know damn well what it's about," Alazar growled. "You have kept me waiting all day and now I find you here meeting with these little monkeys." Alazar eyed the humans like a predator sizing up his next meal.

Now Kunthar rose up and glared at the intruder. "Lord Alazar you may be a powerful warlord in control of many territories, but I am still Shogun, and you will address me with the respect and honor that I am due."

"For now, anyway," Alazar coldly said under his breath.

Kunthar took a slight step toward Alazar. "What? I'm sorry I didn't quite hear you." Reyan calmly continued to serve her guests. As she poured Joenair a cup she bent low and seemed to whisper something to him, unheard by the rest.

"I said yes omo-sama." Alazar bowed, but there was menace in his voice. He turned back to the humans and walked over to where Joenair was seated on the floor. Reyan quietly withdrew with a slight nod to the smaller human.

"And what are these things? They look like hairless monkeys. Like the little monkeys I hunted as a child. I would grab one and bite its head off and laugh as the others ran away screaming. What do you think about that little monkey? Maybe I will bite your head off and watch your friends run away and hide." Alazar flicked his tongue out over his massive canines.

Warrec started to rise and say something, but Joenair waved his hand to sit back down. Joenair slowly got up from the floor and looked straight up at Alazar. "I have a better idea snaggletooth. Why don't I take my little monkey foot and smack it across your ugly face."

Kunthar's nostrils flared. Alazar was going too far threatening his guests. The little male seemed completely calm, however. Kunthar glanced back at Zareem. The elder tiger cocked and eyebrow and stroked one side of his moustache. After a few seconds he nodded, saying let it play out.

Alazar started to laugh, but quickly found himself on the floor dazed with blood running from his mouth. Kunthar couldn't recall later if he had seen Joenair move; it had been so fast. "Would you like to see it again?" Joenair calmly asked.

Alazar roared and lunged at Joenair who easily side stepped and sent the Kathari flying across the room and through one of the paper walls. Alazar slowly picked himself up and shook his head to clear it. He growled again and leapt at Joenair fangs bared and claws ready to rend flesh. He was brought up short as a sword blade slid up against his throat.

"Enough Alazar-dono," Kunthar said. "I will speak with you later. Now go." Zareem gently pulled the sword back from Alazar's throat. Alazar fixed his clothing and left with a huff.

Aluna blinked twice as she tried to figure out what had just happened. "What...what is his problem?" she finally asked.

Kunthar now viewed the humans with much greater respect. That had been impressive. Alazar was no mere cub. There was quite a bit more to them than he had first imagined. The old lion held out his hand to indicate for his guest to again sit. "He wants my job. But that is not a matter for today. Now let's have some tea in quiet." Kunthar answered as he reached for his cup.

Warrec turned to look at Joenair. "Jay what the hell was that?"

Joenair cocked his head and gave his friend a half grin before mock whispering back an answer, though loud enough for everyone to hear. "I was told to tame the tiger."

Kunthar looked over at Reyan. She was pretending to be preparing a tray of biscuits but was clearly trying to hide her laughter. He couldn't help himself. Kunthar started to chuckle too, but it quickly grew into a full belly laugh.

430

Chapter Twenty-eight

Warrec decided that he liked the Kathari. Days and weeks passed as the three of them spent time getting accustomed to the Kathari people. They found them to be a very civilized race with a high degree of formality. Well, most of them anyway. Joenair had come to sense an underlying tension among them; mostly directed at the faction controlled by Alazar.

Warrec slid back the paper door to his room and walked out into the hallway. It was still early, just a little after dawn and he was surprised to see Jay slipping out of his room as well.

"Morning War," Joenair said.

"Morning," Warrec said. "Where are you headed off to? I'm guessing you aren't coming down to the dojo today."

Joenair sucked in air through his teeth and gave a half shrug. "No, well maybe later. I gotta go check with a fisherman about something I heard yesterday, have to keep following that rumor trail."

Warrec shook his head slightly and smiled. "Zareem is going

to make you pay for being late."

Joenair shrugged again. "Hey, you're the one that asked me to keep an eye and ear open, so you should have to take my punishment." Warrec punched him in the shoulder. "Ow, it was worth a shot."

"Are the locals talking to you? We are foreign devils after all." Warrec chuckled. They had heard that insult fairly quickly when talking with the Kathari. They said it simply as a statement of fact and the three of them decided best to not take offense over it. Now it had become a running joke between the three of them.

"That's one of the funnier things," Joenair said with a grin. "Maybe it's because I'm a foreign devil, but the Kathari are huge gossips, at least the worker guys seem to be. And the women, the women will talk your ear off."

Warrec cocked an eyebrow. "Just talk?"

Joenair gave him an exasperated look. "Oh, how little you think of me, granted with my track record it's an accurate opinion but still." He gave a slight chuckle. "No, with the Orc at least the squishy bits and general shape were the same. I've never looked at a cat and gone all, well hello there."

"Just checking, alright I better get a move on or Zareem will have me doing squats till the sun sets."

"Good luck with that." Joenair gave a slight salute and

walked off.

Zareem had been kind enough to show Warrec and Joenair a few moves and fighting techniques that the Kathari used. Joenair had impressed him by flinging Alazar around the room their first day. Impressed enough that he had offered to take the two humans on as students. Unfortunately, much to her chagrin, Aluna had not been included in that offer. The Kathari had an aversion to teaching females the arts of war. The elder tiger rarely took on students and Warrec had quickly found out why.

Zareem was a master of the combative arts the likes of which Warrec had never seen. Kathari came from all over the islands for the chance to train with the great master; very few were found to be worthy. Frankly, Warrec didn't consider himself worthy either, but the elder tiger had obviously seen something.

I better get a move on before he changes his mind, he thought. Warrec turned and practically sprinted down the hallway in the opposite direction. The training yard was on the opposite side of the palace and Zareem's dojo was enclosed off of that.

Warrec spent most of his days training with Zareem. The two had quickly found a mutual respect for each other. Kunthar would sometimes join them when the old lion could find the time to steal away. There the old lion would resume his role of student and assented to the wisdom of his teacher, but these moments were few and far between as the old lion's duties of trying to hold a nation together kept him far busier than he would have liked.

Warrec found this a little odd, he had a hard time imagining some of his superior officers going back through basic training and kowtowing to the training sergeants again. Though the more he thought about it, it probably would have done some of them good.

Warrec suspected Kunthar welcomed the distraction of his and Zareem's sparring. Kunthar was stoic as a mountain, but sometimes briefly when it was just the three or four of them the mask of leadership would slip slightly. Warrec could tell that Kunthar was worried about Alazar. The warlord's name seemed to be on the tip of everyone's tongue. From what he had overheard and the information Joenair had been able to dig up, war seemed imminent.

Warrec skidded to a stop just outside the dojo doors. Panting he desperately tried to make himself not out of breath as quickly as possible. He only gave himself a few seconds before he grabbed the door and slid it open. Walking in he could see that today he and Zareem were alone. The elder tiger knelt on the training mats in the middle of the empty training hall with his back to the door.

"You are late Warrec-kun," the elder tiger said without turning to look at Warrec.

Warrec bowed to Zareem's back. "Sorry sensei."

Zareem flicked a finger in irritation towards one of several weapon racks that lined the walls. "Hozumi the trickster god must have sent you to me to test my patience Warrec-kun. Go; warm up, fifty front kicks and one hundred punches, horse stance. Then grab a bokken, and quickly."

Warrec kicked off his slippers and hurried over to the corner Zareem had indicated. He started kicking as quickly as he dared, knowing if his form was off on any rep he would have to start over. By the time he was finished he was breathing hard, and his heart thudded in his chest. He grabbed one of the wooden training swords and joined the elder tiger on the mat.

Warrec quickly found that his swordsmanship was subpar at best when compared to Zareem. The Kathari had perfected the use of the blade into an art form. The two of them stripped off their top robes to spar in only simple hakama pants. While the lack of clothing and armor provided better freedom of movement Warrec couldn't help but feel a little exposed.

They had barely begun before Zareem already had a ten to three lead on Warrec. One of those three wins had been blind luck and Warrec was fairly certain Zareem had given him the last one. Warrec readied himself as they reset again and prepared to strike.

Warrec brought the bokken down in a quick slash from high

guard, aiming at Zareem's left shoulder. The elder white tiger was a master of voiding, barely moving and letting the strike pass by. Zareem cocked his shoulder back and Warrec's strike slashed through empty air. Before he could recover, he found the edge of Zareem's wooden sword resting against the outside of his throat.

"Eleven to three," Zareem stated with a slight nod as he withdrew. "Remember strike where your opponent will be, not where he is."

Warrec was starting to grow frustrated, more at himself than his opponent. Zareem was calm and collected as always and had the air of trying to teach a child a simple concept, yet there was no condescending tone in his voice or manner. Despite his many losses Warrec felt the teaching was invaluable.

"I'm used to having a shield," Warrec stated as he set his stance for the next round. "I would have blocked it."

"Yet, you do not have a shield and so you are dead again." Zareem feigned a horizontal slash across Warrec's stomach. Warrec easily parried and countered at Zareem's exposed right leg. Again, his bokken struck air as the tiger circled around and slapped him across the buttocks with the flat of the blade.

Warrec sighed deeply and dropped his chin to his chest. "Ok what was that? You had an exposed weakness and I attacked."

Zareem smiled as he readied in a low guard stance. "A

novice leaves himself exposed. A master does not. Know your opponent."

"So, you left your leg exposed so that I would strike there?"

"Correct," Zareem nodded again. "Make your enemy attack where you want him to. Know your enemies' strengths and weaknesses and yours, chose the place of battle and your victory is already won." Warrec nodded as the lesson sank in.

Every time he attacked the Kathari easily moved or dodged. Warrec readied and again slashed downward at Zareem's left shoulder. At the last second, he turned the angle of the attack to strike the tiger's right shoulder. Zareem flicked his sword upward and softly guided Warrec's strike away. Before Warrec could regain his guard the Kathari slashed across his forearms and against the inside of his thigh.

"Thirteen to three," Zareem stated in the same calm tone. Warrec just stared at him trying to figure out what he had done wrong. Zareem bowed and stuck his bokken back into his silk belt. "Come, let us take a break. You are improving. You struck where I would be and not where I was. However, you must never show your opponent your full strength at the beginning. Always guard and hide your true abilities. Display strength when you are weak and feign weakness when you are strong." Warrec nodded and followed after Zareem as they walked over to the water bucket in the corner.

"Tell me Warrec-kun why are you here?" Zareem asked as they drank and rested.

Warrec cocked an eyebrow. "What do you mean sensei? I thought it was obvious, to practice and improve my skills."

Zareem gave a slight smile. "No, my friend, I meant why are you here in our lands."

"Our king wanted to establish diplomatic relations with your people." Warrec answered still not sure where the questioning was going.

"Forgive me, my meaning is not clear. Why are you...you Warrec...why are you here?"

Warrec scratched at his beard still not sure what he was being asked. "I don't follow sensei. What are you asking?"

The white tiger rolled his shoulders and looked the big man up and down. "You are no diplomat Warrec-kun. You are a warrior such as I. You go where you are ordered, kill who needs to be killed and keep the peace in your land. Your friends are also not diplomats."

Warrec slowly nodded as he finally understood what Zareem was asking. It was something he had also been wondering about. He had neither the ability nor authority to broker any type of trade relation or treaty. Joenair was superb at gathering intelligence, but he was certainly no ambassador. Aluna was basically along for the ride. They were an odd trio to send to make first contact.

"I don't really know," Warrec said. "Now that I think about it and have the question voiced." He tapped his finger on his chin. "I suppose it's a cultural exchange. We learn about the Kathari, and you learn about our empire," he finally answered. That didn't seem right, but it was the only thing he could think of.

Zareem nodded. "So, then tell me of your homeland. You say it is an empire, so you have an emperor?"

Warrec shook his head. "Well, no, not anymore. Our emperor died and the empire was split into two equal kingdoms ruled by his twin sons."

"Ah, so your government is a hereditary monarchy," Zareem stated.

"Yes, for the most part. Our king rules, but usually delegates authority to a council of nobles, our senate, to handle day to day issues. You have an emperor do you not? Isn't it the same?"

Zareem shook his head. "Our emperor is but a child. Someday, when he is ready, he will claim his throne and give guidance to our people. His rule is absolute as he is chosen by the gods themselves. Heiko gives authority to the region and clan lords, and they care for their territories. Generally, they are left to their own devices as long as it does not go against the will of the emperor or cause suffering to the people. Heiko, he is the spiritual head and guidance of my people. We have only one emperor. When he dies, he is reborn again and again."

Warrec cocked his head not sure how that would work. "So, it's the same person over and over again?"

Zareem laughed. "No, I see your confusion. Our emperor is not immortal. When he dies his soul is reborn in a new body. He must learn again the lessons of life. Sometimes he remembers things he learned long ago, sometimes not. Each time he passes away our priests must search the land for where he is born again."

"So, then who rules your people? You seem to have a class system."

Zareem nodded again. "Yes, our Shogun rules, until that time, sometimes it is long, sometimes short. Kunthar-sama was elevated to that position. His duty is to maintain the empire until Heiko is ready to resume his place as emperor. It is not an easy or enviable task, at least not to one with sense."

"And Kunthar is from the ruling class," Warrec said. He shaped his hands around his head and neck. "They're the ones with the manes."

Zareem nodded again. "Yes, though not all are of that class. He comes from our daimyos, or you would call nobles or clan lords. He either takes power through military might or is chosen by the other lords. Kunthar is our current Shogun and has been for many, many years. It is a difficult position as he must gain cooperation from the region lords and has little authority to do so without the backing of the others."

"What about using the military," Warrec asked

"The region lords fight amongst themselves for territory and resources regularly. Sometimes the shogun must step in to restore the peace, but it is frowned upon for him to be the aggressor."

Warrec slowly shook his head. "That seems difficult; he is given a sword, but not allowed to use it. Instead, he has to stand back and ask the others to play nicely."

"Indeed," Zareem said "As I said it is not an easy position to maintain, most don't last that long. War breaks outs and a new shogun is chosen if the old one loses."

Warrec stroked his beard. "You have a whole group of people, waiting around for the next fight and putting pressure on the whole situation."

"Correct again Warrec-kun," Zareem said. "Beneath them is the warrior class, such as myself. We serve our lords and pledge our lives to them. A warrior without a lord is said to have no honor, a wander, driftless, so we all seek to serve. Every lord must maintain a host of warriors; these are above the common conscription soldiers. I will admit that my class tends to get bored when there have been no battles for too long. Then there are the peasants that feed us. Last are the artisans and merchants."

Warrec mulled it over in his head before speaking. "You are born into your class. So, a merchant could never become a warrior or even a peasant?"

Zareem nodded again. "Yes, one is born into the destiny chosen for them. If they were meant for other things, then they would have been born to them. But being in a class does not prevent one from learning. A farmer may learn to fight, and a warrior may learn to paint, a merchant may learn to fish but these are not their destinies."

It seemed that the Kathari's appearance had a large part in which class they appeared to be in. Warrec shook his head. "But what about free will? Isn't there a choice? We choose our own destiny, don't we?"

Zareem cocked his head and stroked his drooping whiskers as he thought. "There is choice; one always has a choice in the matter of one's destiny." Zareem motioned for Warrec to rise and the two walked back towards the sparing area. "But perhaps it is an illusion, or perhaps one has more than one destiny. Ones choices lock a person into their destiny. I could have chosen to learn to be a merchant and reject my class, but then I would not be me. My peers would have shamed me and rightly so for dishonoring my class. It does happen on occasion, however." Zareem drew his bokken and set his stance at a mid-guard.

Warrec matched his stance. "But, how would you know which path you have chosen is the correct one?"

"You wouldn't, until you reached the end of the journey." Zareem answered as he lunged forward. The proper counter to the attack would have Warrec parry the strike and guide it away from his body. Each time he had tried it before the Kathari had reversed the strike and brought it back against his throat.

Instead, this time he received the attack, barely moving at the last second. The tip of Zareem's sword lightly grazed against his ribs. Warrec closed the distance and slashed outward bringing the edge of his bokken up against Zareem's neck.

The white tiger nodded and smiled. "Choice, perhaps you are right friend Warrec. Destiny may not be a linear path, but one with many branching roads."

Warrec smiled. "Thirteen to four," he said.

Chapter Twenty-nine

Three days after the battle with the raptors the trio of Duncan, Wildbeard, and Akana found themselves at the location of the lost Elven city of Naacada Niwt. At least, that's where they were supposed to be. All Duncan could see was more endless jungle. The Dwarve walked up beside him and gave a frustrated grumble.

"Are ye sure this is the spot?" Wildbeard asked for probably the hundredth time.

Duncan didn't bother looking down at him as he answered. "Yes, according to the map it should be here." He pulled the map box from his pack and sat down crossed legged on the ground as he began looking at it again. It still said the same thing as the dozen other times they had made him check it. They should be standing in the city now.

"Are you sure you are reading it right?" Akana asked for probably the thousandth time.

"Yes," he said. A low growl had seeped into his voice, and he honestly didn't care. The heat and humidity had been taking its toll on Duncan. Wildbeard didn't appear to be fairing in better and the two of them had become increasingly grumpy, because of it. Which of course Akana found to be quite funny and teased the two of them mercilessly.

The Orc was beginning to weigh on his nerves. He still wasn't completely sure if she had been following them or just encountered them by happenstance. They couldn't just kill her because she was difficult and annoying. At least that's what he had told himself, but that argument was losing strength.

"I hate this place," Wildbeard stated for probably the millionth time that day alone. Duncan grunted in agreement as he studied the puzzle map.

"Oh, I don't know," Akana said. "I think it's actually quite nice here. I love this weather." Duncan could see the vein pulsing on the Dwarve's forehead as she spoke. Her tone was far too happy for Wildbeard's taste.

"Ye would. You're also half naked...more than half," the grumpy Dwarve shot back. Akana cocked a hip at him and placed a hand on the hip. She slowly stroked her hand across her thigh in an inviting gesture, and then laughed as the Dwarve's face turned red.

"Don't act like you're not enjoying the view," she said coyly. "Besides nothing is keeping you from stripping down...other than Dwarven modesty. Come on Whiskers, let me see what you got." She suddenly lunged at the Dwarve and seized him by the waist as she tried to pull his pants down.

"Now see ere woman, unhand me! I'm nae yer plaything," he bellowed. Akana had a little over a foot in height on the Dwarve. However, he had fifty pounds on her and a great deal more raw strength. He easily batted her hands away and shoved her back. Akana fell backward, over dramatically and landed on her back. Akana had been laughing the whole time. Now she propped herself up on her elbows and gave Wildbeard a sultry look as her legs naturally splayed open.

"Among my people we call that foreplay," she said licking her lips.

Wildbeard gave an exasperated huff and threw his hands in the air. "Ye little tart, away with ye woman. I have half a mind to throw those shackles back on ye and leave ye chained up," he said with a snort.

Akana laughed again and pouted her lips. "Yummy, now that could be fun," she said, her voice coming out in a sultry hiss. "You know just what to say to a girl to get her all hot and bothered." Akana squeezed her arms together pushing her ample cleavage up. It was a miracle that the leather straps held them in place.

The Dwarve's eyes bulged for a moment and his cheeks turned an even brighter crimson. He drove his wide palms into his eyes rubbing them. "That's not what I meant, I dinnae mean..." he trailed off. Wildbeard grunted and threw his arms down in a dismissive gesture. He then turned and stomped off with a huff.

Duncan shook his head at the two. He had tried to ignore the two of them, but they didn't make it easy. For the past three days Wildbeard and Akana had been playing the same game nearly nonstop. Or at least Akana was playing; the Dwarve probably didn't find it that amusing. She had quickly learned the Dwarve's buttons and pressed them at every opportunity. Neither he nor Wildbeard were particularly pleased that she had attached herself to them, and Duncan now had to suffer the Dwarve's complaints of the Orc now as well.

"And stop calling me Whiskers!" Wildbeard shouted back over his shoulder.

"Ok, Whiskers!" Akana shouted back. Wildbeard answered with a very audible growl. Akana giggled at the Dwarve as he continued to stomp away. "He is so easy," she said to no one in particular.

She then looked over at Duncan still seated in front of the puzzle map, doing his best to ignore them and concentrate on the map. A wicked grin crossed her face. Akana stretched and rolled over onto all fours arching her back. She then crawled, cat-like toward him.

Akana's blatant sexual advances on the Dwarve had been made

quite clear. Although Duncan wasn't entirely sure if she was genuinely interested in the Dwarve or was merely playing with him. So far, she had done everything shy of forcing him and she had come close to that.

Though perhaps that's part of the game, he thought. *She certainly has gotten under his skin. Though as to why I can't say. There is something more going on than mere sexual attraction, but what I'm not sure,* Duncan thought absently as he studied the map. With the Dwarve she had been fairly aggressive, but he wasn't the only one she had set her sights on. Her advances on Duncan though had been much more subtle.

Duncan watched her moving toward him out of the corner of his eye. Akana moved with the tell-tale signs of a predator stalking its prey. Duncan had been married to the same woman for forty years. He didn't have much experience with women, but he could recognize this and what the Orc was trying to do. Njola had been the love of his life, this Orc wasn't even worthy of her shadow.

Wildbeard didn't trust her and had said as much to Duncan, repeatedly, though whether it was simple prejudice or not the Dwarve couldn't say. Dwarves and Orcs had been bitter enemies for a long time. They were now technically allies, but old hatreds had died hard.

Duncan had thought Wildbeard had been a bit confused by her

and not sure how to respond. The Dwarve had dealt and traded with a few of the prominent Orc tribes after all, the Wolfhelm and Daggerfoot mostly. Wildbeard hadn't been able to place her; she definitely hadn't come from either of those tribes. Her accent and mannerisms had all been off.

They had asked both together and separately where she came from. Her answers had been evasive, but Duncan had managed to get a tribe name out of her. The Salt Hopper tribe was as far away and remote as an Orc tribe could get, past the southern coast and impossible to verify. Wildbeard hadn't mentioned the attempted museum burglary since the first night, but the thought had lingered in Duncan's mind.

Duncan didn't trust her either. He kept going back to the same thing he had told the Dwarve that first night, at least this way they could keep an eye on her. He hadn't failed to realize that she had been working them, or at least was trying to. Duncan still wasn't sure yet if she was just trying to keep herself alive by attaching herself to them or if there was more sinister intent.

Her manner and wanton sexual nature were disarming and distracting to say the least. She spoke her mind with brutal honesty and without a hint of tact. Her frankness and demeanor reminded him of his late wife, Njola, in an odd way.

He quickly shook his head. *I do not want to start*

associating her with Njola, he thought. He had enough painful, disturbing, and tormenting things floating around in his head as it was. The last thing he wanted was for the memories of his wife to become tainted.

Instead, he thought back over the last few days of how the Orc had acted towards their mission. *She hasn't shown any real curiosity about the puzzle box or really why we are out here,* he thought.

She had asked what it was of course. Duncan at first had been hesitant to let her know of it, but he couldn't think of any way to keep it secret. He couldn't go tromping off to check it behind a tree every time. After they had told her it was a map, and they were historians looking for ancient ruins her interest had seemed to drop away to nothing. *Or at least that's what she wants us to believe.*

Her story had made sense in a way. Slavery was relatively common among the Orc clans and accepted as the norm. The Dwarves didn't keep slaves, just indentured servants and debtors and it was a practice that was fairly widespread in the empire. His people kept thralls after all. The only real difference was slaves were owned by individuals while thralls belonged to the whole village or clan.

"How's it going handsome?" Akana practically purred as she finished crawling toward him. She had moved behind Duncan, and he could feel her warm breath on the back of his neck as she looked over his shoulder at the map.

She draped her arms over his shoulders as she knelt behind him. He could feel her pressing her breasts against his back as she looked at the map. Duncan blinked and looked up at the jungle avoiding looking back at her. *Yes, much more subtle, though for an Orc that's a relative term,* he thought.

He did his best to ignore it. Duncan still missed his wife terribly, but it had been a long time since he had felt a female's touch. It had been too long in fact. Akana was an Orc after all, but she was still a woman. Orc or not she was still quite attractive. Duncan wasn't pleased with the feelings she was arousing inside of him. *I'm too old for this crap,* he thought. He grunted in response to her question.

"I don't understand it," he said as he stood up suddenly. Akana fell backward as Duncan had surged up to his feet. A look of dissatisfaction and irritation flashed across her face, quickly replaced with an innocent smile, but he had caught it.

"Don't understand what?" she said with a huff still lying on the ground.

Duncan didn't say anything as he began to pace about. After a minute or so he finally responded. "Naacada Niwt should be here. At least that's what the map says. I know I'm translating the message correctly."

"So why isn't it?" she asked. "Look big guy, I have never heard of any Elven city being anywhere near here. Granted this is pretty remote jungle, but it's not like Orcs have never been through here. Humans probably not, Dwarves certainly not, but us Orcs have, this area has been explored. If there were ruins here, they would have probably found it."

Duncan was not happy with her response. His fist balled up and he looked toward the sky. He said a silent prayer to the AllFather for guidance.

"The only thing I have ever heard about being around here is an old obelisk," Akana said as she rose to her feet. She mimed dusting herself off, causing her breasts to jiggle. She sighed when she noticed that Duncan wasn't really paying attention to her show.

"Wait what did you just say?" Duncan asked as his head snapped back down to look at her.

"About what? That no one has found the ruins of a city here?"

"No...no the other thing. What about an obelisk?"

"Oh, I just heard there was an old obelisk out here somewhere in the area."

"Why didn't you mention this sooner?" he snapped.

"Because you are looking for a city," she said with an exasperated huff. "Besides it's not that important. It's just an old blank obelisk," she said. Akana placed her hands on her hips defiantly.

Duncan clapped his hands together in excitement. "That's it. It has to be." He turned to where the Dwarve had stomped off to. "Wildbeard!" he called after the Dwarve.

"What?" the Dwarve called back, looking up from his pack.

"We need to fan out. I think we found what we're looking for. Or at least we will. Try to find an obelisk. Look carefully it might be covered in overgrown vegetation."

"Bout time," the Dwarve grumbled as he disappeared into the jungle growth. The trio spilt off as they searched the area for the long-forgotten stone pillar. A few minutes of furious searching, that quickly devolved into roughly five hours of slow methodical scouring passed before Wildbeard's voice rang out from the jungle overgrowth. "Over ere," he shouted. "I think I have it."

The sound of snapping branches and vegetation being torn down flowed through the hot humid air. Duncan barreled his way through the jungle flora towards the sound of Wildbeard's voice. Duncan crashed through the vegetation sounding as if a herd of mammoths had suddenly appeared and began stampeding through the undergrowth. He didn't slow as he tore creepers down and swung his machete in wide arcs clearing a path wide enough for a river barge to sail down.

Wildbeard stood before a lone stone pillar in a small clearing. It towered over him, easily three times his height. The pillar seemed to be formed of pure shadow crafted to a fine onyx that shimmered like obsidian glass in the few rays of sunlight that still pierced the jungle canopy.

It should have been overgrown with vines and creeping moss. Long vines descended from the trees to the ground forming a near wall of viridian vegetation surrounding the pillar. Though no vines, leaf, stem nor flower petal grew within a few yards of the ominous structure. The very ground around it was bare dirt devoid of the lush growth that surrounded it. The dark obelisk lay bare in the clearing as if the jungle flora sensed something ominous about its presence and avoided it, a hole in the center of the jungle.

"Well, I reckon this is it," Wildbeard said. "Though I've walked around it twice and I still aven't seen anything on it. It's just bare stone." Wildbeard pulled his pipe out and puffed on it as Duncan slowly walked around the obelisk. "If ye can call it stone," he added. "Looks more like liquid shadow, there is black and then there's this thing."

Akana appeared a few seconds later, neither of the two had heard her approach. Duncan was completely enthralled by the pillar and Wildbeard simply hadn't heard the Orc. The Dwarve nearly jumped out of his boots when she spoke.

"See I told you it was just an old obelisk," she said. "Just dark stone nothing that special." Wildbeard whirled around and fixed her with an icy stare. She glanced at him out of the corner of her eye and blew him a kiss before turning her attention back to the pillar and on Duncan.

Duncan slowly walked around the obelisk for a third time as he studied it. His eyes searched up and down the stone, trying to find any aberration in the fine glassy surface. Finally, after circling the pillar three times he stopped but continued to stare, lost in thought.

"Well? What now. Doesn't seem like much," Wildbeard said with a huff.

"Told you," Akana said with a condescending manner.

"Hush," Duncan said, barely above a whisper. The pair shot him confused looks but fell silent. Gingerly, Duncan reached out a hand toward the obelisk. His hand paused less than an inch from the dark glassy stone surface. His fingers tingled as he held them a hairs breath from the pillar and then he reached out and placed his hand on the black shiny surface. The stone felt warm to his touch. A low humming sound began to fill the small clearing, softly at first then gradually growing louder as it increased in pitch and speed.

"What the hell is that?" Akana said with apprehension in her voice. Wildbeard started to reach out and grab Duncan to pull him away from the stone.

"Wait," Duncan said as Wildbeard's huge meaty hand closed around his free arm. The Dwarve relaxed his grip but didn't let go. The humming had been growing steadily louder and now rose to a piercing whine. Then suddenly it stopped. A flash of light exploded out of the pillar, blinding Wildbeard and Akana. The Orc threw herself flat. The Dwarve staggered back as he inadvertently released Duncan. He tripped and fell to the ground across Akana. She let out a grunt as his weight hit her.

Wildbeard blinked rapidly trying to clear his vision. "Everything gone all blurry, I canna see." He jammed two ham hock sized fists into his eye sockets and began rubbing furiously. Duncan reached down and lifted Wildbeard up into the air and placed back him back on his feet. Akana let out a squeak as she was also set right side up again. The Dwarve slammed a hand down to try and seize whatever had grabbed him by the waist. He felt Duncan's arm as the old giant released his grip.

"Are you two all right?" Duncan asked.

Wildbeard blinked again and shook his head. "Aye, ugh, what…what happened?" The Dwarve asked. Wildbeard kept blinking rapidly as he tried to restore his vision. "It's starting to return I can almost see ye lad."

"To be honest I'm not really sure," Duncan said. "But here come look." He placed a hand on Wildbeard's back and guided him back toward the obelisk.

Akana let out a grunt. "You know Whiskers, I can think of easier ways for you to find an excuse to lay on top of me," she said as she rubbed an eye with the heel of her palm. She slowly stepped after the two of them.

Their eyes now seemed to have cleared as the three stood before the stone pillar. However, now it was no longer blank. Elvish markings and pictographs covered the dark stone. They shone with a light blue light, almost leaping off the black surface.

"What magic is this?" Akana whispered as she placed a hand before her mouth, staring at the magical engravings.

Wildbeard slowly took his pipe out and lit it again. After a few puffs, the Dwarve tapped the stem of the pipe a few times against his temple. "None that I've ever seen or heard of before," the Dwarve said. Cautiously, he tapped the pipe stem on one of the hieroglyphs as he studied the markings.

Duncan's eyes danced across the engravings. "This is old, older than the empire at least," Duncan said with a slow nod. He shook his head twice shaking off the temporary mesmerization he had found himself in. He turned and grinned at the two of them. "Get comfortable, we are going to be here awhile."

Chapter Thirty

Warrec checked himself in the mirror again, for probably the twentieth time. He readjusted the collar on his black doublet, making sure the rank pins were aligned properly. Everything else appeared straight and inline, green longcoat, blue breeches, boots, all looked clean and pressed. The Kathari washer women did fine work. He bent down and grabbed the sword belt and buckled it on. It looked odd being empty with no sword or knife on it.

"I feel a little naked," he said as he looked at the empty belt. There would be no weapons allowed tonight. He didn't like it, but the last thing he wanted was to cause a diplomatic offense by insulting some region lord.

The day of the Kathari emperor's birth, the holiest and highest holiday in the Kathari year, was today. All day the common folk had been dancing and playing music in the streets as the whole city joined in the festivities. At noon, a parade had traveled down from the palace down to the beach front along the bay. Kathari cubs had run through the streets shooting off whizbangers and popping firecrackers.

"I can't wait to see the big ones tonight," he said as he pulled his doublet down again in front. The fireworks were one of the things he enjoyed most about this land. Every full moon there was a little fireworks display at night to celebrate the coming new month. They were one of the things that just couldn't be described but had to be seen. No one in the empire would believe him. Zareem had said that tonight would be the biggest ones of the year.

Kunthar had planned for a large party at his house this evening with invitations going out to all the surrounding warlords. All of them had accepted the invitation except for one. Alazar had sent a short, but polite response that he would be unable to attend. After reading the letter Zareem had bluntly told his master that he would not be missed.

Finally, satisfied with his appearance, Warrec turned and walked out into the hallway to check if Joenair and Aluna were ready. He tapped lightly on the door frame at Jay's room.

"Coming," Jay's voice rang out in a sing song tone. Warrec rolled his eyes at the paper door. After a few seconds, the door slid open and Joenair leaned heavily on the door.

He was dressed in a fine maroon sleeveless doublet over a white linen shirt, with long puffy sleeves. He had matching breeches and what looked like soft new leather boots. Again,

Warrec wondered where he had gotten the clothing, because he hadn't packed any of it, at least not that Warrec had seen.

Joenair smiled seductively, but quickly let it drop into a look of utter disappointment. "You are the ugliest date I have ever had," he said. "I want my money back." He quickly held up a finger to cut Warrec off. "And yes, that includes the Orc, she smelled better too."

Warrec thought about punching him for a good three seconds. "Are you ready?"

Joenair grinned again and clasped Warrec on the shoulder as they started down the hall. "Yep, it's going to be a hell of a party tonight. Too bad there aren't any women. My gods man, do you know how long it has been?" Joenair bit his knuckles. "Cuttersbend!" Joenair clutched at his chest and mimed having a heart attack and slumped against a wooden pillar.

Warrec sighed. "Are you finished?"

Joenair took a deep breath and snapped back to his feet. "I've only started but forget about that. Let's just go get Red the forest nymph and get down there."

Aluna's room was on another floor above them. The Kathari didn't allow unwed males and females to stay on the same floor. They generally tried to keep them as separate as possible. Warrec at first had found their prudish nature a little odd, but it had quickly turned into amusement when Aluna had been told the amount of clothing and makeup a female was required to wear on a daily basis. She had not found it as funny, which made him laugh even more.

"You think she is ready yet?" Warrec said. "It takes them hours to get everything on." He couldn't help but smile at the thought of Aluna having to wait as the Kathari women wrapped her in layer after layer of silk and linen.

"I would hope so, she and Reyan started three hours ago."

As they walked Warrec's hand subconsciously went to rest on the hilt of his sword, which he wasn't wearing. It caused him to half stumble and miss a step. He let out a low grunt of frustration.

"Doesn't feel quite right not having the steel on your side, does it" Joenair said.

"Yes, I still don't know why I can't at least carry a knife. I feel practically naked," Warrec said.

Joenair shrugged. "It's a trust thing. There's a lot of big wigs coming to this shindig tonight. Going to this armed shows you don't trust the other guy, so it causes offense, which leads to duels, which leads to someone dying, which leads to war. So, they don't wear weapons at formal gatherings. Plus, the whole symbolic thing with the spirit of their emperor being here, can't bring weapons in his presence," he trailed off waving his hand in a circle.

"Still seems silly," Warrec said. He then stopped and placed a heavy hand on Joenair's shoulder. "Jay, do you have any weapons on you?" His tone was calm but icy.

Joenair grinned. "War, now would I do something like that?" Warrec just stared at his friend in response. "Look which answer do you want, because I know you don't want to cause an incident, but you also don't like the idea of going somewhere without a way to protect yourself. So, to answer you, yes but also no."

Warrec slowly shook his head and balled up a fist in front of his face. He then bit his knuckles before releasing Joenair and walking away. He quickened his pace and made his way to the entrance to the female quarters. He could feel Joenair's smile on his back.

At the entrance he announced himself to the eunuch guarding the door. The eunuch was a fat tawny cat with large ears. He clapped his paws together and let out a girlish giggle before disappearing down the hallway. After a few minutes Aluna came out to join them.

She was bound in a bright green kimono with cherry blossoms embroidered on the hem. That was just the top visible layer; underneath would be five or six more. A red sash rode low on her hips covering her rear, but at the same time emphasizing the curves of her chest and hips.

Her hair was bound up in a tight bun, held in place with

black lacquered chopsticks. Aluna's face had been painted a bright ivory white, which contrasted significantly with her ruby red lips, dark eyeshadow, and rosy cheeks. She batted her emerald-green eyes at them. She looked stunning.

The image quickly burst as she let out a loud snort and laughed. "I look silly," she said. She raised her arms, her sleeves were huge and covered her hands, and pointed at herself. "I mean look at this. I can't move."

Warrec let out a chuckle. "No, no you look great." He turned and winked at Joenair before walking quickly back down the hallway with quick large steps. "Come on, hurry, we don't want to be late," he said back over his shoulder. After half a second, Joenair nodded and followed after at the same quick pace.

They made it halfway back down the hall before they heard her yell after them. "You assholes, wait, I can't walk that fast in this," she yelled. They both burst out laughing as her little slippered feet rapidly shuffled across the floor trying to match their pace.

They waited for her. Warrec had to wipe away a tear, he was laughing so hard. She swung and tried to hit them, but the poofy sleeves got in the way, which made them laugh even harder. It took them several minutes to calm down as they walked back through the palace, which caused quite a few stares as the

Kathari looked at the odd humans.

The night of the celebration was cool and clear. The party guests were sitting in the courtyard watching a play. Banquet tables had been arranged in a half rectangle around the stage. Warrec, Aluna and Joenair had been given a place of honor seated near Kunthar at the high table. A skeleton crew of the palace staff worked frantically to feed and refresh the guests. Most of the palace staff had been dismissed for the evening to celebrate the holiday and the wives and concubines of the various lords had taken over duty to serve the banquet.

Warrec dug ravishingly into the different food dishes as they were brought around. Some of the food was downright disgusting, fish eye stew and octopus did not look, or smell appetizing and he avoided those. However, the fried meat dishes stuffed in pastry and laid on a bed of yellow rice were particularly good. One thing he did find odd was that the Kathari didn't have anything sweet, instead relying heavily on sour and bitter flavors.

Aluna let out a little squeal beside him. "By the AllFather I love these," she said as she popped a hunk of meat, coated in duck fat and dripping with a bitter tangy black sauce, into her mouth with the two sticks. She bit down and a look of ecstasy passed over her face. She quickly snatched up another one off the communal plate. "So good," she said around her bite. Her skill with the chopsticks was impressive, they were not something Warrec had taken to easily.

"You don't even know what meat that is," Joenair whispered.

"Hush, I don't care, it's delicious," she hissed back at him.

Warrec fumbled with the chopsticks as he tried to pick up a sliver of what looked like beef and onions. He looked up at the high table as he managed to get the food to his mouth.

Next to Kunthar a large and ornate chair had been placed at the center of the tables. The Emperor's chair sat empty as always. Kunthar had of course sent an invitation to the child emperor but was not surprised when he received the reply that Emperor Heiko would not be attending.

The emperor never left his monastery. Like every year before, his chair sat empty, serving only as a place of ceremony. The guests had come by one by one and knelt before the empty chair and swore allegiance. A slow trickle of the lesser lords were still making their way through as the play began. All the important people had already come through and were happily dining.

Aluna glanced up and followed his eyes to the chair. "It seems weird right?" she said.

Warrec shrugged. "They're swearing fealty, since they can't do it in person, they do it to the chair in front of the shogun, who bears witness.

Joenair leaned over and whispered. "Which makes it mighty odd that a certain region lord isn't here," he said.

"Yeah, I caught that too," Warrec said with a nod.

Warrec looked around the tables. There were easily forty of the region lords seated, flanked by one attendant, who most certainly was also a bodyguard, each, and several of their lesser lords. Kunthar had personally gone around and introduced each one to them. Warrec couldn't remember any of their names.

Except for Varoon, who was an old fat leopard and one of the few lords that didn't look lionesque. Varoon was jolly and a bit of a scalawag. He had visited a few weeks earlier and had made time to teach Warrec all the Kathari curse words he knew. Varoon lifted a wine cup in salute as he made eye contact with Warrec. Warrec returned the gesture. He liked Varoon.

Zareem was ever vigilant standing behind his master. Warrec saw his sensei's head snap up as the elder tiger stared at the roof top of the courtyard wall. Warrec turned to look at what had caught Zareem's attention. A cloud drew across the moon and Warrec thought he saw movement in the shadows behind the wall. He stared up at the rooftops but detected nothing more. After a few seconds he turned back to finish watching the play.

"Something up?" Joenair asked.

Warrec slowly shook his head. "Not sure yet, thought I saw

something." He looked back at Zareem, but his sensei had gone back to watching the play as well. "Keep your eyes open just in case."

The play was an old Kathari tale about a young woman who must choose between three suitors. The guests roared with laughter as the actor playing the bumbling old grandfather strutted around the stage. Warrec was having a hard time understanding the plot, but he laughed along with the others when the grandfather clutched his chest and feigned a heart attack at his foolish granddaughter.

An explosion of red and blue light lit up the night. A thunderous boom rattled the courtyard and there was another flash of green and white now. The fireworks exploded high over the banquet. The party guests let out a collection of oohs and aahs as the vibrant multihued bursts exploded overhead and smoke began drifting down into the courtyard.

"Those are early," Aluna said. "Look the play isn't even over yet." The play had stopped, though as the actors along with everyone else watched the booming display.

A sudden bump, between the explosions, of the high table sent a pitcher of wine and a large platter crashing to the floor. Warrec had his attention on the fireworks but turned as he heard the clatter. Kunthar let out a roar of rage and everyone turned back to see what was the matter.

Zareem had lunged forward, bumping the table, and spilling the wine. Warrec's eyes widened as he saw that the white tiger had barely managed to snatch an arrow from the air inches from Kunthar's chest. Reyan screamed as she realized what had happened. Chaos erupted as the courtyard filled with acrid smoke.

"Smoke bombs," Joenair yelled as he ducked underneath the table right before one detonated on the table. Dark figures descended from the rooftops and began slaughtering the guests.

"Shadow-warriors," Zareem roared as he tossed the arrow aside and up ended the high table to make a makeshift barricade.

The dark assassins were clad in black robes and wore only simple black leather armor except for a breastplate that was shaped like a snarling Kathari face. Yellow eyes glowed softly in the night hidden behind black masks. Their bodies seemed to fade and shimmer in and out of the smoke as they moved, disappearing, and reappearing somewhere else.

The shadow-warriors wielded simple short katana blades. Their swords showed none of the elaborate decoration of most of the blades that Warrec had seen so far. The simple blades were purely for utility, though even these simple swords showed the extensive labor that went into every Kathari blade.

It took a few seconds to react, but almost as one the warlords and their bodyguards leapt to their feet. Even unarmed they fought fiercely. Warrec watched as one tiger guard snatched a silver platter off the table and smacked an assassin across the face with it. A region lord jammed chopsticks into the eyes of another, before snatching up the crude katana.

Arrows sniped from the shadows cutting down the guests as they resisted. The night air was filled with flying steel as the shadow-warriors unleashed their hidden weapons.

"Beware the shurikens and chakrams," Zareem yelled out in warning. The words barely left the elder tiger's mouth before he had to heed his own warning. Zareem skillfully used a plate to parry and knocked away three of the razor sharp five-pointed stars as they flew at his face.

Warrec scrambled on all fours searching for some kind of weapon. Half blind and coughing from the smoke and with his ears ringing from the explosions he finally managed to close his hand on a single chopstick. "That's not going to cut it," he grumbled to himself. That Kathari lord had managed to use the slim sliver of wood as a weapon, but Warrec had serious doubts that he would be as capable.

Warrec ducked just in time as a chakram flew over his head. The sharp disc sunk into a tree behind him where his head had been a second ago. Warrec surveyed the courtyard. Each lord and his attendants were solely focused on keeping themselves alive, including Kunthar and Zareem. No one was leaving to alert the palace guards. The sounds of the fireworks display above would cover the sounds of the battle in the courtyard until it was too late.

"Joenair," he shouted. "Take Aluna and go with the rest of the women. Get them out of here and get the guards," Warrec ordered as he regained his feet. His two friends started to make a protest about leaving his side, but he cut them off with a glare.

Joenair nodded and reached into his doublet. Grinning he pulled out an eight-inch stiletto and tossed it to Warrec. Warrec caught the knife and gave his friend a quick salute.

"Who loves ya War," Joenair said. He turned and half carried Aluna towards the garden entrance, ushering the other females along as he did.

The assassin's katanas darted through the air like vicious serpents searching for warm flesh to strike into. Warrec knew that a little knife was no match for a few feet of steel, but it was still better than nothing. Silently, he thanked Jay's paranoia.

He had neither his armor nor his shield and he felt very naked. It didn't help that the shadow-warriors were much faster than he was either. It was everything he could do to keep his insides from becoming his outsides. Warrec fell backward and back peddled away from a shadow-warrior that had nearly opened up his stomach.

Varoon roared out in pain as an assassin's blade found its mark. Warrec cursed in both Highcommon and Kathari for the old leopard. Varoon's murderer turned on him now. Warrec barely ducked in time as an arrow whistled past his ear.

Warrec now found himself facing two of the assassins. Their yellow eyes glowed and narrowed as they moved in for the kill. Warrec swore under his breath as they seemed to be smiling under their mask at this easy kill.

Warrec screamed at them and threw his tiny knife in desperation at the nearest one. This took them off guard for a moment and he seized the opportunity. He leapt and rolled forward covering the distance between them. With a snarl he brought his fist up in an uppercut smashing into the lower jaw of the assassin on his right, sending blood and teeth flying.

Warrec rolled off the assassin's left shoulder and came up behind them. Before the other could turn Warrec bent down and grabbed his tail. Yanking upward with all his might he pulled the shadow warrior violently off his feet. The assassin yowled in pain as several bones in the tail snapped and he sprawled out on the ground.

Warrec spun and brought his heel down hard on his neck breaking it and cutting the yowl off. The first, still clutching his jaw, turned, and slashed at him. Warrec managed to sidestep and backpedaled to a sand garden behind him. The assassin lunged after him barely missing. Warrec quickly swiped at the ground sending a spray of sand at the shadow warrior's face. The assassin hissed in frustration as he was momentarily blinded.

Warrec took the opportunity and dove past him into a roll. He came up beside the one he had just killed and snatched up the fallen katana.

"Ok, grimalkin now we're a bit more even," Warrec snarled at the shadow warrior. The assassin had managed to clear most of his eyes and answered with a snarl of his own. He slashed forward striking at Warrec's stomach.

The enemy's blade caught Warrec across the stomach. Luckily, he had managed to step back fast enough to keep the cut from being deep enough to spill his guts out on the ground. Warrec kicked out and caught the assassin in the knee. His opponent fell and Warrec stabbed him in the back. The shadow-warrior didn't move from where he fell.

The noise of battle began to die down and Warrec looked up to see why. Just then a mighty roar echoed through the courtyard. Warrec saw Kunthar standing on the stage and ran towards him. The old lion was armed with two of the shadow warrior's blades and a pile of bodies at his feet showed testament to how lethal the old lion still was. His top robe was shredded, and multiple cuts could be seen on his bare chest, but none seemed fatal.

Without looking in one fluid motion Kunthar tossed one of the swords to Zareem and caught an assassin out of the air by the throat and lifted the smaller Kathari up with one arm. An audible crack was heard as the old lion snapped his enemy's neck in his hand. At the same time the elder tiger caught the sword and then slashed sideways with two blades cutting down another assassin. Kunthar caught the dropped sword of the assassin he had just killed and spun in place stabbing behind Zareem to stab another shadow warrior through the throat and liver.

The reason the battle had been dying down was because all the other warlords and their bodyguards had fallen. It seemed that every time one shadow-warrior was slain two more seemed to take its place. Now only three warriors remained, Kunthar, Zareem and Warrec. He joined the two elder warriors on the stage. The three found themselves surrounded, as the crowd of assassins slowly circled around them. Zareem walked backward till he was on the stage next to Kunthar and Warrec. The three warriors stood back-to-back in the middle of the stage with an army of assassins closing in. A knowing nod passed among them. They would make their stand here. They would win or they would fall, but they would go down fighting.

Zareem let loose a wild roar and slashed at the approaching assassins. Kunthar roared a horrible sound that shook Warrec to his core and lashed out at the nearest shadow-warrior. Warrec gave his own battle shout and felt rage coursing through his veins. The grimmig surged in his chest and time seemed to slow.

The shadow-warriors wore black leather armor similar to what the Kathari soldiers had worn but lighter. It offered them little protection from Zareem's sword as the elder tiger wove an intricate dance of death among them. Warrec marveled at the white tiger's skill. Zareem had said that he had fought in over one thousand duels and never lost and Warrec could now see how.

The assassins were concentrating on bringing Kunthar down, but they were having no luck. They fell before the mighty lion like wheat before the thresher. His blades did not slow as they cleaved through leather and flesh.

Everything grew still and slowed. Warrec could see everything and took in everything around him all at once. Everything was slowed down, but Warrec did not. He moved at normal speed along with everything that came in contact with him.

Zareem's sword weaved through the still night air, leaving a small trace of its image in its wake. Saliva glistened off Kunthar's fangs as he brought the two swords down on an assassin's shoulders. A pair of dumplings flew lazily through the air as a shadow warrior took a flying leap off the table. Arrows and shurikens glided through the air looking for the three of them. Warrec tinked two off course with his sword, keeping them from hitting Kunthar and him.

Warrec turned his shoulder as a sword slashed down at him. The blade slowly passed down his body as he dodged it. He backhanded the assassin, sending him flying. The shadow warrior snapped back and then seemed to float in the air as Warrec broke contact.

The three were giving out more than they took, and it almost seemed like they were winning, but Warrec could tell that this was a hopeless battle. They slaughtered their enemies left and right, but this failed to put a dent in the assassin's numbers.

Warrec lunged at one of the shadow-warriors, but it disappeared in a puff of smoke. Without turning he reversed the blade and stabbed behind. His new sword found its mark and he felt his blade sink into flesh. When he turned, he thought he saw a look of bewilderment in the glowing eyes of the shadow-warrior.

Warrec grinned and kicked him off his sword. He had been friends with Joenair long enough to know some of the tricks that the assassin used. The vanishing act was one of them. "Strike where they will be not where they are," he said with a grin.

Warrec was too busy congratulating himself to sense the enemy sneaking up behind him. He whirled and brought his sword up to parry the attack, but it wasn't necessary. There was a flash at the garden entrance and a bolt of lightning snaked through the night. It arced through the courtyard and struck the shadow-warrior in the middle of its back, a second later the crack of thunder followed it. The assassin exploded sending a rain of charred fur, bone, and goblets of flesh all over Warrec.

Bewildered, Warrec looked where the lighting had come from and saw Aluna standing at the doorway. She gave a little wave before vomiting in the bushes as the cost of the spell took its toll.

Aluna wiped her mouth and moved to join them. She had torn the kimono up to her hip and ripped the sleeves off. Her makeup was smeared, and her hair flowed freely around her face as she moved. She appeared slowed as the rest of the world as she ran forward. Warrec watched as she ran in slow motion towards him bouncing with each step and her hair like fire floating behind her. She looked mesmerizing. Then as she grew closer, she sped back up to normal speed matching Warrec. He swatted an assassin's blade aside and ran the cat through as he watched her.

Now recovered from vomiting, she ran up behind one of the assassins and seized his head in her hands. Scarlet bands of energy flowed out of the assassin and swirled around her. Aluna's eyes glowed ruby red. Within a few seconds she drained him and dropped the emaciated corpse. Aluna spread her arms wide as the red lines of energy crackled around her.

She let loose a scream, raw and primal. Hurricane force winds ripped out from around her and swept across the courtyard. A torrent of air spun around the three of them on stage. Shadow warriors went flying as the sudden cyclone ripped them from the ground, smashing them against the walls and each other. The sky opened up and a deluge of water fell. Small bolts of lightning crackled and occasionally struck an unlucky assassin.

The miniature hurricane swept up and out over the outer walls, scattering the archers on the roof tops and clearing the smoke. Aluna's spell had managed to stun most of the assassins and cut their numbers down significantly but not all. They were already regaining their feet.

Joenair streaked past her slowly at full sprint and stabbed one of the shadow-warriors in the back. Jay spun and whirled through the air wielding what looked like two long kitchen knives. He slashed, dodged, stabbed, and cut, carving a path through the back of the assassin's numbers. Warrec blinked wiping bits of gore from his eyes. It was surreal watching his friend slowly, but oddly quickly at the same time cut through the shadow warriors ranks.

Heavy pounding feet could be heard coming from inside the palace. Joenair had sprinted out of the palace to the garrison and returned with reinforcements. The assassins began to vanish as Kunthar's soldiers burst into the courtyard. Warrec breathed a heavy sigh of relief. As the storm raged around him Warrec felt the storm inside him subside and the grimmig faded back as the world returned to normal.

Kunthar and Zareem were still engaged in combat, but as the soldiers rushed in their enemies faded away into the night. Kunthar began to shout an order but was interrupted by Zareem's scream.

"Master look out," Zareem screamed as one final arrow flew toward Kunthar. In a last ditch attempt an assassin had cowardly fired an arrow at Kunthar's back. Without thinking twice Zareem launched himself into the air.

As he had before he managed to catch the arrow in flight. Kunthar's smile quickly faded as he saw his former sensei and most trusted friend fall to his knees clutching at the hand that had caught the arrow. The old lion caught his friend before he struck the ground as Zareem went limp in his arms. "Zareem, Zareem hold on!" Kunthar shouted. He could see that the arrowhead had pierced Zareem's hand.

Kunthar gently cradled Zareem as they sat on the ground. "Kunthar-sama I am dying," Zareem said and shuddered. "Sea snake venom, the arrow was poisoned. I can...I can feel it burning through my blood." Zareem broke out in a coughing fit and blood trickled out of his mouth. "It was…it was an honor to serve you. You were my greatest accomplishment. You have made me proud old friend." His eyes gently closed, and his breathing stopped.

Kunthar rolled his head back and let loose a roar so powerful that the palace shook. He held his dying friend and wept bitter tears.

Chapter Thirty-one

Aluna leaned heavily on Joenair as he half pulled; half carried her to the garden entrance as the shadow warriors attacked. Her little slippered feet were a blur as she tried to keep pace. The kimono was bound so tight around her legs she couldn't take a step of more than a few inches at a time. It had been amusing earlier, but now when she actually needed to run, she couldn't.

"Damn this dress," she snarled in Joenair's ear.

"Yeah, I hear ya," he said. He stopped and pushed her sideways separating the two of them as a shadow warrior materialized in front of them trying to cut off the only escape route. Without breaking stride, he shifted sideways as the assassin slashed downwards, cutting the space they had both just been in. Joenair brushed the assassin's arm sideways as he slithered up the arm, grabbing at the wrist and elbow.

In the next step he locked the assassin's arm out straight and spun a hundred and eighty degrees sending the shadow warrior crashing face first into the ground. On the third step, Joenair twisted the stretched-out arm up and back while stepping on the shoulder joint. There was a loud audible pop and tearing sound followed instantly by a scream of pain as the assassin's arm tore out of its socket and snapped at the elbow.

He didn't bother finishing the assassin off as he flowed through to the next step. On the fourth step Joenair reached out and pulled Aluna back to his side, before they continued on. "We have to get them out, they can't move any faster," he said pointing to the other women fleeing the garden.

Aluna glanced back and down at the fallen assassin as he rolled and howled in pain. She blinked twice and continued running as fast as her legs could go. They reached the garden gate before most of the other women and held them open.

Reyan scooted up to the gate. The First Consort looked distressed and near panic. Her hair had come out of its tight bun and looked frazzled. Her makeup was streaked from crying.

Reyan brought her hands up to cover her mouth and turned back to look as her husband fought on the center stage. Reyan turned back to Aluna and started to reach out with shaking hands, before stopping. She stepped forward then turned back, taking a step back towards Kunthar. She shook, unable to decide whether to go or stay.

Aluna seized her, spun her around, and pulled her into a quick embrace. "Go," she said. "You can't help him here and he can't win if he has to protect you." Aluna pushed The First Consort to arm's length and looked her in the eyes. "I swear to you we will do everything we can to help." Reyan's mouth and whiskers quivered, then she nodded twice and hurried through the gate.

It only took a few minutes to get everyone out but felt like an eternity. As the last of the consorts shuffled out Aluna turned back to find Stupid Warrec. She watched as the big man took one of the assassin's down with his bare hands and broke his neck, before turning to face another one.

"Don't you die on me," she whispered. *Don't you dare,* her mind echoed. With a growl she whirled and went through the gate with Joenair. "Plan?" she asked him.

Joenair pointed over to the side kitchen. "There weapons, I can run faster and will get the guards." He dashed across the open ground between the garden walls and palace curtain wall and ducked into the kitchen alcove. Aluna hadn't made it halfway before he came sprinting back out carrying a large kitchen knife and two more tucked in his belt.

He handed the one he was carrying to her. "All they had," he said. He turned and jogged backwards a few steps, still moving to the guard barracks but turning to face her. "What are you going to do?"

Aluna took the knife and drove the blade down between her

legs; savagely she cut downward to her feet. The beautiful and undoubtedly expensive silk parted like paper as the knife sliced through. Despite her complaining she had liked the dress. It had been a gift from Reyan, and she did feel a bit sad to destroy it like this. *Worry about it later,* she chided herself.

She stood back up and answered Joenair with a low growl. "I'm going to bring the storm."

Joenair grinned and gave her two thumbs up. "Have fun killing everyone," he quipped before turning and moving back into a full sprint towards the barracks.

Aluna nodded at his back. She slashed a hole at the shoulder of each sleeve and tore the cumbersome things free. She took two swipes at her face with her hands trying to wipe most of the makeup off but succeeding in mostly just smearing it. Her legs now free, she dashed back to the garden gate as she pulled the chopsticks out of her hair, shaking it free.

As she ran through the gate, she paused to survey the scene. Stupid Warrec, Kunthar and Zareem stood alone on the stage surrounded. The three of them moved and fought like mythical kings, the kind the bards and songsayers sung about, like *Jolback* and the *Saga of Grendimoor*.

She watched mesmerized as Stupid Warrec squared off against an assassin. The shadow warrior vanished in a puff of smoke only to be impaled by Stupid Amazing Warrec's sword. She smiled, then her eyes went wide. Stupid Amazing Warrec wasn't moving to stop the one sneaking up behind him.

No, her mind screamed. *Not my Warrec, you won't take him!* She sucked in a lungful of air, pushing the energy through her body. With an effort of will she pushed and pulled her life's energy through her body and pooled it in her right hand. Aluna focused causing her hands to take on a negative and positive charge. As the polarity increased, she could feel her bones vibrating, desperately wanting to release the built-up charge. With a snarl she let it, discharging the energy from her right hand. Her lifeforce exploded outward forming into lightning. The bolt streaked through the air before striking the assassin in the back causing an explosion of gore and fur.

At the sudden release of energy nausea welled up from inside her. She felt the drain crashing through her body as her body tried to compensate for the sudden loss. Aluna felt like she had just fallen a thousand feet and come to an instant stop. Her stomach lurched and despite her effort to stop it, hurled its contents back up her throat. Pain exploded through her body making her feel like her bones were on fire. She saw Stupid Amazing Warrec looking for her out of the corner of her eye and she waved a hand at him. She would be ok; it would just take a second. She took a few deep breaths, willing her body back under control. A few heartbeats passed and the pain and nausea subsided.

Ok, that, that one hurt, she thought. She shuddered and fought down another wave of nausea. *Can't stop but can't do that again. Have to find another source.* Her mind trudged through the thought process.

She saw a shadow warrior a few steps away, he was still stunned from the bolt of lightning and thunderclap crashing right by him. He reacted slowly and still wasn't aware of her. With a nod, she made her mind up and lurched towards him, seizing his head in her hands.

She pulled. The shadow warrior's lifeforce came shrieking up out of him. Crimson bands of energy ripped through the air and flowed around and through her. The assassin's soul screamed out in pain as she ripped it free and drained the life from the body. His soul shot out wailing out into the night sky searching for a way into the afterlife.

Aluna felt her body pulsing with new sudden power, each pulse increasing in intensity. Each pulse thundered in her blood as she drained the last of the assassin's life. Her body couldn't handle the amount of power of two lives at once for long. It demanded to be released, so she did.

Her vision went red, and she summoned forth the storm. The hurricane tore through the night, bringing thunder, lightning, wind, rain, and pain. It took all her will to keep the eye centered around the three on the stage. She held it in place as long as she could before she had to release it and push it out over the walls, howling into the night.

She felt slightly dizzy as she finished and only a little lightheaded. It was like she had suddenly stood up too fast after hanging upside down. She had used the assassin's energy to build and summon the storm and then hold it in place. Her energy had only had to direct it a little and aim it. It was just enough to make her catch her breath. She leaned a hand against the garden wall.

Joenair surged past her, moving like poured oil. He flowed through the battle scene as a blurry flash of steel. Behind him the palace guards erupted out of the gates, like an ant mound that had been kicked open. They looked furious and wanting blood. Unfortunately, it didn't look like they would get satisfaction tonight. As they poured into the gardens the assassins beat a hasty retreat, vanishing up and over the walls in puffs of smoke.

Aluna felt a wave of relief wash over her. It was over and Stupid Amazing Warrec was still standing. She smiled and began to run to him. A blur of white crossing the stage made her stop. Zareem collapsed into Kunthar's arms. The two old warriors fell to the stage floor.

Kunthar held Zareem for a few seconds before the old lion's

head fell back into a blood curdling roar. Aluna covered her mouth. It was a sound that was eerily similar to the one the shadow warrior's soul had made as it was ripped from its body.

The rest of the night the palace was a flurry of chaos. It had been fairly obvious who had been behind the attack. Every region lord within a few days travel on the main island had been at the party. All except one. Aluna wasn't certain if Alazar had felt certain the attack would succeed or he was just stupid.

"Or both," she mumbled to herself as she finished tearing off the remaining shreds of the once lovely kimono. She stood naked in her room as she frantically assembled her gear. Joenair and Stupid Amazing Warrec had withdrawn to their own rooms to get ready. The entire palace was gearing up for war and would be on the march within a few hours.

She had run by the armory before coming here and had grabbed a scale plate cuirass and a set of bracers and greaves that matched it. Aluna threw the cuirass on over her poncho and checked to see if she could still easily draw her weapons. Satisfied, she finished putting on the greaves over her boots and last the vambraces. She tossed her twin satchels over her shoulder and sprinted out the door and down the hallway to Stupid Amazing Warrec's room.

Stupid Amazing Warrec had returned to his room to retrieve his armor. As she reached it, she didn't bother to knock and violently slid open the door. Stupid Amazing Warrec was standing in the middle of the room with his arms above his head as Joenair fought with his breastplate, trying to get it to lock in place over the gambeson. Getting a knight dressed and fully armored was a two- or three-man job. She stifled a laugh as the two of them spun around each other.

Aluna rolled her eyes and pushed Joenair out of the way. She grabbed the strap and with a savage pull downwards got it to snap down into place to be buckled.

"You didn't knock," Stupid Amazing Warrec said as he was finally able to lower his arms. "What if I had been naked?"

Aluna grinned wickedly and glanced down at his breeches. She felt a bit of satisfaction as his cheeks flushed. Aluna gave a nonchalant shrug. "We used to bathe together, not like I haven't seen it before."

Stupid Amazing Warrec's eyes narrowed. "We were four then. Things have, things have changed."

"I would hope so for Addie's sake," Joenair said. He then quickly ducked out of the way to keep a gauntleted hand from going upside his head.

They worked in silence as they finished attaching the pauldrons, vambraces, fauld and tassets to the big man. Aluna felt much better with all this steel and valentium between Stupid Amazing Warrec and whatever was trying to kill him. She didn't want to admit to herself how worried she had been during the ambush.

"So, we're really going to do this," Joenair asked after a couple of minutes.

"Do what?" Stupid Amazing Warrec said.

Joenair swept his arm over all their armor and weapons. "This. Ride off into battle, joining someone else's war, committing the support of the Maroveyan Empire to this civil war of a foreign power."

All three of them stopped for a second staring at each other. In all the chaos she hadn't even thought about it, and she knew Stupid Amazing Warrec wouldn't have either. Someone had attacked him and his friends, that someone needed to now not be alive. It was the right thing and a simple choice for him. It was one of the things she found amazing about him, one of the reasons why she loved him.

After a second Stupid Amazing Warrec nodded. "Yes, if it comes to it, we acted on our own. But yes, I'm going to fight and see this ended." He looked back and forth from her to Joenair.

"Yes," she said.

Joenair threw his arms up and raised his eyebrows. "Ok, just checking," he said with a chuckle. "See now aren't you glad you hauled all this down here?"

They quickly finished armoring Stupid Amazing Warrec up. He now wore his full plate armor and carried his new valentium shield. He had the Dwarves make the shield in the design of his people instead of the normal tower shields of legionnaires. A large circle nearly four feet in diameter with a center valentium boss, though instead of wood the entire thing was constructed of valentium making it only slightly heavier.

Stupid Amazing Warrec tapped his long sword against the shield, the spatha made the shield ring. "Finally get to use this thing," he said hoisting the shield up. "Cost a good amount of gold but supposed to be indestructible. Well, it cost Addie a good amount of gold," he added sheepishly. Aluna and Joenair both shook their heads at him, and they grabbed what gear they needed before heading out to the assembly grounds.

By dawn Kunthar had assembled the majority of his army and was preparing to march to war. He was a bit calmer now, more focused, but the rage bubbling beneath the surface was easy for everyone to see. He kept muttering under his breath a single name, Alazar.

The three of them marched across the staging grounds towards the shogun. Aluna felt a bit odd as the lines of troops watched the humans break rank and cross the grounds. As they walked up to Kunthar's side the old lion took notice of them even though he didn't turn to look at them.

Kunthar was also dressed in the full armor of his ruling class, but the Kathari armor was far lighter than Stupid Amazing Warrec's plate armor. Kunthar's armor was similar to what his soldiers wore but much more elaborate. The heavy blood red segmented plates made no sound as the old lion moved. The high domed helmet had a skirt of segmented plates around the neck instead of the simple chainmail. A large set of antlers sprouted from the top. A steel mask with his snarling image covered his face, leaving only his eyes visible. Rising from his back the banner of the shogun, a golden lotus on a field of black, above two joining rivers completed the dominant visage of the old lion.

"Friends Warrec-kun, Joenair-kun, Aluna-chan," Kunthar said in casual greeting. The old lion's words were calm and cordial, but Aluna could sense the tension underneath.

"Kunthar, Omo-Sama," Stupid Amazing Warrec said.

Kunthar stared off at the horizon. "Why are you three here?"

"We have come to help you...to fight with you," Stupid Amazing Warrec said.

Kunthar sighed as he shook his head. "This is a personal matter. I cannot ask you to come with me. Alazar has an incredible force and I have no guarantee than you will survive."

"Kunthar-sama you don't have to ask me. We consider you a

friend now and ally. I will fight with you. Besides, I am no diplomat, I am a warrior just as you are. I know death and I am not afraid," Stupid Amazing Warrec said the determination clear in his voice.

"I will fight," Joenair said.

"I will fight," Aluna said.

Kunthar turned now and gazed at each of them in turn. He nodded to each of them. "I have seen humans fight now," he said. "I feel pity for Alazar, pity but not mercy." The old lion pointed at the top post over the main gate to the palace. "I will have his head there."

Stupid Amazing Warrec nodded once. "We will take it."

Satisfied, the old lion nodded his head and turned back to oversee the troops. The four of them stood silently for a minute. They were interrupted by a low deep bellow. The three of them turned to see a soldier bringing up Kunthar's mount.

The creature was a massive beast easily six feet at the shoulder and weighing six or seven tons. Its skin was thick and baggy, colored a deep maroon. A large single horn jutted up from its snout and its mouth ended in a soft leathery beak. A large frill lined with fist size bony knobs jutted out from the back of the creature's head. Two six-foot-long spines or maybe they were tusks, she wasn't sure, swept out from the jawline pointing forward. The beast had a thick three-foot tail covered in quills.

Kunthar took the reins and looked over to where the three of them were standing. He raised his hand to the soldier. "Zareem bring..." Kunthar bit the words off. His body shook for a second and the shogun let out a long breath. "Forgive me. Daichi go and bring mounts for them, they will be joining us." The young tiger bowed and quickly ran off.

Aluna could feel the grief and pain coming off the old lion in waves. She was surprised after a few moments, when the shogun reasserted control, locking his emotions down.

"Think you three are up to riding a gainda?" Kunthar asked.

Stupid Amazing Warrec laughed, he had a great laugh. "If you can put a saddle on it, I can ride it," he said.

The three grew somber as the great column of war moved out. Kunthar rode at the head with his generals and aides buzzing around his sides. The three of them held a few paces back. The scouts were already bringing in reports of Alazar's forces. He had decided to entrench his forces up in his mountains. Kunthar's army would be hard pressed to advance. The terrain was rough, and Alazar had the high ground. This would not be an easy battle to win.

Chapter Thirty-two

Warrec clenched and unclenched his fist around the shaft of the Kathari spear. The eight-foot weapon ended in a thin, foot long blade with a small crescent blade where steel met wood. He found it a suitable replacement for his lance. By the day's end he suspected it would be coated in blood.

"I don't like this forest," Joenair said. Ever since they had entered the dense forest at the foot of the mountain, he had grown increasingly fidgety. His head was constantly moving as his eyes searched for enemies in the trees.

"I know, I feel it too," Warrec said. The rich volcanic soil had given rise to a dense forest of massive conifers, soft pines and a mixture of maples and birches. It had an eerie foreboding atmosphere to it that had clung on them as soon as they had entered the forest. "Aluna, have you sensed anything?"

She nodded. "Everything, this place is filled with life, old and ancient. The animals are similar to back home around The Lake but different. But the mass of our soldiers is keeping me from picking much out."

"Torasamitto, Alazar's home city is at the summit and another day's ride. I don't particularly relish the idea of spending the night here," Joenair said.

Warrec shook his head. "I doubt we make it that far. Alazar doesn't seem the type to sit back and wait. I think we will fight before we reach the summit."

"According to the maps Torasamitto looked more like a mountain fortress than city," Joenair said. "With the lake up there, it looked like an ideal place to withstand a siege."

Warrec nodded and shifted in his saddle. "That would be the smart play and it may still be his plan. Still, I think he will make contact at some point in these woods. It's too good a place for an ambush. Keep your guard up." They both nodded as their gaindas kept trudging forward.

The mist and fog held low over the mountain as Kunthar's army slowly crawled their way up through the mountain passes like a monstrous snake. Alazar had blocked off the main road forcing Kunthar's forces to scrabble across little more than deer trails. The army train stretched out for miles behind the old lion. Trepidation tempered with resolve hung over the army as thick as the fog as they climbed higher and higher.

The slumbering mountain, Eien No, loomed above them. Warrec couldn't see the mountain peak through the trees now, but he could feel it. The snow-capped volcano dominated the region and held sway as its tyrant king. There was a feeling of almost malevolence in the air as they moved closer. The mountain did not want them there.

Visibility was low, and Warrec and Joenair were having difficulty seeing more than a few feet ahead at a time. Aluna didn't seem to be having any difficulty piercing the fog. Warrec cocked his head at her and then realized she wasn't using her eyes to see.

Warrec strained his ears trying to pick out sounds in the forest that didn't belong, though the world sounded muffled through his padded coif and helm. Every crack of a twig, every rustle of leaves could be an enemy or it could be a deer fleeing away from the army. He couldn't tell and his nerves were on edge.

The Kathari seemed to not be at such a great disability. Their amber eyes pierced through the fog, at least a little further than his. Their sense of smell played a large role as they tracked the enemy. Kunthar would stop periodically and stand in his saddle and sniff the wind.

Alazar while brash was no fool. Kunthar outnumbered him five to one, but it was a moot point in the mountains. On an open field such as close to Olasanaka, he would easily crush the halfbreed. Up here though, in the mist covered forest and secluded valley of Torasamitto near the peak Alazar would have the advantage. Here Kunthar's forces were spread thin and easily picked off.

Throughout the day there had come back reports from the scouts that there had been a few guerilla attacks, small sorties by Alazar's forces that had been more probing than forceful. The little scout skirmishes had been expected but had still slowed their advance. Warrec did not expect to reach Alazar's seat of power before coming under full attack.

"It's quiet," Joenair said. "Almost too..."

Warrec cut him off with a quick slashing motion of his hand. "Don't you dare finish that sentence," he said. Joenair just grinned at him. "You two stay here. I'm going to go talk to Kunthar."

Warrec set his heels to the gainda's side and set it into a trot as he moved up the line to meet up with Kunthar. The old lion rode flanked by Daichi and Daiki as they marched along behind their master. The twins kept a wary eye on the swarm of aides and attendants that seemed to orbit around the shogun as he rode. Surprisingly, they didn't bother to hold him back as he rode closer.

"Warrec-san," Daichi said. The young tiger grinned at him amiably. Of the two he was far friendlier and agreeable. Daiki had the disposition of someone that had just found maggots in his rice bowl. They both had an odd colored coat, more brownish grey than orange with wide black strips. Daiki was lean and wiry while Daichi had a bit more floof around his body and middle.

"Warrec-san," Daiki grumbled. At first Warrec had thought the brother tiger was hostile specifically to him. He shortly realized Daiki didn't care that Warrec was human, he simply didn't like anyone. Zareem had called them the sun and moon, the night and day twins.

Warrec gave a half bow, at least as much as he could in the saddle, in greeting. "What's the news," he asked.

"Well, so far the coward Alazar has only poked at our scouts," Daichi said, his words light and animated. "But we have sent his cubs running each time."

"Still, it's only a matter of time, until they decide to come down on us all." Daiki said. He spoke in a droning monotone. "We're spread too thin as anyone can see. We'll all be dead by nightfall, I bet my dinner rations on it."

"Brother, you are mistaken." Daichi said. "Our stretched-out line gives us all greater chance for glory and honor. It's the only way to give Alazar a fair shot after all. Besides if we are all dead who will collect your dinner?" Daichi laughed.

Warrec couldn't help but grin at the two. As the younger tiger's laughter died down Warrec heard something. Or that is he didn't hear anything, the sounds of the forest had shut off and the air grew still, only broken by the occasional bellow of a gainda. The heavily forested mountainside was eerily quiet, almost as if the mountain forest had taken a slow deep breath and was holding it.

Suddenly, Kunthar's arm shot up and the army ground to a halt. A troop of monkeys came screaming through the trees as they swung from branch to branch. Warrec felt something wasn't right as he tried to peer through the fog. Warning horns sounded from down the line. Kunthar gave a shout to form up in defensive formation, but the command came too late. Seconds later Alazar's forces charged through the mist, from both sides of the trail catching Kunthar's forces unaware.

The haphazard line quickly crumbled as the enemy charged through it. Chaos erupted as the frenzied battle raged all around. Before Warrec could even level his spear an enemy spear tip caught him across the head. He was knocked from his saddle and fell to the ground with a heavy thud, dazed.

He heard Daichi call out his name. Warrec shook his head to clear the stars and looked for his friend but couldn't see him. He rose to his feet and quickly drew his sword and shield. Alazar's troops were on him in seconds. Warrec found himself surrounded with several swords and spear points aimed at him.

Warrec let out a yell and charged the nearest one. The Kathari lashed out with its spear, but Warrec easily blocked it with his shield. Warrec heard a soft gurgle as his sword opened up the Kathari's neck.

The enemy wasted no time attacking Warrec. Multiple blows and cuts rained down on him. Warrec laughed at them as his own sword lashed out and answered each of their blows. The Kathari blades bounced off Warrec's armor and shield as if they were blunt practice weapons.

The Kathari were extraordinary swordsmiths, but even their blades were no match for Dwarven forged heavy valentium armor. Even in normal armor Warrec was quick and agile enough having trained in it all his life. But with the lightness of the valentium material itself he could move as if he were wearing only chainmail and cloth.

The only things Warrec was still vulnerable to was a heavy blunt weapon like a hammer or perhaps a great war axe that could still break the bones under the armor or a sharp thrust at the joints. The Kathari used no such weapons. His invulnerability matched with his unbridled skill made the Kathari troops no match for him. Warrec passed through Alazar's forces leaving only death in his wake.

Most of these soldiers looked like conscription forces, farmers and merchants that had been pressed into service to bolster the ranks. They were poorly armed and armored. Most only wore heavy cloth and wood. They made up for it in tenacity.

Warrec spun and slammed the length of his sword down on an

enemy's head. The wooden helmet the Kathari was wearing splintered as the heavy sword smashed through. His eyes bulged and blood streamed down from the top of his head as he collapsed on the ground.

These Kathari did not fight with shields. Warrec found it easy to catch their attacks on his shield and then quickly counter. As long as he kept moving and weaving between them, he could stop them from surrounding him and thrusting with spears until one found a lucky mark.

One of Alazar's soldiers armed only with a long machete furiously slashed at Warrec. Within a few heartbeats three strikes had rung harmlessly across his shield. Warrec snarled as he slammed the shield back into the Kathari's face. The cat stumbled back and Warrec slashed down opening his femoral artery. The Kathari grunted in pain and stumbled to the ground, quickly bleeding out.

Warrec moved on as the Kathari lay bleeding out on the ground. He purposely left himself open as another attacked. His new adversary wielded a long polearm. Warrec grinned as the Kathari confidently slashed across his chest certain of an easy kill, only to have the blow harmlessly glance off. Warrec caught the end of the polearm under his shield arm and stabbed the Kathari through the throat. He gurgled as Warrec pulled his blade free in a spray of crimson.

Despite his battle victories Warrec found himself cut off from the rest of Kunthar's forces. He fought as an island in a sea of enemies. He watched in horror, unable to do anything as the enemy swarmed around Kunthar and his guards.

Daichi spun his spear around in a whirlwind of flashing steel and wood. With expert precision he stabbed an enemy through the eye and withdrew, before snapping the butt up into the chin of another. Daiki slammed his spear down into the foot of an enemy. With blurring sped he stepped forward punching him in the face with fist and spear shaft.

The twins fought fiercely and with the skill of a lifetime of training. It wasn't enough to keep them from getting surrounded and cut off from each other.

An enemy spear caught Daiki in the unarmored back side of his calf. The brother tiger let out a grunt of pain and dropped to a knee. Before he could recover another spear shoved its way through his side. Two more went into his other side and through the inside of his leg. As they withdrew Daiki shuddered and fell face down on the ground, he fell still and did not move from where he had fallen.

"Brother!" Daichi roared. The young tiger leaped into the air and swung his spear in a full circle arc trying to clear away the enemy. Daichi spun the spear up and slammed it down through the leg of one of the soldiers standing over his brother's body. The Kathari yowled in pain collapsing to the ground and pulling Daichi's spear free from his hands.

Before he could draw his sword a torrent of machete and sword blows rained down on him. Daichi fell beside his brother. The twins lay on the ground facing opposite directions, their blood forming a pool around them. As the sun and moon died on the cold mountain ground the forest around them echoed with haunting laughter.

Aluna strained her senses trying to pierce as deeply as possible into the mists. She couldn't see more than a few feet in any direction, but she could feel the soldiers around her. She couldn't see Stupid Amazing Warrec as he had ridden on up ahead. The mists had swallowed him, but she could still sense him a couple hundred yards ahead, talking with the twins.

It was the forest that was the problem. The tree line on either side of the trail held fast, a wall keeping her from looking too deeply. It was like trying to peer into deep murky water. She could sense something every now and then, a deer, squirrels, an occasional bird, but after they moved a few feet deeper they would all but vanish.

Her head snapped to her right and she stared hard into the

mist. Something was there, just beyond the tree line. It was little more than a collection of heartbeats, fast and anxious. The wind shifted and it was gone. Aluna stood in the saddle straining trying to find anything.

"Something is out there," Joenair whispered. "I can..." he trailed off as the air grew still. Aluna counted one heartbeat, two, three, a horn sounded far behind them, then another and another, echoing up the line. Screams and the sound of steel clashing sounded in the forest.

Alazar's forces exploded out of the mists. Within seconds they were swarmed on both sides. Aluna pulled hard to the right on her reigns causing the gainda to slam its massive head into two of the enemy sending them flying.

Joenair whistled and caught her eye. "I'll go high you go low," he shouted. The slim man then jumped from the saddle. He flipped through the air sending a pair of knives spinning out into the air. The blades found their marks lodging in one enemy's eye and another's throat.

Aluna pushed herself backward off the gainda and landed lightly on the ground. With an effort of will she touched the beast's mind sending it rampaging into the enemies still pouring in from the tree line. She pulled her tomahawk and kukri and surged forward towards the closest enemy.

He snarled at her as he thrust at her face with his spear.

Aluna stepped sideways and spun down the length of the shaft, its head missing her face by inches. Within an arm's reach she ducked low sweeping under the spear shaft and closing in fast.

She swung her axe up in an uppercut blow, burying the axe head between the Kathari's legs. The freshly made eunuch howled in pain. She cut the sound off with a quick slash across his throat, before spinning the kukri back around and lodging it between the dying cat's left clavicle.

With her now free hand she reached into the Kathari's neck and coated her hand in warm blood. Aluna reached up and smeared the blood across her face, tasting it and relishing the sudden influx of power. The bloody handprint briefly flared bright crimson as the life energy flowed into her.

Aluna jerked her blade free and grinned a bloody smile at the enemies around her. The sudden savagery of her attack and actions caused Alazar's forces to pause. It was all the time she needed. She stepped back, her arms held wide, eyes bulging manically, and smiled as she vanished.

"Mistwalker, Fogrunner, Dimmaloper; that is my name. Now you will see, now you will see little kitties, you grimalkins, now, you, will, see." As she spoke the fog rolled around her enveloping her. A few of the soldiers let out panicked shouts as she vanished. A few of the smart ones turned and ran.

Blood erupted from several different Kathari at once as

Aluna flowed through their ranks. Her steel fangs bit and tore into flesh, leaving little more than ragged meat in her wake. One of the Kathari started to shout an order but was cut off as a new steel tongue erupted from his mouth. Aluna kicked the dead body off her knife as she pulled it free from the back of the Kathari's head. The mists boiled around her, and she was gone again before they could react.

Alazar's forces in the immediate area now found themselves on the defensive. They grouped up into a tight circle, back-to-back. Their spears forming a thorny barricade to the now hostile fog. They thrust randomly into the mists trying to catch her, desperately probing for her.

Aluna slowly circled them, stalking them. She watched them with predatory eyes. She watched them and she laughed. The rocks around her laughed with her, and then the trees joined in. The fog laughed with her, and the sounds of her laughter drifted and floated through the forest all around her.

Kunthar quickly found himself cut off from the rest of his forces. Daichi and Daiki lay dead nearby. The enemy army mobbed up around him. He whirled around in circles slashing at the enemy as they advanced on him. His gainda used its head like a battering ram and sent the enemy flying in all directions. Kunthar was only able to hold them back for so long, however. His mount had suffered several wounds from the enemy's spears, and it eventually collapsed under the old lion.

He leapt from his now dead mount and landed decapitating three soldiers with one strike of his sword. His free hand shot out and grabbed an enemy soldier. He let out a cry of pain as Kunthar hoisted him into the air and slammed him back into the ground. The banner of the shogun attached to Kunthar's back flailed wildly in the wind as he fought.

Each stroke of the old lion's blade was perfect and precise. With each slash and with every cut another enemy died. There was no unnecessary movement, every strike was direct, and each attack was flawless. Zareem had taught him well and he honored his sensei with every move. The bodies of the enemy quickly piled up around him. Kunthar bellowed out a deep roar.

The enemy started to pull back. Kunthar could now hear laughter and someone clapping coming from behind him. He whirled around and saw Alazar there. The forest echoed with eerie laughter as the halfbreed leaned casually on a tree, his arms loosely crossed.

"Well done, old friend," Alazar said, the compliment sounding more like an insult and dripping with venom.

"You're no friend of mine, but soon you will be dead for

what you have done you dishonorable cur," Kunthar growled back.

Alazar grinned in more of a snarl than a friendly gesture. The tiger wore no mask and his fangs gleamed eagerly for blood, but his sword was sheathed and his hands empty. "Kunthar, my dear shogun, you wound me. I'm shocked, I truly am. I always considered you a good and trustworthy friend and ally. We have our differences politically of course, but this seems excessive even for you. This whole thing has been one great big misunderstanding. We should talk about this; surly we can work out this trivial little disagreement without more unnecessary bloodshed." Alazar fluffed his snow-white mane playing with the twin stripes of black that disappeared down his neck, then brushed some imagined dirt off his shoulder.

Alazar slowly walked towards Kunthar as he spoke, stopping just out of sword reach. Kunthar snorted, not believing a word of what Alazar said. Honor demanded he look his enemy in the face and the old lion slowly removed his mask and glared menacingly at the tiger.

"Misunderstanding, oh the sentiment was quite clear, as was your incompetence. You're a useless fool Alazar, but do not worry, I will make something of you yet. Your head will make a fine ornament for my home." Kunthar swept his sword up into high guard and waited for the cowardly halfbreed to draw his sword.

"Well, then, perhaps not," Alazar said with an evil grin.

His hand shot out and a white powder exploded into Kunthar's face. Kunthar roared in pain and stepped back flailing wildly with his sword in defense. He rubbed his eyes and blinked wildly; his eyes burned as his vision blurred. The world distorted into smears of grey and splotches of black.

Curse him for a coward, Kunthar's mind roared. He couldn't see anything other than blurry blobs and his nose burned along with his eyes. He slashed at a shape and felt his sword hit a tree. Kunthar whirled in place searching.

Alazar laughed at him as Kunthar tried to clear the powder from his eyes blinking rapidly. Kunthar could hear Alazar slowly draw his sword, but the sound came muffled as if from underwater. He could sense Alazar reveling in his apparent triumph.

He slowly circled Kunthar his sword point scrapping along the ground. Kunthar tried to locate where Alazar was, but the powder had completely disorientated him. None of his senses were working properly. The world spun around him dominated by the halfbreed's laughter.

With the sound of battle all around him and the smell of blood and bile filling his nostrils Kunthar turned in a circle his sword held out in defense waiting for the inevitable attack. He breathed in slow deep breaths remembering what Zareem had taught him. Alazar gave a quick laugh as he lunged forward assured of an easy victory. Kunthar managed to sidestep the attack and his elbow caught Alazar square in the mouth.

Alazar let out a low growl as he stepped back. Kunthar's vision was slowly improving but not fast enough. Blood trickled down one of his six-inch fangs. He licked it away and grinned malevolently at Kunthar again. He slashed downward. Kunthar managed to parry the attack and counterattacked making Alazar step back again.

The halfbreed was still confident of his victory but was growing irritated. This time he feinted. Kunthar moved to block the attack that was no longer there, and Alazar caught him across the stomach. Kunthar's armor managed to keep the cut from spilling his guts all over the ground, but the wound was still deep, and he dropped to his knees.

Kunthar knew this was the end. A look of utter hate and defiance crossed his face as he waited for the final blow. Alazar laughed as he brought his sword up. "My head?" the tiger sneered. "No, you old worn-out old fool, it will be your head on my gates." The blade fell.

A sharp metallic clang echoed across the mountainside loud as thunder. Warrec had managed to get his shield there just in time. Alazar's blade actually bit into the valentium shield a few inches but was now stuck in the metal.

A surprised look crossed the halfbreed's face but was

quickly replaced by shock and pain. Kunthar seized the opportunity and surged up and forward stabbing Alazar straight through the heart. Kunthar's katana seemed to scream as it pierced the steel of Alazar's armor. Alazar clutched at the blade sticking into his chest. He fell to his knees with a look of utter disbelief. Kunthar withdrew his blade and with one clean stroke relieved Alazar's massive shoulders of their weight.

The battle quickly ground to a halt as Alazar's forces realized their master was dead, the news spreading down the battle lines like wildfire. They surrendered easily; honor no longer compelling them to fight. With Alazar dead they could now surrender with their honor intact. A look of relief appeared on Kunthar's face. He blinked as his vision finally completely cleared. Kunthar looked at Warrec and nodded. He then promptly passed out from blood loss.

Two days later Kunthar awoke to find himself lying in his own bed. As he sat up, he felt pain and soreness in his abdomen. He looked down and touched his stomach and found it to be heavily bandaged. A familiar scent passed through his nose, and he looked about the room. In the corner he saw Zareem sitting in a chair watching him.

"Zareem? But you're dead. Am I dreaming? Or am I dead now too? Is this the afterlife?" Confusion washed though Kunthar as he tried to understand what was happening. The pain he felt was real enough. Zareem smiled at him.

"No, my student and my master you have not died. You are very much alive, but I am not," Zareem said with a laugh.

"How…how is this possible? I don't understand sensei."

Zareem laughed again. "Always the why with you Kunthar-chan, is it not enough that a teacher wanted to see his favorite student one last time. You have won, that is enough. Be well Kunthar-soma." Zareem slowly faded away, growing more and more transparent till he was gone.

Kunthar bolted upright out of the bed. Now fully awake he snapped his head over to the chair in the corner. It sat empty. He slowly nodded and bowed his head in prayer.

Chapter Thirty-three

Duncan felt as if two Dwarves were using his head as an anvil. He lay on his back in a groggy haze; his eyes shut tight and wondering what had happened. The last thing he could remember was whispering a few of the glyphs to himself as he read them. "Stupid old man, stupid, stupid," he chastised himself. "You know better than that. Never, never read arcane glyphs aloud."

A cool breeze blew across his face and was a pleasant change from the sweltering jungles of Nangonango. Duncan slowly breathed in the dry arid air and that seemed to help clear his head.

Dry? Why is the air dry? he wondered. The air in the jungle had been wet and moist almost to the point of suffocation. He now noticed that he couldn't smell the subtle scent of jungle rot that had permeated the air.

Duncan reached his right hand out and felt it close on dry sand instead of wet leaves. He snapped his eyes open and stared up at a sea of stars instead of the thin rays of sunlight that had filtered through the canopy minutes ago. His dazed head took a few seconds to process that he should not have been able to see the stars through the trees and then to realize that there no longer were any trees.

The old giant sat up with a jolt. Which he immediately regretted as his head began to spin from a wave of vertigo. He fought down a surge of nausea and willed the world to stop spinning so fast. He blinked rapidly to clear his head.

Duncan looked around in disbelief as he tried to piece together what had happened. The jungle was gone and, in its place, lay endless moonlit desert. Duncan ran a hand through his beard, stroking it as he thought.

The twin moons, Strix and its smaller sibling Chiro illuminated the area as their light reflected off the sand, bathing the land in a soft eerie light. The only thing that stood out from the horizon was the black obelisk that moments before had been surrounded by jungle. He then realized that he did not see the Dwarve and Orc lying beside him.

"Wildbeard! Akana!" Duncan bellowed out as he rose to his feet. He turned as he heard the sound of leather softly scraping across the sand behind him. Duncan couldn't help but chuckle at what he saw. "He is never going to live this down," Duncan said to himself.

Both Wildbeard and Akana were still unconscious, but they

were starting to come around. Akana lay on her back with her legs splayed wide. Wildbeard was lying face down and had his face planted firmly in her crotch. He was making soft puttering sounds as he labored to breathe.

Akana was the first to come around. Her eyes fluttered open, and she propped herself up on her elbows. The Orc flashed her infamous wicked grin as she cocked her head and looked at the Dwarve lying between her legs. Akana looked over and saw Duncan looking at the two of them. Her grin grew wider, and she stuck out the tip of her tongue and bit down lightly. Wildbeard was finally starting to come around.

"I think he is dreaming of some old barmaid," Akana said with a wink. The Dwarve's head was stirring back and forth. She let out a giggle as he grunted and coughed. Akana reached out and gently traced a finger across his bald head. "Morning Whiskers," she cooed softly at the Dwarve.

Wildbeard's puttering breaths abruptly stopped as the Dwarve froze. Gingerly he reached up and grabbed Akana by the hips and patted his hands along the outside of her thighs. Heartbeats passed as the fog slowly lifted from the Dwarve's mind and he began to realize just where he was. Wildbeard exploded backward as his mind finally made the connection.

The Dwarve slapped at his face and did his best to wipe his tongue raw and clean. Akana howled with laughter. Duncan covered his mouth with his hand and tried to appear to be looking off in the distance. He was not very convincing.

Wildbeard sat back on the ground and glared at Akana. She winked at him in return and licked her lips. "I can think of worse places to wake up but not many." He grunted and shuddered.

"Oh, please Whiskers, you're not fooling anyone. You loved it!" Akana said in a mocking tone. "Men have paid good gold to be where you were."

"Paid ransom to get away more likely," Wildbeard said with dismissive wave of his hand. He then got up and walked over to Duncan ignoring anything the Orc had to add. "Dunna say a word." He stabbed a sausage sized finger in the air. "Not one word, ye 'ear.

"I wouldn't dream of it." Duncan casually scratched at his beard as Wildbeard gave him a look of disbelief. "I mean whatever the two of you do in private..."

"Oye, I warn ya!" Wildbeard glared at Duncan, trying to look down on the human that had nearly three feet on him. The old giant couldn't help himself but chuckle.

"Fine...fine. Not a word then." Duncan held up his hands in mock surrender.

Wildbeard gave a curt nod. He then looked around at the surrounding moonlit desert, up at the moons, over at the blank obelisk and finally back at Duncan. "You cast some transportation spell I wager," he stated.

Duncan slowly nodded and gave a half shrug. "It would appear so."

Wildbeard shook his head and spat on the ground. "Ye know better than that lad. If I had a ladder, I would box yer ears." The Dwarve half growled.

Duncan sighed and nodded again. He then took a long swig from his flask. "I probably would let you. We could have died." Duncan started to take another swig, but then thought better of it. He stared at the flask in his hand. His mistake could have cost them their lives. Duncan snapped the lid closed and stuffed the flask back in his pocket. He would have to be more careful with his drinking.

Wildbeard sighed and kicked at the sand. He knew Duncan was beating himself over it and there was no more point in pouring salt on the wound. "Where are we?" he asked, changing the subject.

The old giant took a deep breath and then looked around them. He shook his head. "No idea. Looks like a desert. The obelisk is still there."

"So did we move or did the jungle move?" Wildbeard asked as he walked back over towards the obelisk.

"That's the question isn't it," Duncan answered as they both gazed up at the night sky trying to get their bearings.

"The stars are all wrong."

Wildbeard slowly nodded in agreement. "I didna recognize some of the constellations and the ones I do are in the wrong place."

"I'm thinking that the obelisk may be a waystone and it moved us."

"What's a waystone?" Akana asked as she walked over to them.

Wildbeard stroked his beard as he mulled the thought over. "Aye could be, would make sense." The Dwarve waved a hand absently at Akana in acknowledgement and stared at the obelisk. "A waystone is...well it's a link between two places."

"Like a portal. The two stones are connected, and you can move from one to the other," Duncan interjected.

"No matter the distance," the Dwarve finished.

"So, we could be anywhere," Akana said. "That's lovely, just great."

"Aye," both Duncan and Wildbeard spoke in unison.

Akana glared at Wildbeard. "You stupid Dwarve. I told you not to touch it."

Wildbeard snorted at her. "Ere now, I dinna do anything. Duncan spoke the words."

"It's still your fault." The Orc gave a frustrated growl and looked away. Akana raised her hand to her eyes and scanned

the horizon. "There! I see something." She pointed off towards
the east.

Duncan squinted but couldn't see anything. "Are you sure?"
he said.

Wildbeard grunted under his breath, "bloody females." He
threw his arms in the air in frustration and looked out where
she was pointing.

"I canna see 'ah blasted thing with the bloody moons
reflecting off the sand." The Dwarve began rummaging around in
his pack and finally retrieved a pair of goggles.

The goggles appeared to be made of brass with dark rose-
colored lenses. The lens over the right eye could extend out to
magnify. Wildbeard's eyes appeared twice as big through the
goggle lenses. The sight of the Dwarve's bald head, huge flame
colored beard and strange goggles lent to a curious sight.

Duncan cocked an eyebrow as he looked at the Dwarve. "Too
much moonlight?"

"Aye...aye. Used to the tunnels of Hammerfall and the dark
corridors of the museum. Dwarves aren't made to be out in the
desert. What fool lives in a desert."

"I don't know about live," Akana said. "But we are going to
die if we don't find shelter before the sun comes up. We should
head east. It looks like there is a mountain or something." She
reached over and smacked Wildbeard on the ass. "Come on

Whiskers. Don't want that sexy head of yours to get burned."

"Hey, look ere now." Wildbeard grunted.

Duncan shook his head and grabbed his pack and weapon.
"Come on. She does have a point." Duncan said. Wildbeard only
grunted in response.

After a few hours of walking over endless sand dunes the
trio reached the mountain. Except that it wasn't a mountain,
Duncan could now see it was a massive stone pyramid. It was the
largest structure any of the three had ever seen. In the
darkness they couldn't see the top; it just seemed to keep on
rising up into the night sky forever. Duncan marveled at the
massive stones that had been used to construct it. Each was
easily twice his height.

"A mammoth couldna move one of these," Wildbeard said as he
slapped the side of one of the stones.

"Have you ever heard of something like this?" Duncan asked
the Dwarve.

Wildbeard placed his fists on his hips and stared up at the
massive structure. "Aye, some of the ancient texts, older than
the empire and the Dwarven kingdoms tell of a mountain carved by
hand, past the red sand.

"Naacada Niwt?" Duncan said.

"Aye the same," Wildbeard said with a nod.

Akana clapped her hands together in glee. "Then we are

here. We reached it." She looked at the pyramid then back at
Duncan and Wildbeard. The smile quickly faded from her face. "So
now what?"

"More walking," Wildbeard said. The Dwarve gave a
disheartened grunt and pointed to the side of the pyramid.
Akana's shoulders slumped at the answer, but she picked her pack
up off the ground without a word. The three then set out to walk
around the pyramid.

After nearly a quarter of an hour they had only covered two
sides of the massive structure. Wildbeard dropped his rucksack
to the ground with a huff. "Let's stop a moment. The sun is
starting to rise." Duncan and Akana both dropped their packs as
well.

Duncan stared out at the horizon and at the rising sun. The
sky slowly seemed to catch fire as the sun rose over the
horizon. Orange and yellow with streaks of red and purple
clashed with the inky black of the night sky. It was the most
glorious sunrise Duncan had ever seen.

"It's beautiful," he said to himself. Wildbeard looked up
from the ground.

"Gonna be hot too," the Dwarve added. "Look a city!"
Wildbeard pointed towards the north.

Now that the sunlight was chasing away the deceptive glow
of the moonlight, they could see several buildings scattered out

from the north side of the pyramid. Two large trapezoid
buildings rose up from the center. A river cut through the
desert on the far east of the city bordered by palm trees.

"As good a place to start as any," Duncan said with a shrug
of his huge shoulders.

"Let's just hope they are friendly," Akana said.

"Let's just hope someone is there. The ancient Elves have
been gone from this world for a long time," Wildbeard said.

As the trio made their way towards the city, they could see
that it had fallen into disrepair and was little more than
ancient ruins now. Small houses made of sunbaked mud bricks had
collapsed inward. The ancient city was quiet, and nothing moved
among the buildings. After several minutes of walking through
empty streets and climbing over fallen rubble they reached the
large twin buildings that had dominated the city skyline. The
city opened up into a massive courtyard stretched out before the
twin buildings.

While dwarfed by the giant pyramid the twin buildings rose
up to easily twice the height of the gates of Hammerfall. They
were connected in the middle by a smaller third building. A long
wide ramp that could easily have let twenty-six horses ride side
by side led up to a large, cavernous opening in the third
building. Four giant statues carved out of granite stood
guarding the courtyard, two on either side.

Each statue was between twenty and thirty feet in height. On the left stood a human and a Dwarve, their arms raised up to the sky. A giant stone Orc stood on the right beside the entrance. The fourth statue had broken in half long ago. Its broken veiled head lay at the statue's feet.

"Orc, human and Dwarve, but what is the other one?" Akana asked.

The Dwarve and Duncan stared intently at the broken veiled face lying on the ground. "I believe it is or rather was an Elve," Duncan said. He then scanned the rest of the courtyard. Six smaller statues around half the height of the giant ones lined the courtyard and he pointed towards them. "There are smaller ones at the corners"

"That's a Centaur and a Goblin," Wildbeard said pointing to the far corners. "A Savan and a..." The Dwarve paused as he looked at the statue across from the Savan. "I have no clue."

"A Kathari," Duncan said. Wildbeard nodded at the answer, not sure how Duncan knew that.

"And these two here are an ogre, and bless me, a troll." The Dwarve finished with a wave of his hand at the two closest statues, guarding the entrance to the courtyard.

"Do we go in?" Duncan asked with a wink at the Dwarve.

"Of course, dinna come all this way to stop now." Wildbeard grinned. Akana clutched at the handle of her dagger and gazed

uneasily at the giant stone sentinels as they made their way
across the courtyard and up the long ramp.

As they moved, Duncan couldn't help but feel like they were
being watched. Stone sentinels watched as these trespassers
entered into places they shouldn't go and where no one had
walked for millennia. It was an unnerving feeling, and he
couldn't help but have a chill go up his spine.

As they reached the entrance, they found the collapsed
remains of two more statues that had fallen from above. A
massive saurian head lay half buried under the rubble. The other
was a twisted wreck of arms and spines. Akana shivered as she
looked at the two monsters.

"That looks like a dragon....an ancient dragon, not one of
the jungle beasts," Duncan said, pointing at the reptilian head.

"I don't want to know what that other one was," Akana
said. Duncan nodded silently in agreement. If his suspicions
were correct, it was a Xellex and better to not speak their
name.

Wildbeard turned and looked back at the courtyard and
scanned the statues. "Two giants guard the entrance, ogre and
troll. Four corners by creatures of beast and men." The Dwarve
turned and scanned the four sentinels towering over the
courtyard. "The civilized races as we know them. That broken one
is ah Elve, long gone from the world." Wildbeard stooped and

525

picked up a small shard from the broken dragon and then looked up to where it had been perched. "Two for the air. If this is a dragon, then the other must be...blast the name is on the tip of my tongue."

Duncan shuddered as he looked over the mass of spines and arms. "Xellex," he said. "Creatures of death and legend, best gone from this world." He gazed over the broken statues. "The broken statues are of creatures that are lost to history."

"I don't know of Elves, but I never want to meet a dragon and these Xellex seem worse. I'm glad they are gone," Akana stated with a nod. Wildbeard and Duncan nodded in silent agreement and slowly stepped through the entrance.

Several large columns stood like sentinels as they lined the chamber room. Fluted tops carved to resemble tree branches held the ceiling up. They had once been painted with vivid greens and blues that had now faded with time into a dull lackluster shadow of their former brilliance. Elven hieroglyphs covered their bases.

Wildbeard let out a low whistle as they walked toward the center of the room. The Dwarve twirled in a slow circle as he gazed at the ancient and masterful architecture. "Would you look at this. It's incredible. 'Ah canna believe we are here. Never in my life would 'ah think 'ah would see this."

"I know it's..." Duncan stopped midsentence and shook his

head twice. The old giant then fell to one knee.

"Duncan!" Wildbeard shouted rushing to his side. Akana let out a grunt and collapsed to the floor.

Duncan reached out and clutched at the Dwarve. Duncan watched as the Dwarve shuddered and his eyes rolled back in his head before he too collapsed to the floor. Duncan shook him, but then his head began throbbing. Duncan's eyesight turned black, and he slumped to the floor.

With a roar Duncan surged back to his feet. The grimmig thundered in his blood as the world took on a crisp and clear image. Duncan whirled looking for the source of whatever was attacking them, his bardiche held ready to spill blood.

His heart pounded in his chest and energy crackled in the air around him. Two small and dark figures cloaked in shadow stood in a far corner watching him. Duncan roared again, the sound reverberating in the building loud enough to make it shake.

Duncan stepped forward raising the great axe high, making ready to leap and sunder these new enemies. His weapon trembled in his hands and then tore itself from his grip. It flew across the room and stuck fast into the wall.

Duncan snarled and took another step forward. He should have been nearly flying across the room but felt himself moving against a tidal force of energy bearing down on him, crushing him. He felt like he was trying to push against a glacier.

"Ah who, look, look and see. Tis a guardian this one be. Savage and powerful measure beyond mortal compare. Best be quick brother and beware, before he comes and kills both you and me." A shrill high-pitched voice sounded from one of the cloaked figures. This one appeared to be floating in the air.

"Yes, it would appear so good sister." A slightly deeper voice said from the other figure. "Still your hand guardian of the blade. My sister and I bid you welcome to Naacada Niwt. Come and be welcome. There is much we need to discuss. Yes, much indeed."

Chapter Thirty-four

Warrec hastily jammed the pair of hakama pants into his rucksack. After a couple seconds he thought better of it and pulled them back out. He folded them and managed to get them in the bag tighter and not as wrinkly now. Satisfied, he started folding up a few other items of clothing to pack.

He tried to pack quickly, but he wasn't in that big a hurry. His armor and gear had already been packed and stowed on the ship. Now, he just had to get these last few personal items ready. *Besides it's not like they're going to leave without me,* he thought.

Ten days had passed since the battle in the mountain forest on the slopes of Eien No. It had been only a few days after they had returned to Olasanaka that another human ship had sailed into the bay. Warrec and Joenair finally received the news that civil war had broken out across the empire. They were ordered back home at once.

"Leaving a civil war here and going home to another one," he muttered.

Joenair sat in the window seat casually watching outside and eating a kebab of roasted pork and tropical fruit. "One battle is hardly a civil war, I would think," he said. "Barely a skirmish really."

Warrec savagely thrust a shirt into the bag. "Zareem died. Daichi and Daiki died. A lot of good soldiers died. A lot of farmers and merchants and other Kathari that had no desire to be there other than to serve their master, died."

Joenair slowly nodded and then hung his head. "Yeah, yeah, sorry, I wasn't thinking. I'm worried about back home."

"Me too. Fighting our own people." Warrec stopped packing for a moment. He stood there, fists clenched and took a deep breath. He then turned to look at Joenair. "Damn them, damn the both of them for doing this, for doing this to the empire," he said through clenched teeth.

Joenair nodded and then pointed the kebab at Warrec. "You're right but get that out of your system now. You can't be saying things like that once we get back on the ship."

"It needs to be said. Maybe that's the problem, people are too afraid to speak up about the state of the empire."

"Folks back home don't have any problem criticizing the empire and the senate and the nobility," Joenair said before taking another bite. "It's the criticizing the emperor that will get you, you Warrec, a lieutenant in the legions of the

Maroveyan Empire, in trouble," he said around a mouthful of pork.

Warrec slammed the rucksack down on the bedroll. "Jay, we don't have an emperor. That's the whole problem. We have two spoiled jackasses squabbling like children and fighting with toy soldiers. Except the toy soldiers are me and you and the others. The playsets are going to be people's farms and homes that get burned down."

Joenair chewed silently for a few seconds until Warrec looked back over at him. "Not every leader can be Ordias, not every leader can be Kunthar," Joenair said. "We just came back from a hell of a fight, but it was a good fight. The sides were clear and there was no mistaking who the bad guy was. You got to be the hero and it felt good, really good.

"But now we are about to go into another fight, a lot of fights and the sides are murky at best. There are no good guys and bad guys in this one. People are going to die, good people, innocent people. It's going to leave a scar on the empire, on our cities and on all of us. We're not fighting to defeat some evil, we're not fighting for freedom, we're not fighting for glory or honor, conquest or even for money. We're going to go in and fight for one thing and one thing only."

"And what's that?" Warrec said.

"We're fighting to end the fighting. We're fighting for

peace. The quicker we can defeat the west, the quicker we can break the ability of Ptharis to make war, the more people we save. It doesn't really matter who is right or wrong in this, we just have to stop it and we do that by winning and quickly."

Warrec nodded and rubbed his face. "You're right, damn you're right."

Joenair finished the kebab and flicked the stick over into a trash bin. "I'm right quite often, yet everyone seems to be surprised at it."

There was a slight knock at the door, moments before Aluna poked her head in. "Are you two ready yet?"

Warrec hefted the bag and threw it over his shoulder. "Just finished," he said walking to the door.

"I've been ready," Joenair said and jerked a thumb at Warrec. "He had to pack up all his souvenirs."

"Well, hurry up already," Aluna said. "The palace is deserted and it's weird."

Warrec furrowed his brow and nodded. As they left their rooms, they found that the palace did seem deserted. They made their way outside and still didn't see anyone. The only Kathari they saw was Alazar's head perched on a spike at the top of the main gate, his tongue lolling out as flies buzzed around him.

"So long Al," Joenair said.

"You might have been ugly," Aluna said.

"But at least you died doing what you were great at," Warrec said. "Getting your ass kicked." They then all three gave a rude salute to the disembodied head and walked out the palace gates.

"Jay, I have been wondering something," Warrec said. "Aluna has turned into somewhat of a ghost story for what happened in the battle. And I helped Kunthar a bit. But you never really said what happened to you in the fight."

"Yeah," Aluna said. "You just said you would go high and then disappeared into the trees."

Joenair shrugged. "And that's what I did. I got up in the trees and started chucking knives at the enemy."

"How many knives did you take?" Warrec said.

"Twenty-two," Joenair said.

"And how many of Alazar's soldiers did you kill?" Aluna said.

"Twenty-two," Joenair said. "You're welcome by the way," he added with a smirk.

Warrec and Aluna looked at him then each other and then back to him. They both started laughing at the same time. Joenair gave a sheepish grin and then started laughing along with them.

As they walked through the city, they didn't see one Kathari. No one seemed to be at home at the houses around the shogun's palace. Then they found that most of the shops were closed up as they entered the market and found it empty as well.

After several minutes of walking through empty street after empty street they turned the corner to the road that led down to the docks and found where everyone had gone. It seemed the entire city had turned out for their departure. A thunderous shout went up as they walked along the street. The Kathari cheered and the children threw flowers.

An honor guard was set up along the ramp leading up to the ship. They were decked out in full regalia, artfully crafted court armor. Each wore the banner of the shogun on their backs that flapped loudly in the wind. They snapped to attention as the three humans approached.

Kunthar stood beside the gangplank along with his wife. Kunthar wore the full black sokutai of the shogun, something he only did on the most special of occasions. The voluminous robes contrasted sharply with the bright and multicolored sokutai worn by Reyan. The two Kathari bowed deeply; as they did so too did the entire crowd.

"My friends," Kunthar said as he rose. He walked over and took Warrec's hand in his massive paws.

"Kunthar, you didn't have to do all this," Warrec said with stunned modesty.

"Nonsense," Kunthar said with a wave of his hand. "You have

mine and the gratitude of the entire Kathari people. I swear this to you my friends if you ever need our aid the Kathari people will be there."

"I don't know what to say," Warrec said.

"Warrec-san, say only that you will someday return," Kunthar said. "We wish you luck and good fortune."

Warrec's eyes widened for a second as he realized that Kunthar had used the honor title of an equal for him. Warrec nodded and bowed, Aluna and Joenair joining them. Another cheer went up from the crowd.

Warrec, Aluna and Joenair left with a mixture of jubilation, regret, and trepidation. They waved and watched the crowd as the Silver Cloud pulled away from the docks and made its way out into open ocean. They watched long after the city and bay had disappeared from view.

Warrec let out a heavy sigh of relief as their ship entered into the bay surrounding Artania. Finally, after another long, rolling, pitching sea voyage the Silver Cloud pulled into port at Artania.

The Meridiem Ocean had not been kind to Warrec, and the pleasing visage of the twin cities was a welcome sight. Captain

Obar had advised against pulling to port in Snetha with the civil war going on. The conflict didn't seem to really have affected the twin cities, but it was better not to chance it.

"It's good to be home," Joenair said. The three of them stood at the railing watching the ship pull into harbor.

As they watched two sloops, one bearing the twin roses of Artania and the other the sea turtle of Snetha came alongside each other. The two crews shouted and exchanged insults. They threw what appeared to be old pottery filled with rotting fish and excrement at each other before pulling apart and sailing back to their respective harbors.

"Luckily, that seems to be the extent of the war here," Warrec said.

Joenair shrugged. "That's not much different than normal, so that's a good sign."

"What's the plan when we get ashore," Aluna asked.

Warrec scratched at his chin. "Well, I have to report at the garrison and Jay has to swing by the imperial magistrate. Get our orders and go from there I guess."

"First, I need to swing by the dock master's office," Joenair said. "Grab the lasted news and gossip before we head on in."

Warrec nodded. "Good idea," he said.

"I'll go with you," Aluna said. Maybe there will be news

from The Lake.

Warrec was practically giddy as he walked down the gangplank and set foot back onto the solid wood of the dock. He sighed and smiled, dropping his ruck to the planks, and sat down. Warrec closed his eyes and dozed until Joenair, and Aluna came back. It barely seemed like he had closed his eyes before they were back.

"Hey, get up," Joenair said and kicked Warrec's feet softly. "The sailors had mentioned a few rumors, and none sounded good."

Warrec opened his eyes and yawned. "Sailor's rumors never sound good. But what do you got?"

"Well, there's the rumor that the western kingdom has fallen into anarchy for starters," Joenair said. "That king Ptharis has gone mad and is killing his subjects on a whim."

"Rumors spoke of the streets of Eldurania being lit at night by burning corpses locked in cages to serve as streetlamps," Aluna said.

"Right and the implication of the locked cages gives me the impression that whoever had gone into the cages hadn't started out as a corpse," Joenair said. "There are even reports of cannibalism. None of it could be confirmed of course, but it's enough to sow anxiety among the people of the eastern kingdom and get everyone worked up."

"Dammit," Warrec said. "That's worse than I feared." He sighed and got to his feet. "All right, let's get a move on, report in and see if there is anything official."

They grabbed their bags and the three began making their way toward the city garrison. As they threaded their way through the crowded streets a beautiful young woman with long dark hair took notice of them. She had been busy wiping down the tables of an open-air cafe. As she spotted them, she threw her rag to the ground and made her way towards them. With menace in her eyes, she stomped over towards Joenair.

"Pig!" she yelled as she slapped him across the face and walked off without another word.

"Who was that?" Aluna asked a little shocked.

Joenair had a stunned, but not all together surprised look on his face. "Uh, not really sure...Mary...Madalynn...Maddie, it was definitely an M name," Joenair said as he rubbed his cheek.

After a few more steps they turned a corner and passed a flower shop. Another woman hurried out of the shop to catch up to them as they passed. She had a willowy frame, short chestnut colored hair, full lips, and wide hips. This one wrapped her arms around Joenair's neck and kissed him deeply.

"Where have you been? You're gonna come see me later, right?" she asked in a sultry voice and pouted her lips. Joenair just nodded. She smiled and kissed him again and walked away.

Joenair grinned as she walked away. "Ah Farah, it's good to be back home," he mumbled to himself.

As they crossed the main road and turned down by the corner market two more women spotted him and stormed over. "Bastard!" the first one said as she slapped him. The other kicked him in the shins. "Pig," the second said. They stormed off in a huff without another word.

Warrec raised an eyebrow in a question. "The Cappelli sisters?" Joenair simply nodded. "You deserved that then. Didn't you promise to marry one of them?"

"Both actually," Joenair said with a sheepish grin.

Just then they heard a shout. "There he is! I told you guys that was his ship!" A large, fat, angry man yelled. He started running up the street followed by three others.

"Who is that?" Warrec asked about to step in.

"Oh, just some brothers who think I knocked up their sister or maybe I owe them money," Joenair said. "I can't really remember and honestly who can keep track. Don't worry about it, but I, I'll just meet up with you guys later. Good to be home huh."

With a laugh he jumped up and pulled himself onto a roof. He gave a mocking wave to his pursuers and disappeared over the other side. The three men ran right past Warrec and Aluna and tried their best to keep up with Joenair. The fourth, the fat one that had yelled started to say something to Warrec, but quickly thought better of it after the Vatninu glared down at him. He then turned and ran after his brothers.

Warrec watched as the men ran after Joenair, shook his head, and just laughed. Aluna couldn't help but laugh as well.

"So... tell me about the Cappelli sisters," she prodded as the two of them continued to make their way through the city.

Warrec laughed again and shook his head. "Well, it's a long story, but we have a long walk," he said as the two of them ambled on through the city.

Their ship had pulled into port just before noon. After almost an hour of walking through the busy streets they finally made their way up to the hill the city garrison main building sat on. Aluna stopped and looked back over the rooftops as they stretched back to the waterline.

Warrec cocked an eyebrow and looked back with her. "What is it," he asked.

Aluna chewed on her lip a moment and then shook her head. "I guess with our little walk I got to see most of what Artania had to offer. To be honest I'm not that impressed."

Warrec chuckled. "Well, my dear Lady Aluna please explain," he said.

She glowered at him and gave him a shove. "Well, it's just that I noticed that Artania isn't as majestic as Eldurond had been. What the Artanians called gardens don't come close to measuring up to the ones in Olasanaka. The streets are dirty. There are beggars and homeless people all along the sides of the streets. We even saw one old man fighting with a dog over a bone."

She swept her arms around and gestured, indicating everything around them. "The whole city just has a more rundown feel to it. Most of the buildings facing the street don't have windows. Seems that of the few that do they have one or two broken. Streetwalkers plied their trade along the corners. I just, I don't know. I don't get it."

"Don't get what?"

"Well, I thought Joenair had said that Artania was a highly cultured city. Maybe, after being in Olasanaka I'm just jaded," she said. She kicked at a loose stone in the cobblestone street.

Warrec shrugged. "Compared to Snetha it is. But it is a port city after all. Besides, this is Joenair we're talking about after all. To him a wide variety of taverns, gambling halls and brothels is what he considers cultural."

She nodded and laughed. As they reached the door to the garrison she stopped again. "Thank you for letting me come along. You and I have now seen something that the rest of our people have never seen. I'll cherish that experience for the rest of my life." She leaned up and kissed him softly on the cheek. Before he could say anything she quickly turned and walked into the building.

The garrison entry hall was jammed with desks. Scribes worked furiously to copy and send report after report. A constant stream of messengers came and went bringing mail and taking new mail back with them. Warrec made his way to the central desk, a massive old oak monstrosity that held dominion over the area.

The old sergeant behind the desk rose to attention as Warrec walked up but not too quickly. "At ease," Warrec said.

The sergeant had begun sitting back down before Warrec could even finish the sentence. Warrec smiled a little. The sergeant was old and had been through it all and back again. While he would give the respect that was due an officer, he also wasn't gonna take crap off some young pup who thought he was important just because he had an eagle's head on his shoulder.

"Name?" the old sergeant asked.

"Lieutenant Warrec Vornirulf Duncanson." Warrec answered. The desk sergeant began shuffling through a pile of papers on his desk. He pulled out a sealed document and handed it to Warrec and went back to his paperwork without another word.

Warrec took the document and turned with a smile, he had been dismissed. He had learned very quickly in his career that old sergeants secretly outranked everyone except generals.

Warrec knew to treat the sergeants as his equals even if he did out rank them.

Warrec walked back over to Aluna and broke the wax seal to open up his orders. He let out a low whistle as he read them.

"What is it? What do they say?" Aluna asked.

"Me and Joenair are to report back to Legate Silnis' replacement, Legate Lanksver and debrief him on the Kathari mission. I guess that includes you too. And…I'm being promoted to centurion and given command of a centuri," Warrec finished a little stunned.

"Wow Warrec, centurion and a command. That's what a hundred soldiers? You're moving on up," Aluna said excitedly.

"Yeah, not including cavalry and support," he said with a grin as the realization began to sink in. Warrec read the orders again and cocked his head in confusion. "Wait Legate Silnis' replacement. What the hell? It doesn't say where Silnis is."

"Maybe they reassigned him, moved him to the front or something," Aluna said.

Warrec nodded, but then turned and walked back to the desk sergeant. "Excuse me sergeant do you know where Legate Silnis has been reassigned?"

The old sergeant snapped his head back up at the mention of the Legates' name. He had a sad look on his wrinkled face. "Sir, I guess you haven't heard. Course not, no, how could you, just got off the boat and all. The Legate is dead, killed by western forces. It's what sparked this whole war it was."

Cold silent rage flowed through Warrec's veins as he merely nodded and walked out of the garrison to find Joenair.

The future loomed dangerously in his mind. The news of the war already sounded horrible, and he could only suspect that it would get worse. The blow of the legate's death hurt him more than he cared to admit.

Silnis had been like a second father to him. Warrec didn't know where his real father was now either. *The old man could be on the other side of the world for all I know,* he thought.

He wanted to get home, to get to Addie. He missed her and right now he just wanted to be in her arms. These next few months were going to be a hard road, he knew. And to top it off out there somewhere Argis was waiting.

.

www.ingramcontent.com/pod-product-compliance
Lightning Source LLC
Chambersburg PA
CBHW020244030726
47499CB00001B/51